Cindi Myers is the author of more than seventy-five novels. When she's not plotting new romance storylines, she enjoys skiing, gardening, cooking, crafting and daydreaming. A lover of small-town life, she lives with her husband and two spoiled dogs in the Colorado mountains.

Nicole Helm grew up with her nose in a book and the dream of one day becoming a writer. Luckily, after a few failed career choices, she gets to follow that dream—writing down-to-earth contemporary romance and romantic suspense. From farmers to cowboys, Midwest to *the* West, Nicole writes stories about people finding themselves and finding love in the process. She lives in Missouri with her husband and two sons, and dreams of someday owning a barn.

Also by Cindi Myers

Eagle Mountain: Unsolved Mysteries
Canyon Killer
Wilderness Search
Peak Suspicion
High Country Escape

Eagle Mountain: Criminal History
Mile High Mystery
Colorado Kidnapping
Twin Jeopardy
Mountain Captive

Also by Nicole Helm

Bent County Protectors
Vanishing Point
Killer on the Homestead
Fatal Deception

Hudson Sibling Solutions
Cold Case Investigation
Cold Case Scandal
Cold Case Protection
Cold Case Discovery
Cold Case Murder Mystery

Discover more at millsandboon.co.uk

DANGER ZONE

CINDI MYERS

EYEWITNESS IN DANGER

NICOLE HELM

MILLS & BOON

All rights reserved including the right of reproduction in whole or in part in any form. This edition is published by arrangement with Harlequin Enterprises ULC.

This is a work of fiction. Names, characters, places, locations and incidents are purely fictional and bear no relationship to any real life individuals, living or dead, or to any actual places, business establishments, locations, events or incidents. Any resemblance is entirely coincidental.

Without limiting the exclusive rights of any author, contributor or the publisher of this publication, any unauthorised use of this publication to train generative artificial intelligence (AI) technologies is expressly prohibited. HarperCollins also exercise their rights under Article 4(3) of the Digital Single Market Directive 2019/790 and expressly reserve this publication from the text and data mining exception.

® and ™ are trademarks owned and used by the trademark owner and/or its licensee. Trademarks marked with ® are registered with the United Kingdom Patent Office and/or the Office for Harmonisation in the Internal Market and in other countries.

First Published in Great Britain 2026
by Mills & Boon, an imprint of HarperCollins*Publishers* Ltd
1 London Bridge Street, London, SE1 9GF

www.harpercollins.co.uk

HarperCollins*Publishers*
Macken House, 39/40 Mayor Street Upper,
Dublin 1, D01 C9W8, Ireland

Danger Zone © 2026 Cynthia Myers
Eyewitness in Danger © 2026 Nicole Helm

ISBN: 978-0-263-42020-3

0226

Printed and Bound in the UK using 100% Renewable Electricity at
CPI Group (UK) Ltd, Croydon, CR0 4YY

DANGER ZONE

CINDI MYERS

For Gini

Chapter One

"Look at the dog!"

"Oh my gosh, that's so cute!"

"I didn't know they allowed dogs on the ski runs."

"It's a ski patrol dog. Look at its red vest."

"Shelby! Come!"

Patroller Lily Alton skied to a stop a short distance from the tourists clustered around her Belgian Malinois, Shelby. A woman in a purple ski suit, two men in black pants and brightly colored jackets, and two little boys with shark fins on their ski helmets stood with a third man, who was eating a hot dog. The blonde dog with black muzzle was sitting at attention, focused on the hot dog. "Shelby, come!" Lily repeated.

Shelby jumped to all fours and whirled around. Upon spotting Lily she let out an excited bark and bounded across the snow toward her. The dog leaped into the air, slamming her front paws into Lily's chest. Lily bent backward, but managed to stay upright with her arms full of fifty pounds of squirming fur.

All around her, people began to laugh and applaud. Lily forced a smile and managed to set the dog down without injuring either of them. "What's its name?" A teenage girl skied up.

Lily winced as the girl's skis skimmed only a few inches from Shelby's paws. The dog was standing still now, looking from Shelby to the girl, plumed tail gently fanning the air.

"This is Shelby," Lily said. "She's one of seven avalanche search dogs here at SkyCrest Resort."

"Can I pet her?" One of the shark-fin-helmeted boys had joined them.

"You can. And thanks for asking."

Shelby's whole body wiggled with delight as the kids patted her. The dog sat, then slid to the ground, until she was writhing in the snow, both children rubbing her belly and giggling.

"Would you like a trading card?" Lily took two of the cards, which featured a color photo of Shelby on the front and details about her and SkyCrest's avalanche dog program on the back.

"Ooh, yes please," the girl said.

Lily handed out the cards. "You can collect the whole set," she said. "There's one for each of the avalanche dogs here at SkyCrest."

"Thanks!" the boy said.

Lily's radio crackled. "Alton. What's your twenty?" The crisp voice of Patrol Director Scott Linden cut through the static.

"I'm at the bottom of lift one," Lily replied.

"Well, get over here. We're all waiting on you."

"Ten-four." She clicked off the radio. "Shelby, come!" she called.

"Sounds like Scott is in his usual sunny mood," she told the dog when she pranced up to her.

Shelby wagged her tail in reply. Nothing the grumpy patrol director said seemed to affect the dog's sunny mood. If only Lily could adopt the same attitude.

She skied to patrol headquarters, left her skis in the rack at the bottom of the steps, then knocked snow off her boots as she stomped up the steps to the door.

A wave of warmth hit her as she stepped inside, followed by the smell of damp dog. Shelby trotted past her to greet Hunter and Darth, the two black Labs in the corner, then moved on to lick the goldendoodle, Farley, in the face. She ended her rounds at the feet of a tall blond man who frowned down at her. Shelby sat and looked up at the man expectantly.

The man, Ski Patrol Director Scott Linden, turned to Lily. "Why were you late, Alton?" he asked.

"A group of guests stopped me to ask questions," Lily said. Part of their job as ski patrollers was to interact with guests.

"The rest of patrol doesn't seem to have as much trouble getting to meetings on time as you do," Scott said.

"That's because we're not showstopper blonds," patroller Chase Sergeant said from his perch by the lockers. He held up his hands. "I was referring to Shelby, of course."

The dog in question had flopped onto her side, eyes closed. She was definitely a striking pup, her pale gold hair tipped with black, black socks, black upright ears and muzzle, and brown eyes that appeared to be lined with kohl.

Lily had light brown hair worn in a braid that hung from beneath her black ski helmet, an accessory that obscured most other features. So yeah, she was sure Shelby was definitely the one attracting all the attention as the pair traveled through the resort.

Scott stepped over Shelby to reach the middle of the patrol shack. In addition to the four dogs, the small space was crammed with seven patrollers, half a dozen pairs of skis, two toboggans, several backpacks, orange cones, rolls of snow fence, coils of yellow nylon rope, four shovels, a bundle of avalanche probes, two cardboard boxes overflowing with ski patrol T-shirts and an inflatable palm tree. "Sergeant and Donaldson, you're at Buttermilk Basin this morning," he began, reading from a clipboard. "Iverson and Castro, I want you at the Glades. Milk Run is closed to the public for race practice, so you'll want to keep an eye on that. Raz, I want you here at post one. Alton, you're with me at Top of the Mark."

Lily kept her expression neutral, even as she groaned inwardly. Shelby raised her head and met her gaze, always in tune with Lily's mood. Scott had an excellent reputation as a skilled patroller, but he had all the charm of a drill sergeant. At least his dog, Hunter, was a genuine sweetheart. The big black Lab stood now and stretched, front and back, then shook vigorously, his patrol harness jingling.

"Weather reports show a storm coming in after seven tonight." Scott continued reading from the clipboard. "They're calling for three to six inches overnight. Five a.m. start tomorrow."

This elicited groans from the gathered patrollers, though the early callout was routine on mornings after a snowstorm. They would spend hours on avalanche mitigation before the slopes could safely open to visitors.

"I'll have the ammo ready." Connor Donaldson, Farley's handler, was in charge of the explosives used for triggering controlled slides in inbound terrain.

"Alton."

Scott's voice had her sitting at attention. "Yes, sir?"

"We need to schedule Shelby's Level B certification," Scott said.

"Shelby already has her Level B certification," Lily said. "She received it last May."

"That was at Kingdom Mountain," Scott said.

"Yes." Lily had patrolled at Kingdom Mountain ski resort, west of here, for six years before the resort had shut down last spring, the last year with Shelby. They had transferred to SkyCrest, owned by the same corporation, this fall.

"I want you to recertify for SkyCrest," Scott said.

The room had fallen silent, everyone watching and listening to this exchange. "Shelby was certified by Wasatch Backcountry Rescue," Lily said. "She shouldn't need to be recertified."

"She's a new dog for us," Scott said. "I have no idea of her capabilities. I want her recertified. I'll set up the test in a few weeks and get back to you."

She stared, speechless. Part of her wanted to protest that he was only doing this because he hadn't wanted Lily and Shelby on his team to begin with. Management had announced the addition to patrol without consulting him and that, apparently, had irritated him. That didn't give him the right to take it out on her and her dog. But pointing this out wasn't going to win her any points with him. He was going to make her prove herself. She stood. "Fine," she said. Shelby rose also. "We'll be ready."

Her gaze locked to his for a brief moment. She was prepared to see a lot of emotions in his gaze—anger, disdain or even dismissal. What she didn't expect was the flicker of heat his direct stare sent through her. His hazel eyes weren't exactly friendly, but they were definitely—interested. Scott scrutinized her as if she was a puzzle he was trying to figure out. As if he *wanted* to figure her out.

She looked away as he dismissed everyone with his usual "be careful out there."

"I'll meet you up top," she mumbled, and hurried out of the lift shack, Shelby at her heels.

"Hey, Lily!" She paused and waited for Connor to catch up. Farley tackled Shelby and the two dogs rolled in the snow, then popped up and shook themselves, panting happily.

"Don't let Linden get to you," Connor said. With his shaggy ginger hair and clipped beard, he bore a passing resemblance to his dog. They definitely shared the same soulful brown eyes.

"What is his problem?" she asked. "He treats me like I'm a brand-new trainee who's never been on snow before."

Connor grimaced. "I think it's because you're the only dog handler he didn't personally select and train."

"So he knows more than Wasatch Backcountry Rescue and C-RAD?" Colorado Rapid Avalanche Deployment was the premier organization in Colorado for training and deploying avalanche dog teams for immediate response to avalanches anywhere in the state. Lily and Shelby had completed multiple classes with WBR and C-RAD.

Connor shrugged. "Scott founded the dog program here. It's his baby."

"That doesn't give him license to act like a jerk."

The man himself exited ski patrol headquarters in time to hear this announcement. His head snapped up, and he turned in Lily's direction. Now she'd done it. Well, she didn't care if he knew what she thought of him. She raised her chin, defiant, then planted a pole and skied away, Shelby bounding alongside.

As Lily approached the head of the line the liftie, Desi, signaled for the next group of skiers to wait and waved Lily and Shelby forward. The dog jumped into the lift chair, and Lily settled beside her. Shelby lay down, her head in Lily's lap, as the chair rose into the air. Lily buried her gloved fingers in the thick ruff of fur around the dog's neck. She reached the mid-mountain lift and rode it up to Top of the Mark, the highest lift-served terrain. This was the view touted in all the advertising for SkyCrest resort—snow-crowned peaks set against a turquoise sky. In addition to the lift-served runs accessed from "the mark," gates provided access to acres of hike-to terrain.

At the top of the lift, the chair slowed. Lily stood as her skis made contact with the ground and Shelby bounded gracefully off the chair and toward the ski patrol shack at the edge of the tree line a few yards away.

She was opening the door to the shack when Hunter trotted up behind her, followed quickly by Scott. Lily braced herself for a confrontation over her "jerk" remark, but he said nothing. "We'll leave the dogs here while we patrol," he said as he moved past her into the shack.

He was filling a water bowl for the dogs when she joined him inside. Both canines lapped noisily as soon as he set the bowl on the floor. "Come on, Hunter," he said, and opened the door to one of the kennels in the back corner of the hut.

Hunter obediently trotted into the kennel and curled up on the memory-foam pad there. Without Lily even asking, Shelby loaded into her own kennel. She was curled up, plumed tail over her nose, and asleep before Lily even closed the door.

Dogs secured, she followed Scott back out of the lift shack and stepped into her skis again while he secured the door. "Let's make a run down May Day," he said. "On the way up I got a complaint about kids hucking off the rocks there."

Hucking—or jumping—off the rocks above the ski runs presented a real hazard to both the jumpers and skiers below them. Patrol had roped off the area several times, but the ropes were easy enough to take down, and a group of local teens, supplemented by more daring visitors, regularly congregated in the area to test their mettle and the agility of the patrollers. So far, they had all escaped apprehension.

"Hey, Lily!" They had not skied far when a boy hailed her. She slid to a stop as nine-year-old Jackson Endicott skied up to her. Small for his age, with pale blue eyes, Jackson usually wore an earnest, slightly worried expression.

"Hi, Jackson," Lily said. "What are you up to?"

"I'm waiting on Dad." He looked up the slope, where a black-clad man had stopped to talk to a couple in matching red ski suits. "He's always stopping to talk to people." He looked back at Lily. "Where's Shelby?"

"She's taking a nap right now," Lily said. Aware of Scott waiting beside her, she gestured to him. "This is Scott Linden," she said. "Scott, this is Jackson Endicott."

"Nice to meet you, Jackson," Scott said. He even sounded friendly.

"Are you coming over tonight?" Jackson asked.

"I sure am. I'm looking forward to it."

"Cool. Oops, there goes Dad." Jackson jammed his poles in the snow as his dad sped by. "Gotta go." He rushed off, skis scraping as he worked up speed.

Lily and Scott set off behind him at a slower pace. "How do you know Jackson Endicott?" Scott asked.

"I was his nanny when he was a baby," she said. "Before he started school."

"Then I guess you've been inside their chalet."

"Yes." And their summer home in Maine and their winter retreat in Taos. "I still babysit for Jackson sometimes when his dad has to be away." Tonight was a client dinner. Though the Endicotts had a live-in housekeeper, Denny Endicott preferred to have Lily stay with Jackson. And since he paid twenty dollars an hour and all the food she could eat, she was happy to oblige. "How do you know the family?" she asked Scott.

"I don't know them, but I know *of* them. Denton Endicott is always in the news."

"Hmm." Lily didn't pay that much attention to the news.

"*The New York Times* did a profile of him a few months ago, about the proprietary navigational software he's developed. Apparently, it's a pretty lucrative business."

"I guess so."

"He might be a good person to approach about donating to the avy dog program," Scott said. "SkyCrest supports our avalanche dogs with some funds, but you know how expensive training and upkeep can be. We're always looking for private donors."

She gaped at him. "You want me to hit him up for money?"

"Why not? The program is something you're passionate about. Maybe he'd like to support it. You may not think about these things, but I have to." Not waiting for an answer, he sped up, quickly outdistancing her.

She was still processing the exchange when shouting ahead drew her attention. She skied around a curve and almost collided with a boy on a snowboard who zipped in front of her across the slope. A second boy braked to avoid hitting her and fell over backward in the snow. Lily hurried to help him up. "Are you all right?" she asked.

"That man grabbed my brother," he said.

Lily followed his gaze behind him, to where Scott stood, his hand clamped on the arm of a slightly older boy in a baggy blue jacket and wide-legged plaid pants. Lily looked back at the boy at her feet. "Were you hucking off the rocks?" she asked.

He stuck out his lower lip. "We made sure nobody was coming before we did it. We weren't hurting anyone."

"Come on, get up." She offered her hand to the boy. He hesitated, then took it, and she helped him to his feet. Then she pulled out a pair of scissors.

"You're not going to take my pass, are you?" the boy wailed.

"You can pick it up next week in the pass office," she said as she cut the nylon tie that attached his ski pass to his jacket. "That is, if this is your first offense. Second offense means you're done for the season."

"That's not fair!" the boy wailed. Up ahead, his brother was giving Scott grief. Lily skied up to join her boss.

"I got the brother's pass," she said.

"You people are going to hear from our dad," the older brother said. He was red-faced, frost forming on the nascent moustache above his thin upper lip.

"He's welcome to give me a call," Scott said. "I'll tell him how you were trespassing in closed terrain and endangering your own life and the lives of others." He pocketed the boy's pass. "Now ski down and go home."

They watched the two boys head down the run. Scott looked at the rocks above the run. "We need to go up there and restring the ropes."

"Easier to ski over from Daisy Chain," she said, naming the run that led above and behind them.

"Then let's do it."

They spent the next hour restringing the ropes, closing a narrow section of a run where the snow had melted off to expose rock, and redirecting skier traffic away from a lift that was temporarily closed due to a malfunction. Working with Scott wasn't as bad as Lily had feared. He didn't try to tell her how to do her job, and he was pleasant with the public. When two girls skied up to them, he stopped what he was doing and gave them his full attention. "Do you have any trading cards?" one, who looked to be about eight and wore a helmet with bunny ears, asked.

"Of the dogs," her friend with a bright purple helmet asked.

"Here you go." Scott offered cards featuring Hunter at the wheel of a snowmobile.

The girls squealed in delight, and squealed again when Lily passed over cards featuring Shelby's photo. "Where are the dogs?" purple helmet asked.

"They're resting up," Scott said. "Running around in the snow wears them out."

"Give them kisses for me," rabbit ears said. She hugged the cards to her chest. "I just love dogs."

"So do I," Scott said, his grin almost as big as the girls'.

Seeing him like this stunned Lily. "Who knew you were such a softy," she teased.

His smile faded. "Yeah, well, I only wish the rest of our job was as easy as interacting with kids." He checked his watch. "I've got a meeting I need to get to. You should check back in at the ski patrol hut."

"See you later," she said, and skied away. But she stopped at the top to look back at him—a tall, graceful figure gliding down the slope. Working with him this morning hadn't been so bad. He was good at his job, and good with people. If only he could see her as an ally, not an imposition.

Chapter Two

The rest of the day passed in a blur of activity, from marking hazards to tending to injured skiers. By four o'clock, all the lifts on the mountain shut down. Scott and Lily released the dogs from the kennels and closed the patrol shack for the night, switching off lights and the heater and locking the door. At four forty-five, they began their sweep of the runs, making sure everyone was cleared off the mountain before dark.

Lily and Shelby skied May Day, a long, wide run that ran for over a mile, all the way to the base area. This was her favorite time of day, when they had the snow all to themselves. Shelby, rested up and full of puppy energy, ran ahead of Lily, legs stretched out, puffs of snow flying up around her at each landing. Occasionally she stopped and rolled in the snow, the picture of pure joy.

Lily made long, sweeping turns, checking both sides of the run for any skiers or snowboarders who might have fallen or simply stopped to rest. Across the mountain, all the lift chairs hung empty and still, and lights began to bathe the ski village at the base in a golden glow, in anticipation of growing dusk.

Back at the base, she stowed her gear in her locker and fed Shelby her supper. A national pet food supplier donated a diet designed for active dogs to the ski patrol, so whenever they were working, meals were covered. While Shelby ate, Lily swapped her uniform for leggings and a tunic sweater. Then she grabbed her day pack and parka and headed for the shuttle stop. At her apartment, she transferred Shelby and her belongings to her car and set out again.

Fifteen minutes later, Lily was at the gate to the Endicotts' property. She lowered her car window and leaned out to press the intercom button. "Hi, it's Lily Alton," she said.

"Jackson's waiting for you," a gruff but not unfriendly voice said. Mike Swanson was Denny Endicott's right-hand man. The title on his business cards said senior analyst, but after Jackson's mother passed away when the boy was three, Mike had taken over as a kind of household manager/chief adviser to the busy executive. The two had apparently known each other since college. He was actually the person who had hired Lily to be Jackson's nanny six years ago.

The gate swung open, and Lily guided the Subaru up the winding drive and parked in a slot to the left of the garage. Shelby bounded out after Lily and ran to the open back door, where Mike waited. He was only a couple of inches taller than Lily's own five foot six, but he had the muscular build of a wrestler and the round face and bald head of a cherub. He bent to pet the dog, then looked up at Lily. "Denny said he's sorry he couldn't be here to meet you. He's entertaining some important clients."

"You aren't going with him?" she asked. Mike played a big role in the operation of Endicott Industries, also.

"I have a meeting of my own tonight."

The door from the kitchen to the rest of the house burst open and Jackson rushed in. "Shelby!" he cried, and dropped to his knees to embrace the dog.

Shelby, tail wagging exuberantly, licked Jackson's face while the boy giggled wildly.

"That's enough," Mike said. "Remember what happened last time you got Shelby too excited."

Behind his back, Lily made a face. The incident in question involved Shelby racing through the house with an expensive velvet throw in her mouth, flying out behind her like a flag while Jackson, shouting at full volume, raced after her. At least one imported vase—not to mention the throw—were casualties of the chase. Lily had spent most of the rest of the night terrified that she would spend the rest of her life paying back the cost of the damaged items. Fortunately, Denny had only laughed at Jackson's delight over the story. "Jackson says it wasn't your fault, and I believe him," Denny had said. "But try not to let it happen again."

Jackson stood. "No chases, I promise," he said. "What kind of pizza do you want, Lily?"

They had a tradition of ordering pizza whenever she babysat. "How about pepperoni?" she asked. It was Jackson's favorite. Hers too, as it happened.

Mike took a suit jacket from the back of a kitchen chair and slipped it on. "I'll leave you to it," he said. "Don't forget to set the alarm behind me."

She followed him to the back door and waited until he was in his car before she pressed the code to arm all the outside doors and windows. She guessed being a billionaire meant you had to be more careful about security, though she had always felt safe here in this beautiful, quiet home.

They ordered pizza, then headed for the den, where Jackson demolished her in a game of *Slime Rancher*.

The doorbell rang. "Pizza!" Jackson shouted.

"I'll get it." Lily hurried to the door, Shelby trailing behind. She checked the security peep, her hand already on the doorknob, but stopped short. The man on the other side of the door—tall, long-faced, prominent nose, close-cropped dark hair graying at the temples—was not the pizza delivery person. He wore dark slacks and a blazer and carried no delivery bag.

She pressed the intercom. "Can I help you?"

"It's Preston. I'm here to talk to Mike. Who are you?"

"I don't know a Preston."

"I'm a new hire for Endicott Industries. Look, here's my ID." He held up a card with the Endicott Industries logo and his photo. He was identified as *Preston Smith, Data Specialist*. She scrutinized it, then opened the door, leaving the chain on. "Mike isn't here," she said.

"Who are you?" he asked.

His demanding tone annoyed her. "I'm the babysitter."

Jackson moved in beside her. "Hello, Jackson," Preston said. "Would you please tell the babysitter I really do work for your dad?"

Jackson scowled. "He works for Dad," he said.

"Do you want to leave a message for Mike or Mr. Endicott?" Lily said.

"Why don't you let me in, and I'll write a note to leave."

She shook her head. "Not going to happen. I don't care if you are an employee, I don't know you and Mike isn't here."

He frowned and pocketed his ID card once more. "How long have you been babysitting for Mr. Endicott?" he asked.

"That's none of your business."

"Where did Mike go?"

"He said he had a meeting."

"Who was he meeting with?"

"I don't know. I think you'd better leave now." She didn't like this man or his attitude. She started to close the door but saw headlights sweep up the driveway. A battered compact car with a lighted sign for the pizza restaurant on the roof stopped in the driveway, behind a black pickup she assumed belonged to Preston Smith.

Smith turned to watch the young man with the pizza head up the driveway. He stepped to one side. "Good night," he said, and headed for his truck.

The pizza guy looked from the truck to her. "Something wrong?" he asked.

"Just stay here until he's gone," she said. She punched in the code to disarm the security system, then lifted the chain and opened the door all the way.

"Sure." He handed over the pizza, and they waited silently until the truck was out of sight.

"Thanks," she said.

"No problem."

She closed and locked the door, reset the alarm, then carried the pizza into the living room. Jackson sat on the floor in front of the coffee table. Shelby settled beside him, all her focus on the pizza. "I don't like that guy," Jackson said.

"Preston Smith?"

"Uh-huh."

Smith certainly hadn't impressed her. "Why don't you like him?" She opened the pizza, slid a slice onto a plate and passed it to Jackson.

"He's just—sneaky. Like, I caught him coming out of Dad's home office once when Dad wasn't home. He said he left some papers for Dad to look at but I think it was just an excuse to snoop." He took a bite of pizza. "Mike doesn't like him, either."

"Don't talk with your mouth full, please." Lily chose her own slice of pizza. "Why did your dad hire him, I wonder?"

Jackson swallowed and took a drink of Dr Pepper. "He's

supposed to be some genius or something. Anyway, I'm glad you didn't let him in."

"You should never let anyone in the house you don't know," she said. "Especially if your dad or Mike isn't here."

"Yeah. I know." He offered a piece of pizza crust to Shelby, who gobbled it up. "You could have threatened to sic Shelby on him."

Lily smiled at the dog, who was begging for more pizza. Shelby looked fierce, but she was really a cream puff. "Shelby isn't that kind of dog. She's bred to help people, not fight them."

"I guess so." Jackson reached for a second slice of pizza. "Are you working again tomorrow?" he asked.

"I am. Saturday is our busiest day."

"I wish I was going to be there," Jackson said. "But Dad said he won't get home until late, so I have to wait until next week."

"The snow may be even better next week," Lily said.

"Do you like your new job?" he asked.

"I do."

"That guy you were with today—he's your boss?"

"Yes. Scott is in charge of the avalanche dog program."

"He seemed nice."

Scott was…complicated. Like most people, she expected. Not the most charming man she had ever met. But everyone described him as "firm but fair." His insistence that Shelby be recertified for her Level B annoyed her, but he was clearly the kind of her person to cross all his t's and dot all his i's. And she had faith in Shelby. The dog was still young, but so smart and eager to please.

After pizza, they watched a movie. Jackson fell asleep before the end, and Lily woke him to put him to bed. Then she and Shelby relaxed on either end of the sofa, a rom-com she had selected from the Endicotts' endless streaming choices playing low on the television.

She must have dozed off. Shelby's low growl woke her, and she sat up as headlights played across the home's front windows. She waited, tensed, until she heard a key in the lock of the back door. It opened, then the beeping of the alarm keypad told her Denny was shutting off the alarm. She moved to the front hallway, smiling, intending to offer a cheerful greeting.

But the smile faded as she stared at Denton Endicott. The normally impeccably put-together businessman slumped against the wall, his navy-blue suit rumpled, one sleeve hanging loose, his thick graying hair in disarray. He glanced at her, and she gasped—one eye was swollen shut, the skin around it purple, his bottom lip puffy and bloody. "What happened?" she asked, rushing forward, hands outstretched.

But she stopped short of touching him. With effort, he straightened and waved her away. He stood over six feet, and though he had developed a paunch over the years, he still conveyed power. "It's nothing," he said.

He started to move past her, but she blocked his path. "You're hurt," she said. "Do you want me to call an ambulance?"

"No!" His voice was sharp, angry.

She drew back, and his expression softened. "Really, I fell," he said. "I probably had too much to drink." He pulled a wallet from his pocket, opened it and thrust a sheaf of bills at her.

She stared at the wad of twenties—at least two hundred dollars. "This is too much," she protested.

"Go on. Take it. You're always so good with Jackson, and he's crazy about you. In fact, could you come again next Friday night? I have to go out again."

"Of course." She was still staring at the money, afraid to look at his damaged face again.

"Now go on," he said. "I'll be fine." He moved past her, and she stared at his back, still frozen in place. At the bottom of the steps, he turned toward her once more. "No need to tell anyone about this," he said. "It would be too embarrassing."

"Of course not," she said. The last thing she wanted was to embarrass this man who had been so nice to her.

"Go home now, Lily," he said, and even smiled, though at the cost of a fresh trickle of blood from his swollen lip. "I'll be fine. I'll wait and set the alarm as soon as you're out."

She pocketed the money, collected her things, and let herself and Shelby out. In the six years she had known Denny Endicott, he had never been anything but perfectly polished and calm. She had never seen him even tipsy. Had never smelled alcohol on him. She had looked up to him, as a kind of father figure even.

But he was only human, and humans did drink too much. They fell down. But who got a black eye and a busted lip from a fall? And why hadn't the clients he had been entertaining made sure his injuries were treated?

But it was none of her business. Though she thought of Denny Endicott as her friend, he operated in a world far removed from her own. His problems involved billions of dollars and how to raise his son as a single father.

All she had to worry about was training her dog, doing her job as a ski patroller and dealing with an exacting boss. It was enough for any one person—right?

"WE'LL DO SHELBY'S Level B certification tomorrow before the lifts open," Scott informed Lily after morning meeting the next Thursday. "Be at the back bowl off of Lift 12 at seven a.m."

Lily wanted to protest this was a waste of everyone's time, but she knew that wouldn't get her anywhere. "All right," she said.

Shelby had aced her first Level B test, less than eight months ago. There was no reason to think she wouldn't do well this time, either, unless Scott had done something to make the test harder. Did he resent Lily's presence on the team so much he would engineer her failure? She shook her head. Even if Scott had been reluctant to have her as part of his group, he hadn't done anything to make her think he was that vindictive.

So Friday morning found her and Shelby at the appointed location a few minutes before 7:00 a.m. The sun had barely risen over the ridge, casting long shadows over the pristine snow. Lily's teeth chattered, and she swung her arms and stamped her feet, trying to generate warmth.

A tall figure skied up beside her and skid to a stop, snow flying. Fellow patroller Nina Rose grinned at Lily as she stepped out of her skis. "Are you ready for this?" she asked.

"We're ready." Lily tried not to feel self-conscious around Nina, but she, along with everyone else she knew, had been glued to their televisions the last winter Olympic games. They had all seen Nina claim a silver medal in the giant slalom. A few months later she had graced the cover of *Vanity Fair*, wearing a whisper of a gown that showed off her athletic figure.

Nina looked past Lily. "Here comes everyone else."

Lily turned, expecting to see Scott and maybe one other person he had recruited to serve as a judge for this test. Instead, she was startled to see all of the other dog handlers—Brian, Anders and Connor skied up just ahead of Scott. "I didn't expect to see you all here so early," she said.

"We came to cheer you and Shelby on," Connor said.

Scott skied up with a tall man dressed all in black, a full ginger beard obscuring most of his face. "Hello, Lily," Adam Derocher said. "How are you?"

"I'm good," she said. "It's good to see you." She meant the words—Adam had been one of her trainers with C-RAD.

"We're all here. Let's get started," Scott said, without preliminaries. "Adam will be the judge. Lily, are you and Shelby ready?"

"We're ready." She ignored the flutter in her stomach. Shelby had performed well at every trial so far, but she was still a young dog. If she wasn't in the mood to work this morning, they could end up embarrassed in front of friends and people she respected. Not to mention they would probably be kicked off the avy dog team.

Adam stepped forward. "Who are our volunteers?"

A man and a woman held up their hands. "This is Marion and Pete," Scott said. "They live here in town and volunteered to be our victims this morning."

"Great," Adam said. "We'll get a couple of people to show you what to do."

Connor and Nina left with the couple. After the lifts closed yesterday they had dug snow caves where the volunteers would wait for Shelby to find them. Despite the cold and discomfort involved, there was no shortage of other resort employees and townspeople who were willing to volunteer to be buried in the snow for training exercises or certification tests like this one.

"We'll run the obedience test while we wait," Adam said.

"Sure." Lily called Shelby to her side. The dog sat, eyes bright, ears up, the picture of attentiveness.

Lily ran through all the basic obedience commands—sit, stay, lie down, heel and come. "She can fetch, shake hands and bow, if you want to see those," she volunteered.

"Nah, that's good." Adam marked the paper on his clipboard. "Let's go see if the others are ready."

Anders and Brian met them halfway across the wide bowl. "Everything's set," Brian said. "Let's see Shelby do her stuff."

The dog danced around, clearly sensing something was up. Lily asked her to sit and she did, though she practically vibrated with anticipation. "You know the drill," Adam said. "The dog has to find two buried volunteers within twenty minutes." He consulted his watch. "The time is seven ten. She has until seven thirty."

Lily took a deep breath. This was it. The snowfield they were in was the size of a football field. The two volunteers could be hidden anywhere in this expanse of white. "Shelby?"

The dog fixed her gaze on Lily. "Go find!"

Shelby faced the snow, but didn't move. Lily's heart sank. She was about to give the command a second time when the dog took off, racing across the field, snow flying behind her.

Lily ran after the dog, aware of the others behind her. Shelby had her nose to the ground, "casting" back and forth for scent. Unlike search-and-rescue dogs, avalanche dogs weren't trained to fix on one particular person's scent. Rather, they detected any human scent and focused in on it. Supposedly, they could smell a person buried even thirty or forty feet deep.

Shelby let out a bark and began digging. Moments later a hand stuck up from the snow and waved. "Time, six minutes," Adam said.

Lily laughed and rushed to pet Shelby as others pulled Marion from the pit where she had been hiding.

"Good girl!" Marion declared, and hugged Shelby.

"One more to find," Adam reminded them.

"Shelby, go find!" Lily said.

Shelby took off again. She sniffed around Marion's hiding place for a few minutes, then moved farther away. Lily made her hands into fists and tried not to think about the time passing as the dog searched, but found nothing.

"Five minutes." Adam said.

Lily's stomach was in knots. *Come on!* she silently encouraged her dog. *You can do this.*

"Three minutes."

Lily turned to glare at Adam. His countdown wasn't helping.

A bark, then a shout from Brian. Shelby was all the way across the field. Lily hurried to the location as the dog dug frantically. Adam jogged up to her side. "Only one minute left," he said.

Just then, the snow collapsed in front of the dog and Pete poked his head out. "Good girl!" he cried, and patted the dog, who continued to dig at the snow.

"We'll take it from here," Brian said, and gently moved the dog aside and began digging out the grinning volunteer.

Lily took a well-worn rope toy from her pack. Shelby barked and leaped at the toy, then tugged hard in her favorite game—her reward for a job well done.

"Congratulations. You passed." Lily looked up to see Scott standing beside her. "I was a little worried there at the end, but Shelby came through."

"She was great," Lily said.

"Good job," Scott said. "Now let's get to work."

He headed for the lift. Adam moved in where Scott had been standing. "I think Scott was more nervous than you were," he said.

"Why would he be nervous?" she asked.

"Probably because he knew if Shelby failed the certification, he'd have to remove you from the program. He didn't want to do that."

She wasn't sure she believed that. "I suppose it would look bad to lose me when I just joined the team," she said.

"I don't know anyone who takes this work more personally," Adam said. "Frankly, I'd love to have him on my team. But whenever I've asked about hiring him, he talks about how much this program means to him. Anyway, congratulations. Shelby did great. You should be proud. How old is she now?"

"Sixteen months."

"She should be ready for her Level A test by the time she's eighteen months. That's the minimum age we can certify her."

"I'll be in touch." She shook the hand he offered, then put on her skis and headed back toward the base area.

She was greeted by a chorus of "Congratulations!" when she entered patrol headquarters, and Shelby received plenty of pats on her way to her kennel.

"Settle down, everyone," Scott called. "We've got a lot on our schedule today."

And that was it. Another accomplishment ticked off, but just another day on the job. Maybe she and Jackson could raise a toast when she babysat for him tonight.

The rest of the day was a typical busy day. The snow was good and the sun was out, so the resort was packed. Lily helped transport a woman with a knee injury from a steep black run on the back side of the resort to the clinic at the base area, helped move a bunch of fencing to a storage area behind the terrain park, answered questions from tourists, took Shelby out for some exercise and obedience drills, and ran general patrols.

When she stopped for lunch at twelve thirty, she saw

she had missed a call from Denny Endicott. He had left a voicemail. "We won't need you to babysit tonight. Change of plans. Thanks."

She wished she had been able to talk to him. She wanted to know how he was doing. But maybe he would have thought she was being too personal. She thought of him as a friend but really, to him she was probably just the babysitter.

She was collecting her belongings at the end of the day when Nina stopped by her locker. "Big plans for tonight?" Nina asked. She had freed her long blond hair from the braid she usually wore, and it fell about her face in attractive waves. She looked runway-ready in black leggings and a black turtleneck that accentuated every curve.

"I was supposed to babysit, but that got canceled," Lily said.

"Then come out with me. We can celebrate Shelby's certification."

At the mention of her name, the dog nuzzled Nina's hand. Nina obliged by rubbing the dog's ears.

"Where would we go?" Lily asked.

"Just to the Trail's End for a few drinks and something to eat. Nothing fancy. Some of the other patrollers will probably be there. The dogs will be fine here for the few hours we're gone. You can ride with me."

"Thanks. I'd like that. Just give me a sec." Though she had been part of this ski patrol team for a month now, she hadn't socialized much after work. It would be good to have a night out and get to know people better.

Chapter Three

The Trail's End was a popular hangout for locals and tourists alike, and on a Friday night it was packed with people, all talking loudly to be heard over the mix of alternative country that blared over the speakers. Scott pushed his way toward the bar, behind Connor and a lift tech named Hank. The two friends had waylaid Scott outside Ski Patrol headquarters and persuaded him to go out with them for a beer.

While they waited for the bartender, Hank entertained them with an account of the twelve-year-old triplets in matching pink ski suits and blond pigtails who had delighted the crowds in the lift lines by blowing bubbles and handing out candy to celebrate their birthday. "Cutest little girls, and they were eating up the attention, too," he said.

"Hey, it's our turn." Connor pointed to the bar, and they moved forward to place their orders.

Beer in hand, Scott turned to survey the crowd. He recognized a couple of fellow employees from the resort, as well as a few couples he had spotted on the slopes that day. Then the door opened and Nina entered. The tall blonde couldn't help but turn heads. Behind him, Hank gave a low whistle. "Our own Powder Princess," he said softly, a reference to a nickname some sports blog had given Nina in her ski racing days.

But it was the woman behind Nina who made Scott's heart strike an extra beat. Lily wasn't especially tall, but she carried herself with a confidence he admired. But she wasn't arrogant. People liked Lily, from the ski school toddlers to entitled tourists. Whereas he apparently had a talent for rubbing people the wrong way, Lily could charm even the grumpiest complainer.

He wouldn't say she had exactly charmed him, but she did distract him. He'd like to figure out why.

"Hey, Nina! Lily! Over here!" Connor raised one arm and motioned the women over.

"Hello, Connor. Hank. Scott." Lily's smile sent warmth through him, even though she had barely glanced at him.

The bartender approached. "What can I get you ladies?"

"Hah!" Hank said. He was a wiry dark-haired man with soulful brown eyes and a thin moustache. "I had to wait fifteen minutes to place my order."

Nina smiled at the bartender. "I'll have an Avalanche Pale Ale and an order of chili cheese fries." She glanced at Lily. "Is that okay? We can split the fries."

"Sure. I'll have a Snowcap Cider."

"My treat," Hank said, and reached for his wallet.

"No thanks," Nina said. "I always pay my own way." She handed over a credit card, the smile just as warm.

Lily handed over cash to cover her share of the order, then turned her back to the bar. She surveyed the crowd, then glanced at Scott. "Is everything okay?" she asked.

"Sure. Why wouldn't it be?"

"You're staring at me." She brushed a lock of golden-brown hair out of her eyes. "I thought maybe something was wrong."

He looked away. He hadn't meant to stare. He just had a hard time keeping his eyes off of her.

But he wasn't the only person in the bar focused on Lily. "Do you know that guy over there?" he asked, and gestured toward the cash register by the door, where a beefy middle-aged man had his gaze fixed on her.

She looked in the direction he had indicated, then straightened. "Mike?"

The man moved toward them. "Hey, Lily!" he said. He glanced at Scott.

"Um, this is Scott. Scott, this is Mike." No explanation of their relationship. Relative? Friend? Boyfriend? He must be at least fifteen years older than Lily, but some women had a thing for older guys. "How are you, Mike?"

"I'm okay." He moved in closer and lowered his voice. "I guess Denny got in touch with you?"

Scott angled away slightly and pretended not to listen. But it was impossible not to hear everything they said in these close quarters. And the name Denny intrigued him. Denny as in Denton Endicott?

"He left me a voicemail saying he didn't need me to babysit tonight," Lily said. "Is something wrong?"

"No. Not that I know of. The meeting just got canceled at the last minute. I just wondered what he said to you last week. About the shiner." He pointed to his eye.

"He said he drank too much and fell."

"That's what he told me, too," Mike said.

He didn't sound convinced. "He looked really rough when he came in that night," Lily said. The bartender set her drink on the bar, but she made no move to pick it up. "His jacket was torn—like he'd been in a fight."

Denton Endicott in a fight? Scott sipped his beer and pretended to be watching a couple on the dance floor. Tourists, who had clearly drunk too much. They were executing a series of dips and spins Scott bet would have at least one of them falling flat before the song was over. Meanwhile, he could clearly hear Lily's conversation with Mike.

"That doesn't sound like Denny," Mike said. "I mean, I've known him twenty years, and he's never been in a fight."

"What about the client he was with that night?" Lily asked. "Do you know him? Or her?"

"Him. And he's a great guy. Someone else I've known for years. No, it must have been a fall." He laughed. "Denny and I are both getting older. We don't hold our liquor like we used to."

"What about this new employee, Preston Smith?" she asked.

Mike's expression sobered. "How do you know Preston?"

"He came by the house that night, not long after you left. He said he wanted to speak to you. He got kind of annoyed when I wouldn't let him in."

"I'm sorry he bothered you. I had no idea."

"It's all right. I meant to say something to Denny about it, but then he came in looking so awful and it seemed silly. I mean, the guy didn't do anything. Did Smith ever get in touch with you?"

"Not that night, but we work together every day."

"What do you think of him?" she asked.

"He certainly knows his stuff, but I'm not sure he's a good fit for the organization," Mike said. "He's got an attitude."

"Why did Denny hire him?"

"He's got excellent credentials and came highly recommended." Mike shrugged. "As long as he does his work, I guess his personality doesn't matter. I'll tell him to stay away from the house, though. He shouldn't be showing up after hours like that."

"Mike?" a server, holding a brown paper bag, called from the cash register.

"My order's up. I'd better go." He nodded and left.

Lily turned back to the bar and picked up her drink.

Scott moved in closer once more. On his other side, Nina was deep in conversation with Hank and Connor. "Everything okay?" he asked.

She frowned, a single shallow line forming on her forehead. "I hope so. Mike works for Denton Endicott. I was supposed to babysit Jackson again tonight, but his dad called at the last minute to cancel. When I was there last Friday, Denny came in from his dinner meeting with a black eye." She set her drink on the bar and turned to face him. "And I just remembered I promised Denny not to say anything to anyone about that, so if you tell anyone, I swear I'll make you regret it for the rest of your life."

He might have laughed at the threat, coming from such a sweet-faced young woman. But the vehemence with which she spoke gave weight to the words. "I won't say a word," he said. "I promise." And he wouldn't ask about Preston Smith, either, who had apparently annoyed her enough that she thought him worth mentioning to Mike. None of Scott's business.

She picked up her drink again and sipped. "Let's talk about something else," she said.

"Shelby made it interesting for us today," he said. "I was getting worried she wasn't going to find Pete in time."

"I had faith in her," Lily said.

He thought she had looked a little panicked, but whatever. The dog had come through and passed the exam, and that's all that mattered.

"I know you think I was singling you out, insisting you recertify," he said. "But we can't afford to have any of our qualifications questioned. Better to be certain."

"You're the boss," she said. "You don't owe me an explanation."

The dismissal hurt, he could admit it. He didn't like that she thought of him first as "the boss." "I'm in charge of the avy dog program," he said. "But we're all part of the team. It's important that we get along."

She sipped her cider, watching him over the rim of the glass. She had almond-shaped eyes with thick lashes. Her gaze struck him as...troubled. Not what he had expected. "It's a good team," she said. "I don't have any problems with anyone."

"Good. I don't want any problems."

"What do you want?"

The question startled him. It sounded like a challenge. Did she expect him to tell her what he required from her, as a member of his team? But he had given her that spiel her first day on the job. "I want the avalanche dog program to be a success," he said.

"Because then you'll be a success. You'll keep your job."

"No!" The word came out more sharply than he had intended. She visibly flinched. "If someone is caught in a slide, they're depending on us to get them out alive," he added. "That's the only success that really matters."

Her eyes grew glossy, as if she was holding back tears. "You're right," she said, her voice rough. "Of course that's what matters most."

He hadn't expected so much emotion and had to look away. Awkward silence stretched between them.

"I'm going to head out of here." Connor clamped one hand on Scott's shoulder and smiled at Lily. "Have a good night."

"Good night, Connor." Lily set her half-finished drink on the bar. Scott was sure she was going to cry off, too, if only to get away from him.

But Nina moved in beside her and shoved a plate piled

with chili cheese fries toward her. "Eat up," she said, and handed Lily a fork. "Or else I'll devour them all."

Lily hesitated, then stabbed the fork into the fries. Scott didn't blame her: the food looked and smelled amazing.

Hank moved over to flirt more with Nina, and Nina shut him down with practiced finesse. Scott said nothing, but continued to watch Lily while trying to appear not to. He told himself he should leave, but he couldn't bring himself to do that, any more than he could bring himself to move away from her.

"We should go out somewhere nicer than this," Hank said. He grimaced. "Someplace quieter, where we can talk."

"I'm here with my friend Lily," Nina said. "We're celebrating a big accomplishment for her today."

"Lily can come, too," he said. "And Scott." He looked across the women to Scott. "You can come out, can't you?"

"Not tonight," Scott said. He set his empty beer bottle on the counter. "Some of us have to be at work early in the morning."

"I'd better go, too," Lily said. "I can call an Uber to take me back to my place."

"If you're sure you don't mind," Nina said.

"Does that mean you're up for going with me?" Hank asked.

Nina smiled. "Just for a few drinks. A game of pool, maybe."

"Sure. Sure. Just friends."

Lily bit back a smile. Scott had to fight back a laugh. Hank was as eager as a puppy.

"Is your car back at the resort?" Scott asked Lily.

"Shelby and I rode the shuttle in this morning." The free shuttle ran a continuous loop between 6:00 a.m. and 10:00 p.m. She checked her watch. "I don't think I'll make the last bus, though."

"I'll take you home then," he said. "Where do you live?"

"The Ridge condos."

"No problem. I live there, too." The Ridge was a big complex, with four sections of buildings.

"Oh. Well, we'll have to stop by patrol and collect Shelby."

"We can do that."

He led the way outside. "I didn't say that about having to be at work early as some dig at you," he said. "I don't care how long you stay out as long as you're on time in the morning."

"I didn't think you did," she said. "I just didn't want to go out with them."

He glanced at her. "Why not?"

She shrugged. "I wasn't interested. Why didn't you go out with them?"

"Same reason," he said. "I wasn't interested. I did the bar scene in college and when I first got out of the army, but I don't enjoy it now. I'd rather stay home with my dog. Guess that makes me boring."

"Then I'm boring, too. I was supposed to babysit tonight and I was actually looking forward to it. Pepperoni pizza, Dr Pepper, and the rom-com of my choice after the kid went to bed. And Shelby on the couch at my feet, snoring."

"Sounds like the perfect evening."

She laughed, and he joined in. Her low, husky chuckle set a tremor through his stomach that startled him. Yeah, that was definitely some heat there. No surprise. He liked women, and she was an attractive one. Smart and interesting. But not interested in him. She'd made that pretty clear.

THE SCOTT LILY had seen tonight was different from the Scott she saw at work. Less uptight. Friendlier. He wasn't her boss after hours—he was just another guy. A good-looking, interesting guy.

And full of surprises. Instead of crossing the street to the parking lot, as she had expected, he stopped at the curb half a block down from the bar. "Here we are."

She stared at the black, brown and silver motorcycle parked at the curb. Clearly, the bike belonged to Scott—Hunter was standing in the side car, tail wagging. Scott patted the dog, then unlocked a compartment on the rear of the bike, took out a helmet and handed it to her.

"I didn't know you had a motorcycle," she said.

"The bike is easier than a car for getting around town. Cheaper, too." He donned his own helmet and straddled the bike, then looked back at her. "Is something wrong?"

"No. I'm fine." She shoved the helmet onto her head and fumbled with the latch.

"Come here," he beckoned, then reached out to fasten the helmet's strap. A shiver raced through her as his fingertips brushed the sensitive skin beneath her chin. She shook off the sensation and climbed on behind him, while Hunter settled into the sidecar.

"How are we going to get to my place with Shelby?" she asked.

"She can ride in the sidecar with Hunter. There's plenty of room."

He started the engine, and she steadied herself with one hand on his shoulder, aware of the hard muscle bunched beneath her palm. She put as much distance between them as possible—a scant two inches—gripped the seat beneath her thighs, and stifled a squeal when the bike rolled forward and into the street.

They sped through the darkened streets of the resort town. Once they turned off the main drag there were few people on the sidewalks. Cold air stung her cheeks, but the sensation of scenery flying by was exhilarating. Too soon, they turned into the ski resort. But instead of heading to the parking garage, Scott steered the bike down a series of alleys and passages and came out on the snow beside ski patrol headquarters. She was pretty sure he wasn't supposed to have a motorcycle there, but she didn't say anything. Maybe he wasn't the total rule-follower she had pegged him for.

He opened the door to ski patrol headquarters, and Shelby barked at them from her kennel at the back. Lily retrieved her, Scott locked up, and they headed outside again.

Hunter jumped out of the sidecar to greet Shelby, and the two dogs danced around each other. "Let's go, Hunter," Scott commanded.

The Lab hopped into the sidecar and looked up at Scott expectantly. "Get in, Shelby," Scott said.

Shelby looked up at him and wagged her tail.

"She doesn't know that command," Lily said.

Scott bent and scooped the dog into his arms. "Move over, Hunter," he said, and deposited Shelby in the sidecar next to Hunter. "Stay."

Shelby settled down next to Hunter, alert, but not upset. "Good girl," Lily said.

They mounted the bike again and set off. Shelby took her cues from Hunter and sat still, panting and glancing around her. Lily was less relaxed, the rumble of the motorcycle engine vibrating through her. Scott drove faster out on the highway. Lily tried to keep her balance by holding on to the seat, but ended up with her hands on Scott's waist, the rest of her pressed against his back.

The Ridge condos had been constructed ten years previously as affordable housing for workers. Most importantly, the complex allowed pets. Lily had been lucky to snag a vacant unit, though it was a single-bedroom space on the third floor. Still, she had great views and no upstairs neighbors, and it was enough for her and Shelby. "Which building are you in?" Scott asked as he slowed and turned the bike into the main entrance.

"Building Two," she said.

"I'm in Building One." He stopped the bike in the parking lot for Building Two. Lily dismounted, and Shelby sprang out of the sidecar after her.

"Thanks for the lift," Lily said.

"You did a good job today," Scott said. "With Shelby. If I didn't say so already. I'm not always good about that. Giving praise where it's due, I mean. I'm trying to do better."

"Um, thanks," she said. "That means a lot."

She started to turn away, but he called after her. "Don't forget my helmet."

"Oh. Sure." She fumbled again to unfasten the buckle, but her fingers seemed to have lost all dexterity.

Scott reached out and gently pushed her hands away, then unfastened the buckle himself. He lifted the helmet off her head, then reached out to smooth her hair.

The gesture was unexpected, almost tender, and sent a shiver of awareness through her. Which just proved how exhausted she really was. She took a step back. She had learned some things about Scott tonight—that he cared more than she gave him credit for. And that she was more attracted to him than she wanted to be.

THE NEXT DAY—Saturday—was the usual mixture of crowds and chaos. Lily scarcely had time to exchange a few words with the rest of the crew between morning meeting and heading up the slopes to begin work. She responded to three minor injuries before noon. She was starting up the mountain for a last run before lunch when she heard a familiar voice hail her as she waited to board the lift to Top of the Mark. Jackson Endicott skied up to her. He was dressed in black pants, a blue jacket and a black helmet plastered with stickers form the various resorts he had skied. "Can I ride up with you?" he asked.

"Sure." She moved over to make room, and they skied forward when the liftie waved to them.

"How's your dad doing?" Lily asked when they were on the lift chair.

"Have you seen his eye?" Jackson swiveled toward her.

She pretended ignorance. "What happened to his eye?"

"He tripped and fell coming out of the restaurant last Friday. He's got a black eye that looks like something out of a horror movie—all green and purple and yellow. I told him it would make a great Halloween costume."

"Is he okay?" she asked.

"Oh yeah. He's here somewhere." He waved a hand to take in the resort. "I'm supposed to meet him for lunch." He turned back to her. "How's Shelby?"

"Shelby's great. She passed her Level B certification test yesterday."

He frowned. "Is that like, a math test or something?"

"It's a test of how well she can find people buried in the snow. She had to find two people within twenty minutes, and she did it."

"That's great. If I was buried in the snow, do you think she could find me?"

"I bet she could. But don't go burying yourself to see."

"Okay." They approached the top of the lift, and he faced forward. "See you!" he shouted as he sped away.

She spent the rest of the day patrolling at the terrain park and beginner areas, took Shelby out for a patrol midday, and did a safety demonstration—with Shelby's help—for a ski school class. She kept an eye out throughout the day for Denny or Jackson Endicott, but saw neither of them. The image of Denny, torn jacket and beaten face, stuck with her.

The radio attached to her pack strap crackled to life. "All patrollers report to patrol base," Scott's voice was urgent. "I need you here now."

Lily straightened her line and crouched over her skis in a racing stance. She sped past Shelby, who barked and ran after her. She crested the hill above the base and slowed only slightly to avoid the clusters of tourists lingering at the bottom of the run, and skidded to a stop outside the door marked Patrol.

As she was stepping out of her skis, Chase, Connor and Livi Rasmussen—known to all as Raz—arrived. "What's going on?" Chase asked.

"No idea," Connor said, and the others shook their heads as well.

Inside the patrol office Anders Iverson, handler of the team's second black Labrador retriever, Darth, was pulling out stainless steel dog dishes and filling them from one of the barrels, a half circle of attentive dogs focused on his every move.

Scott stopped Lily just inside the door. "Have you seen Jackson Endicott this afternoon?" he asked.

"Jackson? I rode up to Top of the Mark with him before lunch, but I haven't seen him since."

"You haven't even caught sight of him in the distance on a run or while riding the lift?" Scott asked.

"No. Why?"

Scott looked at the other patrollers. "Do any of the rest of you know Jackson Endicott? Nine years old, a little over four feet tall, sixty-nine pounds, light brown hair and blue eyes. He's wearing black ski pants and a blue Spider jacket and a black ski helmet. Atomic skis."

The very precise description alarmed Lily. "What's going on?" she asked.

"Have any of you seen a kid like that this afternoon?" Scott asked.

The others shook their heads. Lily tugged on Scott's arm. "What's going on?" she asked again. "Has something happened to Jackson?"

His gaze met hers, worry deepening the lines at the corners of his eyes. "He's missing. Someone reported seeing him going through the backcountry gates a little before three o'clock. He hasn't been seen since."

Chapter Four

"Jackson is a good skier, but he knows he's not supposed to ski out of bounds." Denton Endicott was a big, burly man with a football linebacker's build and a slight paunch. Incongruously, he also sported a black eye, the bruising faded to a yellowish-green. Though the pictures Scott had seen of him in the media depicted a powerful, commanding presence, worry for his only child had diminished him, hunching his shoulders and reducing his voice to a hoarse croak. "He's never even asked to ski that terrain before," he continued.

"We're sending every patroller on duty to search for him right now," Scott said. "The dogs will search, too."

"Shelby knows him," Lily said. "She'll recognize him right away."

Scott didn't hide his annoyance at her interruption. "All the dogs are trained to seek out human scent," he said. "They'll key in on Jackson, even if he's fallen or in an area where he's hard to see."

"When did you last see your son, Mr. Endicott?" The questioner was Sheriff Van Howard. Denton Endicott had called him in immediately after telling the resort about his concerns for his son. Scott imagined that hadn't gone over very well with the resort's top brass. They would have preferred to keep bad news from the public if at all possible. Even if Jackson had disobeyed his father and headed off-piste, there was a good chance the patrollers would locate him. The resort was big, but it wasn't that big.

"We skied together down May Day right after lunch," Endicott said. "I had a meeting, so I left Jackson to ski on his own. He's been skiing since he was three and knows the resort as well as I do. He often skis by himself or with friends."

"Was he with friends this afternoon?" the sheriff asked.

"No. He told me he was going to go over to the terrain park and play around there for a while."

The terrain park was located off of Daisy Chain, halfway between Top of the Mark and Lift Four. Daisy Chain was also the closest run to the gates leading to the hike-to, inbound terrain. Those gates closed at 3:00 p.m.

"A lift tech reported a boy who fit Jackson's description passing through the gate near Daisy Chain a few minutes before three," Scott said.

"We got there right at three to secure the gate, and the liftie told us about it," Chase said. Beside him, Raz nodded in agreement.

"You didn't try to stop him?" Endicott asked.

"It's not illegal to go through the gate before three o'clock," Chase said. His normally sallow face was flushed, his light brown eyes troubled.

"Was Jackson by himself?" Lily asked.

"The liftie didn't see anyone else," Chase said.

"That gate serves all the terrain in Creek Bowl." Scott indicated a shaded area on the map on the wall behind him. "I'm going to assign a segment of the bowl to each patroller. We'll do a thorough sweep of the area. If Jackson is there, we'll find him."

When they exited the patrol office, dusk was already staining the sky purple and casting long shadows across the snow. With the lifts shut down, they had to snowmobile up the mountain. Chase clapped Lily on the back. "You and Shelby ride with me," he said, and headed toward the row of snowmobiles beside the office.

They stowed their skis on the back, then Lily straddled the seat and Shelby balanced in front of her. While the dog was a pro at riding the lifts or even being transported down the mountain in a sled, she was skittish on the snowmobiles, constantly shifting her weight and trying to find a comfortable position. Lily grabbed the handle on the back of her harness and held on, steadying her as Chase gunned the machine up the mountain.

At the top, Lily clicked into her skis and joined the others standing at the gate—really just a gap in the ropes marking the boundary between lift-served terrain and inbounds backcountry. A large sign informed anyone contemplating passing through this gap of the dangers of skiing off-piste. The patrollers studied the snow, with lines of ski tracks cutting through the powder at the edge of the drop into the big bowl of terrain that swept down toward a forest of trees. Just beyond those trees was the dividing line between the resort and the national forest from which SkyCrest leased terrain. Ropes and signs along this line declared Ski Area Boundary.

"We should look in the trees," Anders said. "It would be easy to get tangled up in there, or turned around." He didn't add that tree skiing presented hazards such as hitting a tree at high speed or falling into the well created when snow collapsed around the tree's roots, but everyone thought about that. They wanted to find Jackson alive, but they had to be prepared for the worst.

Next to Anders, Darth danced impatiently, then let out a short, sharp bark.

"Let's go," Anders said, and skied through the gate and dropped into the bowl. Darth, still barking, raced after him.

The others followed, skiers and dogs spreading out across the terrain that looked smooth and pristine from above, but in reality was rough in places, icy in others, and full of deep, soft powdery snow in others. The fading daylight made it difficult to see variations in terrain, and Lily bent her knees more deeply to avoid being thrown off balance. "Jackson!" she shouted as she reached the edge of the trees.

Shelby darted between the silvered trunks of aspens and bounded over downed trees and boulders. Lily guided her skis in the narrow alleys between trees, sometimes following the tracks of those who had passed through here earlier in the day, sometimes carving her own route. "Jackson!" she called, over and over until her voice was hoarse and her throat was sore.

She kept her radio turned up, positioned high on the strap of her pack where she would be sure to hear it, certain that at any moment one of her fellow patrollers would radio that the boy had been found. Maybe he had fallen and hurt himself, or maybe he had become lost in the trees. Or maybe he had left this bowl long ago and was back at the family's chalet, drinking hot chocolate and unaware of the fuss he had caused.

She was wondering if she should put on her headlamp when the radio finally crackled. "Return to base, everybody," Scott ordered.

Lily keyed her mic. "Have they found Jackson?" she asked.

"Negative, but it's getting too dark to search. Someone is going to get hurt."

She wanted to protest, but here in the trees she could hardly see two feet in front of her. More than once she had had to extricate herself from a snow-covered pile of branches. She was shivering from the cold, and Shelby plodded along beside her, tongue hanging out, clearly spent.

But first they had to climb up out of the bowl. She found the track used by those who braved the area during the day. Connor and Raz were there, clicking out of their skis. Chase and Anders, with Darth, were climbing ahead of them. Lily shouldered her skis and whistled for Shelby. Bent forward, she began the hike up to the lifts, kicking the toes of her boots into the icy snow, following the rough stairs made by the skiers who had climbed out of the bowl before her.

Scott was waiting at the gate, Hunter stretched out on the snow at his side. As each patroller passed through, they moved to the side and clicked back in their skies, then waited, until everyone was accounted for. "Any word on the boy?" Anders asked.

"Nothing." Scott looked grim. "The resort is sending up a helicopter first thing in the morning to do an aerial search. This area will remain closed tomorrow. We're going to have someone at the gate all day to enforce the closure. Everyone go home now. Try to get some sleep. We're back on at five."

Lily was so cold she could no longer feel her fingers and toes, and her legs ached. But she still had to ski down to the base. She squatted down. "Are you ready, Shelby?" she asked.

Shelby was always ready. She jumped into Lily's arms, then scrambled up onto her shoulders. Lily stood, made sure she and the dog were balanced, and skied down. The other patrollers with dogs assumed the same posture. This was one of the first things Shelby had learned in her preparation to be an avalanche dog. Running long distances on snow was hard on a dog's joints, especially when they were already tired, either from a search or from patrolling all day. Sometimes they were taken down the mountain on snowmobiles, or in sleds, but carrying them down was often the most expedient mode of transport.

"Watch your claws," Lily said, as one of Shelby's back paws dug into her neck. She put up a hand to a furry haunch. Shelby was a lot bigger now than when Lily had trained her as a pup, but she didn't mind. No matter what kind of day she had had, ending it with her dog literally wrapped around her was comforting.

But even Shelby couldn't completely console her this evening. What had happened to Jackson? He was such an appealing combination of smart and naive, daring and timid. Not being able to find him filled her with dread. Already the temperature was below freezing, and weather reports called for up to six inches of snow. A little boy alone out there was in real danger of freezing to death.

She and Shelby had trained for months in order to save lives. She felt so helpless now, not being able to do anything.

SCOTT GAVE UP trying to sleep at 3:00 a.m. He went out at three thirty to shovel a path to the street. As predicted, about five inches of soft snow now blanketed the area. The motorcycle wasn't ideal for these conditions, but he had good tires and would take it slow. Fortunately, he didn't have far to go. The temperature was sitting at zero, which would make for an uncomfortable ride. He tried to avoid thinking of the little boy who had spent the night out in this, but his mind kept returning to the memory of Denton Endicott, distraught over his son's disappearance.

By four fifty he was unlocking the door of the patrol office. Hunter trotted in after him and began sniffing his empty food dish. "It's not breakfast time yet," Scott told him, then fished a jerky treat from his pocket and passed it over. Satisfied, Hunter took the treat to a dog bed along the wall to eat.

Ten minutes later, the resort operations manager, Doug Elam, entered the office. Fifty, with dark hair just graying at the temples and the chiseled features of a movie star, Elam was the third generation of his family to head Sky-Crest resort. When the property had sold to Brugenhoff Resorts five years before, Elam had been part of the deal and had continued to guide operations ever since. "I saw your light," he said.

"Any news?" Scott asked.

"We built a bonfire in Creek Bowl last night," Doug said. "Figured the boy might see it and make his way to it. His dad and some other family spent the night out there. I think they might still be there, but I haven't heard anything."

"The sheriff said the helicopter would be here first light," Scott said.

"As long as the snow stops," Doug said. He moved to stand beside the desk where Scott sat. "What have you got on tap this morning?"

"We'll hit the usual trouble spots with charges," Scott said. "That cornice on Baker Ridge builds up in weather like this. We'll want to make sure to bring it down before we open the runs below it. And we have to hit the slopes above Buttermilk Basin and Tessa's Trees. We usually mitigate in Creek Bowl, too, but I think we need to hold off on that for now. Especially since the area is closed."

"Right." Neither of them mentioned they didn't want to bury the kid's body, if it was there.

"Nobody goes into that area without a beacon, though," Scott said. "There's not a big slide risk on those slopes, but there's some."

"You've got six dogs who can find people without beacons," Doug said.

"They can, but do you want to be the seventh person under the snow if a slide lets loose?"

"You know I just like to give you a hard time," Doug said.

Scott glared. Though Doug had declared himself in favor of the avalanche dog program at SkyCrest, Scott knew he was getting pressure from people higher up in the organization to cut the expensive, and what they saw as unnecessary, program.

Voices approaching drew his attention. The door to the office opened and patroller Nina Rose walked in, her red golden retriever, Sky, prancing beside her. Nina was SkyCrest's biggest celebrity, and Scott had worried fans would distract her from her work with ski patrol, but it turned out that the ski patrol uniform—complete with helmet and goggles—rendered her anonymous, which she seemed to prefer.

"Lily called and told me last night about the missing little boy," Nina said as she patted Hunter, who had come forward to greet her and Sky. She hadn't worked the day before, but it didn't surprise Scott that she already knew what was going on. Theirs was a small, close community.

"How is Lily doing?" Doug asked. He directed the question at Scott.

"She's fine," Scott said. He had already voiced his objections to Doug when Lily was hired—mainly, that he had had no say in her selection or training. Doug had made it clear that he was obligated to take in any Kingdom Mountain employees who wanted jobs with SkyCrest.

Two other patrollers—David Reagan and Trey Manuel—had also transferred from Kingdom Mountain, but they were different. They didn't have dogs. Scott had put his job on the line to lobby for formation of the avalanche dog program, and one screwup—say, by a person with a poorly trained dog—could bring the ax down on what Doug still referred to as an experiment. But he didn't think Lily was going to be that screwup. "She's working out okay," he added.

The door opened again, and Lily and Shelby entered. The dog made a beeline for Scott and shoved her nose right between his legs.

"Hey!" he yelled, and pushed her away.

"She likes you," Nina said, stifling laughter.

Lily's face was red. "Come here, Shelby," she said. "Don't be such a goof."

"I'd better not catch her doing that to a guest," Scott said.

Lily turned away, fussing with the straps on her pack, and once again he regretted being so quick to rebuke her. Why did he find it so difficult to relax around her?

One by one, the rest of the team reported for duty—not merely the patrollers who were scheduled to work that day, but all of them. "I figured I could help look for the boy," Brian Weeks, who with his golden retriever, Daisy, was supposed to be off this week, said. Part-timers Carson Slade and Charli Castro arrived, too.

"We're waiting for a report from the helicopter that's doing an aerial search this morning," Scott told them. "In the meantime, everyone can help with mitigation."

A murmur of agreement. This was active work that required concentration—just the thing to keep their minds off the missing child. Scott handed out assignments, and they prepared to exit patrol headquarters. Scott left them with his familiar parting words, "Be careful out there."

THE PATROLLERS SPLIT into teams, each assigned a different area. Lily and Connor were together this morning, their dogs kenneled at headquarters while they hauled backpacks full of explosive charges—essentially grenades—up the mountain via snowmobile to lob onto any slopes that might be holding snow. Other teams would ride up to bomb other slopes, while still others would take to the air in the resort's helicopter to reach high-angle slopes that would otherwise be inaccessible.

Over the more than fifty years SkyCrest had been in operation, generations of patrollers had learned the tendencies of the snow in every area of the resort. But the constantly changing weather and terrain required continual reassessment. At Top of the Mark, Connor and Lily dug snow pits to assess the characteristics of the snow. They consulted records and their own memories to determine what kind of charges they should use and where they should target them for the best effect.

They were setting their final charges of the day when a helicopter skimmed overhead, Forest Service green stripes clear on its side. "I hope they find the little guy," Connor said as he and Lily watched the chopper disappear from view.

"I hope they find him alive," Lily said.

The lower slopes had to be cleared before the lifts started operating at 9:00 a.m. Higher elevations sometimes delayed opening if more time was needed to clear them, but the goal was to have everything open no later than 10:00 a.m. barring extreme storm conditions.

With so many extra hands, all the runs were open by nine. The patrollers spread out across the resort to post up at various lift shacks around the mountain. From there they would respond to calls for assistance from guests and their fellow employees. Sometimes they needed to set up ropes to keep people out of hazardous areas, or make an appearance to slow down speedy skiers. They gave directions, answered questions, and offered advice to guests, handed out avy dog trading cards and resort maps, and even posed for pictures. Their primary job was ensuring guest safety, but they were also there to be ambassadors for SkyCrest.

Lily reported back to the main patrol office at nine thirty to feed Shelby and take her out for a break. The dogs spent most of their days kenneled, with breaks to socialize and run around, or to run training drills, but their primary purpose was to be ready if needed.

Scott was on the phone when she entered the office, his face animated. When he wasn't frowning, he was a good-looking guy—strong jaw, cleft chin, intense hazel eyes. Though today those eyes were underscored with half-moon shadows, and his jaw was dusted with a day's growth of beard. "Just the single set of tracks? You're sure they don't belong to anyone who was at the bonfire last night? You really think it could be him? Of course I'll be right there. Two of us. With dogs."

He hung up the phone. "They've found something?" Lily asked.

"The helicopter saw a sets of ski tracks exiting the woods at the resort boundary line," he said. "The imprint was pretty shallow, and he thought it looked shorter than most adult skis." He stood and shrugged into his jacket.

"Shorter kids' skis," she said. "Less weight on the snow."

"That's what they're thinking." He grabbed an avalanche beacon from the cubby behind him and checked the battery level.

"The chopper is going to pick me up at heli-ski operations." He clipped on the beacon and grabbed his pack. "They lost the tracks when they went into the trees again. I'm taking Hunter. The helicopter can set us down near the tracks. With luck we can catch up with them. I'll radio Connor and Farley to meet us there and go with me."

Lily stepped in front of him, blocking his exit. "Take me and Shelby. Jackson knows us. He's been out all night by this time. He's probably terrified. A familiar face is going to make things easier on everyone."

He hesitated. "Have you trained for backcountry rescue?"

"Not wilderness search-and-rescue, but I've trained with C-RAD on avalanche rescue—search techniques and first aid."

"It's not the same as search-and-rescue."

He tried to move past her, but she remained where she was, refusing to give way. "Jackson knows me. If two men he doesn't know are out there calling for him, he's liable to be afraid. He might even hide from you."

He looked at Shelby, who was standing at the door of the kennel, poised to come out. "Has Shelby ridden a helicopter before?"

"Of course." This was a lie. They hadn't reached the level of training that included riding in helicopters. But she had faith in her dog. Shelby wasn't the type to freak out over anything.

"All right," he said. "But you have to keep up."

She released Shelby from her kennel and grabbed a beacon, then raced after Scott.

Chapter Five

Scott hadn't asked if Lily herself had ridden in a helicopter before. She hadn't thought it mattered, but now that they were inside the noisy beast, rising straight into the air while her stomach stayed on the ground, she was having second thoughts about volunteering for this mission.

She gritted her teeth and focused on not losing her breakfast. Shelby lay between Lily's feet, head up and ears back, but obedient to the command Lily had given her to stay.

Next to them, between Scott's feet, Hunter let out a high-pitched whine. "It's okay, boy." Scott patted the dog. He glanced at Lily. "He's never liked flying."

"Have the two of you flown a lot?" she asked.

"A few times."

"For avalanche rescue work?"

"Yeah. Nothing inbounds, but we've responded to several backcountry slides."

"Has Hunter found people who were buried?" She and Shelby had spent hours training with people who volunteered to be buried in snow caves and "rescued" by the dogs, but she had yet to participate in a real rescue effort.

"He has. He made his first find less than five minutes into his very first search."

She almost smiled at the pride in his voice. She got it.

Seeing your dog succeed was every bit as satisfying as achieving something yourself.

Scott glanced at her, his expression more sober now. "None of them were alive," he said. "The people he found, I mean. Even though we got to them within half an hour in one case, we were still too late."

"They tell us that in the training," she said. *Most searches are body searches*, she remembered her first instructor saying.

"That's just the reality of what we do," he said.

"Dogs do make live finds sometimes," she said. "There was a handler who spoke to us at my last WBR training class."

"Was it Ed Hayes?" he asked.

"Yes. And his dog."

"Xena. Yeah, I know him. Everybody knows Ed and Xena. Because he's the only person most of us have ever met who did have a live find. Or at least one that wasn't made immediately after the avalanche. Most of the time our dogs aren't on scene that quickly."

"Do you ever think about that?" she asked. "I mean, why we're even doing this if the chances are so minuscule that we'll save someone?"

"I think about it all the time," he said. "Especially every time I have to justify requesting more money for people who think they're just paying for patrollers to have an excuse to bring their dog to work each day."

"What do you tell them?"

He looked down at Hunter, who was silent now and lying at Scott's feet. "I point out that dogs are great PR. Customers love dogs. They love seeing them on the slopes. Then I tell them if there's a chance to save even one life we should take it. And I tell them that every single person who has ever lost a loved one due to an avalanche would say the same."

She looked away, voice rendered useless by the tears that clogged her throat. But she would choke to death before she cried in front of Scott. So she dug her fingernails into her palms and looked straight ahead, staring at the back of the pilot's head and wondering how deep the snow would be where they were going.

SCOTT THOUGHT ABOUT Clark on days like today, all blue sky and deep powder. His best friend's idea of heaven was first tracks on snow as light as feathers. Clark whooped and hollered as he skimmed over the surface with all the speed and agility of a cheetah.

He was doing just that the last time Scott saw him, leaving lines in the snow like a swooping signature on clean white paper. One moment Scott was admiring the way Clark made it look so easy and listening to his friend's shouts echoing off the surrounding mountains, and the next he was watching in horror as the whole top of a mountain fell down on him, like a building toppling.

Clark was wearing an avalanche beacon, but Scott couldn't find the signal. Much later, they would discover the beacon had been torn from his body by the force of the avalanche. It was two days before they found him, after hundreds of hours of probing by dozens of volunteers.

A dog could have found him sooner. Maybe not soon enough to save his life, but it would have saved his family and friends two days of agony. Even that was worth something, wasn't it?

"Look down there!" the pilot shouted over the roar of the engines and rotors and pointed to their right. Scott leaned forward and craned to see out the right side of the aircraft. There, as if a giant had dragged two fingers through cake frosting, was the clear outline of ski tracks, leading from the woods that marked the ski area border, across a clearing and into the national forest.

The chopper rose and circled back, then arced down to hover low to the far left of the tracks. "I can't land in this snow!" the pilot shouted. "You're going to have to throw out your gear and jump out after it."

Lily stared at him, wide-eyed. Scott picked up his skis and tossed them out the door. His pack followed, then her skis and pack. When he reached for Shelby, Lily finally sprang to action. "You're not *throwing* her anywhere," she said. Before he could say anything, she hoisted the dog into her arms, moved to the door, and jumped.

THE SNOW WAS deep and soft as a featherbed, but it still made for an awkward landing. Lily landed on her back, with Shelby sprawled across her. The dog scrambled away, and she sat up just in time to see Scott, with Hunter in his arms, make his exit. As soon as he hit the ground, the chopper rose again.

She got up and started collecting their gear. She had to dig for one ski, but they recovered everything, and within a few minutes she was upright and ready to go. She stomped her feet, making an even place to stand on her skis.

Scott skied up beside her. "I wasn't going to throw your dog," he said. "I wouldn't do that."

She nodded. One thing she did know about him was that he took care of his dog. "It got me out of the chopper in a hurry, anyway," she said. She looked around them. "Where are the tracks?" Except for the spot where they had landed, the landscape appeared to be a smooth expanse of white.

"This way." Scott started to follow the tree line east. In a few minutes he stopped and pointed one pole at the line of ski tracks. Lily was startled at how faint they were. "Later in the day, they'll be invisible in the sun," he said.

"It's only the way the light is slanting right now that helps them stand out."

They decided to flank the tracks, the better to keep them in sight, and set out. There was enough of a downhill slant to the terrain to help them navigate without much problem on skis, but the dogs had to fight the snow, porpoising through the deepest stashes. "They're going to wear themselves out," Lily said.

"Ski behind me," Scott said. "The dogs can follow in our tracks."

She fell in behind him, and they commanded the dogs to do the same. The canines still struggled at times, but the going was a little easier. The tracks they had been following led into another thick stand of trees. Scott slid in between two trunks, and Lily followed. They wound their way in and out, stopping from time to time to reorient and make sure they were still following the faint track.

"We're almost out of the trees," Scott said when they had been skiing about fifteen minutes.

Five minutes later, they emerged, then stopped and stared. Two sets of tracks extended across the snow in front of them.

"Is that the track we were following?" She pointed with one ski pole to the smaller, fainter lines on the left.

"I think so," Scott said.

"Then who is that?" She indicated the second set of tracks—longer skis and deeper indentations, laid out scarcely a foot from the smaller, fainter tracks.

Scott looked back over his shoulder. "I don't know. But I didn't see any other tracks back there."

"Neither did I," she said. "Do we keep following them?"

"Let's backtrack and see if we can figure out where these came from."

They skied along the edge of the clearing and found the

place where the second tracks emerged. Then they followed the trail back into the woods. The tracks wound in and out among the trees, sometimes crossing the boy's tracks, sometimes taking a different path. Lily was following Scott and almost collided with his back when he stopped suddenly. She lurched to one side to avoid running over his skis.

"What is it?" she asked.

"It's a campsite." He moved forward, and she was able to see around him. The snow was beaten down, and someone had built a lean-to covered with pine boughs, snow thick on top of the boughs. Directly in front of the lean-to was the remains of a campfire, a thin tendril of smoke rising from the ashes. "They must have been here last night," she said.

Scott leaned over and fished something bright yellow from the snow. A candy wrapper. He walked to the lean-to and looked inside. "Looks like a couple of people spent the night here," he said. "There are depressions in the snow."

He took out his radio and attempted to transmit, but all they could hear was static. "Let's get out from under these trees," he said, and skied past her.

She followed him away from the campsite. By the time she reached his side, he was talking on the radio. "I'm sure someone spent the night here. Two people. And the two sets of ski tracks look like a kid and an adult."

"We can try to get some other searchers into the area." Lily thought she recognized the voice of the sheriff. "But there's another storm cell headed this way. Forecasters are saying it could drop another three to five inches of snow."

"Let us follow the tracks a little farther," Scott said. "They can't have left the camp very long ago. The ashes of the fire are still warm."

They set out once more. The two ski tracks traveled in an almost straight line across the snow, on a slope that grew progressively steeper. If not for the seriousness of their mission, Lily might have enjoyed the almost unblemished powder and the crisp air.

The two humans might have skied for hours, but they had to stop to water the dogs and give them something to eat. She and Scott drank from their water bottles and ate gorp and beef jerky. "Where do you think they're going?" she asked. "I mean, besides farther into the woods? Are there any roads out here?"

"I'd have to check on a map to be sure, but I think this is all designated wilderness. No roads. The only town is the ghost town of Pandora. I think there are some summer homes there, and a general store that operates in the summer months. But I'm pretty sure you have to cross two ridges to get there from here. Not an easy trip to make any time of year, but especially in winter."

"Jackson isn't strong enough to ski all day in this terrain," she said. "He's just a kid. And he's not especially big for his age."

"At least we know as long as he's moving, he's alive, and the exercise will keep him warmer." He stowed his water bottle and adjusted his pack. "Come on. You're right about a kid not being able to ski all day. And he'll ski slower. That should give us a chance to catch up with them."

"If someone found Jackson and decided to spend the night rather than try to make it back to the resort in the snowstorm, why didn't they turn around this morning and head for the resort?" she asked. "Why move farther away?"

"I don't know," Scott said. "Maybe they got confused? We'll have to ask them when we find them."

"What are we going to do if we see them?" Lily asked.

"I don't know," Scott said. "I guess that depends on how they act."

They hadn't gone much farther before it began to snow again—big flakes, drifting gently down at first, but gradually getting heavier and heavier, until it was like standing in a swirl of feathers. "Hurry," Scott said. "The snow is going to fill in the tracks."

Lily tried to hurry, but she was exhausted, and the snow clung to her goggles, so that she had to pause every few feet to wipe them clear. At last, Scott stopped. "I can't see the tracks anymore," he said.

"We have to stop, for the dogs' sake, if not our own," she said. Both dogs lagged behind now, tongues hanging out, fur coats caked with snow.

"You're right." He pulled out a water dish and filled it for the pups.

Lily looked around them. She had no idea where they were. Scott's radio popped and crackled. "Scott, are you there?"

"I'm here," Scott answered.

"Were you able to follow the tracks?" the sheriff asked.

"We were, until it started snowing hard. We can scarcely make out anything now."

"The storm came in faster than we expected," the sheriff said.

"I don't think there's anything more we can do out here right now," Scott said.

"Can they pick us up?" Lily asked. Now that she was standing still, she was shivering, and fatigue dragged at her, as if she were hauling a sled full of bricks behind her.

"The helicopter is grounded until the weather clears," the sheriff said.

Scott looked at her. "I heard," she said. "What are we going to do?"

"You can try to ski out," the sheriff said.

They both looked back the way they had come—the route was rough, and the last half of the journey would be uphill. "I can't do it," Lily said. "And I don't think the dogs can, either."

"We've got emergency supplies," Scott said. "We'll make camp and spend the night. In the morning we can decide on our next steps."

"Roger that. We'll be in touch."

Scott hooked the radio back onto his pack. Silence closed in around them. Snow had gathered on their shoulders and the tops of their helmets. "Come on," Scott said. "Let's ski back into the woods. We'll have more shelter there."

The woods were farther away than Lily remembered. "Tell me again why we didn't come out here on snowmobile," she said.

"It's a wilderness area," he said. "No motorized vehicle traffic allowed."

"Not even in an emergency?" she asked, her voice rising sharply on the last word.

"Maybe there wasn't time to get permission," Scott said.

She fell silent. There was no sense debating what they might have done. They needed to focus on getting through the night.

At last, they entered the trees. Immediately the brunt of the storm lessened. By silent consensus they avoided the camp where they believed Jackson and his companion had spent the night. Scott led them to a small clearing and stopped. "This looks good," he said.

They stood still for a moment, not speaking. The silence of the snowy woods closed around them, making her feel a million miles away from anyone else. If the loneliness of this place spooked her, what would it feel like to a little boy, so far from everyone he knew and loved?

Chapter Six

This was not how Lily wanted to spend the night. She was cold, tired and hungry. The thought of trying to sleep in the snow without even a sleeping bag made her want to cry. But worse yet was the thought of spending long, idle hours with Scott. They had gotten along well enough all afternoon, and the other night at the bar, but she couldn't shake the feeling that he was judging her, and she could never relax around him. He was so freaking calm and competent—anything she said or did wasn't going to be good enough.

But she wasn't going to tell him any of this. She wouldn't give him the opportunity to label her as a complainer. Instead, she looked him in the eye and said, "What can I do to help?"

"We need a fire, and we need shelter," Scott said. "I'll start the fire. See if you can find some dry wood." He knelt and began clearing snow from a patch of ground. Both dogs lay down to watch.

She turned in a slow circle. Everything was covered in snow. The few tree branches she spotted on the ground would be soaking wet.

"Look underneath trees and deeper in the undergrowth," Scott said, not looking up. He had taken out a knife and was shaving a twig into small pieces.

She turned and walked away, heading for the far side of the clearing. She plunged into the undergrowth, snow dumping onto her back, head and arms. She shook off the deluge and pulled at a tangle of branches. What she came up with wasn't exactly dry, but she supposed it was drier.

Shelby plunged in beside her and began tugging at a branch and biting at the snow. She looked up at Lily, snow crowning her head and back, then shook hard, filling the air around her with a cloud of icy white. Lily laughed. The pup made it impossible to stay in a bad mood.

"What are you doing?" Scott called.

"Getting firewood," she called, and gathered branches into her arms.

She dumped the wood beside Scott. He frowned at her offering. "That doesn't look very dry."

"If you think you can do better, you're welcome to try." She studied the small blaze he had made. If it snowed much harder, the fire didn't stand a chance.

Scott stood. "We need to make a shelter," he said.

"With tree branches?" She pictured the one they had found at the other campsite.

"A snow cave would be warmer." He pulled the collapsible shovel from the back of his pack. "Help me pile up a bunch of snow to work with."

For twenty minutes they shoveled, clearing an eight-foot circle and piling the fresh, wet snow around the perimeter. "That's a good start," Scott said finally. He stuck his shovel in one pile and pulled a multi-tool from his pocket, opened it and folded out a sawtooth blade, then handed it to her, handle first. "See if you can cut some pine branches. We can pile them beneath us to help insulate us from the cold ground."

For the next half hour she sawed away at green pine

branches, until her fingers ached and her gloves were sticky with sap. She managed to cut a decent-sized pile of leafy branches, and dragged them back to where Scott was putting the finishing touches on a sort of igloo, with built-up snow sides and tarp-covered branches for a roof. "Get inside and I'll pass the branches to you and you can lay them out on the floor," he said.

Inside, there was scarcely enough room for her to rise up on her knees. When she stretched her arms out, she could almost touch the sides. "Is this going to be big enough?" she asked.

"We'll need to huddle together with the dogs for warmth," he said.

She recognized the logic of what he was saying, but her stomach fluttered nervously. She wasn't worried Scott would try anything…improper. But the thought of being that close to him unnerved her.

"Here. Take this branch."

She took the pine boughs he passed her and spread them on top of the snow floor of their shelter. When she was done, he handed her a second orange tarp. "Lay this over the branches. Do you have an emergency blanket in your pack?"

"Yes." The Mylar blankets were standard first aid supplies.

"Good. We can wrap up in those. Now come out and let's see what we have to eat."

She joined him by the fire as he fed in larger twigs from which he had shaved the bark, revealing mostly dry wood beneath. The blaze wasn't large, but it burned bright and hot. "How did you get the fire going so fast?" she asked.

"Cotton balls soaked in petroleum jelly."

"Huh. I bet you were a Boy Scout."

"Eagle Scout."

"I guess that's where you learned to be so prepared."

"That and the army."

"When were you in the army?"

"Eight year ago." He turned his attention from the fire to his pack. "What have you got in the way of food?"

She opened her pack and pulled out everything she had shoved in there before she left her apartment this morning: protein bars, peanut butter pouches, cheese sticks, nuts, four candy bars, two peanut butter and jelly sandwiches, energy gels, two water bottles, instant hot cocoa mix, and two tiny bottles of peppermint schnapps.

Scott cradled the schnapps in his hand. "What made you bring these?"

"For medicinal purposes."

He laughed—one of the few times she had heard him laugh. It was a nice laugh, deep and rumbling, and it set up a flutter in her chest.

He surveyed the items she had laid out. "You must have been hungry when you packed all this," he said.

"I thought we would be searching again, and when we found Jackson he would be hungry."

He nodded, all mirth gone. "Yeah, he probably is. Though maybe whoever is with him has food."

"We found that candy wrapper," she said. "I hope that means Jackson is eating something."

His own contribution to their stores included chicken bouillon cubes, more protein bars, beef jerky, instant coffee, energy gels, and two ham and cheese sandwiches. "We won't go hungry," she said.

He took out a metal mug, filled it with snow, and set it on a rock beside the fire. "I only have the one cup, but we can share."

He made cocoa and added a slug of the schnapps, then

offered the mug to her. The hot, sweet liquid was heavenly, sending a jolt of warmth through her. She refrained from gulping it all and passed it back to him.

They shared the sandwiches and a candy bar each, and a second cup of fortified hot chocolate. By the end of the meal she was drowsy and mostly warm.

The dogs ate jerky and one of the ham sandwiches, and some of the bottled water.

"I feel almost human again," she said as she passed over the empty cup.

"I'm sorry I got you into this situation," Scott said.

The comment surprised her. "I don't think you could have predicted this. And I volunteered to come with you, remember?"

"I should have come by myself. I shouldn't have risked someone else."

"Isn't one of the chief rules for recreating in the wilderness not to go out alone?" she asked.

"I should have gone with my original plan to take Connor."

"Why? Because he's a man?" Her contented mood had vanished, replaced by weary annoyance.

"No. Because he's more experienced."

"What would he have done that I haven't?" she asked. "Except that he would eat more food and take up more room in the snow cave."

He nodded. "You're right. I shouldn't have said that."

She leaned toward him. "What is it about me, exactly, that you don't like?" she asked. "Because if it's just the fact that you didn't personally handpick me for your exclusive team, then you need to get over yourself." She clamped her lips shut. Had she really said that out loud? Maybe the schnapps had been stronger than she anticipated.

He stared at her, his face flushed. This was it. He was going to fire her, and management would back him up. She'd been out of line—even if what she said was true.

"That's not it at all," he said.

She remained silent, waiting.

He leaned forward, hands gripping his upraised knees. "I didn't want to add you to the avy dog team," he said. "But it had nothing to do with you, personally. I didn't want to add anyone else to the team."

"Why not?"

"Because there are some members of the corporation's board of directors who think the program is too expensive and unnecessary. There's a big push to cut costs these days. It's why Kingdom Mountain was shut down—it wasn't proving profitable enough."

"Kingdom Mountain was at a lower elevation than Sky-Crest," she said. "The season became too short to be profitable."

"Right, but they could have added snowmaking or tried to expand terrain. Instead, they shut it down. Some people at the corporate level are pushing to shut down the avy dog program here, too."

"And one more patroller and dog makes the program that much more expensive," she said. "But if they really want to cut the program, one team more or less isn't going to make that much difference."

He began rubbing Hunter's ears. "I know that. I was just grasping at straws. I didn't mean it personally."

"Instead of keeping this to yourself, you should tell all of us what's going on," she said. "Maybe if we all work together, we can come up with new donors or ways to cut costs or improve our image to the board members."

"I don't like to worry people that their jobs are in jeopardy."

"Except it's the kind of thing we need to know."

He fed another piece of wood to the fire. The temperature had dropped and while the front of her was warm enough, cold seeped through her clothing into her back. Shelby lay on her side between Lily and the fire, snoring softly.

"I hate that a child is in danger," he said. "But if we can find him, it might persuade people who matter that the avy dog program is worth it."

"Do you think Jackson is the one who made that camp we found?" she asked.

"You know him better than I do. Do you think he could have built that shelter and started that fire?"

"He's really smart, but it's hard for me to picture any nine-year-old doing all that. Where would he have gotten the tools, or even the skills to do those things? It's not like his dad is a big outdoorsman, teaching his kid how to survive in the wilderness."

"It definitely looked to me like two people had slept in that shelter," Scott said.

"So Jackson and who else?"

"Another searcher? Everyone in town must know by now that a little boy is missing. Maybe someone decided on their own to go out and look."

"It's strange that you and I didn't see whoever it was," she said.

"Maybe they're trying to remain anonymous."

"They must not have found Jackson," she said. "Or we would have heard." She inched a little closer to the fire and shoved her hands deeper into her pockets. "So maybe what we saw was two completely differently people. Other searchers, or even tourists who don't know about the missing boy.

I'm really worried about him. How is he going to survive a second night in this weather, alone? He might have had a few snacks with him, but they would be gone by now."

"Is he the type to panic or give up easily?" Scott asked.

"He's smart and he's quiet. In some ways he's very mature for his age. He's traveled all over the world and is pretty comfortable around all kinds of people. But he's also been very sheltered. Spoiled, even. He's a good kid, but I wouldn't say he's faced much physical hardship."

"Has he done much backcountry skiing? Do you know?"

She shook her head. "I have no idea."

"Why did you leave the job with the Endicotts?" he asked.

"Because Jackson didn't need me. When he turned six he started school full-time."

"What do you do in the summers now?" he asked.

"Different things. Wait tables. Work retail. What about you?"

"I work for the resort," he said. "Maintenance staff. Hunter still gets to come to work with me every day."

"How old is Hunter?" The dog was looking at each of them in turn, having recognized his name.

"He's four. He's been training as an avy dog since he was two months old."

"Same as Shelby."

Shelby gave a single thump of her tail, but didn't raise her head. "So she's about eighteen months old now?" he asked.

"Sixteen. And she's doing great." She dared him to say otherwise.

"What made you want to train an avalanche dog?" He scooped snow into the mug and set it beside the fire to melt.

She could have made up a story about seeing other patrollers work with their dogs, or about coming across the perfect dog to train for the work. Maybe it was the darkness, or the lingering effects of the food and the schnapps, or the novelty of being stranded together, but she decided to opt for the truth. "My brother, Ben, was a ski patroller. He was six years older than me and was training an avy dog, Cache, when he was killed in an avalanche. He was training Cache that day, and was being careful. But a slab of snow let loose and caught him. Friends dug him out, but by the time they found him, it was too late."

"I'm sorry," he said. "That's really tough."

She took a deep breath, steadying herself. "I tried to take over where he left off, training Cache, but I was only seventeen, and I just didn't have the experience, or the time, to do a good job. But I kept the idea in the back of my head. I worked ski patrol for five years before an opening came up in the avalanche dog program at Kingdom Mountain. I applied and was accepted."

"Where did you get Shelby?"

"From a breeder in Steamboat Springs. She comes from a long line of avalanche and search-and-rescue dogs." She reached out to stroke the dog. "My parents helped me buy her. I could never have swung the cost on my own. The resort gave me some money for training, and I scrounged up the rest. But it was worth it. She's been great. Ben would have loved her, too."

"I'm sorry about your brother," he said. "What happened to his dog?"

"Oh, he's living the good life with my parents. He's a pampered senior now. What about you—how did you get into avalanche dogs?"

"Similar story to yours," he said. "My best friend was killed in an avalanche. It took two days to find his body. When I learned that a dog could probably have found him much faster, I wanted to do that for other people—to not make them wait to know what really happened to their loved one. And you always hope that you'll be able to save someone."

"I'm sorry about your friend."

"Yeah." He looked up, snow sifting down onto his cheeks. "He would have loved being out here like this. He would rather be outside in bad weather than cooped up inside almost any time. I try to take comfort in the fact that he died doing something he loved, but I'd rather he was still around."

"How old was he when he died?" she asked.

"He was twenty-six. If he had lived he'd be thirty-three now. A year younger than me."

Ben would be thirty-four if he had lived. The same age as Scott. The two men were nothing alike—except that they both loved dogs and snow.

It was getting colder. She tried to hide her discomfort, but doing a poor job. "You're shivering," Scott said. "Let's turn in. We'll be warmer inside."

"I hope so," she said, and followed him into the snow cave.

She had been nervous about sharing the close quarters, but there was nothing intimate about curling up in a crinkly Mylar blanket while wearing all her clothing. The dogs settled between them. Lily pulled a knit beanie down low over her forehead, gripped the blanket with mittened hands, and waited as warmth gradually seeped into her body and she drifted to sleep.

WHEN SHE WOKE it was still dark. Her whole body ached with cold. Disoriented, she groped beside her, startled to find herself alone. As sleep receded, she sat up and found her headlamp and switched it on. A figure darkened the doorway of the snow cave and she gasped.

"It's just me," Scott said. He crawled past her. The dogs followed and curled into tight balls, tails over noses. "I'm sorry I woke you," Scott said. "Go back to sleep."

"Yes, sir."

"Sorry. I don't mean to sound bossy."

"I get it. You're used to giving orders."

"I guess that's true." Order or not, she wasn't going to be getting back to sleep anytime soon. Her head ached—probably from a combination of schnapps and not enough water. She found her water bottle, but the contents had frozen.

"Here." Scott passed over his. "You have to keep it tucked in next to your body or it freezes."

She should have thought of that. "Thanks." She drank, greedily, then passed it back.

He drank also. The gesture struck her as intimate, even though he was only being practical.

"I should have asked earlier," he said. "Do you have someone who will be worrying about you—a romantic partner, or your parents?"

"My parents are in Vermont. And I don't have a partner. What about you?"

"My parents are in Utah."

"That must be nice, having them so close."

"I guess. I don't really see them much."

There had to be a whole story there. She was debating whether to ask when he said, "I broke up with my girlfriend four months ago."

His tone of voice made her think the breakup hadn't been his idea. "Rough," she said.

"She said she couldn't see a future with a man who had so little ambition."

"Ouch."

"I get it. Working resort maintenance and ski patrol isn't

going to pay for a six-figure lifestyle. For what it's worth, my parents agree with her. They think I'm throwing my life away."

Ouch. "There's something to be said for enjoying the work you do," she said.

"Oh, I think those guys drawing six-figure salaries probably enjoy their jobs, too. I'm just not them."

She understood. The thought of spending every day in an office made her anxious. "Not every woman sees things the way they do," she said.

He didn't answer, except for a soft exhalation of breath that told her he was asleep.

SCOTT WOKE, ON HIS SIDE, his arm draped over someone soft and warm and definitely female. He smiled to himself and moved closer, until he was pressed against her back. She stirred against him, and awareness edged out sleep as he realized this wasn't Madison, his former lover. He froze, and other facts became clear. He and the woman were both wearing a lot of clothing, and lying on the ground.

He sat up and switched on his headlamp. Lily turned onto her back and looked up at him, eyes wide.

"I'm sorry," he said, dread hollowing his chest. "I was asleep. I didn't realize." If she complained to management, he'd be out of a job, the avy dog program ended permanently.

She lay still a moment longer. "It's okay," she said finally, and sat up. She didn't look at him, but didn't seem angry, either. "Where are the dogs?" she asked.

"I don't know. Hunter!"

"Shelby!" she called.

Both dogs came squeezing in, all wagging tails and wiggling bodies. He hugged Hunter to him and buried his face in the dog's thick fur, while Lily did the same to Shelby. "What time is it?" she asked after a bit.

He checked his watch. "Five thirty-two."

She untangled herself from the Mylar blanket and began folding it up. He did the same with his. She left the shelter, Shelby bounding after her. He folded the tarp they had been lying on and by the time he emerged from the snow cave, she was squatting beside the fire, blowing on the tiny flame that licked at a pile of pine needles.

He collected water in the cup he had washed out last night and boiled water for instant coffee. They shared the cup and ate protein bars for breakfast. The dogs ate the last of the jerky.

Afterward, they took down the shelter, scattered the fire and reloaded their packs. At 7:00 a.m. they emerged into open space once more, and he radioed to headquarters. Doug Elam answered. "Scott? You and Lily okay?"

"We're fine," Scott said. "What's the plan for today?"

"I was just talking to the helicopter pilot," Doug said. "They're going to pick you up in...in twenty minutes. Where are you?"

Scott read off the GPS coordinates he had marked. "There's a big clearing here. We shouldn't be too hard to spot."

"Have they heard anything about Jackson?" Lily asked.

"Any sign of Jackson?" Scott asked.

Another long pause. "We haven't found him," Doug said. "But there's been a development."

Doug's voice wasn't reassuring. Scott's gaze met Lily's. She looked as ill as he felt. "What kind of development?" he asked.

"That boy didn't wander out there and get lost," Doug said. "He was taken."

Chapter Seven

The sheriff and Doug were waiting when Lily and Scott and the dogs arrived back at the SkyCrest heliport Monday morning. "What have you heard about Jackson?" Lily demanded as soon as she stepped off the helicopter. "Do you know where he is? Is he safe?"

"Mr. Endicott is meeting us at my office," Doug said, one hand at her back, urging her forward. "We'll know more then."

They piled into a resort SUV, Scott and Lily together in the back seat, the dogs sprawled across their laps. Doug drove, but no one spoke on the short drive to the resort offices. The SUV's heater was pumping out warmth, and Lily found herself drifting off, the exertions of the previous day and her uneasy sleep the night before catching up with her.

She woke abruptly when the SUV parked in the underground garage, and followed the sheriff and the others into the elevator to Doug's office. Denny Endicott met them at the door. His lip had healed and the bruising around his eye had faded to a sickly yellow and brown, but it was the look of hope on his face that was so painful Lily had to look away. "We don't have anything new," the sheriff said.

Denny turned away, but his hunched shoulders and clenched fists were the image of a man fighting to hold himself together. "Mr. Endicott, do you have the note you received?" Sheriff Howard asked.

"Yes. It's right here." Denny reached into the pocket of his flannel shirt and took out a plastic bag and passed it over to the sheriff.

"Did it come to you in this bag?" the sheriff asked.

"No," Denny said. "The envelope was delivered with the day's mail. I put everything in the bag after I read it. Maybe I didn't mess up any other prints too much."

Sheriff Howard lay the bag on Doug's desk, then pulled on a pair of nitrile gloves and eased an envelope from the bag. "No return address," he said. "Local postmark. We'll check with the post office, see if anyone remembers when this came through, but it could have been dropped in a postal box anywhere in the area." He opened the envelope and removed a single sheet of paper. "Looks like a page torn from a spiral notebook. Lined paper, three-hole punched, no perforations. The message is hand-printed in block letters. 'We have Jackson safe. Cooperate and he won't be hurt.'" He looked up at Endicott. "What do they mean—cooperate? What do they want you to do?"

"I don't know," Endicott said. "I haven't heard anything before or since."

"You never had any previous threats to you or your family, or attempts to extort you in any way?" the sheriff asked.

"None."

"What about that black eye?" the sheriff asked. "Who gave you that?"

Denny touched one finger to his bruised eye. "I had too much to drink at a client dinner and tripped and fell. It doesn't have anything to do with Jackson." He leaned forward, fingers gripping the back of a chair. "We're always security conscious. We have a good alarm system at home, and I've taught Jackson not to talk to strangers or to go with anyone he doesn't know. I don't understand how this happened."

"Do you have cameras around your house?" the sheriff asked.

"Yes. More than one."

"We're going to want to see all the footage, as far back as you've got. The person or persons responsible for Jackson's kidnapping may have been watching you for a while now."

Endicott straightened. "I thought he was safe here at the resort," he said.

"We've turned over all our surveillance camera footage to the sheriff's department as well," Doug said. "We're also gathering data on every skier whose ticket was scanned yesterday. Something like this never should have happened."

"We've asked for assistance from the Colorado Bureau of Investigation as well," the sheriff said. "We're putting as much manpower as possible on this."

Endicott turned away from them. For the first time, he noticed Lily and Scott on the sofa. "You two were out searching last night, right?" he asked.

Lily took off the knit cap she had been wearing and stood. "Hi, Denny, it's me, Lily Alton."

"Oh, Lily. I'm sorry I didn't recognize you." He swiped a hand over his face. "I'm operating on not much sleep."

"It's okay," she said. His normally full and open face looked thin and drawn, deep lines on either side of his mouth.

Scott rose and came to stand beside her. "We were out searching for Jackson last night," he said. "We followed ski tracks we thought might be his for a long way. He was by himself, and then he wasn't."

"Where did the second set of ski tracks meet up with

him?" Doug asked. He walked to a color map of the resort and the surrounding national forest that took up much of one wall of the office.

Scott and Lily moved to the map, along with the sheriff and Endicott. "Right at this second clump of woods." Scott indicated the spot on the map.

"We found a camp," Lily said. "Where two people spent the night. There was a fire and a shelter."

"Where was this camp?" the sheriff asked.

Scott and Lily studied the map. "About here, do you think?" Lily pointed to a location, and looked to Scott for confirmation.

"Yes, I think that's right." Scott moved his finger a few inches south and west of the spot she indicated. "We spent the night somewhere in here, I think."

"You're sure the camp was recently occupied?" Doug asked.

"Positive," Scott said. "The fire was still smoking."

"There was a shelter there, made of branches and a tarp," Lily said. "I'm sure someone spent the night before last there."

"There were two indentations in the shelter, like two people slept there," Scott said.

"Jackson and the kidnapper," Denny said.

"We don't know that for sure," the sheriff said.

"But who else would be out there in a snowstorm?" Denny asked.

"We followed the tracks as far as we could," Scott said. "Until the snow obliterated them."

"What's out there?" Denny asked. "Where would they be headed?"

"That's all designated wilderness," Doug said. "There aren't any roads." He frowned at the map. "The kidnapper might have arranged for a helicopter to pick them up, but we're not aware of any flights into the area except our own helicopter."

"We'll follow up on that," the sheriff said.

"Someone could have picked them up in a snowmobile," Denny said.

"Maybe," the sheriff said. "But we've been flying drones every time the weather clears enough to allow it and we hadn't seen any tracks."

"Does that mean they're still out there?" Endicott asked. "Jackson must be exhausted."

"They could be heading for Pandora," Scott said.

"Where's Pandora?" Denny asked.

"It's a ghost town on the other side of this ridge of mountains." The sheriff indicated a jagged ridge near the top of the map. "But you'd have to be crazy to try to make it all the way there on skis, especially with a kid in tow."

"Crazy or desperate," Denny said.

"If you received that letter today, wouldn't it have had to be posted by Saturday or earlier?" Scott asked.

Endicott looked to the sheriff. "I would think so," he said. "Don't you, Sheriff?"

"The stamp is canceled," the sheriff said. "According to the postmark, it was mailed Friday."

"That's taking a big risk, isn't it?" Lily asked. "What if their plan failed and they weren't able to grab Jackson? What if the weather didn't cooperate?"

"Or what if the letter was lost?" Scott asked. "Why not just send an email or a text, or make a phone call or hand-deliver a note?"

"The Endicotts' security may have scared them away from the house," the sheriff said. "And the kidnapper may not have been tech-savvy enough to send an electronic message without us being able to trace it."

"If the kidnapping didn't happen, it would be easy to dismiss the letter as a crank message," Doug said. "Mr. Endicott might have even thrown it away without reporting it to the sheriff."

Denny nodded. "I might have."

"We think it likely there are a group of individuals involved," the sheriff said. "We'll get a team to Pandora and see if we can intercept them. We'll also continue to fly surveillance in the area."

"What can we do to help?" Scott asked.

"Go home and get some rest," the sheriff said. "We'll take it from here."

"Thank you for your help," Doug said. "You can go now."

Reluctantly, Lily followed Scott and the dogs out of the room. She waited until they were in the elevator headed to the ground floor before she spoke. "I notice no one offered us a ride home," she said.

"I'll take you," he said.

He led her to the motorcycle, parked in a back corner of the parking garage. This time, Shelby didn't hesitate to hop into the sidecar. Lily was able to fasten her helmet without help, and the ride to her apartment—in the daylight this time—wasn't as unnerving. Scott drove slowly, and she clung to him, as much for the bodily warmth as to steady herself. The clock tower in the middle of the ski village indicated it was almost noon. Crowds of skiers convened in the cobblestoned courtyard that fronted many of the restaurants and shops. People in brightly colored pants and jackets lounged on benches or carried skis and snowboards toward the lifts. Children laughed and dogs barked. Shelby's ears were straight up, but she maintained discipline—or maybe she was too frightened to risk leaping from the moving vehicle. Scott guided the bike between pedestrians and parked cars, and turned onto the main road leading away from the village.

Minutes later, he turned into the apartment complex. "Thanks," she said again, after he had parked and she had returned his helmet. "I guess I'll see you tomorrow."

"Let me know if you hear any news about Jackson," he said.

"Yeah. You, too." She waved, then turned and followed Shelby into the building.

She waited inside, out of sight, and listened to the roar of the motorcycle recede as he headed toward his own building. The complex had an elevator, but it was primarily used for freight. Lily always used the stairs, considering the climb part of her exercise routine. Even weary as she was, it didn't feel right to resort to the elevator, so she started up the stairs.

Shelby bounded up ahead of her, still full of puppy energy.

Inside, she fed and watered the dog first. She debated making tea, but decided on the shower first. The hot water elicited a blissful groan as it sluiced over her. For the first time in almost two days she began to feel truly warm. Lavender-scented steam surrounded her, and she fought the urge to lean against the tile wall and fall asleep standing up.

Her intention was to make tea, eat something, then go to bed. But instead of feeling sleepy, after she ate she had the jangly, electrified feeling of having been awake too long to relax. Her mind replayed the events of the previous two days like a poorly plotted movie. Jackson had been so happy when she had spoken to him two days ago. How could he have just…disappeared? The thought of him in the wilderness somewhere, with a stranger or strangers, cold and frightened and maybe even hurt, tore at her.

She powered up her laptop and searched until she found a map similar to the one on Doug's office wall. From what she had seen yesterday and this morning, the wilderness area was rugged, the direct route to anywhere interrupted by dense woods, imposing ridges or deep ravines. Reaching Pandora would mean a traverse of a pair of rocky mountain ridges full of dangerous obstacles obscured by snow, steep drop-offs, the near-constant threat of avalanches, and bitter winds. How was a child supposed to survive all of that?

She stared at the map until her vision blurred, and was about to close the screen when another thought occurred to her. If going over the mountain to reach Pandora was so difficult, was it possible to go *around*? She traced a Forest Service road that led from town, skirting the wilderness area and ending a couple of miles before Pandora. The kidnapper would have to be careful to keep himself and Jackson out of sight, and the journey to get to the road from the place where they had spent the night would require navigating around dense woodlands and uneven terrain. But that route would also afford more places to hide or seek shelter from the weather.

She punched in the number for the sheriff's office. When a woman answered, Lily identified herself, explained that she had been part of the search for Jackson and asked to speak to the sheriff. The woman transferred the call, but the person who answered wasn't the sheriff. "Sheriff Howard is very busy right now," the man said. "I'll be sure he gets your message."

"Who am I speaking to?" she asked.

"I'm one of the deputies. That's really all you need to know."

That was not all she needed to know, but weariness was stealing over her once more. "This is Lily Alton," she said. "I was with the sheriff earlier today. Tell him that I think instead of traveling over the mountain, Jackson's kidnapper might try to go around. It would be safer, and they'd have more places to hide."

"That's an interesting theory," the deputy said. "But I don't think you're right."

"Just tell the sheriff what I said and let him decide," she said.

"Thanks for calling," the deputy said, and hung up.

She stared at the phone, shaking with anger. She scrolled and found Scott's number. Wait until he heard about this. But she hesitated with her finger over the number. Scott was exhausted. He was probably already asleep. He wouldn't welcome her calling and waking him up to complain about a dismissive deputy.

She set down the phone. As much as she wanted to help Jackson, there really wasn't anything she could do right now. All she could do was rest up and be ready if she was needed. And wait.

Chapter Eight

On Tuesday Lily and Shelby went back to their regular post with Ski Patrol. Scott and the rest of the group were there, and everything at the resort was running normally. "I don't have an update on Jackson Endicott," Scott told them at the beginning of the patrol meeting.

"News reports said he'd been kidnapped," Brian said. "His family received a ransom note or something."

"I heard the family was contacted," Scott said. "I don't know if there was a ransom request or not." He consulted the clipboard in his hand. "Law enforcement is dealing with that. We need to focus on our work here. I need a dog and handler to talk about safety to the ski school kids at ten a.m. Lily, can you take that?"

"Sure." She sat up a little straighter. "Shelby loves kids."

"We've got a set of posters you can use for your presentation," Scott said. "Just go through those and you should be good."

He moved on to patrol assignments, then dismissed them. She waited until everyone else had left before she approached Scott. "You really haven't heard anything about Jackson?" she asked.

He slotted the clipboard onto a shelf in the ski patrol office. "They're more likely to tell you news than me. After all, you know the family."

"I've thought about calling Denny and asking, but I hate to bother him." She nibbled her thumbnail. "I'm so worried about Jackson."

"We all are, but there's nothing we can do. Let's just get on with our work." He opened a file drawer and took out a large envelope. "Here are the posters for the safety talk. You'll be talking to the second-and third-grade kids. I think there's two classes. Meet them midway down Easy Street at ten o'clock."

At ten, she skied up to a group of ski school children waiting at the edge of the trees, midway down a beginner's run. Shelby, newly released from her kennel and sporting a new baby-blue SkyCrest bandanna, danced with excitement as they approached the children. "Patroller Lily is here to talk to us about ski safety," Kristen Waters, one of the instructors, introduced her.

"Hey, everybody," Lily said. "This is avalanche dog Shelby. She's going to help me with today's presentation."

"Can we pet her?" a little girl in a pink snowsuit and helmet asked.

"You can all pet her after the talk," Lily said. "First, I want you all to listen carefully. At the end I'm going to ask some questions and if you answer a question correctly, I have prizes." She held up the stickers and trading cards she had brought along to hand out to them.

The posters featured cartoons of the SkyCrest mascot, a baby-blue dinosaur named Shred, demonstrating lift etiquette, the importance of respecting other skiers and other tips for safe skiing. Lily enlisted Shelby to demonstrate points such as taking turns, and looking up the slope before you merged on a new trail. "What happens if you don't stay still on the chairlift?" Lily asked.

"You can fall off," a little boy in a helmet with flames painted on the side said.

"That's right." Lily looked at Shelby. "Show them how you fall, Shelby."

Shelby dramatically plopped onto her side in the snow, sending the children into fits of giggles.

"You get a prize for answering my question," Lily said. The boy chose a sticker.

"I want a trading card!"

"I want a sticker." Other children clamored for the prizes.

Lily asked more questions about the material they had just covered and handed out stickers and cards to all the children. Every one of the children was so adorable, she thought. Some of them weren't much younger than Jackson. "Do any of you know Jackson Endicott?" she asked as a little girl deliberated over her choice of prize.

"I heard about him on the news last night," one boy, the tallest of the group said. "But I didn't know him."

"What happened to him?" a little girl asked.

"He disappeared," the boy said.

"I'm sure they're going to find him very soon," Kristen said. She sent Lily a warning look.

"Hey everybody, you've been such a great group," Lily said. "If you take your skis off, you can come pet Shelby."

"Why do we have to take off our skis?" a girl asked.

"Ski edges are very sharp," Lily said. "They can cut a dog's paws and hurt them very badly. So never ski close to a dog."

The kids raced to kick off their skis, then descended on the dog, who greeted them with a wagging tail. Lily moved over to Kristen. "Sorry I mentioned Jackson," Lily said. "I didn't mean to upset anyone."

"It's okay," Kristen said. "What a terrible thing to happen. I'm afraid to let any of these kids out of my sight now."

"Have you seen anyone hanging around the children?" Lily asked. "Watching them or anything?" Though the note Denton Endicott had received seemed to indicate that Jackson was the deliberate target, maybe the kidnapper had looked for him first among the other kids at the resort.

Kristen shook her head. "I haven't seen anyone. And we do watch for things like that. Anyone hanging around the kids who we don't know for sure is a parent gets reported to security."

"How often do you have to report someone?" Lily asked.

"Not often, but even once is too much."

Lily was packing up the posters and preparing to call the kids off Shelby when a familiar figure in a black helmet skied up. Scott nodded to her. "Don't let me interrupt."

"I was just finished."

"Is everybody ready for lunch?" Kristen called.

"Yes!" The children scrambled to line up.

"Shelby, come!" Lily called.

The dog loped over to her side, while the ski school students returned to their skis. "Did you need me for something?" she asked Scott.

"What were you and Kristen talking about?" Scott asked.

She frowned. Why did he care about that? "I asked her if she had seen anyone suspicious hanging around the kids," she said. "I thought maybe whoever took Jackson might have looked for him with other children."

"It's not your job to investigate this," he said.

"I happen to think it's every person's job to look out for kids," she said. "A little boy's life is at stake, and I'll do anything I can to help."

She braced herself for an angry reaction, but he appeared unfazed. He watched the ski school class head down the hill, an undulating line following their instructor. "You're really good with the kids," he said. "I bet you were a good nanny."

Was he complimenting her, or insinuating she should leave patrol and go back to taking care of children? She wished he wasn't so hard to read. "I try to do my best at every job," she said. "Whether that's changing diapers or training an avalanche search dog."

He was still watching the retreating children. "I've been thinking a lot about Jackson."

"I have, too," she said. "I looked at a map again last night, and I don't think the kidnapper would try to go directly over the ridge to Pandora."

He turned to look at her, though she couldn't see his eyes clearly through the amber goggles he wore. "Why do you say that?"

"Going over the ridge is the shortest route, but it's also really risky and really hard. It would be a lot easier to go around the mountain."

"A lot farther, too."

"Yes, but safer."

"Maybe you should talk to the sheriff about your idea."

"I tried calling and leaving a message last night. The deputy who took my call was pretty dismissive."

"I've been thinking about going over to Pandora myself and looking around," he said.

"Could you even get there?" she asked. "I mean, don't you think the place is crawling with law enforcement?"

"I don't know. But it's worth checking out, I think."

"When would you go?"

"It's my regular day off tomorrow," he said. "If I get an early start I can get there and back in no time. If you drive up Matlock Road there's a trail at the end that goes right into the wilderness area."

"Can you make it up there on a motorcycle this time of year?"

"Probably. From there it's probably only a couple hours' hike to Pandora."

"You shouldn't go by yourself," she said.

"I'd have Hunter with me."

"Is Hunter Lassie now? Does he know how to go for help?"

The corners of his mouth twitched, almost as if he was holding back laughter. "I thought maybe you'd like to go with me."

"I'm on the schedule for tomorrow."

"Anders wants next Sunday off. You could switch with him."

Her heart jumped. "Then yes, I'll go with you."

"You sure? You don't want to think about it?"

"I told you, I want to help Jackson."

"Good." He paused, then added, "Let's take your car. That way we'll for sure get to the trailhead. I'll be at your place tomorrow morning at six." Without waiting for more, he planted a pole and skied away. She watched him go, struck once more by how much he stood out among the crowds of skiers—tall and graceful, but skiing with purpose. A man on a mission, even if the mission was to get to the bottom of the mountain. His suggestion to look for Jackson on their own had surprised her. One more bit of proof that he didn't always play strictly by the rules.

DARKNESS STILL PAINTED the world in shades of gray as Scott stood beside his motorcycle waiting for Lily to emerge from her apartment. She had texted she would be out in five minutes. He stamped his feet and watched his breath fog the air. The thermometer at his apartment had registered minus nine degrees Fahrenheit when he left.

A sharp bark from Hunter alerted him to Lily and Shelby's approach. Shelby shot toward them and tackled Hunter. The two dogs rolled on the snowy pavement then leaped up, tails waving.

"Good morning," Lily said. "My car is over here." She led the way two rows over to a blue Subaru Outback, and stood on tiptoe to heft her skis into the rack on the car's roof. Scott followed and added his own skis, then they shoved packs, boots and poles in to the back of the vehicle. "Do you have your beacon?" he asked.

"Yes. And it's fully charged."

"Just checking."

She grinned. Was she amused at his inability to stop being the boss? Or because he was so predictable she had anticipated what he would say?

She pulled an insulated mug from the side of her pack, slid the top open and sipped. The tantalizing aroma of cinnamon filled the air.

"What are you drinking?" he asked.

"Black tea with cinnamon and cloves." She tilted her head and considered him. "Let me guess—you drink black coffee."

She wasn't wrong. "Let's go," he said.

She slid into the driver's seat and buckled her safety belt. Shelby arranged herself on the back seat next to Hunter. "Have you heard anything from the sheriff?" she asked as he settled into the passenger seat.

"No. I called Doug last night and he said a couple of agents from the Colorado Bureau of Investigation interviewed him, but they wouldn't say anything about the case."

She started the car and backed out of her parking space. "I

called the Endicott house last night," she said. "The man who answered said they weren't taking calls and there was no news. I didn't recognize his voice, so I thought maybe he was a cop."

"We may get to Pandora and find the place crawling with cops," Scott said.

"What are we going to tell them if they ask what we're doing?" She turned onto the road that led to the back country.

"We tell them we came to ski," he said. "Plead ignorance."

She chuckled softly.

"What's so funny?" he asked.

"You don't look that clueless."

"What do you mean?"

"Everything about your screams 'competent and informed.' I mean that as a compliment, but no cop is going to believe you live in a cave and haven't heard a thing about a boy being kidnapped. You can't help looking like you know exactly what you're doing."

"Then I've fooled you," he said. "I have no idea if we'll find Jackson or not, but I have a hard time sitting around doing nothing."

"Then you and Shelby have a lot in common."

There she went, making him the butt of a joke again. "I'm glad you find me so entertaining," he said.

"Would you rather I be intimidated?" She sipped her tea.

"I'm not trying to intimidate anyone."

"When I first started work here, you were pretty forbidding," she said. "Until I figured you out."

"Oh, you figured me out, did you?" Whereas she confounded him more every minute.

"You're like a lot of guys I've met—cool and detached on the outside, but inside you care deeply about things. I think it frustrates you when other people don't care as much, like with the avalanche dog program."

The assessment hit him like a punch in the gut—he didn't like being so transparent. "Were you a psychology major?" he asked.

"No, but I pay attention to people." Another sip of tea. "It's my superpower."

"Too bad your superpower can't tell us what happened to Jackson."

She sighed. "Yeah. Too bad."

They both grew quiet, though he was aware of her, only a few inches away, focused on her driving. He had seldom been around someone so self-contained, content with silence.

She turned the car onto the snow-packed Forest Service road that led to the trail they wanted. "Have you been here before?" he asked.

"No. I looked up the directions last night online. And I read about Pandora. Apparently, it used to be a gold mining town."

"Right. There are half a dozen log buildings still standing, some of them in pretty good shape. It's a popular destination for hikers in the summer, and there are a few more modern summer cabins near the town site that are still kept up, but hardly anyone comes up here in winter, except occasional cross-country skiers."

At the end of the road, she parked at a locked gate. "It looks like a lot of people were parked here recently," she said, pointing to the packed snow on either side of the road.

They let the dogs out to run around while they collected their gear. They both donned packs, boots and skis. "It's about two hours, maybe a little less, to Pandora from here," he said.

"Should we turn on our beacons?" she asked.

"Not yet. We have to go a ways before needing to worry

about avalanche danger." He took a pistol from his pack and slid it into the pocket of his jacket. She watched him, eyes wide. "We don't know what we might be up against here, or who we might run into," he said. "I want to be ready."

"Okay." He couldn't read the emotion behind that single word.

"I was military police," he added.

"Ah. That explains a lot."

It explained the gun, maybe. He wasn't sure what else she meant, and he hesitated to ask. No doubt she would have an interesting explanation, but he wasn't ready for more dissecting of his character right now. "Come on."

They squeezed around the gate and set out skiing side by side down the closed roadway. Dark green firs and the bare white trunks of aspen thickly lined the road on either side. They had been skiing about fifteen minutes when the road curved and the woods opened onto a view across a meadow up against the mountains. Rosy light bathed the snow-filled meadow in a pink glow and painted the mountain peaks in gold. Lily stopped and stared, her lips parted.

He skied up beside her. "What is it?" he asked. "What do you see?"

She turned toward him. She hadn't lowered her goggles yet, and her eyes were damp. "It's so beautiful," she said.

She was beautiful, her face flushed from exertion and cold, lips so soft and inviting. Had he ever felt as awed as she looked now?

He forced his gaze away. "It's too cold to stand around," he said, and skied off.

She caught up with him, and they skied hard for the next mile, the dogs running ahead, then falling back to lope along in their tracks. After another half hour, they stopped and put on their avalanche beacons. They left the trees behind and steadily climbed, the only sound the squeak of their skis on the snow and their own labored breathing.

The sun was climbing overhead before they came to a wooden signpost that directed them to Pandora. The town itself was tucked into an open flat, or park, between two peaks. The buildings sat in the shadow of the mountains, snow piled halfway up the sides of most of the structures. The largest building, a former dormitory for miners, was missing half its roof and leaned precariously to one side, but several of the smaller structures—mine offices and miners' homes—appeared intact except for a few broken windows.

"Why isn't there anyone here?" Lily asked. She turned to him. "The sheriff's deputies should be here, and Colorado Bureau of Investigation people. This should have been the first place they came."

"Maybe they were here and left when they didn't find anyone," he said.

She turned to study the scene again. "I don't see any tracks. It doesn't look like anyone has been here since it snowed on Sunday."

"Maybe this elevation got more snow last night," he said.

She moved forward on skis, sliding right up to the front of the closest building. She leaned forward to peer into the window.

"See anything?" he called.

She shook her head. "And I don't smell smoke. If someone was sheltering here, they'd have to build a fire, wouldn't they, as cold as it's been at night."

It was still cold. Well below freezing, he guessed. The arctic chill stung his bare cheeks and had him tucking his gloved fingers into his jacket to try to thaw them.

They skied all the way around the ruins, but found nothing but a set of fox tracks and the smaller imprints of rodents.

"How did people ever live up here in the winter?" she asked when they were back at the entrance to the town. She glanced at the steep slopes on three sides. "Weren't they worried about avalanches?"

"Avalanches are what finally drove people to abandon the town," he said. "For a while I think they worked the mines in summer only, but then the gold played out completely. Everyone left shortly after the turn of the twentieth century."

She hugged her arms across her chest and rubbed her shoulders. "It's creepy."

"Maybe we should go back," he said. Initially, he had planned to ski past the town, maybe even over the ridge above. They might spot Jackson or his kidnapper. But looking up that steep slope, with its heavy blanket of snow, sent danger warnings through him. Steep slopes and fresh, heavy snow were prime conditions for an avalanche. He wouldn't risk his life—much less Lily's—on such a reckless foray.

"I'm ready to get out of here," she said, and turned toward the trail back to her car.

The return trip took less time. They were traveling downhill and said little. As she was unlocking the car, Scott's phone rang. He waited until they were inside, engine on and heater running, before he looked at the missed call. "I've got a message from Doug Elam," he said. "I'd better see what he wants."

He called his voicemail. Doug's Georgia drawl was thick with agitation. "If you get this in the next five minutes, I need you and Hunter to the staging area below Axis Ridge. We've got a big slide, two people potentially involved."

Chapter Nine

"Two people? Do they think Jackson and his kidnapper were caught in the avalanche?" Lily asked, the words coming out as fast as the hammering of her heart.

"Doug didn't say." Scott studied his phone for a moment longer, then tossed it on the dash. "There's a Forest Service road that cuts across to the base of the ridge," he said. "I'll tell you where to turn."

"Shelby and I are only certified for inbound searches," she said, and felt foolish as soon as the words were out of her mouth. Scott knew this—and it wasn't as if she didn't want to help.

"Just do what I tell you," he said. "It'll be fine."

She turned the car around and headed back the way they had come. She drove as fast as she dared on the narrow, snow-packed road, teeth clenched, gripping the steering wheel so hard her fingers ached. She lost traction on every curve, and fought to bring the fishtailing car back under control. Scott gripped the dash with one hand and said nothing.

Phrases from her training played in her head. *A person caught in an avalanche has a 92 percent chance of surviving if they are rescued within fifteen minutes. Survival rates drop by 3 percent for every additional minute someone is buried.* Those were just one set of statistics. A Canadian study put the survival rate at 86 percent after ten minutes and only 10 percent after thirty-five minutes. The whole point of training dogs was to get to victims as quickly as possible, increasing their chances of surviving.

She had been so focused on training Shelby to locate someone quickly that she hadn't thought about how long it could take to reach the site of a slide to even begin the search.

She pressed down harder on the accelerator and thought of Jackson. *Hang on*, she silently told him. *Please hang on*.

They reached the cutoff road and followed the ruts left by other vehicles to where the track abruptly ended at a six-foot berm of packed snow. Half a dozen vehicles were parked haphazardly in front of the berm. Lily fit the Subaru in between a Jeep and a lifted 4X4 pickup and cut the engine. Scott retrieved his phone and checked the screen. "Twenty minutes," he said.

She followed him to the back of the Subaru and retrieved her pack. "Put your beacon in receive mode," he said.

She did so. "What about Shelby?" she asked. The dog had her head over the back of the seat and was whining softly.

"She can search with Hunter," Scott said.

The dogs raced ahead of them, to the group standing at the edge of the snowfield. The jagged tops of trees jutted through boulder-sized clumps of snow that marked the path of the snow slide, pine needles scattered across the surface like confetti. Dirt, broken branches and boulders littered an area as wide as a football field.

Some people were already searching, moving in a line across the snow, pausing every step to plunge long, flexible poles into the snow. They were feeling for anything soft enough to be human.

Adam Derocher from C-RAD jogged over to them. "A

helicopter searching for the boy who went missing from SkyCrest saw the slide run and called it in at 11:56," he said.

Lily did the math—twenty-seven minutes had passed since that call. "The spotter saw two people skinning up the ridge just before the snow turned loose," Adam continued. "He didn't have anywhere to land."

"Where were these two people?" Scott asked.

"On the east side." Adam pointed. "I want the dogs to search over there."

Like Scott, Adam knew Shelby was only certified to search inbounds, but he apparently wasn't going to pass up the chance to use her now that she was on the scene. Both dogs were eager to go. Hunter had done this before, and was communicating his excitement to Shelby, who raced between him and Lily. Shelby had been part of dozens of training exercises by now, and she knew searching meant a reward of playing with her favorite toy. But she had only found volunteers hiding in man-made snow caves, never anyone buried by an actual avalanche.

Tugging on Shelby's lead, Lily followed Scott and Hunter across the snowfield, stumbling over blocks of compacted snow, dodging chunks of rock and broken trees, then sinking to her knees in an unexpected drift. By the time Scott halted at the far edge of the field, she was breathless, one knee throbbing where she had twisted it.

"I'm going to release Hunter first," Scott said. "After he takes off, let Shelby go and give her search command."

Hunter sat, trembling with anticipation, his attention fixated on Scott. Scott unclipped the dog's lead. "Hunter, find!" he commanded, and Hunter took off, nose to the ground.

"Shelby!" Lily had to repeat the dog's name twice before Shelby focused on her. She removed the leash. "Go find!" she said.

Shelby took off in Hunter's wake, head down and moving back and forth, casting for scent.

Less than three minutes later, Hunter gave one sharp bark and sat, gaze fixed on a patch of snow. "He's found something!" Scott shouted, and raced toward his dog.

Lily followed. She dug at the compacted snow with her hands while Scott used the folding shovel from his pack. Hunter dug, too, sending plumes of snow flying between his legs. Other searchers joined in.

"I've got a leg," someone shouted, and the searchers shifted their efforts to several feet above this location, hoping to uncover the person's head.

Five frantic minutes later someone uncovered hair, and then the whole face and upper torso. The man's skin was blue, his lips frozen in a grimace, his head at an unnatural angle. Adam knelt beside the body and felt for a pulse, then shook his head. "He's gone," he said. "Looks like his neck was broken."

Lily looked away. The body in the snow didn't even look real, but was still shocking. Scott led Hunter away. He praised the dog and offered the rope toy that was his reward for a successful find, but the dog knew something wasn't right and kept looking back toward the unknown man's icy grave.

While the others worked to free the rest of the body, Lucy looked around for her dog. "Shelby!" she shouted, hands cupped to her face. "Shelby, come!"

Finally, she spotted the dog at the very edge of the snowfield, pawing at something. Lily made her way to the dog, who by this time had a piece of blue fabric in her mouth. "What have you got?" Lily asked.

She wrested the cloth away from the dog and was examining it when Scott and Hunter joined them. "What is it?" Scott asked.

"It looks like blue nylon," she said. "Is it part of a jacket?" Jackson had been wearing a blue jacket, she remembered that.

Scott examined the scrap of fabric, which was about as big as his gloved hand. "Maybe it's part of a backpack," he said.

Both dogs had returned to the spot and were worrying at something. Scott and Lily shoved them out of the way and began digging. Within minutes, they had unearthed a small backpack with an internal hydration bladder—a style favored by skiers and snowboarders. Lily stared at the battered pack and tried to remember what Jackson had been wearing when she had spoken to him on Saturday.

"There's a name on the inside flap," Scott said. He turned the pack around so he could read the name written in black marker, but fell silent.

"What does it say?" Lily demanded.

He met her gaze, looking every bit as hollowed-out as she felt. "It's Jackson Endicott."

THE VOLUNTEERS PROBED and dug in the compacted snow for the next two hours and found no sign of Jackson, or of anyone else. Denton Endicott arrived, along with the sheriff, and they stood over the pack, Endicott's normally ruddy face slack and devoid of color. "Jackson got that pack for Christmas," he said. "I'm the one who wrote his name in it." He bowed his head, jaw clenched, but after a moment he looked up at the snow spread out like a rumpled blanket. "How could the pack be here and you haven't found my boy?"

"Avalanches have tremendous power," Adam said. "They can tear the clothes from a man."

Avalanches could also break bones and crush skulls. Scott had seen bodies recovered that looked practically untouched, while others were battered almost beyond recognition.

The sheriff put a hand to Endicott's back. "I need you to look at the man we found and see if you recognize him," he said.

Scott followed the two men, wanting to hear what they would say. He had taken Hunter back to the truck an hour before, the dog exhausted from repeated fruitless searches. Lily and Shelby had disappeared in the mass of volunteers. He needed to find her soon, but for now he stuck close to the sheriff and Endicott.

The man's body had been placed on a litter and covered with a blanket, then slid into the back of one of the two ambulances that waited on scene. The driver opened the doors and stood aside to allow the sheriff and Endicott to lean in. Scott waited to one side. He'd gotten a good look at the body earlier—a fit white male in his mid-to late thirties, clean-shaven with light brown hair and brown eyes, dressed in good-quality but not top-of-the-line ski gear. "I don't recognize him," Endicott said after a moment. "But he looks so ordinary. Not the kind of guy to stand out."

"No," the sheriff said. "Apparently, there's no identification on him. Maybe we'll get lucky when we take his fingerprints. We found these things with him." He moved to a tarp on the ground nearby and pulled it aside to reveal a large backpack. "It looks like he was prepared to survive out here for some time. There's a lot of food and cold weather gear in there."

"Maybe he came out here to search for Jackson," Endicott said.

"Then why not have ID with him?" the sheriff asked. "There was also this." He pulled an evidence bag from inside his parka and showed it to Endicott. Inside was a handgun.

Endicott face went even paler. "My poor boy," he whispered.

"You're sure you've never seen the dead man before?" the sheriff asked.

Endicott shook his head. "Never."

They retreated from the ambulance. Suddenly, Endicott turned to Scott. "Are you the one who found him?" he asked. "You and your dog?"

"Yes, sir."

"And you found Jackson's pack?"

"Lily and Shelby found that," he said.

"Then why haven't you found Jackson? What do you think happened to him?"

"I don't know, sir. If he was buried very deeply, that can make things more difficult."

"How long has it been since the avalanche?" Endicott asked.

"Almost three hours," Scott said.

"Then if Jackson is under there, he's dead," Endicott said.

Scott said nothing.

"Don't try to shield me," Endicott said. "If Jackson was buried and you haven't found him by now, he's dead, isn't he?"

Scott nodded. "I'm sorry," he whispered.

Endicott stared out across the snow again, blinking rapidly. "We might not find him until spring," he muttered.

"We're going to bring heavy equipment out here to dig starting tomorrow," the sheriff said. "We need to uncover all the evidence we can, and if your boy is here, we'll find him."

The sheriff led Endicott away. Scott started toward the parking area, then stopped and scanned the scene for Lily and Shelby. Lines of volunteers continued to probe the snow, but Adam had agreed there was no need to exhaust the dogs further, now that the chance of finding anyone alive was virtually zero. Yet there were Lily and Shelby, on the far side of the slide, the dog's plumed tail waving like a signal flag.

Scott trudged over to them. "What do you think you're doing?" he demanded. "Are you trying to kill your dog?"

She stared at him, wide-eyed. "I've been trying to get Shelby to come back to the car for the last hour," she said. "But she keeps searching this same section of the slide. She actually tried to lead me into the woods three times, but when I follow her, she loses the trail after about a dozen yards."

"You're the one in charge, not your dog."

"But why is she acting this way?" Lily asked. "She's never done anything like this before."

"She's frustrated because she didn't find a person, only a pack. And it's obvious to anyone she's exhausted."

Shelby lay on the snow, tongue lolling, though her head remained up, ears alert.

Lily shifted the leash to her other hand. "Come on, girl," she said. "We have to call it a day."

The dog rose, but looked back toward the edge of the snowfield, not moving. "Come!" Lily commanded.

Shelby's ears twitched, but she didn't move, not even when Lily yanked on her leash. Clearly, Lily hadn't taught the dog who was in charge. "You're wasting my time," Scott said, and bent and scooped the dog up. Then he stalked back across the snow, Lily trailing behind him.

The dog was small for a Malinois, but she still weighed at least fifty pounds. Scott, worn out from the day's activities, struggled to carry her over the rough terrain. "Put her down," Lily said. "I can carry her."

Scott could hardly manage. There was no way Lily, who looked ready to drop where she stood, was going to be able to carry the dog. As for Shelby, she had become an inert mass in Scott's arms, like a dog cast in lead.

When they exited the avalanche field he did set the dog down. Lily grabbed the leash and stalked ahead, pulling the dog after her. She might be tired, but clearly she was angry, too. She was waiting beside the car when he reached it. "I would never do anything to harm my dog," she said.

"I don't believe you would, intentionally," he said. "But the thing about dogs is that they are so devoted and tenacious that they will literally work until they drop. It's up to us to see that that doesn't happen."

She loaded Shelby into the car, then slid into the driver's seat. "I'm sorry," she said as she started the engine. "I was too focused on finding Jackson, and not enough on Shelby. I won't let that happen again."

He nodded and fastened his seat belt. She backed the car out of the parking spot. "Nobody feels good about days like today," he said.

"How could we find Jackson's pack and not find Jackson?" she asked. "If he was skinning up that ridge, he would have had it on."

"Maybe he stopped to get something out of it and took it off right before the slide triggered," Scott said. He could picture it. Skinning was hard work. Maybe Jackson wanted to shed a layer of clothing, or put away his gloves, or check the water level in his hydration bladder. "When the slide released, it would have been torn from his hand."

"Then where is Jackson?"

"He could be anywhere in that debris field," Scott said. "Under feet of snow."

"What if he's not there?" she asked. "What if he got pushed out of the way to the side? That's why I kept following Shelby into the woods. I thought Jackson might have run in that direction."

"If that happened, why didn't he come back when he saw all the searchers?" Scott asked. "Even if he didn't know his kidnapper was dead, he should have known there were people in that crowd who would help him."

"I don't know," she said. "And I don't know why Shelby lost the scent trail every time after only a few feet."

She stared straight ahead, and he wondered if she was crying. "I'm sorry about Jackson," he said. "Knowing him the way you do makes this harder."

She sniffed, but still didn't look at him.

"I saw his father a few minutes before I found you," he said. "He identified the pack as Jackson's. He said he didn't recognize the man. The sheriff said he hopes they can match the man's fingerprints to a known person."

"The sheriff said they're bringing heavy equipment out to dig tomorrow. They're looking for more evidence. Maybe he means the pack."

"Maybe they'll find Jackson's body," she said. "As awful as that is for his family, not knowing for sure what happened to him must be worse."

When they reached the townhomes where they both lived, Lily had to wake Shelby to get her out of the back seat. "Oh honey, I'm sorry." Lily knelt and hugged the dog. "I shouldn't have let you work so long."

"She'll be okay," Scott said. "She's young, and she doesn't appear to be limping."

She kept her cheek pressed to the dog's fur, not looking

at him. "You're not going to kick me out of the avy dog program because of this, are you?"

"No! What made you think that?"

"You were so furious with me. And I understand why. A big part of our training is protecting our dogs, and I wasn't doing that."

"We all make mistakes," he said. "The lessons we learn by screwing up are the ones that really stick." He hadn't been wrong to correct her, though maybe he could have been gentler. The anguish he had heard behind her question made him feel like the worst kind of heel. "I know I wasn't exactly welcoming, but I'm glad you're in the program. And you and Shelby did a good job today. She found Jackson's pack."

"I wish she had found Jackson."

"We all wish that." He patted her shoulder. She looked up at him, and his gaze shifted to her lips. She appeared delicate, but he had seen how strong she could be. Her lips were soft like her, but they would be strong, too. Expressive. Communicating what they wanted.

He took a step back. "Good night." Without waiting for a reply, he turned and hurried off toward his apartment. He was Lily's supervisor. He had no business kissing her, especially when she was exhausted and vulnerable.

He prided himself on always doing the right thing. But why was the right thing so hard this time?

Chapter Ten

Scott slept fitfully, reliving the afternoon's search for Jackson Endicott over and over again. Then the search for Jackson morphed into the search for Clark—the frantic probing and digging, the desperate effort to cling to hope, the surrender to despair. And then the waiting and not knowing, trying not to think about the suffering Clark might have endured in his last moments, and everything Scott might have done to save his friend.

He rose early Thursday and tried to banish the nightmares with a shower and hot coffee, but the gray mood clung to him like a second skin as he rode into the silent ski village just as the sun rose. On his way to the ski patrol office he saw the light was on in Doug's office. He detoured there and found the resort director behind his desk, looking like a Ralph Lauren ad, in a Nordic sweater and dark jeans, the scent of some expensive cologne hovering around him. He looked up when Scott tapped on the door. "Come in, Scott," Doug said. "What can you tell me about the avalanche yesterday?"

Scott sank into a chair in front of Doug's desk. "Hunter found a body. Maybe the kidnapper."

"Alleged kidnapper," Doug said. "They still haven't identified him. And we don't know for sure he was the person who took Jackson."

"You sound like a lawyer," Scott said.

"Only a man who was married to one. Do you want coffee?"

Scott shook his head. "Have you heard anything else from the sheriff? Besides the fact that they don't have an identity for the dead man?"

"I had to meet them here at six a.m. so they could collect every recording from every camera in the resort," Doug said. "They're looking for images of the man."

"I thought they already looked at the footage," Scott said.

"Not everything. And when they viewed the video before, they were focused on Jackson and anyone he might have talked to. This time they have a specific face they're trying to find."

"Too bad finding him doesn't help us locate Jackson."

"The sheriff said it's pretty certain the kid's dead," Doug said.

Scott winced. "We found his backpack. At the edge of the avalanche field. Until we find a body, we won't know for sure what happened to him."

"You think there's a chance he escaped? Where did he go?"

"I don't know. And he's probably dead." He didn't like saying it, but there was no sense ignoring harsh reality.

"They're still conducting air searches," Doug said.

"They are?"

"One flight a day. But until they have a clue where to look, that's a shot in the dark. An expensive one. If the kid's last name wasn't Endicott, I doubt they'd be doing that."

"Lily and I skied over to Pandora yesterday," he said. "No one was there. It didn't look like anyone had been there since the first snow."

"You and Lily Alton?"

"She was Jackson's nanny. He'd be more likely to come to her than a stranger."

"Guess so. Was there something in particular you needed to see me about this morning?"

"No." Scott shoved to his feet. "I just wanted to know if you'd heard anything about Jackson."

"I'll let you know if I do."

From Doug's office, he made his way to ski patrol headquarters. Lily was waiting at the door, Shelby at her side. "You're early," he said as he unlocked the door.

"Only by a few minutes," she said. She moved quickly past him into the office, but not before he saw the shadows beneath her eyes. She was probably as exhausted as he was. He was tempted to tell her to take a sick day and go home, but he couldn't play favorites. She would probably resent the suggestion, anyway.

Over the next quarter of an hour, the rest of the team reported in. They fed the dogs, gathered their gear and assembled for the morning meeting. With light snow overnight, they had some routine avalanche mitigation to do, targeting the areas most likely to be unstable. "We need to plan on a delayed opening for Lifts 11 and 12," Scott said. "After all the lifts are running, we need to reposition the pads on the lift towers for Lift 6. And the snow fence is down in part of the mid-mountain terrain park, so Raz, you and Trey take care of that."

He read off each team member's duties for the day, then dismissed them. As Lily gathered her gear, Scott found her. "How are you feeling this morning?" he asked.

She stowed a water bottle in her pack and zipped it shut. "I'm fine."

"How is Shelby?"

"She's fine, too. We both crashed after we got home yesterday."

"I'm sorry if I was too hard on you yesterday," he said.

She finally looked at him, clearly surprised. "You weren't. You were right. If I'm going to do this work, I need to protect Shelby, even when she won't protect herself." She leaned closer, her voice a little softer. "Are you okay?"

"I'm fine."

"I was remembering what you told me, about your friend. The one who was killed in an avalanche. You must think of him every time you're called out to search."

"Yeah. I do." He had to force the words out over the sudden constriction in his throat. "But you probably think about your brother."

"Yes…but I don't think it's the same for me. I wasn't with him when he died. I wasn't there for the search, either. It was only after I started training with Shelby that I even thought about it much."

"I don't think these searches are easy on anyone. Maybe that's something we need to stress more in training—the emotional toll this can take."

She shrugged on her pack, then donned her helmet. "We'll get through it," she said, and left.

He followed her out the door a few moments later and spotted her standing with Denny Endicott. "Scott!" she called, and waved him over.

He jogged over to them. "Everything okay?" he asked, looking from her to Endicott. The grieving father didn't look any better than he had the day before, his skin pale, eyes hollow. "Do you know where I can find Doug?" Endicott asked. "He isn't in his office."

"I can see if I can raise him on the radio." Scott unclipped the radio from his pack. "What do you need?"

"I got another message this morning. From the kidnapper. They say they still have Jackson. They say I have to cooperate if I want to see my son again."

TEN MINUTES LATER, Lily stood with Scott and Denny in Doug Elam's office. Doug had summoned the sheriff, but he wasn't waiting to question Endicott. "What do they mean, cooperate?" he asked. "What do they want you to do?"

"I don't know. Someone called right after I received the note and said there would be more instructions later." He looked down at the note that lay on the corner of Doug's desk. Like the first, it was written on plain paper, and Denny had placed it into a clear plastic bag. "I asked to speak to Jackson, to prove he really is alive, but they wouldn't let me."

"If they say they have him, that must mean he's alive," Lily said.

"It could be a hoax."

She winced at Scott's words. Maybe he was right, but did he have to dash Denny's hopes so plainly?

"That's why I asked for proof that Jackson is okay," Denny said. "I want to believe he's alive, but after yesterday…" His voice trailed away.

The door opened and Sheriff Howard entered, accompanied by the undersheriff, Tricia Dees. "What's this about another note?" the sheriff asked.

Denny showed him the note and told him about the phone call that had followed. "If they won't give me proof Jackson is alive, does that mean he really is dead?" he asked.

"Mr. Endicott, you must know the odds of your son having escaped that avalanche yesterday afternoon were slim to none," the sheriff said. "I'm sorry, but I won't lie to you."

Denny nodded.

"I think this is a desperate attempt by the kidnappers to get what they want, even though they know they've lost Jackson," Howard said.

"Have you been able to identify the man who was killed yesterday?" Denny asked.

"Not yet," the sheriff said.

"What about the excavation at the avalanche site?" Denny asked. "Has that started?"

The sheriff looked as if his shoes were pinching his feet. "We've run into a snag there. The avalanche occurred in a designated wilderness area. The Forest Service doesn't want heavy equipment in there tearing things up."

"We're trying to get a special permit," Tricia said.

"So far, no one's budging," the sheriff added.

"What else are you doing to find my son?" Denny asked.

"We're reviewing footage of all the video at the resort," Howard said. "We're trying to find the man whose body we recovered. We hope that will help identify him or find his connection to Jackson. We're still interviewing people who were at the resort that day and might have seen Jackson with someone. We've sent the man's fingerprints and image to the CBI and the FBI for help in identifying him. We're analyzing records for any similar crimes. We've put the word out to the public, asking anyone with information to contact us. We have Jackson's picture on social and traditional media."

"But you're not physically searching for Jackson," Denny said. "Why not?"

Lily was thankful she wasn't facing the hard look Denny gave the sheriff, but the lawman didn't wilt. "We're a small department, assisted by two agents from the Colorado Bureau of Investigation. We're doing everything we can, but we don't have the manpower to continue a ground search.

We have to focus our resources on where we have the chance of getting the best results."

He didn't say *we can't waste our time looking for a body*, but Lily thought that was probably what he meant.

Denny's expression hardened. "I'm going to use every resource at *my* disposal to find out what happened to my son," he said, then left the room.

Doug was the first to break the silence that blanketed them after Endicott's departure. "I think we all need to get back to work," he said.

"Come on," Scott said, and headed for the door.

Lily followed. She caught up with Scott at the elevator. "Do you really think Jackson is dead?" she asked.

The look he sent her stung—a mixture of pity and impatience. "You know the statistics about surviving an avalanche. I'm sorry, but that boy is buried under feet of snow right now."

She bowed her head, not wanting him to see the disbelief in her eyes. He would think she was foolish. Everyone else clearly thought Jackson was dead, killed by that wall of snow that had broken away from the ridge yesterday afternoon. Everything in Lily's training told her that, too, but she couldn't give up. Not on the boy she had fed and bathed and played with from the time he was a toddler. Jackson wasn't any missing child. He was part of her. And she couldn't give up on him, no matter how foolish that might seem to some.

SCOTT LOOKED FOR Lily at the end of the day. Not finding Jackson had hit her hard, and he wanted to make sure she wasn't blaming herself for what had happened. Shelby wasn't in her kennel at patrol headquarters, so that probably meant Lily had taken the dog out for some exercise. He released Hunter from his kennel as well. They could help sweep the runs for any stragglers and look for Lily and Shelby at the same time.

He spotted Connor as he exited the lift office and flagged him down. "Have you seen Lily and Shelby?" Scott asked.

"I saw them headed up Lift 4 a few minutes ago," Connor said. "I was just headed up 2 to start sweeping Buttermilk Basin."

"Good," Scott said. "I'll see if I can catch up with Lily and we'll head down the front side." This section of beginner and easy intermediate runs was often the last of the day to clear of eager skiers hoping to get in one final run.

The last few skiers were boarding Lift 4 when Scott and Hunter arrived. The liftie, a lanky blond from New Zealand, grinned as the pair approached. "How's it going, mate?" he asked.

"We're doing okay, Noah," Scott said as he looked back at the approaching chair. "How are you?"

"Can't complain, though I wouldn't mind a sweet pup like this one." He leaned over to pat Hunter.

"Did Lily and Shelby ride up ahead of us?" Scott asked.

"Sure did. Shelby batted those big brown eyes at me like the flirt she is." He leaned over to boost the dog into the lift chair. "Have a good run, mate."

As they rode the lift up, Scott scanned the terrain below for Lily and her dog. The crowds were thinning, the sun low in the sky and temperatures cooler. He made note of the need to reposition the snow fence that marked the beginning of the terrain park. A snow dump had partially obscured a couple of trail signs. They'd need to check those first thing tomorrow. Snow was in the forecast tonight. They'd need to set charges to clear the slopes above Tessa's Trees and the Glades.

At the top of the lift, Hunter bounded off and Scott skied

out after him. "Have you seen Lily and Shelby?" he asked the liftie, a tall woman name Gigi.

"They headed down May Day about ten minutes ago," she said.

May Day was a wide blue run that opened to views of the distant snowcapped peaks. Two-thirds of the way to the bottom, he spotted Lily and Shelby, surrounded by half a dozen preteens. Hunter let out a bark and raced to join them, but Scott called the dog back. He stopped a few feet upslope and ordered Hunter to sit. Lily was running Shelby through a bunch of basic obedience exercises—sit, stay, roll over— to the delight of the children. Scott watched for a while. She had pushed her goggles up on top of her helmet and was smiling at the children, who cast adoring glances at her and the dog. Wisps of light brown hair had escaped from the helmet and framed her face, and her cheeks were flushed pink from the cold. Most of the time, he avoided looking at her directly, but now, with all her focus on the dog and the children, he felt free to do so. Her beauty hit him like a kick in the gut, leaving him breathless and staggered. He'd felt it the very first time he laid eyes on her, and recognized the danger in the feeling. He was her boss. He wasn't supposed to feel this way about her. Or at least, he wasn't supposed to act on his feelings. And he wouldn't. He respected her, admired her even, though her presence on the team made him uncomfortable. That was his problem, not hers.

She looked up, and for a fraction of a second their gazes locked. Another kick in the gut. Her smile had vanished, and she quickly looked away. Yeah, she definitely didn't feel the same attraction he did.

"I have to go now, kids," she said.

"No!"

"Show us one more trick!"

"Please!"

Smiling, she shook her head and called Shelby to her side. She lowered her goggles and gripped her poles.

"Is that your boyfriend?" a girl with brown braids and braces asked.

Lily glanced at Scott again. "No, it's my boss." She turned from the children and skied over to join him. "Did you need something?" she asked.

"How are you doing?" he asked.

"I'm fine."

Her tone was brusque, and she didn't look at him. "What did you need to see me about?"

I needed to make sure you were okay. But he couldn't say that. "I need to get a copy of Shelby's certification for our files."

Her head snapped up. "You're worried about that *now*?"

He had been trying to come up with something innocuous when the words popped out. He looked away, face burning. "Just get it to me whenever you get a chance."

She shook her head. "I can't really think about that right now."

He started to walk away, but that was the coward's path. Instead, he faced her. "What's wrong?" he asked.

She didn't answer.

"Is it Jackson?" he asked. "It's natural you're upset about him. It's always harder when you know the victim."

"Don't say that word."

"What word?"

She grimaced. "Victim."

"Lily." He tried to make his voice gentle. "You know the odds of Jackson still being alive are slim to none."

"You don't know that." He couldn't see her eyes behind the reflective goggles, but he was sure she was glaring at him. "His backpack was found at the edge of the avalanche field. Jackson could have been thrown free. He could have skied out of the path of the avalanche. He could be out there alone in the woods, without his pack." Her voice broke, and she pressed her lips together.

He wanted to pull her close and comfort her. To hold her and tell her he understood her grief. He had lost people he cared about before. He knew that feeling of helplessness, of not being able to do anything to bring them back.

But of course, he couldn't do that. "I know it's hard," he said. "But you can't beat yourself up like this."

"You're not listening!" Her voice rang in the stillness. They were alone on the run now, the shadows from the tall trees alongside the run stretching out to embrace them. "As long as there's a chance he's alive, we should look for him," she said. "That's our job, isn't it—to rescue people? Not to leave a child to freeze to death in the woods." Her voice shook, and her bottom lip trembled.

"Lily..."

She turned and drove one ski pole into the snow and sped away. Shelby barked and raced after her.

Scott let her go. He wouldn't get through to her now. She would have to come to terms with the situation by herself. She was right. They were supposed to help people.

He hated that he couldn't do anything to help her.

Chapter Eleven

Icy wind froze the tears that streamed from her eyes as Lily raced, blindly, down the slope. Thankfully, there were no guests left for her to collide with. At the bottom of the run, she stopped and tried to clear her vision. Shelby sat at her feet and looked up, whining, the picture of distress.

"Oh, girl, it's okay." Lily sniffed, then bent and hugged the dog. She glanced back to see if Scott had followed her, but the run was empty. Good. She didn't want to hear any more of his talk of "victims" and "accepting the situation."

She hurried to headquarters, collected her belongings and headed for the shuttle stop.

But when she got off at her apartment, she didn't go inside. Instead, she climbed into her car and drove to the Endicott home. The gates at the end of the long driveway were closed, but she pressed the intercom. "This is Lily Alton," she said. "I really need to see Denny."

"Lily?" a man's deep voice asked.

"Is that you, Mike?"

"Denton isn't seeing anyone right now, Lily," Mike said.

"Please," she said. "I need to talk to him about Jackson."

A long pause. Had Mike gone to consult Denny? She wondered if she should press the intercom button again, but then the gate began to swing open. "Come on up," Mike said.

Mike was waiting in the doorway as she mounted the steps, Shelby beside her. He didn't say anything, merely held the door open wider, then shut it when they were all inside. "How is Denny?" Lily asked.

"About as wrecked as you would expect," Mike said. "But he said he wanted to see you."

She followed him toward the back of the house, to Denny's home office. Mike knocked, then opened the door and held it for her.

Denny rose from the sofa and came to meet her, taking both her hands in his. "It's good to see you, Lily," he said.

She nodded, her throat too tight to speak. Denton Endicott looked beaten and deflated. Deep bags under his bloodshot eyes spoke of sleepless nights, and his shoulders sagged as if bearing the weight of the world. He glanced behind her at Mike. "You can leave us, Mike. Thanks."

When they were alone, he returned to the sofa. "Come sit with me," he said.

She sat, and Shelby lay on the floor between them. Denny rubbed the dog's ears. "Thank you for looking for Jackson," he said.

"I want to do anything I can to help."

She waited, thinking he might have questions about what had happened. But he fell silent, his hand stroking the dog's head, over and over. Shelby sat, eyes closed, clearly enjoying the attention.

After a long while, Lily cleared her throat. "I wanted to talk to you about Jackson," she said.

He nodded. "You were one of his favorite people," he said. "He told me all about how you were training Shelby to be an avalanche rescue dog."

"Jackson is a great kid." She refused to speak of him in the past tense. "So smart, and interested in so many things."

"He's a smart kid," Denny said. "Quiet, but he's always thinking."

"Do you remember when he was five years old and figured out how to reprogram the sprinkler system to flood the yard at night?" she asked.

Denny smiled. "He thought it would freeze overnight and make an ice rink. I had to explain it wasn't cold enough yet."

"I've been wondering about some things," she said. "How did the kidnapper know Jackson was going to be at the resort that day?"

"I've wondered that, too," he said. "But Jackson would have told anyone who asked that he planned to go skiing. Or maybe whoever it was had been there every Saturday, just waiting for him to show up."

"But why kidnap Jackson? Did the kidnapper ask for ransom?"

He hesitated, then said, "Not money."

"Something else?"

He looked away and blew out a breath. "You can't tell anyone," he said. "No one knows this."

She waited, afraid to speak. Denny shoved to his feet and began to pace. "Did you know my company has contracts with the federal government?"

She shook her head. "No."

"It's not all of our business, but it's an important segment. Most of the stuff we do is for the United States military, and it's all top secret." He raked a hand through his thinning hair. "Right now, we're developing a new guidance system for weapons. State-of-the-art stuff."

"I'm not sure I understand what this has to do with Jackson's kidnapping."

"These people who have contacted me want the plans for that guidance system."

"Did you tell the police that?"

"No."

At her surprised look, he turned on her. "The system is top secret. Everyone who works on it has a top security clearance. I took an oath that I wouldn't share the information with anyone. I can't risk some loose-lipped clerk in the sheriff's department sharing this information with the media or someone who turns out to be a Russian spy."

He spoke with such fervor she shivered. But on the other hand, this sounded almost cartoonish—Russian spies? Here in the mountains of Colorado? "Is that who you think is behind this?" she asked. "Russians?"

"I have no idea. Certainly all of the people on my team are Americans."

"How many people know about this system?" she asked.

"Only the team working on the project. They're all sworn to secrecy, but it's possible one of them let something slip. People talk."

"I think you should at least tell the sheriff," she said.

"I don't have a lot of faith in that lot," he said. "They think everything is over now that Jackson is…now that he's gone."

"But something like this—wouldn't the FBI get involved?"

"Maybe. I haven't decided if I want that, either."

"Is that how you ended up with a black eye and a split lip the week before Jackson was taken?" she asked. "Because someone was trying to intimidate you?"

He slumped into his chair once more. "I guess no one really believes I was that clumsy," he said. "Yes. A couple of thugs waylaid me after my meeting that night. They told me I had to leave the information they wanted in a drop box the next day. If I didn't, they would kill me."

"But you didn't do that?"

"No. I won't betray my country that way."

Even now, battered and grieving, his voice was full of conviction. "Did you tell anyone about this—the sheriff or someone else?" she asked.

"No. I didn't think they'd take me seriously. I didn't really believe the threats, either. Not at first." He buried his head in his hands.

"Do you have any idea who is doing this?" she asked.

He lifted his head. "I can't think it could be anyone who works for me," he said. "Most of them have been with me for years. But maybe one of them said something to a friend or relative who's not as trustworthy."

"What about Preston Smith?" she asked. "He's a new employee, isn't he?"

Denny sat up straight again. "Mike told me Preston came by the house that night and upset you. But I don't think Preston would do anything like this. He has an impeccable résumé and is excellent at his job. He passed the background check and received his security clearance with no problems at all. And he's reported for work every day since Jackson went missing and doesn't act any differently."

"Maybe he's part of a group of people. I mean, if we're talking foreign governments and spies, maybe they recruited a bunch of different people to work for them." Wasn't that how it worked in movies? She reached out and touched the back of his hand. "Maybe you should contact the FBI."

He sighed. "You're right. I... I just can't think with Jackson gone. I don't care about anything else."

"Had Jackson had much experience out-of-doors?" she asked, remembering the questions Scott had asked her. "Besides skiing at the resort, I mean."

"I'd taken him fishing a few times. Hiking in the summer. Why do you ask?"

"I was thinking. If Jackson was kidnapped, he would be the type to try to get away, don't you think? I mean, he'd try to figure out a plan that would let him get away."

"Probably. But he couldn't have counted on an avalanche."

"What if he did?" She leaned toward him, hands on her knees. "What if he set that avalanche on purpose?"

"How would he do that?"

"If he had read much at all about avalanches, he could have been familiar with the kinds of conditions that make them more likely—steep, exposed slopes, especially if they're south-facing. Windblown slopes or cornices. He would have known that skiing across such terrain could trigger a slide."

He looked dismayed. "Are you saying Jackson caused his own death?"

"No! No!"

"Then what are you saying?"

"I don't want to give you false hope. And I may be completely wrong. But the place where we found Jackson's backpack—that was on the edge of the snowfield. And there was no sign of Jackson."

"Adam said the backpack was probably torn from his body."

"Maybe. But the straps on the backpack weren't ripped. It looked to me more like someone took it off and set it down and it was caught up in the avalanche."

"What are you saying?"

She sat up straighter and took a deep breath. "I'm wondering if Jackson got away. Maybe he fled his kidnapper. He shed the backpack so that he could travel faster, and as a distraction. The kidnapper would see the backpack and stop to investigate. But what if in pursuing Jackson, the kidnapper triggered the avalanche? He was caught in the slide, but Jackson was far enough ahead to get away."

"Do you really think that's what happened?"

"I don't know. Maybe everyone else is right and Jackson was killed in the avalanche. But I think it's possible."

"Adam Derocher said we might not find his body until spring."

"In the meantime, what's the harm in looking for him outside the avalanche?" she asked.

Denny's gaze remain fixed on her. "The sheriff says he doesn't have the resources."

"I want your permission to look for Jackson—me and Shelby." At the sound of her name, the dog's ears pricked.

"You don't need my permission for that."

"I don't want to do it without your knowledge," she said.

"Do you need money? Supplies?"

"No. Just your permission."

"It might not be safe," he said. "I don't know the people I'm dealing with on this, but they could very well be from a foreign government, or aligned with one."

"I'm just a skier with a dog. They won't be looking for me."

He considered this for a moment, then nodded. "All right. Are you sure there isn't anything I can give you to help?"

She thought for a moment. "Do you have a satellite phone?"

"I can get one."

"It would be good to have. Cell phone coverage isn't very good out there."

"Do you need anything else?"

"Maybe some of Jackson's warmest clothes? If I find him, he'll need them."

He nodded again. "When do you want to start?"

"In the morning. First light."

"What about your job?"

"I'll call in sick. My boss knows I'm upset about Jackson. I'll tell him I'm not doing well and I need time." Scott would probably be relieved to hear she planned to stay home. "Or I'll just find someone to trade shifts. We do that all the time." It would be better if she didn't have to talk to Scott.

Denny stood, and she rose also. "Be back here first thing in the morning," he said. "I'll have the phone and the clothing for you."

When ski patrol members gathered the next morning, Scott surveyed the group. Brian and Anders were there with their dogs, along with Renee Castro, Chase Sergeant, Livi "Raz" Rasmussen, and Carson Slade. "Where's Lily?" he asked, a knot of worry already forming in his chest.

"She called early this morning and asked if I would switch with her." Nina spoke up from a back corner.

Scott checked his clipboard. Sure enough, Nina wasn't on the schedule. "Is Lily sick?" he asked.

"I don't think so," Nina said. "She just said she had something to do."

Scott nodded and forced himself to move on to the day's assignments. But when the meeting was over, he waylaid Nina. "What did Lily say, exactly?" he asked.

She frowned. "What I told you—she said she had something to do today and asked if I would trade with her. She's going to work next Saturday for me."

"Did she sound upset about anything?"

"No. I don't know. It was six in the morning. I wasn't exactly awake."

"She didn't say anything about me?"

Nina's eyes widened. "Why? What did you do?"

What had he done? Not been sensitive enough? Pushed

her too hard? "She was just a little upset when I left her yesterday."

"She knew that kid who was kidnapped and ended up dying in that avalanche, right?"

"Who told you that?" he asked.

"Lily told me she knew the kid," Nina said.

"I mean, who told you he died?" Scott asked.

"It's all over the news this morning." Nina pulled out her phone and showed him. A headline declared Son of Endicott Industries Owner Killed in Avalanche.

Right. So Scott wasn't the only one who made the logical assumption that Jackson Endicott had been killed in that avalanche. But Lily couldn't accept that. She was such a kind and caring person. Of course it hurt her to think of a child killed, especially one she knew.

"She probably just needed a day to get her head together," Nina said. "You're not going to give her a hard time about it, are you?"

"No. Of course not."

Nina looked doubtful, but said nothing.

Scott headed out toward the helicopter pad to help with the morning's avalanche control. But all day as he worked his thoughts kept returning to Lily. He made the last sweep of the day down May Day, and the memory of her and Shelby entertaining the children the day before pained him. He had handled the whole situation with her and Jackson so badly.

He loaded Hunter into the motorcycle's sidecar and headed home, but instead of parking in his usual spot, he drove around to Lily's side of the apartments. He needed to apologize—to make her understand he hadn't meant to be so rough on her. "Come on Hunter," he told the dog. "Let's go see Lily and Shelby."

Chapter Twelve

Friday morning, Lily and Shelby slogged through the snow-choked forest between the avalanche site and Pandora. They had been out here for hours and made little progress. At six thirty that morning she had met Denny at a side door of his home. Like a spy passing on top secret documents, he had handed over the satellite phone and a fresh set of clothing for Jackson. "Let me know the minute you find anything," he said.

"I will," she said, as she stowed the items in her backpack. "But I may not find anything."

He nodded. "I didn't tell anyone what you're doing."

"No sense embarrassing us both if this turns out to be for nothing." She slipped the backpack onto her shoulders.

"It's not that." He glanced around. They were alone, standing in the light from a single fixture over this side door, darkness surrounding them. Their breath hung in clouds between them, and biting cold seeped beneath her coat collar. "I've been thinking a lot about our conversation last night—about who could be behind this," he said. "I'll admit I made a mistake, not taking this threat seriously. I think someone on my team has to be involved in this, and I'm going to ask the FBI to take a closer look at Preston Smith."

"That's a good idea," she said. "The FBI is bound to have resources the local cops don't."

"But this kidnapping," he said. "It's so personal. So close to home. It makes me wonder if someone in my own household might be involved."

Her heart jumped. "Do you really think so? Why would anyone who knows Jackson put him in danger?"

"I don't know. But what you said—about someone knowing Jackson was going to be at the ski resort that day—it got me thinking. Maybe the kidnapper was guessing—but what if someone here told them about our plans?" He shook his head. "I just don't want to take a chance."

"Yeah. I guess that's smart." She shifted her feet, trying to fight off the cold. "I'll let you know what I find, either way." She turned away.

"Lily?"

She paused to look back. "Yes?"

"Be careful."

She liked to think she was always careful. That was one reason it had taken most of the day to get even this far in her search. She had parked her car a little after seven, tucking it into the trees down the road from the area that had been cleared for parking. First, she had to skirt the avalanche area itself. At that early hour, no one was around, though the evidence of the previous day's work was scattered across the snowfield. Long avalanche probes stuck up from the ground like the stems of dandelions whose heads had been scattered by heedless children. In places the snow had begun to melt, exposing the jagged chunks of trees and dirt-spotted boulders.

She and Shelby stopped at the place where they had found Jackson's pack. Shelby sniffed around, but alerted on nothing. The dog wasn't trained to search for anything other than people buried in snow, but Lily decided it wouldn't hurt to try her out. She pointed toward the woods and gave the command, "Go find."

Shelby tilted her head in a questioning look, then put her nose to the ground and moved into the trees.

Five yards in, the trees were so thick it was difficult to maneuver. Thick white aspen trunks stuck up like pickets, and the fallen remains of older trees were hidden beneath the snow, dangerous traps for a skier. Lily finally took off her skis and her pack. She strapped the skis to her pack, then shimmied sideways through the tree trunks. Was this why Jackson had removed his pack? It would certainly have made fleeing through the woods faster.

She tried calling for him. "Jackson! It's me, Lily!" But the trees and snow swallowed up her words. Jackson would have to be standing very close for him to hear her.

Shelby climbed over yet another fallen tree and came to stand beside her, tongue lolling. Scott's words, berating her for wearing the dog out, came back to her. She slipped off the pack and took out a bottle of water and a foldable bowl. "I know this is tough," she told the dog. "You're doing great." She checked the dog's paws for any cuts or signs of frostbite, but all looked well.

She set down the bowl, and Shelby drank. Lily took a few swallows of water from the bottle, then stowed it and the bowl. She checked the GPS on her phone. They were traveling in the right direction to reach Pandora, but was this the way Jackson had come? He might have tried to head back toward the ski resort. Or he might be wandering lost in the woods.

Or he might be dead. If he hadn't been killed in the avalanche, would he have frozen to death overnight? He didn't have his pack with him, which meant no extra clothing, food or water. His dad said he had spent a little time in the outdoors, but would he know how to seek shelter or start a fire?

The thought of finding Jackson dead made her wish she wasn't out here alone. Over the years it had been drilled into her how risky it could be to ski or hike or climb solo. But what choice had she had? No one else believed Jackson had survived the avalanche.

She checked her phone. Ordinarily about this time she would be skiing the runs at the resort, on the lookout for anyone in trouble. She might take Shelby out for a run and visit some ski school classes, or even help ferry an injured skier to the clinic at the base of the runs.

Had Scott been angry that she had traded shifts with Nina without checking with him first? Maybe *angry* was too strong a word, but he had probably been annoyed. He always wanted everything to be perfect and orderly under his command. Too bad he was overseeing ordinary people and not robots. People were messy a lot of the time.

Shelby pawed at Lily's leg, bringing her out of her reverie. "Come on," she told the dog. "We have to keep searching." She couldn't give up on Jackson yet.

NO ONE ANSWERED Scott's knock on Lily's apartment door shortly after four thirty Friday afternoon. He had tried texting, then calling, but she wasn't answering. Was she that upset with him? He pounded on the door again, harder this time.

The door of the apartment next to Lily's opened. A scowling man leaned out. "She's not home," he said.

Scott stepped back and sized up the man. Mid-forties, bags under his eyes, in need of a shave. "Do you know where she went?" he asked.

"She and her dog left early this morning. I was heading

out to for my shift driving a county plow just as she was coming out. She works ski patrol."

"Right. But she wasn't at work today. I'm her boss."

"Huh." Bushy eyebrows drew together in a sharp vee. "She had her skis and pack and the dog and everything, all loaded into her car. I don't know where she was heading."

Her car. But she usually took the shuttle to work. "Thanks." He turned to leave.

"I hope she's okay," the man called after him. "She's a sweet girl. Great dog, too."

Scott returned to his motorcycle, but stopped beside it to survey the cars in the lot. Lily's Outback wasn't there—so where was she?

She had called Nina at six this morning, and said she had "something she had to take care of." Then she had left here with her skis, gear and dog. She was worried about Jackson. She thought he was still alive, alone in the wilderness.

A cold knot formed in his stomach. She had gone to search for Jackson—he was sure of it. She had gone by herself, not telling anyone where she was headed. It broke every rule of wilderness safety.

But understanding softened the edge of his anger. Lily had gone out because she cared. He hadn't let himself believe her conviction that Jackson was still alive, so she hadn't been able to turn to him for help. Maybe his dismissal of her concerns had kept her from confiding in anyone else. She probably felt she had no choice but to conduct a search on her own.

Hunter hopped into the sidecar, and Scott mounted the motorcycle and started it. "We're not headed home just yet," Scott said, and patted the dog's neck. The first thing he had to do was find some transportation that wasn't a motorcycle. He'd never make it where he needed to go on the bike.

He pulled out his phone and scrolled through his contacts, then selected a name. "Hey, Brian, it's Scott. I need a favor."

"Sure, Scott." The easygoing patroller and his golden retriever, Daisy, had similar sunny attitudes, though both were good at their jobs.

"I need to borrow your truck," Scott said. "Maybe overnight. Something's come up and the motorcycle isn't going to cut it traveling any distance in this weather."

"Sure. You can use my truck. Is everything all right? Anything I can do?"

"Thanks. I really appreciate it. Could I come get it now?"

"Sure."

Scott ended the call before Brian could ask for more details. He started the motorcycle and rode the few miles to Brian's duplex. He exchanged his bike keys for the truck keys, loaded up Hunter, then headed back to his apartment, where he collected skis, avalanche beacon, and a pack full of food, water and emergency gear. He had enough supplies to at least get him to Lily and bring her to safety.

All he had to do now was find her.

He drove to the avalanche site. Long shadows stretched over the snowfield, darker pools where people had been digging, lighter shades where the snow was still untouched. The cleared-out space where rescue vehicles had parked was empty. He drove slowly past the lot, back onto the road. She wouldn't have wanted to leave her car where it would stand out. So she would have left it nearby, but not in an obvious place.

He found it a few hundred feet from the parking area, a blue Subaru Outback snugged up against a tall pine. He was sure this was Lily's car.

Scott parked the truck next to the Outback, let Hunter out, then began unloading his gear. He shoved extra supplies in his pack and called for the dog. The big Lab was sniffing all around the Subaru, tail wagging. "Do you smell Lily and Shelby?" Scott asked.

He walked over and peered through the windows of the Subaru. Nothing to see. Of more interest were the ski tracks leading away from the vehicle. He followed the tracks along the edge of the avalanche field, to the place where they had discovered Jackson's pack. He spotted tracks of a dog, headed into the woods, the ski tracks alongside them.

He wasn't a trained tracker, but it didn't take an expert to identify the place where Lily had removed her skis. The terrain was too crowded with obstacles to make skiing safe, which was why he had left his own skis behind at the truck. He continued on foot, sinking to his knees in softer snow only occasionally, following Lily's and Shelby's tracks. A few feet into the woods, the shadows deepened. Cold crowded around him. He shoved his goggles on top of his helmet and donned a head lamp. "Lily!" he shouted. "Shelby!"

He stepped into a hole, lost his balance and ended up sprawled in the snow. He lay there for a moment, trying to catch his breath. Hunter bounded over and nudged at him, whining.

"I'm okay." He shoved onto his knees, then stood. Now he was the one being foolish, stumbling around in the dark. He should go home. If Lily hadn't returned to her apartment by morning, he could call the sheriff.

But the thought of leaving her out here alone, in the cold, tore at him. He cupped his gloved hands to either side of his mouth. "Lily!" he shouted again.

Hunter barked, then bounded away. "Hunter! Come back here!" Scott stumbled after the dog. "Where are you going?"

Then Scott saw the light—a small bluish moon bobbing through the trees in the shrouded darkness.

Hunter barked again, and raced toward the light.

"Over here!" a woman called. "I've found something!"

LILY HAD SPOTTED the shoe print half an hour before, just when she was about to turn around and make her way back to her car. It was the clear impression of a single ski boot, but boy-sized, about twelve inches long. Just the one clear print in a line of trampled snow, as if someone had traveled this way.

She followed that trail of disturbed snow, Shelby right in front of her. The dog began to whine. "Do you smell Jackson?" Lily asked.

Heart in her throat, she tried to move faster. The narrow beam of the light from her headlamp allowed her to avoid the largest obstacles in her path, but outside of that light was a black void.

Shelby barked again, then whirled and barreled past Lily, almost knocking her over.

"Shelby!" Lily shouted, but the dog paid no attention.

Lily peered ahead, trying to determine what had made the dog change direction so suddenly. Was there a big animal up ahead—a mountain lion?

In the distance, another dog barked. Not Shelby. Lily turned to look behind her again. Shelby barked in answer, then Lily heard someone calling her name.

Relief surged through her. She wasn't going to have to do this alone. "Over here!" she shouted. "I've found something."

She told herself she should have been surprised to see Scott moving toward her, but she wasn't. He knew her feelings about Jackson's possible fate, and he was just stubborn enough to venture out in the darkness to look for her.

He arrived just behind the two excited dogs—red-faced and scowling. "What are you doing out here by yourself?" he growled.

"I think you already know the answer to that question," she said. She dipped her head to illuminate the path at their feet. "I've been following this trail. I think it's Jackson's."

His frown didn't fade. "This trail could have been made by anything. You could be following an elk, or even a moose."

"Earlier, there was a boot print. A clear impression, just the size of a boy Jackson's age. Come on. Maybe we can catch up with him."

She started forward, but he grabbed her arm and pulled her back. "You're going to get hurt if you keep floundering around in the dark."

She tipped her head enough to shine her light right in his eyes, fully prepared to tell him he had no right to lecture her as if she were a child. But then she realized all of the redness on his face wasn't due to the cold. She lifted her hand to his cheek, but stopped just short of touching him. "You're bleeding."

He put a hand up and smeared the trickle of blood. "It's nothing. I tripped and fell a little way back."

"You can't just stand there bleeding. Do you have a first aid kit?"

"It's nothing," he repeated. "I'll deal with it back at the cars."

She turned away. "I'm not going back. Not when I finally found Jackson's trail. If he's out here, I'm not going to leave him."

He took out his phone. "I'll make note of the GPS coordinates and we can come out here in the morning, with the search-and-rescue team."

"No. By then it might be too late."

"Lily!"

"Scott!" she mimicked his tone and glared at him. "I'll be fine. I know how to take care of myself, and I have a satellite phone if I run into trouble."

"Where did you get a satellite phone?"

"I borrowed it from a friend."

He drew himself up taller. "I'm ordering you to go back with me."

"Or what? You're only my boss during work hours. And if that's how you're going to act, I don't want to work for you anyway."

His shoulders sagged. "Please come with me? I'm not asking as your boss. I'm asking as your friend."

Were they friends? Sometimes it didn't feel that way, and yet who else would be out here with her in the freezing darkness? "I can't," she said. "I can't leave Jackson out here in the cold. What if he's lost, or hurt? What if someone is still after him?"

She couldn't see Scott's expression clearly in the darkness, but he shifted from foot to foot, as if physically wrestling with the problem. Then he hooked his thumbs beneath the front straps of his pack. "Then let's get going and see where this trail leads."

Slogging along in full dark now, the thin beams from their headlamps scarcely penetrating the gloom, they did their best to stay on either side of the trail. The only sounds were the crunch of boots on snow and their own labored breathing. Were they getting any closer to Jackson—or only headed farther away from safety?

A sharp whistle pierced the air, and a rush of wind

brushed past Lily's cheek. Bark flew from the trunk of a tree. Then she was on the ground, flat on her stomach in the snow with Scott on top of her. He was big and heavy, crushing the breath out of her. She raised her head to yell at him to get off of her, but he shoved her back into the snow. He spoke softly, his mouth next to her ear. "Stay down! That was a gunshot."

Chapter Thirteen

Lily froze, heart pounding painfully. Someone was shooting at them?

"Turn off your headlamp," Scott whispered, and his own light went out.

"I can't move," she said.

Scott slid off of her to lie beside her. He was breathing hard, and he kept one hand firmly on her back, as if prepared to shove her down once more. "Turn it off now," he whispered.

She did so. "Why is someone shooting at us?" she asked, keeping her voice low.

"I don't know. But they came too close to hitting us for me to think it was a random shot. They could have a night vision scope or goggles or something."

She started to ask him how he knew that, then remembered he had been in the military. "What are we going to do?" she asked. "We can't just lie here and wait for him to find us."

"We're going to have to crawl." He turned his head to one side, then pointed in that direction. "Over that way. The tree cover is more dense."

The trees were growing so close together they had to

squeeze through them, negotiating an obstacle course of tree roots, trunks, rocks and thick snow. By the time they reached the massive trunk of a fallen lodgepole pine, she was sodden with melted snow and shivering from the cold. "When I give the word, vault over this log and flatten yourself behind it," Scott said.

"Okay." She tensed, waiting. After what seemed like an eternity, but was probably only a few seconds, he said, "Now!"

She pulled herself up onto the log, while he pushed from behind. On the other side, she flattened herself to the ground, pushing up under the tree for a few inches. Scott landed just past her and did the same.

She strained her ears to hear the sound of anyone approaching, but her head was too full of her own ragged breathing and the pounding of her heartbeat. "I don't hear anyone," Scott said after a long moment.

"I don't either." Then a terrifying thought made her raise her head. "Where are the dogs?"

Scott shoved her down once more. "Stay down!"

"Where are the dogs?" she asked again. "If whoever that was shot Shelby or Hunter…"

"They both ran off when the gunshot was fired," he said. "It probably terrified them."

The shot had terrified her. But now she was just angry. "If he hurt my dog…"

"I know," Scott said. "Don't think about that now."

She lay with her face to the ground, shivering hard now, colder than she had ever been in her life. "He won't have to shoot us," she muttered. "We'll freeze to death, lying here."

"Shhh. Someone's coming."

Panic squeezed at her, and she had to bite her lip hard enough to taste blood in order to keep from crying out.

Something was definitely shuffling toward them, but it didn't sound like a person exactly. More like an animal. Or a couple of animals.

Shelby, then Hunter, climbed over the fallen tree and began licking their faces, tails wagging. Lily pulled Shelby down beside her and held the squirming dog tightly, imagining at any moment that another bullet would come their way.

But all was silent.

Hunter lay beside Scott, panting softly. After a long while, Scott raised one ski pole into the air. Then the other. Nothing happened. He raised a hand. Nothing.

Finally, he sat up. "I think whoever was out there left."

"Why did they leave?" She wanted to stay down, safe, but feared freezing to death almost as much as she feared the person with the gun. Stiffly, she pushed into a sitting position. Shelby jumped up and shook.

"Maybe they realized we weren't who they were after," Scott said.

It took a moment before her fear-and-frost-numbed brain realized what he meant. "Do you think he's looking for Jackson?"

"Maybe you aren't the only one who didn't believe he died in that avalanche."

"Oh." The single syllable came out like a moan. "Jackson's dad said he thinks people from another country might be behind all this."

"If that's true, they could be really dangerous," Scott said. "But why does he think that?"

"They've contacted him before. Two people beat him up the night I was babysitting. That's how he got the black eye. They told him if he didn't hand over the information they wanted they would kill him. But when he didn't back down, they kidnapped Jackson."

"What do they want?"

"I can't tell you—I promised. He said it was top secret."

"Why didn't he tell the sheriff this?" Scott asked.

"He doesn't trust the sheriff's department. But he doesn't want to involve the FBI, either."

"Why not?"

She rubbed her hands together, trying to get circulation into her numb fingers. "He wouldn't say, but I wonder if it isn't because he's thinking he'll have to cooperate with the kidnappers to get his son back. He doesn't want to, but he would do anything to save Jackson. What parent wouldn't?"

"Does Endicott know who is behind this?" Scott asked. "Specific people, I mean."

"No. But this morning when I picked up the satellite phone he told me he's afraid it might be someone in his household. Or someone who works for him. Otherwise, how did they know Jackson would be skiing the day he was taken?"

"They could have had someone watching the house," Scott said. "It's easy enough to see people loading up and driving away with skis on top of the vehicle."

"That's true. He's being careful, all the same."

"I don't blame him for that." He stood, then held out his hand. "Come on. We need to get moving and warm up. We should think about where we're going to spend the night."

She took his hand and let him pull her to her feet. Exhaustion had rolled in as the fear receded. She was shivering with cold and clumsy with stiffness.

"Here." Scott shoved something into her hands. "Eat this."

"I'm okay," she said, and tried to push him away.

"When was the last time you ate?" he asked.

"I had a protein bar a few hours ago," she said.

"Your blood sugar is probably dropping. Eat."

She looked at the item in your hand. "A candy bar? Really?"

"It has nuts in it and chocolate. Quick sugar. Eat it."

"Sheesh. You are so bossy!" But she peeled off the wrapper and took a bite, and had to suppress a groan. When had anything tasted so good?

While she ate, he gave the dogs treats and consulted his phone. "Looks like we're headed toward Pandora," he said.

"The tracks seemed to be leading that way."

He looked around them, at the impenetrable darkness. "Jackson has a forty-eight-hour head start on us. He could be at Pandora by now."

She finished the last of the candy bar, crumpled the wrapper and tucked it into the pocket of her parka. "If he thought of heading to Pandora, don't you think whoever is after him thought of that, too?"

"Maybe. But we can't do anything about that tonight. Right now, we need to find a place to spend the night."

"What about right here?" She looked at the flattened space where they had been lying. "I don't want to lose Jackson's trail."

He looked around. "I'd feel better if we moved into denser brush," he said. "We need a fire to try to warm up, but we need to keep it hidden."

"Fine. Just remember where the trail is so we can pick it up in the morning."

She followed him into a section of woods choked with scrub oak and service berry, the dense network of twigs and branches grabbing at her clothing like bony fingers. They came to a bowl-shaped depression maybe six feet in diameter. "This should do," he said. He dropped his pack, pulled out a knife, and began hacking at the scrub around them. "I'll build a shelter. See if you can gather some wood for a fire."

She was so exhausted all she wanted to do was drop where she stood, but she made herself turn away in search of wood. Everything she found was wet with snow, but by digging into the undergrowth she was able to snag a few drier pieces. By the time she returned, Scott had constructed a lean-to and spread a tarp on the ground in its shelter. He was arranging rocks in a circle for a fire ring. She dropped the wood she had collected beside him, removed her pack, and took out her sleeping bag and a pair of dry socks.

With dry feet, and seated on the insulating sleeping bag, she began to feel better. Scott got a fire going, using a lighter and fire starters from his pack, then he set snow to melt in a small coffeepot. She dug into her pack and pulled out the food she had brought with her and contributed to the pile of provisions he had unearthed from his own supplies. The dogs moved in close, sniffing at everything with interest.

"You were prepared to spend the night out," he said.

"I didn't want to, but I knew I would if I thought I was close to finding Jackson."

He nodded and fed each dog a piece of jerky. Shelby brought hers over to the sleeping bag and lay beside Lily. "I take it Mr. Endicott thinks more than one person is involved in the kidnapping—not just the man who was killed?" Scott asked.

"It looks that way." She took off one glove and buried her hand in the dog's thick ruff of fur. "Especially if whoever was shooting at us was after Jackson."

"We don't know that."

"No, but how many other criminals are out here in the wilderness?"

He fed larger branches into the fire. "What could be so important a whole group of people would take such a big risk? They're bound to know everyone will be searching for a missing kid."

"You and I are the only ones searching for Jackson right now."

"I thought Endicott was a software developer. What could kidnappers want from that?"

"You're not going to let this go, are you?"

"I'm just trying to make sense of things."

"Endicott Industries has a lot of government contracts," she said.

He looked at her. The light from the fire lit one side of his face with an orange glow, highlighting the hard line of his jaw and the strong jut of his nose. The other half of his face was all darkness, his expression unreadable. "Are they military contracts?" he asked.

"I can't say."

He nodded. "I get the picture. What else did Endicott tell you?"

"He said Jackson had gone fishing and hiking and stuff like that, but nothing more." She stared out into the darkness. There were so many ways to get hurt out here—the cold, a fall, attacks by animals—both four-and two-legged.

"He's a nine-year-old kid," Scott said.

"A really smart kid."

"But a kid."

"Why are you like this?"

He sat up straighter. "Like what?"

"Always assuming the worst. Why can't you wait to pronounce him done for until we know for sure?"

"You can't go around blind to reality. Most of the time things don't turn out for the best."

"But sometimes they do. I'm not naive, but I'm not going to give up too soon."

He said nothing, but turned to the stack of provisions. "I'm going to make us something hot to drink. We'll both feel a lot better when we've had some food."

He made hot chocolate and filled two mugs, then they ate ham and cheese sandwiches. The cocoa and the food did make her feel better. "Thanks for pushing me down earlier," she said. "You probably saved my life."

"Sorry if I was too rough."

"You didn't hurt me. I guess you recognized gunfire right away because of your experiences in the war."

"Yeah."

"Do you ever have, like, flashbacks?" Was that too personal a question to ask?

"Not in a long time."

Had war made him cynical? Or was that just his nature? He wasn't the first person to accuse her of being too optimistic—that was her nature.

He repacked the rest of their provisions and rinsed the mugs with hot water from the kettle. She stared into the fire, sleep dragging at her. She was trying to work up the energy to say good night and crawl into her sleeping bag when he said, "I'm sorry I was so hard on you yesterday."

The apology startled her awake. "I'm not some fragile flower who's going to wilt when someone yells at me," she said.

"Did I yell?"

"No. You were just a little…brusque."

"Sorry." He smoothed his hand down Hunter's side. Both dogs were already asleep, curled by the fire and snoring. "I've always been better with dogs than people."

"Maybe when I've been doing this work as long as you have, I'll be more cynical, too," she said. "But I'm not there yet."

"This work didn't make me cynical. Not really."

"What did?"

He didn't answer. Maybe that was the question that was too personal to answer.

"Maybe it's just my disposition," he said. "Or the war—I lost people I cared about over there. And then I lost Clark."

"Your friend who died in the avalanche."

"Yeah. Add that I've never pulled a live person from a snowslide, and I guess that has made me cynical."

"I get it. You don't have to apologize. And neither do I." She shrugged. "We feel what we feel."

"I hope you're the one who's right in this case. About Jackson, I mean."

"Yeah, me too." She crawled into her sleeping bag and lay down, waiting for warmth and sleep. She thought of Jackson, and sent up a silent prayer that he was somewhere warm and safe. And that tomorrow they would find him, and everything would be all right.

Chapter Fourteen

Scott woke next to Lily, his arms wrapped tightly around her. The floral scent of her hair teased him to consciousness, then he became aware of the hard line of her spine, pressed against him, and the soft curve of her bottom. She was curled into a fetal position, buried deep in her sleeping bag, a ball of warmth in the frigid predawn. Shelby lay on Lily's other side, so that she was sandwiched between his warmth and the dog's.

Not that he was very warm. Hunter had moved to lie beside what was left of the campfire. Scott couldn't feel his toes or his fingers, and every few minutes a violent shiver rocked him.

He carefully extricated himself from around her. She stirred. "You okay?" he asked.

The sleeping bag wriggled and shifted, then her head emerged. Her face was puffy, hair a wild tangle hiding half her features. She looked soft and vulnerable and younger than her years. "I'm cold."

"Yeah. I'll get the fire started."

When he had a blaze going, she fought the rest of the way out of her sleeping bag and staggered to her feet. "Be right back," she mumbled, and shuffled off into the woods.

By the time she returned, he had the kettle over the flames

and both dogs were eating the kibble he had packed. "I'm going to give them the first water I melt," he said. "Then I'll heat some for us."

"I've got instant coffee crystals," she said. "And oatmeal and peanut butter."

"I've got boiled eggs."

She made a face. "Don't those get crushed in your pack?"

He shrugged. "They're good protein. And I don't care what they look like. I'm going to eat them anyway."

The coffee, when it was finally ready, was scalding hot. The warmth spread through him, driving the last of the sleep from his brain and making him feel halfway human. They ate, the cold making them ravenous. Even oatmeal—not his favorite—tasted good when he was this hungry.

Breakfast over, he stood. "If you'll pack up everything, I'm going to look around a little bit," he said.

"What are you looking for?"

"I want to see if I can find some sign of whoever was shooting at us."

He moved away from the clearing where they had sheltered, both dogs accompanying him. He crossed over the trail they had been following yesterday. The brush thinned, giving way to thick stands of aspens, slender white trunks all leaning slightly to one side, like grass bent by the wind. He studied the snow, which was thinner here, until he found what he was looking for—a single boot print. Not a ski boot, but with lug soles, like a hiking or work boot. Another partial print farther on. He moved more slowly now, carefully placing each step, trying to be as silent as possible. The rising sun slanting through the trees glinted on something at the base of one aspen trunk. Scott bent to look and found two brass shell casings. Forty-five caliber. A new cold slithered up his spine. Too close for comfort. Had the shooter spent the night nearby? He could have killed them in their sleep.

He took out his phone, intending to note the GPS coordinates of this location, but the device had switched itself off and refused to power up again. He swore to himself. Why hadn't he remembered that cold drained batteries? He should have slept with the phone next to him in his sleeping bag instead of stuffed into the side of his pack. He hoped Lily had been smarter.

He went a little farther, but saw no more boot prints or shell casings. No sign of a camp. The shooter must have moved on after he had determined they weren't a threat. Maybe he had decided they were a couple of hikers or skiers out for adventure. Maybe he decided to leave before they spotted him.

He returned to camp. Lily had packed up their belongings and was scooping snow over the fire to douse it. "Did you find anything?" she asked.

He shook his head. He'd keep the information about the bullets to himself for now. "Let's keep heading toward Pandora," he said. "Maybe we'll find Jackson there."

"It's a week today since he was taken," she said. "That's a long time to be out in this cold."

"The kidnapper was probably taking care of him before he was killed," Scott said. "We found their camp, with a fire and shelter."

"But now Jackson is out here without a pack or anyone to help."

"Don't think about that," he said. "Just focus on finding him."

They picked up where they had left off, following the trail of disturbed snow. It could have been a trail made by a boy, but it could have just as easily been a path followed by wildlife—mule deer or elk or even moose. They saw no more boot prints, nothing to tell them for sure that they were on the right track.

The trail ended abruptly, at the base of a large pine, the furrowed reddish bark bright against the paler aspen and white snow. Shelby barked, then planted her front feet against the trunk of the tree. The dog stared up into the limbs, then barked again.

"What is it, girl?" Lily asked.

Scott craned his head to look up into the tree. The branches were thick, a tangle of needles so dark they were almost black. "I don't see anything," he said. "Maybe she treed a squirrel. Come on, Hunter." He turned to move on.

"Wait!" Lily said. She shifted position, craning her neck. "Jackson, is that you? It's me, Lily."

The tree limbs shifted and a pale face—familiar to Scott from the posters stuck up everywhere around the resort—poked out. "Lily! What are you doing here?"

"We're looking for you," she said. "We've come to take you home."

The boy started crying. He was sobbing so hard Scott was afraid he was going to fall out of the tree. "Do you need help getting down from there?" Scott asked.

The boy sniffed and frowned at Scott. "Who are you?"

"This is Scott Linden," Lily said. "He's head of ski patrol. Remember? I introduced you one time."

Shelby barked again. Hunter came to stand beside them and he started barking also. "You'd better come down," Lily said. "The dogs aren't going to quiet down until you do."

"Let me help." Scott reached up toward the boy.

"I can do it." Jackson slowly began climbing down. When he reached the ground, he turned to face them. Strands of blond hair stuck out from beneath his ski helmet. His cheeks were red and streaked with dirt. His blue parka was dirty, too, with a jagged rip in the front. Lily pulled him into a hug. "I'm so glad to see you," she said. "We were so worried."

He squirmed, and she loosened her hold on him and stepped back. "Oh my gosh—you're bleeding!" She pointed to his hand.

The boy looked down at the bare hand, at the gash on the web of flesh between his thumb and forefinger. He flexed his fingers. "It's not that bad," he said.

"What happened to you?" she asked. "Why do you only have one glove?"

"I dropped the other one somewhere."

"We found your pack," she said. "Why did you leave it behind?"

He shifted from foot to foot, eyes darting, not fixing on any one point. "I can tell you all of that later. Can we get out of here now?"

"We'll go," Scott said. "But you need a couple of things first." He removed his pack and dug out a spare pair of gloves and another candy bar. He passed these items, and a bottle of water, over to Jackson.

"Thanks." Jackson tore into the candy bar and ate it in four bites, then chugged the water. He handed the empty bottle to Scott. "When I realized I'd dropped a glove, I wanted to go back and look for it, but I was too afraid. I was terrified they'd find it and be able to track me."

"Who would find it?" Lily asked.

"The people who've been after me. One of them even took a couple of shots at me last night. That was before I went up the tree. I guess they lost my trail in the dark and didn't see me up there."

"Come on." Scott put his hand on the boy's shoulder. The kid's story was making him nervous. "Let's get moving." He wanted to put some distance between Jackson's hiding place and themselves, in case the kidnappers were tracking him again in daylight. Which they would surely do. It sounded like they'd been pretty stubborn about keeping after the kid.

He led the way, Jackson behind him and Lily bringing up the rear, the dogs ranged between them. They were leaving a pretty big track through the woods that would be easy to follow. He glanced over his shoulder at Jackson. "How many people are after you?" he asked.

"Just the one guy, now that DJ is dead. But I'm pretty sure there are others. DJ was taking me somewhere, I just don't know where."

"Who is DJ?" Scott asked.

"The guy who grabbed me at the ski resort. That's what he told me to call him. I don't know what DJ stands for."

"He died in the avalanche?" Lily asked.

"Yeah. He triggered the avalanche when we were crossing this big snowfield. I guess I was lucky—I was on the very edge of the slide and it kind of tossed me off into the woods."

"You left your backpack behind," Lily said.

"I didn't want to, but I figured I had to. I knew DJ had friends. He had been in touch with them a couple of times on a satellite telephone. I thought if they came looking and found my backpack, they would think I had died in the avalanche, too."

"What was DJ doing with you out here in the wilderness all this time?" Lily asked. Scott had been wondering this, too. Even given the weather and the terrain, Jackson and his captor should have been able to reach Pandora in two or three days at most. Or they could have hiked to a road, where an accomplice could pick them up.

"We walked and camped." Jackson scowled. "At first, he tried to make it sound like we were on a big, fun adventure. But it was just cold and boring. The last couple of days he was begging whoever was on the other end of the phone to come and get us. But they told him we had to stay out here until they told us we could come in. DJ said they were waiting for my dad to pay the ransom." His face crumpled. "I couldn't understand why he didn't just pay."

"Oh, honey." Lily held him close. "Your dad has spent every spare minute trying to find you."

Jackson pulled away from her and scrubbed at his eyes with his fists. He sniffed, then said, "After the avalanche, I was worried Dad would think I had died, too. I decided I needed to hike out to a road or a house or someplace where I could get help. But I ended up getting disoriented in the woods and wandering around for a long time. And then somebody started shooting and I climbed that tree."

"That was smart," Lily said.

"It was freezing cold, and I was scared if I didn't die by gunshot, I'd die falling out of the tree and breaking my neck."

"You're safe now," Lily said.

"Do you have a gun?" Jackson asked.

"I don't," Lily said.

"What about him?"

Scott assumed this referred to him. He looked back over his shoulder. "I have a gun," he said. "I hope I don't have to use it."

"The guys who are after me have guns," Jackson said. "DJ forced me to come with him by threatening to shoot me."

Scott looked past Jackson to Lily. His gaze met hers, and she raised both eyebrows, eyes wide.

He faced forward again. "We'll just have to avoid the people with guns," he said. And night vision scopes and who knew what else.

"I could call for help on my satellite phone," Lily said. "I should call your dad and let him know you're okay."

"That's a good idea," Scott said. "Where are you going to tell the cavalry to meet us?"

She glanced around them. "We can give them our GPS coordinates, right?"

"My phone battery died sometime last night," he said. "What about yours?"

She fumbled with her pack and pulled out her phone. "I turned it off last night to save battery." She pressed the button on the side, but nothing happened. "I can't get it back on."

"Below-freezing temperatures drain batteries," he said.

"Maybe they can triangulate our location from the sat phone signal," she said. "Or we could tell them we're headed to Pandora and they can meet us there."

"That's not a bad idea," Scott said. "We can probably make it to Pandora in three or four hours." He didn't think they were far from the last ridge before the ghost town, but it would take a while to make that climb. "Are you up to walking that far?" he asked Jackson. The boy looked dead on his feet.

Jackson lifted his chin and squared his shoulders. "I'll walk as far as I have to to get away from those guys."

Lily took out the satellite phone and switched it on. "At least this battery hasn't died," she said after a moment when the phone lit up. She waited, frowning at the screen. "It's searching for a signal."

"You may have to wait until we get out of these trees to make a call," Scott said. "Satellite phones need a clear line of sight to the sky."

She continued to study the phone. "It says it's unable to connect."

"Switch it off, and you can try again when we're on the ridge, without as much tree cover," Scott said.

They trudged on, heads down, not talking. Lily tried warming her cell phone next to her body, but if still refused to turn on. They made slow progress, all three of them too exhausted to hurry. She kept an eye on Jackson, who walked just in front of her. The boy stumbled from time to time, practically asleep on his feet, but he refused any suggestion that he needed help.

Scott had an old-fashioned compass to navigate, and kept them headed toward Pandora. They began to climb the ridge that separated the old mining town from this more wooded terrain, and the tree cover began to thin. Lily tried not to think what a target they might present for anyone watching them through binoculars—or a spotting scope.

"Let's stop a minute and have some more food and water," Scott said after a while. He halted in the shelter of a car-sized boulder, and they crouched behind it, hidden from view. Within a minute, Jackson was shivering again, and Lily removed the extra clothing she had brought with her from her pack and handed it to him. "I'm sorry I didn't remember before now," she said.

He removed his jacket to pull on the sweatshirt, and as he did so, the sleeve of the fleece top he wore beneath his jacket slid up, revealing a purpling bruise. "What happened there?" she asked.

He shoved the sleeve down over the bruise. "I refused to go with DJ, so he dragged me along." He rubbed at his side. "He jammed the gun pretty hard in my ribs. There's probably a bruise there, too."

"How did you cut your finger?" Lily asked.

"I was trying to start a fire by rubbing sticks together. I've read about it, but it's a lot harder than it looks. I jammed a sharp stick into my hand and never did get a fire going."

Lily took his hand and examined the injury. "You can't let that get infected. Let me get the first aid kit." She pulled out the first aid supplies and began tending the hand.

To distract the boy, Scott crouched in front of him. "Do you know who was working with DJ?" he asked.

"I don't know. DJ complained about getting stuck out in the middle of nowhere with me while everyone else got to sit around in a cushy rental."

"Why take you out into the wilderness anyway?" Lily asked as she dabbed antibiotic ointment onto the wound.

"DJ said nobody would ever look for me out here. They'd look for the kidnapper to get away in a car, not on skis. And even if they did figure out we were here, we'd be hard to find, with all the trees and snow. I guess he thought it was a pretty smart idea, until we were actually out here freezing and falling over logs and stuff."

"We saw your tracks that first afternoon," Scott said. "And we had a helicopter up looking right after that."

"I heard the helicopter," he said. "I wanted to find a way to signal to it, but DJ was watching me too closely."

Lily stuck a bandage on his hand, then closed the lid of the first aid kit. "That should keep it from getting infected."

"Thanks." Jackson pulled on the gloves Scott had given him. There were much too big, but warm. "Where are we going now?"

"Pandora is closest," Scott said.

"That old ghost town?" Jackson asked. "Is it near here?"

"Just on the other side of a ridge," Scott said. "There are buildings there we can shelter in."

"Won't the kidnappers know that, too?" Jackson asked. "We could get there and find them waiting."

"We could, but other people go there, too," Scott said. "Even in winter, it's a popular destination for cross-country skiers. And I'm pretty sure there are no fancy rentals there. Once we get there, we can call for help. We'll have shelter where we can wait."

"I hope we can get someone to meet us there," Lily said. She took out the satellite phone again and switched it on.

After a few seconds, a grin erased the weariness on her face. "We have a connection." She punched in a number. "I'm calling your dad," she told Jackson.

"Hello?" The man on the other end of the phone spoke so loudly and clearly Scott and Jackson could both hear him.

"Denny?" Lily asked.

"This is Mike. Lily, is that you? Are you okay?"

"Mike? Why are you answering Denny's personal phone? Is he okay?"

"He's tied up with something else right now, but he asked me to monitor his personal phone in case you or Jackson called. We've been worried sick."

"Jackson is with me now. That's why I'm calling."

"Is Jackson all right? Where are you?"

"He's fine. We're both fine."

"Thank God for that. Where are you?"

"We're near Nickel Ridge," she said. "We're on our way to Pandora."

"Pandora. That's great. I'll send someone right away."

"Let the sheriff know what's going on. And the resort? I'm sure people are wondering where I am. And Scott Linden. He's with us."

"Don't worry about a thing. I'll take care of it. You get to Pandora and you'll be safe. I'm so glad you called. Denny is going to be overjoyed. Now let me make some calls and get you taken care of."

Lily took the phone from her ear. "He hung up before I could talk to Denny or ask him any questions," she said.

"It doesn't matter," Scott said. "He'll send help. All we have to do is get to Pandora. We don't have much farther to go."

Lily looked up, at the low bank of clouds moving in. "It looks like we could get more snow," she said.

"Then let's get moving." Scott stood and slipped on his pack. "Let's try to get ahead of the storm."

Lily stowed the phone and donned her own pack, then the three of them, plus the two dogs, set out again. The route grew steeper, devoid of trees or even brush. "We don't have far to go now," Scott said. "We should be able see Pandora from the top."

It began to snow, big, soft flakes flitting down. But the scattering of flakes became a deluge, and wind blew the snow sideways. It hit their faces like shards of ice, and the swirling snow blinded them. The flakes piled in miniature drifts on their shoulders and the tops of their helmets, and soon obscured the rocky ground. At every breath, Lily inhaled snow. "Do you even know where we're going?" she gasped.

"Just keep climbing," Scott said. "We should be more sheltered on the other side of this ridge."

At last, they reached the top of the ridge. They paused and looked down the other side. "Do you see Pandora?" Jackson asked.

Lily couldn't see anything but snow. All that white could be covering boulders or buildings—at this point, she couldn't tell.

"I think it's over this direction," Scott said, and raised his arm to point.

A thud, like a fist punching a pillow, made a dull, hollow sound. Scott grunted, then sank to his knees. A second dull thud sounded to his right, and Lily recognized the sound of a bullet striking a target. She screamed and shoved Jackson to the ground. "Scott!" she shouted. "Scott, what happened?"

"Stay down," he said, his voice surprisingly calm.

She stayed down, but she crawled toward him. "What happened?" she asked.

"Stay away," he cautioned. "I've been shot."

Chapter Fifteen

Scott lay prone in the snow, fighting to breathe, heart drumming painfully in his chest. He braced himself against the pain he expected—but felt nothing. With one hand he probed at his chest, but found no exit wound. No blood. His back hurt as if he had been punched. Careful to stay low, he felt at his back. His fingers found a hole in his backpack, the coffeepot beneath it, dented now. There was still no pain, and he could move freely, now that he had caught his breath.

"Are you all right?" Lily asked from her spot, prone in the snow a few feet to his left. Jackson lay beside her—the dogs were nowhere in sight.

"I think so." He rose up on all fours. "I think the bullet struck the coffeepot in my pack. I don't think I'm bleeding."

"There's a hole in your backpack," she said.

"Yeah." He started to his feet, intending to remove the backpack and examine it more closely, but another shot rang out, sending him flat to the ground once more. A quick glance around told him they were in a terrible position—pinned down on the side of the ridge, easily standing out from the snow. But just downslope was a grove of small trees, and below that even deeper woods. All they needed was a chance to get to cover.

"On the count of three, I want you both to jump up and

run as fast as you can for that grove of trees just below us and to the left," he said. "Can you do that?"

"What are you going to do?" she asked.

"I'm going to fire in the direction I think those shots came from. The shooter will focus on me instead of the two of you and you can get away."

"Scott!" she protested. "They'll shoot you."

"No they won't." They might, but he wasn't going to think about that. "I'll stay down. You and Jackson have to get away. Promise me you'll run."

"All right." She didn't sound enthusiastic, but he was counting on her putting the boy's safety first.

"Jackson?" he asked.

"Yes," the boy said, his voice a little shaky, but clear. "I'll run."

Scott found the gun, checked that it was loaded and clicked off the safety. "On the count of three," he said. "One, two, three." He fired twice up the slope. A shot immediately answered, striking the ground to his left. He army-crawled a few feet upslope and fired again. More return fire, though again only a single shot. Was the shooter conserving ammunition?

Scott looked over his shoulder to where Lily and Jackson had been huddled together. They were no longer there. He waited, counting to a hundred. Time to get himself out of here.

He slid the pistol into the waistband of his pants, snugged against the small of his back. Then he grabbed the pack firmly by the sides. "One. Two. Three." He hoisted the pack over his head. Another bullet tore the pack from his hand. He flung the pack to one side, shoved to his feet and ran. He fully expected to feel a bullet slam into him at any moment, but no impact came. He stumbled through the thick snow in his boots, scrambling for purchase, trying to stay low, aiming for the grove of trees.

He crashed into the copse of trees, snow flying from the branches of pinion trees. "Over here!" Lily cried.

She was crouched at the base of an ancient juniper, the trunk two feet in diameter, feathery branches weighted down by snow forming an umbrella over her. He moved in beside her. "I had to leave my pack," he said, gasping for breath.

"Better your pack than the rest of you."

"Where's Jackson?" he asked.

"I don't know," she said. "He was ahead of me, and then I couldn't see him anymore." She raised her head. "Jackson! Jackson, where are you?"

No answer. "Hunter!" Scott shouted.

"Shelby!" Lily called. She whistled and clapped, but the snow absorbed all sound before it went very far.

"We can't go on without Jackson and the dogs." Her voice was tight with fear.

He gripped her arm. "Jackson probably just ran ahead of us. Maybe the dogs are with him." He was trying to comfort her, and himself, too. After all the trouble they had gone to to find him, surely they couldn't have lost the boy now.

Snow continued to fall, hard. Lily turned a complete circle, peering into the wall of white. "How are we ever going to find them?" she asked, sounding as if she might burst into tears.

Scott nudged her. "We need to get out of here before someone comes looking for us. It won't be difficult for them to find us." Even with the heavy snow, they were close enough to the top of the ridge that it probably wouldn't be that far for whoever had fired those shots to come after them.

"What if they have Jackson?" she asked.

"Then we can't help him if we let them find us, too."

He reloaded the gun, then led the way down the slope, moving in a zigzag path from the cover of tree to tree. Periodically they stopped, and he strained his ears, listening for sounds of pursuit. But the woods around them were silent except for the occasional soft "whump" as a tree released its burden of snow. At least the continued snowfall did a good job of erasing their tracks.

They headed steadily downhill, stumbling and stopping to help each other up. Scott searched for any sign that Jackson and the dogs had come this way, but found nothing.

"Stop!" Lily called when they had been trudging along for a quarter of an hour. She pulled her pack to the front and began rummaging in it. "I'm going to call the sheriff and let them know what happened, see if I can find out where our rescuers are."

"Good idea." Scott looked around them, seeing nothing in the swirling snow. He felt half naked without his pack. Maybe he'd made a mistake, sacrificing it that way. He hadn't had any food left in it, but he had first aid supplies and his sleeping bag.

"I can't find the phone."

Lily's words jerked him out of his stupor. "What do you mean you can't find it?"

"It's not in my pack. I swear I stowed it back in here after I spoke with Mike."

"Where did you put the phone?" Scott asked.

"In the outside pocket." She indicated the pocket.

"Was it unfastened like that?" Scott asked.

"I thought I closed it, but it was open when I went to look for the phone." She met his gaze. "I fell a couple of times. Maybe it came out then."

He looked back the way they had come, at an expanse

of smooth white, their tracks already buried under fresh snowfall. Finding a phone that had fallen in all that could take hours, or even days. And they still might never find it.

"What are we going to do?" Lily looked at Scott, her expression bereft.

"I don't think we can risk going back to Pandora," he said. "I think the kidnappers were probably the ones shooting at us. They probably figured Pandora was the closest place for us to seek shelter and stationed a guard on the ridge to watch for us."

"But the sheriff and his officers should be in Pandora soon," Lily said. "They should be able to deal with the kidnappers."

"Maybe the snow has delayed them," Scott said. "They could be waiting on a SWAT team or other reinforcements."

"I'm not sure I want to find them if we have to tell them we lost Jackson," she said. "What if the kidnappers found him first? What if they hurt Jackson? What if they hurt the dogs?"

He put his arm around her. "The only way we're going to get out of this is to stay calm," he said.

She leaned into him, head on his shoulder. She was trembling slightly—was that from cold or fear, or something else? After a moment, she looked up at him. "When you were in the army did you ever feel scared and hopeless?"

"I was afraid plenty of times," he said. "Anyone who says they aren't is lying. But I never let myself feel hopeless. I had too many other people depending on me for that."

She pressed her lips tightly together, then nodded. "Right. Jackson is depending on us. Denny and Mike and all the people who care about Jackson, too. And Hunter and Shelby are depending on us."

She gripped the straps of her pack and looked around

them. The snow had let up a little, but was still falling steadily, the blanket of white obscuring most features of the landscape. "Can you even tell which way we're headed?" she asked.

"If we keep heading downhill, we'll reach the bottom of the ridge," he said.

"Then what?" she asked.

"Then we'll decide what to do next."

She said nothing, but set off again. He hurried to catch up with her. "I don't think anyone is following us," she said.

"It doesn't sound like it, no."

Scott's back hurt, they were almost out of food, and it was only going to get colder as the day wore on. "We'll have to head back toward the ski resort," he said. "The kidnappers are probably counting on us coming back to Pandora, since it's closer. But if we can reach SkyCrest, we should be safe."

"We don't have to go all the way to SkyCrest," she said. "We only have to get to the avalanche site at Axis Ridge. My car is parked near there."

"And Brian's truck is beside your car." At her puzzled look, he added, "I borrowed it from him."

"How long is that going to take?" she asked.

He tried to calculate. They had been out here almost two days already, but part of that time they were unsure of their destination. The terrain and the weather had been against them. He still had his compass, and they would be traveling over territory they had covered before. They would have to stop when darkness set in, but they could set out again at first light tomorrow. "We should be able to make it tomorrow," he said. "We'll push on in as straight a line as possible."

Lily stared at him. He couldn't read her expression, between the goggles shielding her eyes and the fleece gaiter pulled up to her nose. But her shoulders slumped with fatigue, and she was surely as cold as he was. "The sooner we reach the resort, the sooner we can get other people out here looking for Jackson and the dogs," he said.

She nodded. "Right."

They reached the bottom of the ridge—and the almost impenetrable walls of trees. He had hoped to find the path through the woods they had followed before, but fresh snow had obscured their tracks, leaving them to fight their way through the heavy growth, sinking in snow to their knees at times, and tripping over hidden logs and boulders. When she had fallen for the sixth time in an hour, Lily pushed to her feet once more with a curse.

"We need to stop and build a fire," Scott said.

"I thought you said we need to keep going."

"We can't keep going like this. We're both clumsier than usual because we're so cold. We're getting hypothermic. We need to stop, have a hot drink and try to plot a course out of here."

He expected her to argue, but instead, she merely sat down on a snow-covered log and slumped forward, elbows on knees.

He cleared snow from a hollow in front of the log on which she sat, piling more snow in a wall to shield the blaze from the wind. Then he dug beneath a tangle of fallen logs and pulled out drier kindling. "What do you have in your pack to start a fire?" he asked when he had the beginnings of a campfire laid.

She removed the pack and opened it, then pulled out a plastic bag containing a lighter, waterproof matches and an old prescription bottle. He popped the cap on the bottle and found it filled with cotton balls coated in petroleum jelly. "After you told me what you used as a fire starter, I decided that was a good idea," she said.

He nodded and shoved a couple of the cotton balls in among the kindling and flicked the lighter.

Five minutes later, he was feeding slightly larger pieces of wood into the bright flames. Lily still hadn't moved. "It's going to be okay," he said gently.

"Jackson is nine!" The fierceness of her words had him sitting back on his heels. "He's just a kid. He's cold and hungry and afraid." Her voice choked. "His mom died. His dad works all the time. I was one person who always tried to be there for him and now even I've let him down."

She began to sob. Scott moved onto the log beside her and pulled her close. "You didn't let anyone down," he said. "You couldn't have done anything about whoever was shooting at us. Jackson did the right thing, running away from the shooter. It's no one's fault we got separated in the snowstorm."

She sniffed. "I'm worried about Shelby and Hunter, too. They're cold and hungry. What if they freeze to death?"

"They're both healthy, thick-coated dogs. They won't freeze to death." At least he hoped not. "Our job now is to keep from freezing to death ourselves and get to help."

She said nothing, so after a moment he pulled his arm from around her. "What have you got to eat in your pack?" he asked.

She took out several packets of electrolyte drink powder, the instant coffee, some jerky, plastic pouches of peanut butter, some tea bags and a single metal mug. He considered the array, selected the peanut butter and the electrolyte packets, and the mug. "I'll melt some snow," he said, and stood.

They passed the mug of hot electrolyte drink back and forth between them, and each had a stick of jerky. By the time they were done, Lily was sitting up straighter and Scott could think more clearly. "Are you ready to keep going?" he asked.

"Yes. But which way?" She gestured to the woods surrounding them. "All I can see are trees."

"We still have the compass." He took the instrument from his pocket. "We just have to keep heading east until we reach Axis Ridge."

They set out again, Lily in front, Scott trailing. He sighted in the compass. "Head for that tall ponderosa with the broken limb hanging down," he said.

When they reached the ponderosa, they checked the compass and set a course toward a large blue spruce. So far, keeping due east had been easy. But then they had to fight their way around a thicket of scrub oak and wild roses, the thorny canes of the roses snagging their clothing.

Scott crashed through the underbrush behind her, attempting to keep them on the right path, but after the fourth time he told her she was veering too far left she turned and glared at him. "If you think you can do better, you walk in the front."

He didn't fare much better breaking trail, and by four in the afternoon he was dazed with exhaustion. Lily stumbled after him, silent. All he could see was more trees, trunks sprouting like hair on the head of a giant as far as the eye could see. Which proved how exhausted he was, if he was thinking in those kind of fanciful metaphors. He stopped, and Lily walked right into him.

He caught her by the shoulders to keep her from falling, then just held on to her. "We need to stop," he said.

"Yeah," she said.

"How did Jackson and his kidnapper ever survive out here for a week?" she asked.

"They were really lucky," he said. "And not that bright to have come up with that as a plan."

"I guess if Denny's suspicions are right and a foreign power is behind the attempt to get the weapons technology, maybe they have no concept of what winter is like here. Or what a mountain wilderness is like." She hugged her arms more tightly around herself.

"You'd think they would do more research," he said.

"Maybe greed makes people take shortcuts," she said. "Or they thought it would only take a day or two before Denny would give in to their demands."

If Jackson had frozen to death, or died in the avalanche, would that have ruined the kidnappers' plans? Or would they have gone forward anyway, lying about Jackson's fate? Maybe that's what the note Denton Endicott had received after the avalanche had been—a lie to make him hand over the information the kidnappers wanted.

Scott tended the fire while she rummaged through her pack. "Looks like coffee and peanut butter for dinner," she said. "Or you can have tea." She held up one of the bags.

"Coffee," he said.

"Then I'll have coffee, too," she said. "It's easier to share if we choose the same thing. Besides, I think I need the caffeine."

He sat beside her on a log while they waited for the water in the cup to boil. "I'm trying really hard not to think about Jackson out there alone in the cold," she said. "But I'm not doing a very good job."

He put his arm around her, and she leaned into him. All the boundaries that had made him careful not to touch her in their everyday life had vanished here in the woods. "How are you feeling?" she asked after a moment. "I mean, where you were shot?"

"A little bruised," he said.

"Let me look," she said. "I mean, what if you have a bullet in you after all?"

"I think I'd know if I had a bullet in me."

"I've read that adrenaline can mask pain."

He swiveled so that his back was to her and shed his jacket. The cold air traveled quickly through his fleece and base layer top, and he shivered involuntarily.

But the shivering ceased when Lily pushed his clothing up to his shoulders and trailed her bare fingers up his back. Heat scorched him along the path of her touch. She stroked lightly at a place near the middle of his spine. "There's a bruise here," she said.

"Yeah." Though what he felt wasn't exactly pain. Every part of him had tensed at her touch, fighting the urge to lean into her.

She traced the line of one of his ribs. "You have a scar here," she said.

He had to think a minute to remember. "Rock climbing accident. I was seventeen. Fell and broke a couple of ribs. Decided it wasn't for me." He had lost the capacity to form complete sentences as her hand drifted lower. If her fingers felt this good, he imagined what it would be like to have her kiss her way down his body…

She pulled the shirts down. "You can put your jacket back on now," she said.

THE WEATHER WAS FREEZING, but warmth flooded Lily. The sight of Scott's bare back sent a liquid heat through her. Smooth skin and firm muscle sculpted over a masculine frame left her breathless. Even as she indulged in the sensation of her fingers gliding over him, she longed to touch even more.

She told herself she was being absurd. Inappropriate even, lusting after her boss. But Scott hadn't been authoritarian or demanding today—only kind and encouraging. His bravery made her less daunted by their circumstances. She was still afraid. Still worried and grieving. But being with him comforted her. And thinking about him—how she wanted to pull off the rest of his clothing, kiss her way down his body and have him kiss her—was a welcome distraction from the fears that threatened to overwhelm her.

They shared their meager meal, passing the cup of coffee back and forth between them, then making a second cup. Even without sugar and creamer the bitter caffeine was a welcome jolt, the hot liquid beating back the cold. They built up the fire until it was a roaring blaze, then huddled before it on the fallen log, soaking up the heat. Neither of them mentioned the risk they were taking—that the blaze might lead pursuers to them. But without the warmth of the fire, they would surely freeze to death. "How are you doing?" Scott asked after a while.

"I'm warmer now," she said. "Not as hungry as I was. What about you?"

"I'm okay. Warmer is most important. And the coffee helped, too."

"I take supplies in my pack every year, hiking and skiing," she said. "It's been drilled in to me by every wilderness guide I ever read and every instructor I ever had. But I never had to use them before this week. This is the second time in a few days that I've had to spend the night out when I didn't intend to."

"I've spent nights out on missions," he said. "I stayed out two nights before they found Clark."

His words were matter-of-fact, but she heard the loss behind them. "Were you alone?"

"I didn't really want to be around anyone else."

"After my brother, Ben, died, I didn't want to talk to anyone else either," she said. "It's like grief put a wall between me and other people. I was angry that Ben was gone—and angry at everyone else because they couldn't understand how much I hurt."

"I was mostly angry at myself. That I couldn't save him."

She wanted to tell him his friend's death wasn't his fault. But people always said things like that to suffering people, and the words didn't help. Instead, she slipped her hand into his and leaned on his arm. He held on tightly. They didn't say anything for a long time. The fire popped and sent up orange sparks, and the wet wood on the edge of the blaze sizzled and steamed. She breathed in the sweet, smoky aroma of burning pinion and juniper and felt her eyes drifting shut.

"We should try to get some sleep," Scott said. He unwound his fingers from hers.

"We should share my sleeping bag," she said. His was with his pack, up on the ridge.

"I'll just sit up and tend the fire."

"That's ridiculous." She stood and grabbed the bag from her pack, unrolled and unzipped it and spread it by the fire. "Two of us will generate more heat than one." Then she bit her lip, holding back laughter at her unintentional joke.

Maybe he was thinking the same thing. She thought his cheeks flushed, though perhaps that was merely from the cold. She turned her back to him and stripped down to socks and thermal top and pants, then lay down on the sleeping bag and beckoned him. "Come on. If I let you freeze to death I'll never get out of these woods."

Chapter Sixteen

Scott's expression in the firelight was grim, but he peeled down to his long underwear and slid in beside her. With the bag mostly zipped it was a tight fit, but if they spooned together they could manage. It was comfortable even, and much warmer.

Those classes she had taken had taught that this was what people did to survive in the cold. But they never talked about the intimacy of lying with her bottom snugged against his crotch, his very evident erection pressed against her in a way that had her struggling to control her breathing. She wriggled, trying to get comfortable, and heard his gasp. At this rate, neither of them was going to sleep tonight.

She reached back and took his hand and wrapped his arm around her, his fingers splayed across her stomach. "Maybe this isn't such a good idea," he said, his voice soft in her ear.

"Are you saying you won't respect me in the morning?" She meant it as a joke, but part of her was serious. If she gave in to desire and had sex with him tonight, would it jeopardize her job?

"I will always respect you," he said. "But how will you feel about me?"

She wanted to turn and face him, to try to read the expression in his eyes. But that was impossible to do in the confines of the sleeping bag. "Scott, I don't know what's going to happen tomorrow," she said. "All I know is that right now, I want you." To make sure he got the message, she guided his hand down, toward her crotch. He cupped her hard, and she caught her breath before releasing a long sigh.

He kissed her neck, and his tongue traced the line of her collarbone. "Maybe I've been harder on you than everyone else because I was afraid of how much I'm attracted to you," he said. His voice was low and rough, abrading her nerves. She squirmed against him, and he squeezed her hip, stilling her.

"You're…attracted to me?" she asked, the last word a squeak as he gently rolled her nipple between his thumb and forefinger.

"I've had dreams about you." He slid his hand beneath her shirt and cupped her breast.

"What kind of dreams?"

"Inappropriate ones."

All she could do was moan as he slid his hand down her body, coming to rest between her legs once more. When he didn't do anything more, she ground against him. "I need you to touch me," she said.

He pressed his forehead against the back of her head, breathing hard. "I want that. More than anything right now. But are you sure?"

"Yes. Yes, I'm sure." When he didn't answer, she added, "We're two consenting adults. There's nothing in our employment contracts that says we can't be together, and it's certainly not against the law. And if you do ever try to take advantage of me at work—my dad's a lawyer and he'll sue you for everything you have."

He laughed, a deep, sexy chuckle that had her squirming back against him. He slid his hand beneath the waistband of her long underwear bottoms and began to fondle her. She closed her eyes, seeing stars. He was kissing her neck again, doing amazing things with his fingers. Then he slid one finger into her, and she dug the nails of one hand into his thigh. He stilled. "Do you want me to stop?" he asked.

"You'd better not."

He laughed again and began to stroke and fondle in earnest, until she was gasping, back bowed against him. "You feel amazing," he said, his lips against the back of her neck. Those whispered words, and his skilled touch, were her undoing. She climaxed hard, straining against him.

He held her for a long moment before he slid his hand to rest over her stomach once more. She was warm clear to her toes, but feeling a little guilty, too. She tried to reach back for him, but he stilled her hand. "Let's just stay like this," he said.

"That doesn't seem fair." She could still feel his erection, hard and insistent.

He blew out a breath. "We don't have a condom, and we don't have room in this sleeping bag to do what I'd really like to do. I can wait."

This simple statement left her momentarily speechless. The men she had been with before were not ones to wait. She was more often the one waiting on them, and sometimes left unfulfilled altogether while they snored beside her. "I'll make it worth the wait, I promise," she said, then felt embarrassed at the boast. As if she were some femme fatale.

He chuckled again, a sound she was growing to like very much. "I'm sure you will," he said. He pulled her close. "Now get some sleep."

SCOTT WOKE AS gray light was just beginning to filter through the trees. It had stopped snowing, and overnight the fire had died down. At least the campfire he had built had died down. He was still burning for Lily, who slept deeply, curled against him. He carefully lowered the zipper on his side of the sleeping bag and eased out. The cold hit him like an electric shock, but staying in there with her would have been worse torture. He pulled on clothes and began poking at the fire.

Lily groaned and rolled onto her back. "What time is it?" she asked.

"I don't know," he said. "Early. Stay there until I get the fire going."

She ignored him and wriggled out of the bag, then gasped as the cold hit her. She hurriedly dressed while he tried not to watch, though his gaze kept drifting back to her slender form. "I'll be right back," she said, and moved off into the woods.

When she returned he had the fire blazing, and it was his turn to move into the woods to relieve himself. While he was there, he circled their camp, looking for any sign of a predator—human or animal. He found none.

"Breakfast is coffee," she said, and nodded to the cup of snow she had set beside the fire to melt.

His stomach growled, but he nodded. "We should reach Axis Ridge in a couple of hours," he said. "Then we can drive to the resort."

"I would have thought someone would have come looking for us by now," she said.

"The weather yesterday made searching difficult," he said. "But it's clear now. They should be able to get a helicopter up. With luck, they'll spot us on the road. That will speed things up."

They drank their coffee and packed their belongs. Scott was putting out the fire when she grabbed his arm. "Listen!"

He stilled, ears straining. At first he heard nothing, then thought he heard a distant bark.

Then an ear-splitting whistle almost deafened him. He looked over to see Lily, pinkie fingers hooked in the corners of her mouth. She whistled again. "Shelby!" she shouted.

A commotion to their left had them both moving in that direction. The blonde Malinois burst into the clearing and almost bowled Lily over. Hunter was right behind her and leaped into Scott's arms. He staggered back and hugged the dog tightly. Until now, he hadn't allowed himself to admit how worried he had been about the dog.

"Lily!" Jackson staggered from the woods. He was disheveled and pale, tears streaming down his cheeks.

Lily rushed to embrace him. "Oh, Jackson, I'm so glad to see you," she said. "We were so worried."

"I… I got lost," he sobbed. "I… I thought I'd never… never see you again."

Scott was already raking up coals and feeding wood onto the fire. "You're safe now," he said. "Let's get you warm, and you can tell us what happened."

He put warm rocks from the fire under the boy's feet, and Lily wrapped her sleeping bag around him. They heated water and gave him a cup of weak coffee. "You won't like the taste, but drink it," Lily said.

He drained the cup and held it out. "Can I have some more? And do you have anything to eat? I'm hungry."

Scott's own stomach rumbled again.

"I'm sorry, we don't." Lily rubbed the boy's shoulder. "But by tonight you should be home and safe and eating whatever you want."

Scott hoped she was right. Nothing had gone their way lately. "What happened after we ran from the top of the ridge?" he asked. "We looked and couldn't find you."

"I looked for you guys and couldn't find *you*!"

"Where were you?" Lily asked.

"I don't know. After Scott was shot I just ran as fast as I could." He frowned at Scott. "You were shot, weren't you?"

"I was, but fortunately for me, the bullet hit something in my pack. It knocked me over, but I was okay. But in getting away from the shooter, I lost my pack."

"What did you do when you couldn't find us?" Lily asked. "How did you spend the night?"

"Shelby and Hunter found me," he said. Both dogs looked up at the mention of their names. Scott had given them water, and they had laid on their sides in the snow, exhausted. "They both came running up and stayed with me. I was hoping they would lead me to you two, but they didn't. I wandered around looking for you and they stuck with me. Then, when it got to be too dark to look anymore, I found a hollow space at the base of a big tree and crawled into that. The dogs lay on top of me." He smiled a little. "It was kind of like sleeping under two heavy, furry blankets, but they kept me warm. And they made me feel less scared."

"Good dogs!" Lily reached out and stroked each dog in turn. "They must be really hungry, too."

"Not as hungry as I am," Jackson said. "One of them caught a squirrel, and they ate it." He wrinkled his nose. "It was gross, but I was so hungry I almost tried to get part of it."

"Good dogs," Scott echoed Lily's praise. Despite Hunter's name, he had never thought of his pet as a predator. He supposed even a tame dog still had wild instincts.

Jackson finished his second cup of coffee and handed Scott the empty cup. "Are the shooters still after us?" he asked. "Have you heard from my dad? Or the sheriff?"

"I lost the sat phone when we ran down the ridge," Lily

said. "But it doesn't seem like anyone has been following us."

Scott squatted down in front of the boy, so that they were eye to eye. "I know you said you don't know who kidnapped you, but do you have any idea why you were taken?" he asked. "What is it the kidnappers want from your dad?"

"I've been thinking about that," Jackson said. "I thought about it a lot before I fell asleep last night. And I remembered Preston asked me if I had seen any people who spoke with a foreign accent at the house. He was being real weird about it. I asked did he mean French people or people from Mexico, or what? Then he asked if I had seen my dad talking to any people from China, or people who looked Chinese. I told him no, but I thought it was a weird question."

"Does your father do business with people in China?" Scott asked.

Jackson pulled the sleeping bag more tightly around him. "I don't know. Maybe. He does business all over the world. It's all high-tech stuff, but I don't know much about it. I told Preston that, and he finally left me alone."

Scott glanced at Lily. She looked as puzzled as he felt. "Preston works for your dad?" Scott asked. He thought he had the connection right.

"Yeah. He's a new hire. I don't like him."

"I don't like him either," Lily said. "And it wouldn't surprise me to find out he was involved in all of this."

"What are we going to do now?" Jackson asked.

Scott stood. "We're going to keep walking," he said. "Until we get out of these woods. We'll be near the ridge where you escaped the avalanche. From there, we can get to our vehicles." Scott unwrapped the sleeping bag from around the boy. "Come on. The sooner we get going, the sooner we'll reach help."

Scott led the way, Jackson between him and Lily, the dogs ranging on either side. The snow had stopped and the sky had cleared, but without the cloud cover, temperatures had dropped. He set a rapid pace, as much to generate warmth as to hasten the journey. After the first hour, he thought he recognized some of the terrain. The trees began to thin. Suddenly, they were standing on the edge of the forest, looking out across the expanse of broken snow. Sections of earth showed where equipment had been digging, and the terrain was strewn with shattered trees, giant boulders and slabs of snow like icebergs emerging from the ocean.

"How are we going to get over all of that?" Jackson asked.

It was going to be brutal. Scott wondered how far he could carry the boy.

"We can send the dogs ahead of us," Lily said. "They'll pick out the best path."

"We don't have to cross the whole field," Scott said. "We just have to get to the cleared area for parking. The vehicles are just beyond that."

They started toward the parking area, repeatedly falling, helping each other up. In the end, they took turns carrying Jackson. The dogs led the way, guiding them around the toughest obstacles.

By the time they reached the cleared parking area, they were sweating and winded. Several inches of fresh snow had partially filled in the parking area. "It doesn't look like anyone has been here in a few days," Lily said.

Her eyes met his, weary and sad. "They must have halted the search."

"Just as well," Scott said. "They weren't going to find anything, because Jackson is with us. Just like you said all along." He would never forget her reminding him that their job was to save people—no matter what.

"How far is it to the cars?" Jackson asked.

"Not far." Scott swung the boy onto his hip, steeling himself against the sharp pain in his back. He could do this. Only a little farther to go.

Brian's truck was still there, parked beside Lily's Subaru. But they hadn't gone far before Scott realized something was wrong. "What the—?" Lily asked, failing to finish the sentence.

All four tires of the truck were slashed, and the front windshield had been shattered. The tires on the Subaru were ruined as well, only the driver's side window broken. But someone had raised the hood. When Scott reached the car and looked inside the engine compartment, he could see the battery was missing.

"Who would do something like this?" she asked.

"Someone who doesn't want us to be able to go for help," Scott said.

She turned to him, her face pale. Then she looked around them. He could read her thoughts. Was someone watching them now?

Jackson began to cry again. "I'm never going to get home!" he wailed.

Scott passed the boy to her. She rocked Jackson in her arms and kissed the top of his head. "What are we going to do?" she asked.

He looked at the snow-covered road. It was miles to any home or business, but what choice did they have? "We'll have to keep walking," he said. "At least it will be easier terrain to cover than the woods or the avalanche field."

She set Jackson on his feet once more. "I've got a better idea," she said. "I'll ski ahead of you. You two can follow on foot with the dogs, but I'm bound to get there faster. With a little bit of luck, I can send people back to meet you."

She had already removed her pack and was unfastening her skis. She dropped them on the ground and stepped into the bindings.

"I want to go with Lily!" Jackson wailed.

Scott wanted to go with her, too, but instead he put a restraining hand on the boy's shoulder. "Lily will be a lot faster than us," he said. "She'll reach help sooner. We'll follow along at our own pace."

Lily shouldered her pack once more. "I'll send help as soon as I can," she said. Shelby danced beside her. She looked down at the dog. "You'd better keep her here," she said. "She's already worn out. I don't think running all that way would be good for her, and I'm too tired to carry her."

"Shelby, come." Scott beckoned. The dog glanced at Lily, then hurried to his side. He took hold of her harness. "Good luck," he said to Lily. If Jackson hadn't been with them, he might have kissed her.

She nodded, then turned her back to them, planted a ski pole and set out.

Chapter Seventeen

The memory of a shot ringing out, the bullet felling Scott, haunted Lily as she skied down the snowy road. Anyone could be hiding in the trees on either side of her, maybe whoever had vandalized their vehicles. She forced the thought from her mind. She didn't have any choice but to keep going. Jackson was weakening fast. She didn't know how much longer he could do without food and shelter in the cold. She concentrated on sliding one ski forward and then the other, poles planting rhythmically. The road sloped downward slightly, and she began to pick up speed, the cold air stinging her cheeks even as her muscles warmed. After so many hours of trudging along in difficult terrain, the sensation of floating across the snow untied some of the knots in her shoulders and stomach.

She didn't know how long she had been skiing or how far she had traveled when she spotted the lights of a car moving toward her. She slowed and waited, torn between darting into the woods to hide and waving her hands to flag down what could be her rescuer.

The car slammed on its brakes, skidding a little in the snow, and the driver's door popped open. "Lily! Lily, you're safe!" The familiar stocky figure of Mike Swanson emerged from the car and hurried to her. He stopped directly in front of her and pushed sunglasses to the top of his head.

"Mike!" Relief surged through her. "Oh my gosh, I'm so glad to see you."

"I'm relieved to see you, too." He hugged her tightly, then stepped back and looked over her shoulder. "Where are Jackson and Scott?"

"I left them back down the road just a little ways. We decided that since I was the only one with skis, I should go ahead to bring back help."

"Terrific." He lowered his glasses. "Let's go get them."

"Where is the sheriff?" she asked. "Did he send officers to Pandora?"

Mike frowned. "The sheriff refused to take my report about your phone call seriously. I don't know what he's doing, but he isn't looking for you and Scott. I'm not even sure he's looking for Jackson anymore."

"What do you mean he wouldn't take you seriously? You told him Jackson was with me, right? And you told Denny?"

"Denny is as frustrated as I am. We decided to give up on Howard and put together our own team to rescue you all."

"Where is Denny now?"

"He's tied up at a meeting across town."

"A business meeting?" She stared, incredulous. How could Denny even think about business when his son was missing?

"A press conference or something, I think." Mike put a hand on her shoulder. "Come on. I'll radio the team and they'll catch up with us. Take me back to Jackson and Scott."

"Now that I'm here, I can talk to the sheriff," she said. She started to move past him, but he blocked her way.

"We don't have time for that," he said. "I didn't want to upset you before, but the truth is, Preston Smith is ahead of us. We can't let him get to Jackson before we do."

"Preston? The new employee?" A shiver ran through her at the name. The man Jackson had said had questioned him about Chinese visitors.

"He's the one behind the kidnapping," Mike said. "At least, that's what Denny and I think. The sheriff isn't listening to us about that, either."

"Why wouldn't the sheriff believe you?"

"He questioned Preston and apparently believed whatever lies Preston told him. But Denny and I are sure he's involved. He's been behaving oddly ever since we hired him. You met him, right?"

She nodded. And something about him had struck her as odd. "But if I talk to the sheriff…"

"Do you want to be responsible for Jackson's death? That's what will happen if Preston gets to him first."

His words—and the harsh tone in which they were delivered—shook her. "All right," she said. "I'll take you to them."

He nodded, then pulled out a radio and clicked a button. "I'm with Lily," he said. "We're going to pick up Jackson and Scott. Have the team meet us at the intersection of Forest Service roads 723 and 787."

A garbled voice spoke through static. Lily couldn't make out the words, but Mike seemed to understand. "Ten-four." He pocketed the radio again, and turned to Lily. "Let's go," he said.

She shed her skis, stowed them and her pack in the back seat, then slid into the passenger seat. Warmth enveloped her, and she almost moaned with happiness. Just sitting down on something soft, and in such warmth, was luxurious. She forced her eyes open, fearing if she closed them she might fall asleep before they reached Scott and Jackson.

"I'M FREEZING." JACKSON SAT on a boulder by the side of the road and hugged his arms across his chest. He was so exhausted he kept falling in the snow, and Scott could no longer carry him, so they had decided to sit down and wait. "When is Lily going to come back?"

"She'll be here as soon as she can," Scott said. "Or she'll send someone to us." Realistically he knew she hadn't been gone that long, but standing here in this desolate place, cold seeping in and hunger gnawing at him, the minutes stretched to uncomfortable lengths. Even the dogs were miserable, alternately pacing and whining.

"I'm so hungry!" Jackson groaned and doubled over.

"So am I," Scott said. "Try not to think about it."

"How can I not think about it when I'm starving?"

Scott reminded himself that Jackson was only nine. He looked around for something to distract them both. Why hadn't he at least thought to ask Lily to leave her pack, with the fire starters and mug for melting water?

Shelby sat up and growled, low in her throat. Hunter leaped to his feet. Both dogs stared toward the woods behind them. Hunter barked. Jackson sat up straight. "Someone's coming!" he shouted.

Both dogs were barking now, the hair along their backs standing at attention. A figure in black emerged from the woods. A lean man with a square jaw and Roman nose stepped into their small clearing. "Call off the dogs!" he said in a commanding voice.

"Preston!" Jackson moved to stand next to Scott. "What are you doing here?"

Scott wasn't sure Preston even heard the question over the racket the dogs were making. "Call off those dogs!" Preston shouted.

"Hunter! Shelby! Quiet!" Scott ordered.

Both dogs glanced back at him, as if to ask if he was sure. "Quiet," he repeated. "Come. Sit."

They moved to flank him and Jackson and sat, though all their attention was still riveted on Preston.

"Who are you?" Preston addressed Scott. "What are you doing with Jackson?"

"Who are *you*?" Scott countered. Jackson had one hand on Scott's hip, and was nibbling the thumbnail on his other hand.

"I'm Preston Smith. I work for Endicott Industries. Jackson, are you okay?"

Jackson didn't answer.

Scott put his hand on the boy's shoulder. "I'm Scott Linden. I work for SkyCrest Resort. What are you doing here?"

Preston studied him. Scott stood at attention, a soldier under inspection. Whatever this Preston Smith was up to now, Scott would bet he had a military background. He had the bearing of an officer.

Preston unzipped his parka and reached inside. Jackson whimpered. "Is he going to shoot us?"

Scott reached for the pistol at his back, but the other man was faster. Preston wrenched the gun away from him, jammed an elbow at the side of Scott's head, then kicked out, knocking Scott's feet out from under him. Scott clawed at the other man's face and grabbed at his arm, and Preston drove another elbow into his ribs. Scott was flat on his back, sure he was about to be shot—at close range this time—when a woman's scream cut through the air.

The sound froze all action. Preston stood over Scott with one hand raised. Scott lay on the ground, his head turned toward the sound. Jackson was crouched, arms wrapped around his knees, small sounds of distress emanating from him. The dogs still flanked the boy, on their feet once more, but silent as they studied the tableau before them.

"What are you doing!" Lily emerged from a car that had

parked in the middle of the road. A man in black followed her. She looked from Jackson to Scott to Preston.

"Special Agent Preston Shipman, with the FBI," Preston said, and pulled a gun from his jacket.

Lily started to scream again, but the sound was choked off by an arm tightened around her throat. Mike held a gun to her head. "Drop that weapon, Agent Shipman, or Lily is a dead woman."

LILY'S HEART BEAT so hard she thought it would burst. Her vision blurred, and she forced herself to breathe deeply, though doing so made her even more aware of Mike's arm crushing her windpipe. When she squirmed, trying to ease the pressure, he tightened his grip even more and pressed the barrel of the pistol—hard and ice cold—against her temple.

"Mike, what are you doing?" Jackson asked.

"Shut up, kid, or I'll shoot you instead," Mike growled.

This didn't even sound like the Mike she knew—the good-natured, easygoing friend. "Where is Denny?" she asked. "Does he know what you're doing?"

"I told you. Denny is in a meeting. With some associates of mine. As long as he cooperates, they won't hurt him. Much."

Terror shuddered through her. She looked for Scott, but he was out of her field of vision. So she focused on the man across from her, the one who said he was an FBI agent. She recognized Preston Smith, the new employee who had questioned her that night at Denny's house. "Are you really with the FBI?" she asked.

"Shut up!" Mike ordered. "Throw your gun into the woods," he directed Preston.

Preston—Agent Shipman—hurled the gun away from

him. It sailed out of sight into the trees. "You can't kill all of them before I kill you," he said.

"I'm betting I can get the woman and the boy before you get off a shot at me," Mike said. "Do you really want to take that chance?"

Then they all stood there, staring at one another. Lily closed her eyes, but the images were imprinted on the inside of her eyelids, like a still from a bad movie. Whoever flinched first would be the loser—but in the end, no one would win.

Mike's grip on her throat had loosened a fraction, though the barrel of the gun still dug into her temple. He outweighed her by at least fifty pounds, and any attempt to lash out at him had a chance of making him pull the trigger—either willingly or involuntarily.

"So what are you going to do now?" Preston asked. Lily marveled at how calm he sounded. Maybe because his head wasn't the one with a gun to it.

"I'm going to take Jackson and Lily with me and leave," Mike said. "I just have to get you out of the way first."

He moved the gun away from her and pointed it at the FBI agent. Lily yelped and squirmed against him. And then she and Mike were both on the ground, Shelby on top of them, her teeth clamped down on Mike's hand as he screamed and kicked.

The three of them struggled briefly, then Preston said, "Call off your dog. I've got him now." Preston stood over them, gun in one hand, cuffs in the other.

"Shelby! No! Sit!" Lily struggled to a sitting position herself. She had to give the commands again before the dog released her hold on Mike. Preston pulled Mike to his feet and cuffed his hands behind his back.

"I'm bleeding!" Mike complained. "That dog tried to kill me."

Preston only shook his head.

"I should have known you'd have another gun," Mike said.

"The gun isn't his, it's mine." Scott moved in to help Lily up. Scott held her tightly for a long moment, neither of them speaking.

"It was close enough for me to grab," Preston said. He pocketed Scott's pistol. "Come on. We need to get out of here. We have a couple of choppers coming to meet us."

Moments later, as the five people and two dogs stepped from the woods into the clearing once more, the throb of helicopter rotors cut the air. The first had barely touched down on the snow when the door opened and Denton Endicott leaped out. "Jackson!" he shouted over the din of the helicopter.

"Dad!" Jackson raced toward his father, and Denny knelt to embrace him. Lily was relieved to see him. Had Mike lied when he said Denny was being held by his associates?

Preston turned to them. "You two and the boy can go with Endicott," he said. "I'll take Mike with me."

"What about the dogs?" Lily asked.

Preston looked down at the two dogs, who were sitting at Scott's and Lily's feet. "There isn't room for them in the helicopter," he said.

"If it wasn't for them, you might not even be here," Lily said. She crossed her arms. "The helicopter can take Jackson and his dad and Scott first and come back for me and the dogs."

"I'll wait with you." Scott put his arm around her.

"You two go with the Endicotts," Preston said. "We'll send someone for the dogs."

"I don't go without my dog," Lily said.

"Me either," Scott said. "And I'd like my gun back."

Agent Shipman glared at them, then shook his head, turned and walked away, prodding Mike along in front of him.

"Don't worry. I'll make sure they come back for you and the dogs," Denny said. "Or we could probably take Lily and Shelby and come back for Scott and Hunter."

Scott turned to Lily. "Go on," he said. "I'll be fine out here."

"No. I'm not going to leave you now."

She braced herself for a lecture on not being stubborn. Maybe he would even try to order her to leave, as her boss. She could read the impulse in his eyes. He could probably read her refusal in hers. He opened his mouth, then closed it. "Go on, Mr. Endicott," he said. "We'll wait together."

They stood back and watched the helicopters lift off, one after the other. When they were gone, silence descended like a muffling pillow. "Are you okay?" Scott asked.

"I will be." She looked up at him. "I don't think I've ever been so terrified in my life."

"Me either." He squeezed her tight against his side.

"Are you okay?" she asked. She touched a bruise forming on the side of his face.

"Agent Preston objected when I pulled a gun on him. I guess I can't blame him. He probably thought I was one of the kidnappers."

"Mike has worked for Denny for twenty-five years," she said. "They were best friends in college! Why would he do something like this?"

"Greed? Or maybe he resented that Endicott had more than he did. Who knows." He shook his head. "I thought Preston was the villain in this story. When he stepped out of the woods and demanded to know who I was, I was sure he was behind Jackson's kidnapping."

"Denny will tell me later what's going on." She shook her head. "It's all so unbelievable. And Shelby!" She looked down at the dog, then bent to pat her side. "You would think she was a trained attack dog or something."

"She was protecting you," he said. "You're her person. The one she loves most in the world."

She swallowed past a sudden knot in her throat. "I am. That's the thing about dogs, isn't it? They love you with everything they have." Unlike people, who were always holding back. At least she was holding back. Afraid of loving too much. Afraid of hurting too much.

She looked away from Scott, her feelings in turmoil. This ordeal had changed things between them, but what did that mean going forward? He was still her boss. Still prickly and particular, hard to read. She knew him better now, but did that mean they could be a couple?

She wanted that, she thought. She wanted to try. But what did he want?

He sighed, like someone setting down a heavy weight. "I want to go home, take a shower, eat half the refrigerator and sleep for two days," he said.

She laughed—because he was answering the question she hadn't asked out loud, and because the answer was so basic. Except for the bath, it was the same things their dogs probably wanted. "Yeah," she said. "I want that, too." Later, she would think past those basic needs. Later, she would try to ferret out the answer to the riddle people were always trying to solve—what they wanted. What was within their reach and what was impossible.

Chapter Eighteen

Lily did not sleep two days, but she did stay in bed for ten hours before Special Agent Shipman rang her doorbell until she was forced to answer it. This time he held up his identification. "We need to interview you about what happened with you and Jackson," he said.

A woman with a long, narrow dark face and carefully braided hair stepped out from behind him. "I'm Special Agent Green," she said. She held up a cardboard to-go cup. "I have coffee."

Shelby peered out from around Lily's legs and growled. Preston frowned at the dog. "That dog doesn't like me much," he said.

That makes two of us, Lily thought. "She's very protective," she said. She held the door open wider. "Don't make any sudden moves and you'll be fine." She really didn't believe Shelby would attack him unprovoked, but she enjoyed the uneasy look on his face after she said the words. "Let me get dressed, and I'll talk to you." She didn't give him time to respond, merely left the room, Shelby close after her.

By the time she had dressed, combed her hair and brushed her teeth, she was feeling more human. "Thanks for the coffee," she said to Agent Green, and sipped from the cup. It was still fairly hot, and tasted wonderful, full of cream and caramel syrup. Far superior to the weak black brew they had drunk in the woods.

"We need your statement about everything that happened, starting when you found Jackson," Preston said.

"First, tell me what's going on with Mike," she asked. "Was he behind Jackson's kidnapping?"

The two agents exchanged looks. "I can't reveal details of our case," Shipman said.

She set down the coffee and leaned toward him. "The man tried to kill me. He held a gun to my head. He kidnapped a little boy I care about very much. You can at least tell me something—or I won't tell you anything."

"We can have the court compel you to provide evidence," Shipman said.

She crossed her arms over her chest. "Go ahead. Or you could tell me what Mike was up to and I'll tell you everything right now."

"We believe Michael Swanson had made a deal with the Chinese government to sell them the details for technology Endicott Industries developed for the US military," Agent Green said. She ignored Preston's scowl. "Agent Shipman was embedded in the company to look for evidence to refute or support these suspicions."

"Did Denny Endicott know about this?" Lily asked. She held her breath, waiting for the answer. She didn't want to think her friend could be involved in such a scheme.

"We don't believe so, no," Green said. "But at some point in the past few months, he did become suspicious that someone was leaking confidential information. He tightened security. This made it impossible for Swanson to help himself to the information he needed."

"We believe the Chinese put pressure on him to deliver more information," Shipman took up the story. "At first,

Swanson arranged for a couple of guys to rough up Endicott and threaten him if he didn't hand over the information they wanted."

"That was the night I was babysitting," Lily said. "The night you came to the house and threatened me when I wouldn't let you in. What was that all about?"

Shipman scowled. "I was looking for evidence of Endicott's involvement."

"You were out of line, treating me that way."

"I was focused on doing my job," Shipman said. "It doesn't matter anyway, since you wouldn't let me in."

"We've never found evidence that Mr. Endicott was involved," Agent Green said.

"Denny said he refused to cooperate with the people who threatened him that night," Lily said.

Shipman nodded. "The threats didn't work, so the next phase was to kidnap Jackson. The idea was that Mike would volunteer to intercede with the kidnappers on Endicott's behalf. He would turn over the classified information they wanted and return with Jackson. He'd be a hero, Endicott would trust him even more, and the kidnappers would disappear back to China—until the next time Mike had secrets to sell."

"Why would Mike betray his friend that way?" Lily asked.

"He says he didn't have a choice," Green said. "That the Chinese threatened to kill him if he didn't do what they wanted."

"People like this always have an excuse," Shipman said. "They offered him a million dollars in an offshore account. That's plenty of motivation for a lot of people."

"Who was the man who actually took Jackson from the ski resort?" Lily asked.

"His name was Donald Johanson," Green said. "He was

married to a Chinese national and lived in the country for twenty years before he returned to the States to do dirty work for his handlers. He took charge of the boy as a way of having more leverage over Mike. When the avalanche killed him, Mike was frantic. He ended up kidnapping Endicott himself. But without his son, Endicott would reveal nothing."

"But Denny was in the first helicopter that arrived," she said. "How did he escape?"

"The sheriff's department became suspicious when they couldn't contact Endicott and went to his plant. They found him tied up in a vacant conference room and freed him. He told them about Mike."

"Endicott thought Mike and Preston were working together," Agent Green said. Her face was expressionless, but Lily thought she detected a gleam in the agent's eye.

"We cleared that up soon enough," Preston said. "Though I wasn't there at the time. I was trying to track you down."

"Who shot at Scott at the top of the ridge?" Lily asked.

"That was another of the kidnappers," Preston said. "They were supposed to rendezvous with him once Mike handed over the information from Endicott. They planned to leave Jackson somewhere and communicate his whereabouts once they were safely out of the country."

"At least, that's according to the one man who agreed to talk to us," Agent Green said.

"Do you have everyone involved in custody now?" Lily asked.

"Not everyone." Preston's face was as expressionless as a mannequin. "We believe some of the group have left the country."

"We would appreciate it if you'd give us your statement now," Agent Green said.

"All right." She drank the last of the coffee, took a deep breath and told them everything, beginning with the day Jackson disappeared until the helicopters touched down in the valley. By the time she was done, she felt drained emotionally and physically. She wanted to crawl back under the covers and stay there.

Agent Green switched off the recorder that had sat between them. "Thank you," she said. "We may have more questions later, but that should do for now."

"Did you interview Jackson?" Lily asked. "And Scott?"

"We're going to talk to Jackson later today," Green said. "With his father and the family attorney present."

"We talked to your boyfriend," Preston said. "His story matches up with yours."

She started to tell him Scott wasn't her boyfriend, but held her tongue. She didn't know what he was, but clearly he was more to her now than a boss. And more than a friend. At least, she wanted him to be more.

"He wouldn't talk to us until we returned his gun," Green said. "And he asked about you. If you were all right."

Warmth bloomed in her chest at the words. Surely that meant he cared.

The agents left and she went back to bed, and back to sleep. She slept fitfully, and was disoriented and out of sorts when she awoke. She checked her phone and found messages from Nina and Connor, asking how she was doing. But nothing from Scott. She didn't like how much this silence from him stung, but told herself he was probably still sleeping.

By the next morning, she was feeling more like herself. She was on the calendar to work that day, so she dressed, harnessed Shelby and took the shuttle to the ski resort. Most of the rest of the crew was there, and they greeted her with hugs and pats on the back, asked how she was doing, and praised and patted Shelby. Word had spread that the dog had been a hero, and there were jokes about how she should have been a police dog.

"All right, everybody, we'd better get started."

The words were the ones Scott always used, but the person who said them was Connor. He stood while the rest of them sat or leaned against the walls of the patrol shack. "As most of you have probably heard by now, Scott turned in his resignation, effective immediately. I'm filling in as interim while corporate decides what they want to do about the job."

"What!" Lily's cry of alarm made everyone turn to look at her. "Scott resigned? When?"

Connor looked down at the clipboard in his hand. "Yesterday morning. I thought you knew."

No, she had not known. "Did he say why? Is he all right?"

"I was as surprised as you are," Connor said. "So I stopped by his place to see him. He was fine. Just said he had another opportunity he wanted to pursue. He seemed happy about it."

He had told Connor all of this, but not her. The knowledge hurt. She sat back. "Okay. Sorry I interrupted."

He read down the list of patrol assignments and tasks that needed to be seen to. She half listened, still dazed at this turn of events. When Connor stopped talking and everyone prepared to leave, she pulled on her jacket, then stood still, realizing she had no idea what she was supposed to do.

"You're with me this morning," Nina said. "We're patrolling the Glades."

Nina waited until they were on the lift before she spoke. "Real shocker about Scott, huh?"

"Yeah," Lily agreed. "He created the avy dog program. Why would he quit?"

"Did something happen while you were out there, looking for Jackson?" Nina asked. "Something to change his mind?"

So much had happened. Scott had been shot, but hadn't died. They had been cold and hungry and lost and desperate. They had shared a sleeping bag, and she had never felt closer to another person.

Was she the reason he had resigned his job and left the program he loved? That was beyond ridiculous. Maybe escaping death had made him rethink his whole life, and he had decided to move away and what—he didn't seem the type to join a monastery or decide to get a PhD in philosophy. But how well did she know him?

Not at all, it appeared. "I don't know what happened," she said.

"Connor says Scott is happy about it, whatever the reason," Nina said. "And Connor will do a good job."

They reached the patrol station at the top of Lift 7 to find a family from Chicago waiting to buy T-shirts and ask questions. Then they were called to attend a woman who had fallen and injured her knee on a difficult run.

Lily moved from one task to the next in a fog. At the end of the day she headed back to patrol headquarters at the base area, only to be hailed before she could reach the office. "Lily! Wait up!"

She turned to see Denny Endicott and Jackson walking toward her. She smiled. "It's good to see you both looking so well."

Denny hugged her tightly, holding on for just a moment. "I can't thank you enough for all you did for me and Jackson," he said.

"You don't have to thank me," she said. "I'm just so glad everything worked out. Are you both okay? Really?"

"I'm okay," Jackson said. "I ate a cheeseburger and slept for, like, a day and a half."

"I'm still dealing with the fact that the man I trusted with my life tried to take my son away from me," Denny said. "But I have Jackson, and I still have my business and my good name, and that's all that matters. And you're okay. And Scott. The two of you will always be heroes in my book."

She nodded, the mention of Scott's name a heaviness in her stomach.

"I was just talking to Doug Elam about the avalanche dog program," Denny said.

"Oh?"

"Jackson told me how Shelby and Hunter kept him warm and safe after he got separated from you and Scott, and how Shelby attacked Mike when he tried to shoot Agent Shipman. In light of that, I want to make sure the avalanche dog program here at the resort keeps going."

"Dad's giving the resort a lot of money just for the dogs," Jackson said.

"Well, and their handlers and trainers and such," Denny said.

"That's so generous of you," Lily said. *Scott would love this*, she thought. *Why hadn't he stayed to hear this?*

"It's the least I could do." Denny patted her shoulder. "You're sure you're all right now? If you need anything at all, you let me know."

"I'm fine, really."

"That's good to know. I'm glad I ran into you. We won't be needing you to stay with Jackson for a while." He looked down at his son, who grinned up at him. "We're going to take a little vacation, something we've been putting off too long."

"We're going to Disney World!" Jackson said. "We're going to ride all the rides at least twice."

Lily laughed at the boy's enthusiasm, then stooped to hug him. "You have a wonderful time, and when you get home I want to hear all about it."

After they left, she retrieved Shelby and her belongings and headed home. As she stepped off the shuttle at the entrance to her apartment complex, she glanced across the lot and saw Scott's motorcycle parked in its customary place. Before she could lose her nerve, she got out of the car and marched across the complex and up the steps to his apartment.

She leaned hard on the bell, then listened as heavy footsteps crossed to the door. After a moment, it opened. "Lily? What are you doing here?"

"I came to ask you what you think you're doing." She pushed past him. Shelby followed and hurried to greet Hunter.

Scott closed the door behind her. He was barefoot, wearing joggers cinched at the hips, and a long-sleeved T-shirt advertising a long-defunct brewery, the lettering flaking and faded. She turned to face him. "I showed up at work this morning and learned I was the only person on the team who didn't know you'd quit the program," she said. "The program you started. The program you gave everything to. The program Denny Endicott just gave a bunch of money to in order to keep us going. How could you do that?"

She was horrified when her voice broke on the last sentence, and tears spilled down her face. Why did she care so much what Scott Linden did with his life? He was betraying the program, not her.

He raked his hand through his hair. "I was going to tell you," he said. "I was just waiting."

"Waiting for what?"

"For you to, you know, recover. From your ordeal in the woods."

"I'm recovered, okay?" She glared at him. "So what the hell are you doing, Scott? Are you running away? Because of what happened between us? And what did happen, exactly? Did it mean anything to you?"

He met her gaze at last. "Did it mean anything to *you*?" he asked.

She looked away, fresh tears forming. She didn't want to be this woman, crying over a man who was leaving. But she didn't want to be a person who pretended things were all right when they weren't. "You were there," she said, her voice scarcely above a whisper. "You held me in your arms. How can you even ask that?" That moment had meant everything, not because of the intimacy—though that had been pretty special—but because of everything that came before and after. The things they had said to each other. The things they had felt for each other.

"Oh, Lily." He wrapped his arms around her, and she didn't resist. She wanted to be stronger than that. Later, she would be. Later, she would tell him everything she thought about him. But for just this moment she stood, eyes closed, feeling his strength support her, his warmth seep into her, the spice and musk scent of him enveloping her.

She waited for him to say something. Anything. But he only stood there, arms around her, chin resting on the top of her head, as if time had stopped.

She wriggled away from him. "Why did you resign from the avy dog program?" she asked.

"I'm going to work for C-RAD," he said. "Adam has been after me for months to come work for him, and I decided it's time."

"Oh." She studied his face. "And you would rather do that than stay with the avy dog program and SkyCrest?"

"I think I can make a bigger impact with C-RAD." He

looked at his feet, then up at her again. "And I want to be at a place where I'm not your boss."

She blinked, not sure she had heard him correctly. He moved closer, and stroked her cheek with the back of one hand. "I knew you were special almost from the first," he said. "But these few days alone with you…and that night…" He kissed her temple. "I knew after that night that I didn't want to lose you. Not if there was a chance…"

She turned her head and found his lips with her own. This was what she wanted—what she needed. To be this close to him. His mouth was warm and supple, sparking every nerve in her. His tongue was silken against hers, the pressure of his lips telegraphing how much he wanted her. Need surged through her, and she tugged blindly at his clothing, impatient. He picked her up, and she wrapped her legs around his waist, their lips still pressed together.

He carried her from the room, into his bedroom, and kicked the door shut behind him. When he spilled her onto the bed and collapsed beside her, she climbed onto him, tugging his shirt up, kissing her way up from his navel, tracing the contours of his abdomen and ribs, teeth scraping his erect nipples.

He pushed her away long enough for him to pull her fleece top over her head, then strip off his own T-shirt. She tossed her bra across the room, feeling reckless. Then he rolled her to her back and began making his way down her body, his lips heated and insistent. He took his time, stroking and kissing until she was wild with wanting him.

He pushed her leggings and underwear to her hips and clamped his mouth over her with such intensity she gasped. He stilled. "Did I hurt you?"

"No." She pushed his head down. "No." Somehow, that was the only word she could muster. He took the hint and returned to attending to her with the kind of attention she imagined an artist paid to his work.

By the time he rolled away from her she was gasping, and protested at his abandoning her. He smiled and kissed the tip of her nose. "I'll be right back," he said.

She closed her eyes, trying to pull herself together, but before she had recovered enough to sit up, he was back, a foil packet in hand, divested now of the rest of his clothing. She stared at him, appreciating his lean and muscular body—not the physique of a bodybuilder, but the form of a man who spent hours on skis—muscular legs and toned buttocks, broad shoulders and a trim waist.

She raised up on her elbows and watched as he rolled on the condom. Only when he reached for her again did she realize his hand was shaking. She grasped his fingers. "Are you okay?" she asked.

"More than okay," he said, and pulled her to him once more.

Their earlier desperate fervor had transformed to a quiet intensity. They moved more deliberately, exploring the contours and curves of each other's bodies, testing out positions and techniques, watching each other's faces to gauge the results of each new experiment. But as pleasurable as this was, the tension could only be borne so long. She clutched at him and whispered in his ear. "Now. Please."

His answer was a deep and lingering kiss, and then he was easing into her, grasping her hips and guiding her until they found a rhythm they both enjoyed, a rocking cadence that left her breathless and soaring. He reached between them to fondle her, and the combination of sensations had her keening with pleasure. When she dropped over the edge she may have moaned his name, and then he was moving faster, his face a mask of concentration.

His climax shuddered through them both, and she held him tightly, hands digging into the muscles of his back, his forehead pressed to her shoulder. They lay together for a long time after, until their breathing slowed and settled, and he eased away from her. He got up and went into the bathroom and returned a few moments later and lay beside her. She cradled her head on his shoulder and closed her eyes.

"I'm not an easy person to be with," he said, his voice cutting through the quiet.

She let the words and their meaning settle into her. Was this a confession? A statement of fact? Or a tentative promise for the future? "Neither am I," she said. She rested her palm against his chest, over his heart. "I'll tell you what I think without always worrying about sparing your feelings."

"I already figured that one out. I'd rather that than be left trying to read your mind."

She lifted her head enough to look at him. "I reserve the right to make you do that, too." She laughed at the flare of panic in his eyes.

"What's so funny?" he asked.

"You. Nobody's perfect. I don't expect you to be."

"I'm probably never going to be rich. The kind of work I'm drawn to isn't always the best paid."

She remembered what he had told her about his former girlfriend—and his parents—berating him for not being ambitious. "That's just one of the things I admire about you," she said. "Money's nice, but it's not the most important thing. And I know you love dogs. That's a big one."

"Yeah. I love dogs. And kids."

She stilled. "Too soon?" he asked. "No pressure or anything."

Again, she laughed. "I already knew you liked children,"

she said. "You're really good with them. But we'll table this discussion until later." Much later.

"Fair enough. I'm just trying to put all my cards on the table."

"Oh. And why is that?"

"I think we could build something real between us," he said. "I want to try." He covered her hand with his own. "I'm pretty sure I'm in love with you."

Her heart beat faster at the words. Frightening words. Thrilling words. Sometimes the two emotions were so close to being the same. "I love you, too," she said. She kissed his cheek. "I'm here right now, and I'm not going anywhere. That's a good start, don't you think?"

"Yeah." He cradled her against him, and she closed her eyes once more. It wasn't a dramatic declaration or an ardent proposal of marriage, but either of those things would have made her suspicious or scared her away. This was better—a tentative agreement to do their best to love each other. To see where walking this path together would lead.

Epilogue

Three months later

The sun on the snow shone so brightly Lily had to squint through the tinted lenses on her goggles. The blue sky promised a perfect day for skiing, the spring snow the texture of raw sugar, crunching beneath her feet with each step. Shelby raced ahead of her across the ski run and skidded to a stop, snow flying, at Scott's feet. He greeted her enthusiastically, and the dog wagged her tail furiously.

"Are you ready for this?" Scott asked.

"We are." Lily looked around. "It's been ages since I've been to Vail. I'm looking forward to skiing a few runs when this is over."

"Yeah, that'll be fun."

Level A certification for avalanche rescue dogs had to be conducted at a resort other than their home resort. Scott and Adam had arranged for Shelby's certification test to be conducted at Vail, though Scott had recused himself from judging, and Marcie Stevens from Wasatch Backcountry was filling in.

Adam and Marcie skied over to join them. "We need to get started so we're out of here before the lifts open," Adam said.

"Let's do it," Lily said.

"You know the drill," Adam said. "Volunteers, are you ready?"

"I'm ready." Jackson stuck up his hand.

"Me too," Denny said.

Lily grinned at them. She had asked these two if they would be the "victims" Shelby needed to find for today's test.

Nina and Brian led Denny and Jackson away. They would seal them up in the ice caves, then sweep the area to camouflage the hiding spots. Scott moved over and took Lily's hand. "Are you nervous?"

"Of course."

"Shelby is going to do great."

"Everybody ready?" Adam asked.

"Yes," a half dozen voices answered.

He clicked his stopwatch. "Now."

Lily looked into Shelby's eyes—so attentive and eager to please. "Go find," she commanded. The dog spun around and was off.

It took ten minutes for Shelby to find Denny, but five minutes later she was barking and digging out Jackson, who emerged from his hiding place laughing and waving a tug toy, which Shelby grabbed and used to pull him the rest of the way onto the snow. Boy and dog rolled on the ground while Lily's fellow ski patrollers cheered.

"Congratulations," Adam said. "Shelby has passed her Level A certification."

Scott pulled her close and kissed her. "I knew you could do it."

"That's not what you said when we first met."

"That was before I knew how stubborn you could be."

"I prefer tenacious." She looked into his eyes. "I'm not one to give up on something worth having."

"I'm thankful every day for that." He kissed her again, until those around them began whistling and hooting. They smiled at each other, not caring about the good-natured teasing. *I love you*, he said with his eyes. *Love you more*, she answered. What had started out as an experiment to see if they could make it was starting to feel like forever. A bond stronger than the things they had overcome, or the challenges they might meet in the future.

* * * * *

EYEWITNESS IN DANGER

NICOLE HELM

For Franny and my allergy boys

Chapter One

Franny Perkins had plenty of experience being the odd one out. She was an only child who'd grown up with her nose in books, her head lost in her own imagination and no one around her quite knowing where she *fit*. Including herself.

She'd fit here, for a while. The Young Ranch in rural Wyoming. Oh, she was no rancher—she was allergic to just about every animal known to man. But she liked the mountains, the quiet landscapes. She even liked the cold—though deep in a Wyoming summer cold was a bit of a fond memory at the moment.

What she didn't like, at all, was playing third wheel. And with Copeland Beckett moved into the ranch house now that he and her cousin, Audra Young, were engaged, Franny was once again relegated to odd man out.

She'd stayed awhile. She didn't want Audra to feel bad, or think that Copeland's moving to the ranch had made her leave. Audra was the kind of person who would take the blame like that. So, Franny had taken her time, built her story, and now was putting it into action.

"It's only temporary," Franny assured Audra, even though it was a lie. "Just while I write the book. My agent was really excited about the idea of being able to sell it based on real-life experience." She'd just about finished packing everything she would need to move into the little apartment in Hope Town only a thirty-minute drive away. That was nothing. Especially around here.

Audra watched her pack her toiletry bag with mounting suspicion, but Franny kept the easy, breezy expression on her face. "It'll give you and Copeland some time to learn how to live together before I come back."

"You *are* coming back."

"Of course I am." It was a lie, and Franny hated to lie, but she'd hate it more if Audra felt guilty for a choice Franny had made. "Once the novel is finished."

By then, Copeland and Audra would likely be married, maybe even starting a family if she stretched it out long enough. If needed, Franny would create a new excuse. She would *not* horn in on her cousin's new life. Not like that.

Franny shouldered the pack of things she'd need tonight, then hefted her last box. She'd left a few things behind to give Audra the illusion that she'd be back. Some old clothes she didn't wear, a few books she'd never read again.

Audra followed her down the stairs to where Copeland was carrying the heaviest of Franny's belongings into the moving truck. He looked like he was just about done, so it was perfect timing. He'd drive her out to Hope Town in the intimidating moving truck, then go return it for her since the return center was close to his work at the police station where he had a cruiser.

It'd give Franny some time to unpack before Rosalie picked her up on her way out to the ranch so Franny could come back and get her car, eat one last dinner with her cousins while the men made themselves scarce and then make that final break—driving to her new place. Alone.

"I can ride with and help you unpack and—"

Franny turned to Audra and spoke firmly. "And you have

chores to see to. I'm thirty minutes away, Audra. Besides, I'll be back after we unload the truck to pick up my car. We'll have our girls' night dinner. You *are* making brownies, right?"

"Yes, right." Audra frowned. Her gaze drifted toward the back—where her ranch stretched out and there were indeed chores to be done and responsibilities to be met.

So Franny marched herself to the truck, put the box she'd carried in the back before Copeland brought down the door.

He walked over to where Audra now stood on the porch stairs. He murmured something to her Franny couldn't hear, then gave her a quick kiss before heading for the driver's side. Franny made sure her smile was cheerful and easy as she got into the passenger side.

Without much discussion, they started off the ranch and out to the highway. Franny wouldn't let herself wring her hands, though that's what she wanted to do. She didn't understand why she felt so damn nervous when she knew that this was what needed to be done.

New beginnings. Life steps. It was natural to feel…to *feel*. Wasn't that one of the biggest reasons she'd had to move away from her parents? She had shoved down her feelings so much so as to never worry or hurt them that she was afraid she didn't have them anymore.

Feelings were good. Feelings were her job. And her life was fairly sheltered, more or less, but less since coming to Wyoming. Life experience helped her write better books.

So this was all good. She'd never lived alone before. It was long past time she checked off that life experience.

"Thanks for the help, Copeland," she said, wanting to distract herself from her thoughts at least a little bit. Copeland wasn't much of a conversationalist, but she was desperate.

"I'm supposed to talk you out of it on the way."

"But you're not going to. Because I've already decided." She slid him a sideways glance. "And because you don't want to talk me out of it."

He sighed, looking seriously at the road as he drove. "It's a big house, Franny. There's room. I don't want you to think you're not welcome any more than Audra does."

"It's not about being welcome. It's not about…you guys." Another lie. She wrinkled her nose, trying to focus on the positives rather than her lies. "Besides, you two *lovebirds* deserve to have all that room to yourselves."

Copeland pulled a face. "Please never use that word again in my presence."

She grinned. Copeland wasn't the most affable guy— not like Rosalie's husband, Duncan. But it was obvious, no matter how prickly he was, he loved Audra *so much*, and made her *so happy*, and that was all that mattered to Franny. That her cousins, who were also her *friends*, were happy.

She didn't mind being the odd man out on that front. She was young, and sure, who wouldn't like a little romance? But she hadn't moved to the middle-of-nowhere Wyoming to find a man, even if she had the occasional fantasy about being whisked away by an upstanding taciturn cowboy.

She was here to write. To discover…who she was. She loved her parents, they were amazing, but as an only child, she'd known if she stayed in Washington, she would have lost herself in not ever hurting their feelings.

She'd needed a break, some independence. But she'd also needed some built-in friends so she didn't fully immerse herself in hermithood. Something that was far too easy for her to do.

As much as she'd enjoyed living with the Young sisters, Franny also liked being on her own. She liked solitude. Sometimes too much. Sometimes so much her life narrowed down to nothing but fictional worlds. It wasn't good for her.

But neither was trying to constantly please people. So moving out here had been her first step toward meeting her personal goals, and now living on her own without falling into bad habits would be the next step.

It was good. It was *right*.

And she held on to that assertion as she watched Bent County pass by on her way to Hope Town.

"I'M SO PROUD of you!"

Royal Campbell stood on the porch of his sister's ranch house and grimaced as his sister squeezed him tight. He figured he owed her, more or less, though he didn't like to admit it out loud. Especially in the presence of her husband.

Zeke Daniels was an irritating SOB, but he loved Brooke, so Royal figured it gave him enough of a pass, but that didn't mean he was ever going to air any of his feelings in front of his brother-in-law.

Royal detangled himself from his sister gently. Because the whole baby bump thing she had going on freaked him out. Shouldn't she be lying down or something? But she was always moving around, that bump getting bigger every week that went by.

"Don't sound so surprised I made it off field training, Chick," he said, easing away. He was wearing a *gun* since he was in uniform and on his way into work. She shouldn't be that close.

"Why not?" Zeke muttered. Brooke gave him a little slap to the chest with no heat behind it.

"I'm not surprised at all. I am proud and happy." She beamed at him.

She deserved to be happy. And if him getting his life together made her happy, Royal figured that was reason enough to do it.

But somewhere along the line he'd figured out he wanted to get his life together for a lot of reasons. For Brooke. To spite their father who'd been a high-level member of a horrible biker gang. And strangest of all, at least to him, was the desire to get it figured out for himself.

He'd spent his entire life reacting to the bad hand he'd been dealt. Now he wanted to turn that hand into something. Stop reacting, stop running, stop *fighting* every damn thing stacked against him and build something of his own.

"I've got to get to work. Just wanted to drop by and tell you." He took a step down from the porch so she couldn't hug him again.

"Come to dinner on your next day off."

"You're supposed to be taking it easy," Zeke reminded her. "No big meals."

"It won't be a big meal. Just an extra seat at the table." She beamed at Royal. "What day?"

Royal looked from Brooke to Zeke. He didn't relish getting in the middle of any marital arguments, but if he did, he'd be on Brooke's side. Except when it came to taking care of herself. "Thursday. I'll bring pizza."

She frowned a little, but when Zeke's arm came around her shoulders she sighed. "All right. Bring pizza."

He offered a wave then strode back to his Bent County Sheriff's Department cruiser. He got in the car, and once again reveled in having it to himself. He'd had a good field training officer, but part of why he'd applied for Bent County after the police academy had been that there was a certain amount of autonomy once you were off field training.

And now he was. He glanced at the clock. And he needed to get into the station for roll call.

It was a surprise, even to him, that he liked it. That he seemed to fit. Taking orders and following rules had never been his style. A little difficult to learn respect for authority when you grew up in a dangerous biker gang.

It wasn't *easy* to suddenly *yes, sir* everybody. It wasn't *easy* to be the rookie, knowing he got treated a little less for it, especially considering he was older than every single other rookie, and even some of the guys with a few years under their belts. More often than not, it put his back up and had those old rebellious tendencies kicking up a fuss.

But he pushed them down.

He tried to look at it as every rule followed, every pointless-feeling *yes, sir* allowed him to help someone who needed it.

And he knew the depths of needing help that some people faced. He knew the desperate lengths a person could go to in order to *help*. So any time he was tempted to tell a superior to go to hell, he remembered what he'd done in the name of justice as a boy—and how different his life might have been if there'd been someone bigger and stronger to help.

He'd be the bigger and stronger for somebody now. This time, on the right side of the law.

It still gave him a pause, now and again. The ingrained belief that the *system* was bad, and he was an idiot for falling into it. But he fought back those doubts.

Brooke was proud of him, and that held weight. He supposed he was learning to be proud of himself too.

His FTO had been pretty strict about speed limits, setting an example while in his patrol car, so Royal was careful not to speed past the slow-going truck in front of him like he wanted to. But eventually, he couldn't take it any longer, and he eased around the moving truck.

He passed, and on a sideways glance he recognized Copeland Beckett at the wheel. Beckett was a detective at Bent County, and Royal wasn't sure what to make of him yet. As a road deputy, Royal hadn't had much interaction with the detective bureau. A lot of people at the county respected the guy though, but Royal liked to make his own conclusions about people.

Case in point, the one thing he did know about Copeland Beckett was that the cute brunette in his passenger seat was *not* Copeland Beckett's fiancée.

Cops, he thought bitterly—an old habit.

He looked down at his uniform and laughed. Sometimes, life really was a kick in the pants.

Chapter Two

Franny didn't bother to unpack. She'd save that annoying chore for when she wanted something specific or when she hit a rough patch in the book and needed something to occupy her hands. Everything she absolutely required for the first few days was packed in a separate bag anyway—some clothes, toiletries, her inhaler and the like.

She did set up her workspace. She'd learned over the years that she could work anywhere, at any time, with just about any background noise, but she still liked having one organized space to go to when everything started to feel too fractured. A center.

The apartment above the Hope Town Bakery was small—one bedroom, one bathroom and then a kitchen/dining/living room area that was really just one large room. She'd had Copeland put her writing desk and office drawers up against the far wall that was dominated by three tall, narrow windows that looked out over Main Street—the only street—in Hope Town.

She took a moment to enjoy the view. Too bad she wasn't writing a historical. She could almost imagine herself as some mysterious woman from "back East," looking for a fresh start in a Wild West frontier town.

Maybe she could make the book a dual timeline. Maybe her next book should be a historical Western. Maybe...

"One book a time," she muttered to herself.

But she liked that so many ideas were already percolating. It meant she'd made the right choice.

Hope Town was an interesting place with a mysterious history. It had been a ghost town years ago, completely abandoned. Then a man named Zach Simmons, who'd been an FBI agent before he'd settled in Bent, had bought up a bunch of land and buildings and begun to revitalize the town.

The mystery was why Mr. Simmons, who owned all the land and buildings, wouldn't allow anything in that didn't meet his approval. Not a business, not a renter, no one.

Franny had needed to meet with Mr. Simmons with her rental application, answer a few questions. Provide references. He had been professional, kind, and friendly. But he'd been pretty...vague in answering her questions about Hope Town.

A little disappointing, because she wanted to get a better understanding of how the town had come to be. Not because she was writing nonfiction, just because she wanted...some framework for her idea that was based in truth and reality.

So she didn't have to get all the details right exactly as they were, but she wanted to know as much as she could. She wanted everything to feel real, authentic, and she wanted to do right by the story that had been simmering in her brain for a while now.

In her book, this town would see tragedy and fear, death and mystery, and then justice, hard won, with maybe a little romance thrown in.

On that thought, she turned away from the window, grabbed her laptop, and got to work sketching out some ideas.

Royal didn't complain about his zone assignment. Out loud. He was the rookie. He'd get the grunt work for a while yet.

A zone that included Hope Town and a handful of ranches would result in a fat lot of nothing to do. He probably wouldn't even be able to pull anyone over for a speeding ticket. If he got a call, it'd likely be for... Hell, he didn't even know out here.

One thing he'd learned about the citizens of Bent County was that a lot of them—especially the ones who lived more isolated—liked to handle their own issues. They didn't call the police for just anything.

Frustrated, he stood and moved through the room to Corporal Gardner Fairhurst, Gard to his friends—and Royal felt he'd earned the *friends* label by now. Gard had been his FTO and had been just the kind of trainer a person had to be thankful for. Calm, patient, willing to answer any question, giving solid advice, and also had given Royal the room to develop his own confidence as an officer of the law.

And since he liked and trusted Gard, Royal voiced his frustration to him, though he made sure to be quiet about it.

"Shouldn't I be put somewhere I might actually get some experience?"

"You will."

"When?"

Gard looked at Captain Kraig who still stood at the front of the room, then back at Royal. He didn't answer the question. Royal scowled in spite of himself.

"He hates me." Royal knew his past could be used against him, but he'd figured he wouldn't have been hired if the sheriff held that past against him. His record *had* been expunged. That was how he'd even gotten into the police academy, that and some of Zeke's family greasing the wheels.

But Royal hadn't considered some of the men between him and the sheriff might see it all differently.

"He doesn't trust you just yet. You'll get there. Be conscientious, ask questions or for help when you need to and for the love of God, don't complain to anyone but me." Gard clapped him on the shoulder and nudged him out of the conference room. "It'll make its way back to the captain faster than you can blink."

Royal only grunted as they made their way through the building and outside to the waiting patrol cars.

"You've got this, Campbell. *If* you can learn to swallow your tongue."

"Big if," Royal muttered.

Gard laughed. "There's always bartending," he said. "You wouldn't have to hide those tattoos then."

Royal snarled, then split off from Gard toward his patrol car. It *was* hot to be wearing this damned long-sleeved uniform, but those were the rules and somehow he'd become not just a man who had to follow pointless rules, but a man whose job it was to enforce them.

With his current zone, he had two main jobs today. Run radar on the highway outside of Hope Town, do a walk-through of Hope Town in the afternoon, and respond to any calls that came over the radio for his zone.

So, he went about his business and didn't allow himself to dwell on the fact that no calls came through for *him*, while pretty much every other deputy on the road was getting called constantly.

He'd get there, he reminded himself. Gard had said he would, and Gard hadn't steered him wrong yet.

After noon, he headed over to Hope Town, parked at the end of Main Street. The assignment here was to walk up one side of Main, then down the other. Mostly just looking for things that didn't fit in.

He'd only done this duty with Gard twice on field training, and now that Royal was handling it himself, he wondered why Hope Town got special treatment. There were other tiny map dot towns in Bent County, but this was the only one that got a Bent County daily walk-through.

Besides, what would ever "stand out" here? They had a handful of shops—a bakery, an antique store and a bookstore. There was one other building that looked like maybe it was getting a new business, but he couldn't tell what it was.

Maybe there might be some theft because of the businesses, but you'd have to be a pretty stupid thief to come all the way out here to get…what? None of these cash registers could be holding that much money.

He wouldn't complain about it though, he reminded himself. Maybe it didn't make sense, but being able to get out of the car, stretch his long legs, get some fresh air, that was definitely a positive for him.

It was eerily quiet for a sunny summer afternoon, but as he passed different storefronts, he realized that all of them that advertised their store hours said they were closed on Mondays. Still, there were people living in the apartments above the businesses, in the houses farther down the road.

It was weird to be this quiet. As he walked, he noticed up the street there was the antique store with a few cars in the lot. Somewhere a ways off a dog barked. There were signs of life here and there, he supposed.

When he came back on the opposite side of the antique store, things had cleared out again, but it wasn't quiet. He heard…swearing? He stood still, and listened to the stream of creative, threatening profanity.

Was someone in trouble? Excited for some potential action, he moved quickly toward the sounds. Behind the bakery building. He turned the corner to find a woman at the bottom of a rickety-looking set of iron stairs that led to the upper floor of the building. Maybe an apartment above the bakery.

"You okay?" he asked.

The woman stilled for a moment, before she turned toward him and blew the bangs out of her face. She looked vaguely familiar, but Royal couldn't place her. She had a bookshelf half her size leaning precariously against the wrought iron staircase.

"Just made the idiotic decision to purchase this from the antique store across the way." She gestured in the direction of the antique store. "Then thinking, oh, it's just right there, I could carry it back to my place. It's small. And it is, but it's an *antique*, so it's *heavy*. Which would have been doable, if I didn't have stairs to navigate." She sighed dramatically. Studied him for a moment, then flashed a smile. "I don't suppose you could give me a hand?"

"Not really in the job description."

"No, I don't suppose it is," she said, her gaze moving over his uniform in a way that left him…oddly uncomfortable. It was like she was filing away every button, snap, pocket and item on his belt.

"Does Hope Town have its own police dep—" She shook her head before finishing the question. "No, you're Bent County. But a deputy. How does the sheriff's department decide how to police Hope Town?"

Not quite sure where she was going with this, Royal answered the question watching the teetering bookcase and the odd—if pretty—woman. "We get assigned zones. Zone's a lot bigger than Hope Town."

"Do you get a lot of trouble here?"

He frowned at her. He wasn't used to being peppered with questions. That was usually his job. "You looking to apply?"

She laughed, the sound was surprisingly husky when she was kind of a tiny thing. "No, but I suppose the questions are a bit of a professional hazard. I'm a writer. Currently working on a story sort of based on Hope Town. Maybe. Brain is constantly in book mode at the moment."

Royal wasn't sure what to make of that. Her. This.

Before he could decide, a car pulled up and parked in the little lot behind the building.

"Oh, that'll be Rosalie," the woman said.

But Royal would have known the woman even without the name supplied. Vaguely anyway. Rosalie Kirk was a private investigator with Fools Gold Investigations out of Wilde. She harassed the detectives a lot, and occasionally the deputies if she had a case that lined up with police work.

Plus, she was married to Duncan Kirk, former professional baseball player. Pretty well-known around these parts, even if Royal had only been in these parts a few years instead of his whole life like most of them.

Rosalie walked up, carrying a big potted plant. She looked Royal up and down. "You harassing my cousin?"

"Why would I do that?"

"He's not harassing. He was asking if I needed help," the woman supplied. She smiled kindly at him. "Thank you. But I bet Rosalie and I can handle it."

He didn't point out to either one of them that he *hadn't* offered to help. Just nodded and walked away. Maybe he gave the lady a backward glance, just because she was…he didn't have the right word for it. Something about her was… *off-putting*, and he didn't know what. And he was supposed to be looking for things that felt off, wasn't he?

"I'll run up and put your *happy new place* plant inside, then come down and help," he heard Rosalie tell her.

Happy new place. New shelves. She was moving in. Rosalie's cousin.

Which was when it clicked—why she looked familiar. The moving truck.

She'd been the brunette in the truck with Copeland Beckett, though out here in the sun her hair edged toward red.

But Royal figured that was all he needed to know about her.

Even if that laugh kept coming back to him throughout the day, a haunting sound he couldn't quite get rid of.

Chapter Three

Three Weeks Later

Franny felt like she'd settled in quite well. She had a routine—one that got her out of the house most mornings for a walk, a coffee—except on Mondays, and soaking up the whole ambience of the town. Then she'd be home late morning, make some lunch and get to work…or trying to work anyway.

On Mondays, since the town businesses were mostly closed, she went to either the library in Sunrise or Bent to do some research, then swung by Audra's or Rosalie's for dinner—or they all met in town and ate out, sometimes with Vi and her kids.

Vi was Audra and Rosalie's cousin on their dad's side who lived in Bent with her husband and kids. Her husband who was a detective at Bent County with Copeland.

Those little ties always made Franny smile. Back in Washington, her life had always been so…small. They didn't have family, and while she'd had *friends*, it wasn't like her life here.

Which was good. She was feeling really positive about it…or tried to be, since she didn't have much to show for three weeks of work. She didn't usually get hung up on research when she was writing, preferring to focus on character and emotional arcs. The mystery when she got toward the end and had to figure out the bad guy, but she'd learned over the years that no book was the same and apparently this one was going to be difficult in the beginning.

That was fine. She had time.

She told herself that while lying in bed one morning, up *far* too early, but her mind turning in circles.

She'd found out so little about Hope Town, aside from its early history as a frontier town. But it's new history? Basically nothing. And when she asked a few of the residents, she'd been met with a lot of changes in subject.

Maybe that's all she needed, she told herself as she got out of bed, giving up on sleeping to a normal hour. A mysterious town. She could make up the mystery. She didn't need to discover Hope Town's.

"But I *want* to," she muttered to herself. Which wasn't a way to get things accomplished, meet her deadlines or make herself happy, but she just felt...stuck in this need to know.

Well, feeling stuck was for people who didn't have to make a living. Today she was writing that first chapter come hell or high water.

But first she needed coffee and, with any luck, a cinnamon roll the size of her face. She went to the window in her bedroom. It looked out over the parking lot behind the bakery. If Albennie's or Lia's cars were there, she'd head downstairs and beg for some before-hours service. If it was empty, she'd have to make do with the healthy food she'd been foolish enough to stock her place with, thinking living above a bakery meant she shouldn't have snacks on hand.

She glanced out the window, did a little celebratory butt shake when she saw a car in the lot, but stopped and frowned when she saw it was a big SUV.

None of the women who worked at the bakery had a big car like that. She'd never seen a car like that...anywhere in Hope Town.

"Don't be ridiculous," she muttered to herself. Just because she'd lived here a few weeks didn't mean she knew every car, even if it was a small town without a lot of residents. She didn't care about cars. Why would she know if there were cars around like that?

Then why did it stick out? Why did it feel—

She heard something. A faint crash? Her heartbeat kicked up as she strained to hear, but she only heard the thump, thump, thump of her own pulse.

She moved closer to the window, looked down at the car. Knowing she was being ridiculous, she picked up the pen and notepad she kept on her nightstand and jotted down the license number she saw, and some details about the car.

Paranoid, paranoid, paranoid.

Before she could set down the notepad, she saw a figure. No, *two* shadowy figures come out the back door of the bakery. Muffled sounds. Sounds of distress?

It was too dark to see, but it would be easier as they moved toward the streetlight that dimly illuminated the SUV.

"This is an absolute overreaction," she told herself, out loud, but she moved closer to the window, squinting through the dark. Two figures, one much larger than the other. They were moving in kind of fits and starts.

She couldn't make out the smaller figure. It was like they had a hat or a hood completely over their head, but Franny got the impression it was a woman.

"Oh God." The smaller figure was definitely fighting back while the larger figure—a man—pulled her along.

Franny dropped the pad and pen and made a grab for her

cell phone sitting on the nightstand. She cursed when she fumbled it, and it fell to the ground. She picked it back up and ran, dialing 911 as she did so.

She didn't own a gun. She didn't have a weapon, but Rosalie had left her a baseball bat by the door and Franny grabbed the bat and ran. Her exit was just the stairs to the alley, so she'd have to run down the stairs then around to the back of the building.

"911. What's your emergency?" a competent-sounding voice answered.

Franny rattled off her address as she flicked off the security system and jerked her door open. "Send the police please. Someone's being…kidnapped, I guess? Forced out of the building and she's fighting back."

"Who? Can you give me a name?"

"No, I don't know who. It's too dark, but she's fighting him." Franny made it to the bottom of the stairs. "They're in the parking lot behind the bakery, the address I gave you."

"And where are you?"

"I saw it through my apartment window. I ran downstairs—"

"Ma'am, I'm going to need you to remain inside. I'm dispatching a deputy to the address. You need to stay inside—do you understand?"

But Hope Town was so isolated. How long would it take for a deputy to get here? The woman was being dragged to the car now.

Franny looked down at her bat, the woman in her ear just a buzzing now. She clicked End on the call. She didn't want to do anything stupid, but how could she just let someone be taken against their will?

Resolutely, Franny crept forward, trying to keep her breathing even. She wouldn't run forward. She would be smart about this. She would help if she could. She'd called for help, and now she would help if she could.

At the corner of the building she could hear the scuffle. A grunt, a hushed word. But it was just…male sounding. Like the woman wasn't making any sound now.

Heart in her throat, Franny leaned forward so she could see around the corner. She saw the SUV, and a big, hulking figure all but toss the smaller figure in the back seat. It didn't seem like the woman moved.

Oh, no.

The man was in the driver's seat now. His hat had fallen off in the struggle and Franny could see him clearly in the dome light of the car. White, bald, but a short brown beard. A mark on his neck—not a tattoo, maybe a birthmark or injury? She couldn't tell from her vantage point.

She could hear sirens now, blue and red lights flashing somewhere in the distance. She looked toward the sound, willing it to hurry.

When she looked back at the SUV, it was rolling away, but the driver had looked toward the lights too.

And her.

Their gazes met. She couldn't tell the color of his eyes from this far away, but she could make out their shape—narrow, wide set.

She held her breath, frozen with fear, then demanded herself be brave. She made a step forward, lifting the bat. She'd…throw it at the windshield. She'd…

But the tires squealed into acceleration and sped off before she could do anything.

They were gone.

ROYAL WAS FIRST on the scene. He'd just gotten on duty when the call had come out. Potential kidnapping in Hope Town.

He pulled up to the parking lot behind the bakery and saw the woman from a few weeks ago standing in the glow of the parking lot light. She was in pajamas, barefoot, and held a baseball bat.

Dawn was a hint on the horizon, and nothing about the bakery or the parking lot looked particularly amiss, but he parked his patrol car and got out.

The woman rushed forward. "You have to follow them," she shouted at him. "You have to find her. They went that way."

"Who is they?"

"I don't know. I don't know. It was an SUV. She didn't want to go with him. She was fighting him. She… You have to go after them."

"We will. What kind of SUV?"

She blinked up at him, eyes lost and panicked. "I… I wrote down a description of the car, the plate. It's upstairs."

"Good. Good. Let's go." He took her gently by the arm, nudged her toward the side of the building and the stairs. Once she took the nudge, she seemed to get a hold of herself and then she rushed—jogging up the stairs two at a time, so Royal followed.

Into the apartment, through a tidy living area that included the bookcase from a few weeks ago, now full of books. She went into a room, a bedroom and straight for the bed. She bent down, picked up a notepad from the ground and then shoved it at him.

She had neat, printed handwriting. A clear description and license plate number. "This is good," he told her reassuringly. He radioed the detailed description of the SUV, the plate number so dispatch could get it sent out. Stop the car wherever it was headed.

"I—I couldn't see who it was, but if he pulled her from

the bakery at this hour it had to be Albennie or Lia. They always work the morning shift. Albennie Ward and Lia Blair. Lia owns the bakery, or maybe she rents it from Mr. Simmons. I'm not sure, but she runs the bakery."

"That's all good information. Let's go back downstairs. You can show me exactly what you saw."

She led him through it. She was shaky, sometimes rambling a bit, but she recounted the crime with enough clarity Royal could see exactly how it had played out.

Gard was the second officer to come to the scene, and he helped Royal cordon off the area. Day was breaking and some of the townspeople were coming out, asking questions. Royal got relegated to keeping people out of the way. Occasionally, he caught a glimpse of his witness. She just sat, by herself, at the bottom of her staircase watching the goings-on and looking miserable.

He felt an odd wave of sympathy for her, but didn't have time to really deal with it.

When the detective showed up, Royal and Gard walked over to his car to fill him in. The fact it was Copeland Beckett had Royal remembering the moving truck. Still, he focused on the case. That was the job.

Bringing home the woman who'd been kidnapped.

"I've done a welfare check on both the names the witness gave me," Royal said to Copeland. "It seems most likely our victim is Albennie Ward. She works morning shift at the bakery. Unknown assailant, but the witness gave us a description of the suspect and the car he drove away in. Dispatch has radioed out car and descriptions. You have those?"

Copeland nodded.

"I guess you know the witness."

Copeland's gaze moved from the parking lot to Royal. "Yeah, Franny's my fiancée's cousin."

"You always help your fiancée's cousin move house?"

Copeland gave him an odd look, confusion laced with distrust. No guilt. "When my fiancée asks me to."

Which left Royal a little confused himself, like maybe he'd somehow...misjudged? Before he could determine how he felt about that, another car pulled up. Not a police vehicle, at least not marked and not one Royal recognized. He also didn't recognize the man who got out—but that gait, that grim expression. To Royal that read *all* cop.

Or worse, he determined as the man came up to them: federal agent.

Copeland cursed and Gard looked frustrated, like they both knew the guy and weren't too happy to see him. He ducked under the police tape like he'd been doing it his whole life. Maybe he was in some kind of undercover unit Royal hadn't been introduced to?

But something danced along the back of his neck, reminded him of his old life, and what it looked like when the FBI waltzed into something.

"Zach Simmons," the man said, holding out a hand to Royal, and only Royal. He didn't use the word *agent*. He didn't offer any identification, so he couldn't be FBI.

Royal took his hand and shook. "Deputy Campbell."

Zach nodded, then looked from Royal to Copeland. "Bad news. This is going to be out of your jurisdiction pretty quick."

Copeland groaned. "You didn't."

"I had to."

"Had to what?" Royal demanded.

"He's bringing in the FBI," Copeland muttered disgustedly. "Once the Feds get here, this all goes to hell."

"If it makes you feel better, it had already gone to hell," Simmons said.

Chapter Four

Franny sat at the bottom of her outside stairs and watched as the police officers did their work. She tried to focus on that—pretend like she was observing for research—rather than deal with the actual thing that had happened. The officer who wore long sleeves even in this heat drew her attention at times. She wasn't sure why. He held himself... differently than everyone else.

Sometimes she could distract herself wondering what it was. Just discomfort in this heat? Was he a secret criminal hiding behind a badge? Did he carry some horrible inner pain—watching his partner die?

But she could only distract herself with that for a few minutes at a time before the reality poked at her brain.

Albennie had been kidnapped.

Franny didn't know the woman that well. They were friendly though. Albennie had quickly learned Franny's preferred coffee order. They smiled and chatted in the mornings when Franny hung out at the bakery, but no one at the bakery encouraged...getting to know one another on any kind of deeper level. There was an odd...distance, that was unlike the stoic Wyoming rancher personality she was used to. Not natural quietness or loner characteristics. There was something far more *careful* about it.

There was something under the surface in Hope Town and Franny had a feeling she'd stumbled into the deep end—but no one wanted to tell her what that deep end was.

Frustrating, and Franny liked the frustration over the fear, so she nursed it.

She surveyed the scene. Cops everywhere. Worried people everywhere. But no answers. She'd written down that license plate, described the kidnapper, and still it had been hours with no answers.

And then some guys in suits had showed up. Franny didn't think it was her impressive imagination that the guys screamed *federal agents*. They flashed badges to the cops and looked very, very, *very* serious.

When the deputy in long sleeves pointed to her, one of the agents made their way over to where she sat.

His questions were not really all that different than any of the police officers she had talked to. She had to go through the whole thing again. Why she'd been awake. Why she'd looked out the window. Why she'd thought to write down the license plate number.

Why, why, why.

She was about to tell the agent about the driver seeing her, but he was hailed over to another part of the parking lot and excused himself.

Franny sighed and went back to observing the scene. She should probably eat or drink something, maybe get a hat or move into the shade, but she couldn't bring herself to move.

A little while later when Copeland approached, Franny tried not to grimace. She didn't want to have to answer the same questions she'd already answered *again*, even to someone she knew.

Though she had started to piece together that the federal agents had different questions for the people who really knew Albennie than the local officers had. She'd filed that away to consider later. Sitting here had allowed her to eavesdrop on quite a few questioning conversations, and she was getting a picture of two very different investigations.

"Franny."

She smiled at Copeland, then wondered why she was trying to be polite when what she really wanted to do was cry.

"We might or the Feds might have more questions for you later, but I've made sure everyone has your contact information. I haven't called Audra, but—"

Franny pushed to her feet. "I'm not going back to the ranch, Copeland."

He frowned. "Yeah, I had a feeling you'd say that. Look, a kidnapping happened right below where you live."

"It did. Are you telling anyone else in Hope Town to leave?"

He didn't say anything. He didn't have to. And before he could try a different angle, Mr. Simmons approached.

"Detective Beckett." He nodded at both of them. "Ms. Perkins. As the landlord, I just wanted to make sure that you've got everything you need."

Copeland snorted at the word *landlord*, though Franny wasn't sure why.

"I'm fine, Mr. Simmons."

He nodded. "Good. Listen, it's important for a lot of the residents of Hope Town that this…stays below the radar. Obviously we've got a police presence, and people who know Albennie are worried, myself included, but we want to keep things…safe and calm. I'm hoping you'll stay."

"Come on, Simmons. What are you playing at?" Copeland demanded.

"Not playing," he said, not even sparing Copeland a glance. "I've talked with the sheriff," Mr. Simmons said.

The sun reflected off his sunglasses, and he looked very... official even though he wasn't in a uniform and didn't carry any badge. "Hope Town will have an officer posted twenty-four-seven until the kidnapper is found. I know you're a newer tenant, and this is the kind of thing that's going to scare people off, but I'd like to extend a personal invitation for you to stay, knowing there will be extra security and precautions for Hope Town residents."

"Thank you," she said. Then smiled at Copeland. "I plan on staying."

Copeland rolled his eyes and shook his head, but he didn't offer up any compelling argument not to stay. Maybe she was a little scared, but it seemed like the safest place to be was Hope Town if there was going to be a police presence and extra security.

The deputy who'd first arrived came up to Mr. Simmons.

"Simmons. Fed wants to show you something." The deputy glanced her way, but his gaze didn't linger.

Mr. Simmons nodded. "You let me know if you need anything, Ms. Perkins."

Franny nodded, turned to Copeland. "Can I head upstairs now, Detective?" She only *kind of* said *detective* in a way that sounded dismissive—something she'd picked up from Rosalie.

Copeland scowled. "Yeah, but don't blame me if Audra and Rosalie break down your door and demand you come home. I'll come with you, Simmons," he said turning to the man. "I want to hear anything the Feds have to say to you."

Mr. Simmons didn't bristle at that, but the deputy did.

"You can't let her just go," the deputy said, looking at them all like they were crazy.

Mr. Simmons eyed him. "I've already arranged with the sheriff to ramp up Hope Town security and—"

"I don't think you guys understand. She didn't just *witness* the kidnapping." The man's gaze was dark and fierce. "The kidnapper *saw* her."

Slowly Copeland and Mr. Simmons's eyes turned to her, both with an arrested kind of concern in their expressions.

Apparently *that* hadn't made the rounds yet. Or maybe she hadn't expressly told anyone but this deputy.

"Well, hell, Franny," Copeland muttered. "That changes everything."

"Sheriff wants to see you," Gard said, grabbing Royal before he headed out of the station.

Royal raised an eyebrow but didn't mount an argument. It had been a long day out in the heat dealing with the Hope Town kidnapping and Royal was ready to go home, have a beer and maybe sit in an ice bath for the rest of the night just to get the heat of the day off him.

But the sheriff wanted to see him. "Bad see me or good see me?"

"Remains to be seen," Gard said. "But you did good today. No reason it should be bad."

Royal couldn't think of a place where he'd screwed up, and Gard's reassurance helped, but being summoned into the sheriff's office long past the sheriff's usual office hours didn't feel *promising* regardless.

Royal moved through the building, headed for the sheriff's office. In one of the waiting rooms, he spotted the kidnapping witness along with Rosalie Kirk and another redhead—he was pretty sure that was Beckett's fiancée—all sitting together talking earnestly.

He still couldn't believe she hadn't been telling everyone who questioned her about the fact that the kidnapper *saw* her. What was wrong with her anyway?

None of his business.

She looked up at him as he passed. She had a set of eyes on her—big and green, dominating a pretty, fairy-ish face. Franny Perkins. He didn't think that face quite suited the name. Then again, nothing about the woman quite added up in a sensible way, and Royal had spent most of his life making sure he sized everyone around him up with sense and reason and *reality* over emotion.

But now was not the time to ruminate on the oddity of the witness. He knocked on the sheriff's door since Miranda, the sheriff's administrative assistant, was gone for the day. At the brisk order to *come in*, Royal stepped inside.

But it wasn't just Sheriff Buckley waiting for him. It was the Simmons guy. And Copeland Beckett.

Royal didn't know what to make of any of them, or why he was here. But he didn't let that show. He nodded at his boss. "Sheriff," he greeted him. "Corporal Fairhurst said you wanted to see me."

"Deputy Campbell. You got good marks from everyone today. Handled this unique situation just as we would have wanted you to. One of those Feds said he was surprised you were a rookie. You did good."

"Thank you, sir."

"Since you've got some experience now with Hope Town, and you were the responding officer, I'm recommending you to a special assignment. Mr. Simmons here has requested extra police presence in Hope Town while the search for the missing person is going on. I'm happy to oblige, but Mr. Simmons has a…unique request."

Simmons turned to him. No one had filled him in on just what this guy's deal was, but Royal'd be damned if he wasn't some kind of Fed.

"I'd like a deputy living in Hope Town for the time

being," Simmons said. "My preference would be a female officer, but the sheriff has suggested you instead." Simmons looked him up and down. Clearly not liking the idea, but he didn't voice that. "You'll be provided an apartment above one of the empty storefronts. You'll have off time, of course, but we want someone right there, just in case something happens."

"You expecting something else to happen?"

Simmons didn't say anything for a few ticking seconds. "What we have here is a delicate situation. While the FBI work to bring Ms. Ward home, it's my job to keep Hope Town safe. We're asking for Bent County's help. And the sheriff has nominated you."

Royal looked from Simmons to the sheriff. He didn't know why this should fall on him, the rookie, but it sounded a hell of a lot more interesting than what he'd been doing. Besides, he'd taken an oath to keep things safe in Bent County. That's what he'd put on this badge to do.

"All right."

"Good. I'll get an apartment ready. Sheriff gave me your contact info. I'll text you an address in the morning with a time to meet me." Simmons turned to the sheriff. "Sheriff, I appreciate your cooperation. I'll be in touch." And with that, he strode out of the office.

Once Simmons was gone, the door closed behind him, Royal glanced at the sheriff. "What aren't you telling the Feds?"

Sheriff shook his head. "It's more what the Feds aren't telling us," he said on a sigh, nodding toward Beckett.

"There's something more to this, and Simmons is in the thick of it," Beckett said with some disgust. "I'd like to bring Franny back to the ranch, keep an eye on her myself, but… Simmons has his reasons for wanting her to stay put, and

I don't think they're wrong." Beckett looked beyond frustrated. "I just wish I knew what they were."

"We've stumbled into a federal case," the sheriff said grimly. "They want our help, but they don't want us to know what it is we're helping with. We'll help, because this is our county. But I'd also like to know what they're up to and just what I'm helping with and why. Normally I would have gone along with Mr. Simmons's request for a female deputy, but you've got personal experience with federal agents."

Yeah, on the *other* side of things. The *being investigated* side of things, but Royal didn't say it out loud, even if everyone in this room probably knew. Maybe his record had been expunged, but that didn't make his past a full-on secret.

"My guess is you could sniff them out a mile away."

Yeah, the gang he'd grown up in had taught identifying Feds and cops at a glance before they'd worried about any kid being able to read. And since the sheriff was giving him that kind of credit, he figured it was worth an ask. "Simmons?"

"Former FBI, so you're not far off," Beckett confirmed. "And still neck-deep in FBI things from the looks of it since he had them on speed dial when this went down."

"I want your expertise," Sheriff Buckley said to Royal. "I want your eyes, Campbell. Normally I wouldn't give this to a rookie. These are very special circumstances. So if you don't think you can handle it, tell me now."

Royal didn't hesitate. The need to prove himself was too ingrained, even if bringing up his past made him uncomfortable. "I can handle it."

"Good. You'll still work a twelve-hour shift, focusing on Hope Town exclusively instead of the whole zone. Another deputy will handle the night shift, but you're to be on call, as well. And regardless of whether you're on duty or not, I want you watching and paying attention. Particularly to any federal agents who come around, whether they announce themselves or not."

"Yes, sir."

"Added to that, Detective Beckett has requested you keep a special eye on Ms. Perkins. The Feds didn't seem too concerned about the kidnapper coming back—another thing that makes me think there's more to this than meets the eye, but we want to ensure that no one comes sniffing around our eyewitness. And I don't just mean someone connected to the kidnapping. I want to know if the Feds are talking to her, and what they're asking."

Royal wasn't quite sure how he'd accomplish that, but he was hardly going to say he couldn't handle this. Not when it was a real assignment, and right out the gate. No, he couldn't screw this up. "All right."

"I'll expect a debrief in my email from you every night. And if you handle this well, deputy, it'll go a long way in making your rookie year a lot smoother."

"I'll handle it, Sheriff."

"Good. Go home and pack up what you need. Your Hope Town assignment starts first thing in the morning."

Chapter Five

Franny didn't sleep even though by the time she got back to her apartment she was exhausted.

She'd spent her entire evening at the sheriff's department, assuring Audra and Rosalie she was fine, listening to Copeland and the sheriff and even Mr. Simmons lay out all the reasons she wasn't in any danger.

Then repeating that to her cousins ad nauseam until they *finally* relented.

She'd showered the day off when she'd gotten back, crawled into bed and then…stared at the ceiling replaying the scene in her head, over and over again, trying to remember new details. A detail that might help.

But it was the same scene. The same feeling that if she'd been smarter or stronger she might have stepped in and *done* something about it.

Instead, the kidnapper's eyes had met hers and she had done *nothing*.

And, like both the federal agent she'd spoken to and the sheriff, she thought if the kidnapper was worried about witnesses, he would have done something about it at the time.

She considered the deputy who'd been so appalled Copeland and Mr. Simmons were going to let her go back to her apartment. He seemed to be the only one with concerns.

She rolled over onto her stomach, buried her head into her pillow. She wasn't *afraid* exactly. Not for herself anyway. She was afraid for Albennie, afraid of what this all was, but she didn't think a kidnapper who'd gotten exactly what he wanted was going to concern himself with *her*.

But she was…tense. Wound up.

"And not kidnapped so maybe stop feeling sorry for yourself," she muttered into the pillow before shoving up onto her elbows and blowing out a breath.

Okay, she wasn't going to sleep. Maybe she could work. She reached over to her nightstand where she always left her laptop and pulled it onto her lap as she sank into the covers. She didn't often let herself work in bed, because it tended to turn into a two-or three-day marathon of *sloth*, but she got to make an exception for kidnap witnessing.

She opened her book document, looked at the last paragraph she'd written…then immediately pulled up her internet browser.

She typed *Albennie Ward* into the search engine. And then spent the next thirty minutes getting more and more frustrated.

Albennie Ward didn't really seem to exist on the internet. No social media Franny could find, no public records, and that was weird considering how unique a name Albennie was. But there wasn't even the stray mention of her in the obituary of a family member or on Hope Town's bakery website.

Or anyone else for that matter.

Maybe Albennie was a nickname or a middle name, but that didn't help Franny's search any since she didn't know what her real name might be. She didn't even know how old Albennie was.

Not that finding out more about Albennie was going to

do anything. It was none of her business, and she wasn't some TV show character. She didn't think she was going to solve a crime before the FBI or the local police department.

But she was *curious*, and curiosity had led her to her career. If you asked questions, followed clues, you came up with a story.

Maybe it wouldn't be the right story, or the true story, but it felt like…something. Something better than staring at the ceiling wishing she could have been braver and stronger and *better* in a scary moment.

Maybe she could ask Lia if Albennie went by a different name, or what her background was, or if Lia had any ideas about what had happened. Except that Lia was obviously close to Albennie, and questioning Lia felt insensitive at the moment. Poking around like she thought she was a detective when Lia had no doubt already fielded tons of questions wouldn't be right.

What about Mr. Simmons? What was *his* deal?

Which lead to the next question. What was Hope Town's deal?

That was why she was here, trying to write a book, so looking into *that* was work.

She typed *Zach Simmons* into the search engine and then added FBI to the search. And a few articles showed up. Zach Simmons was a much more common name than Albennie Ward, but it was still too much of a coincidence that there was a court document from about seven years ago that included a Special Agent Zach Simmons. Something about cult members.

In Wyoming.

But he hadn't been with the other federal agents yesterday. Was he some kind of…supervisor? Was Albennie part of some… FBI thing? A cult? It would explain some weirdness.

But not the sheriff department weirdness.

Did Lia know about Mr. Simmons? It clearly wasn't a secret if it was easily searched on the internet, but had anyone in Hope Town put it together? Was Franny the only one out of the loop, or was everyone?

Franny glanced at the time on her computer. It was nearly seven now. Would the bakery open today? Would it be bustling or empty? If empty, she could maybe get some face time with Lia, but if *she* was Lia, she'd damn well be taking the day off.

She didn't think Lia was the type.

Well, there was only one way to find out. She pushed the laptop away and went to get dressed.

Sleeping be damned.

ROYAL SURVEYED THE apartment Simmons had led him into. It was above an empty storefront and across the street from the bakery and Franny Perkins's second-story apartment. If he looked out the big window in the living room, he could watch the comings and goings of both.

He could even see a little sliver of the parking lot behind the bakery building. He wouldn't be able to see the comings and goings out the back of the building, but he could see any car that came in or out of the parking lot if he was watching.

"It's a nice place. Updated," Simmons was saying. "But if you have any issues, you can call the number on the fridge. Mr. Poole handles any fix-it stuff around here. Obviously if there's something going on with the case, I'll want to know."

"Last time I checked, I report to the sheriff, not you," Royal replied without any heat.

The man didn't get offended, and also didn't offer an argument. He looked at his watch, edgier than he'd been yesterday. Not quite so cool and calm—not so *FBI*-like.

Instead, he was fidgety. Like he was waiting for something.

"Got somewhere to be, Simmons?"

He looked up at Royal. There was a moment's hesitation, then a shrug. "My wife is waiting on me downstairs. I forgot we were getting family pictures today. Felt like a normal thing to do instead of worry about Albennie. So this is a quick stop before we head into Fairmont."

Wife? Family pictures? Zach Simmons having a real life? It didn't quite compute.

But before Royal could come up with something to say to *that*, he heard the distinct sounds of footsteps on stairs. And a baby crying.

Simmons swore. "Give me a sec." He opened the front door, and on the other side of it was a woman. She had long blond hair pulled back in a clip and a screaming baby with a giant bow on her head in her arms.

She didn't look like she did on stage, but Royal recognized her immediately anyway.

"Zach, I'm losing it." She shoved the baby at Simmons, then gave Royal a pinched smile over Zach's shoulder. "Sorry to interrupt, but this one is a daddy's girl, and she's driving me insane."

Royal blinked at her once. Twice. "You're…" He didn't finish the sentence. She knew who she was.

But she did flash him a grin this time, maybe because the baby had in fact immediately quieted once she'd tucked her head into Simmons's neck.

"See?" she said, jabbing a thumb in the air toward the baby. "You do the work of carting them around in your body for nine months, shove them out and this is how they repay you."

Royal knew he shouldn't say it. He *knew* he should sound

less like a moron, but something had short-circuited in his brain, probably seeing one of his favorite singers in person. "You're Daisy Delaney."

She winked at him. "In the flesh. I go by Lucy Simmons around these parts though. What's your name, Deputy?"

Daisy Delaney was asking his name, and since he was still in some kind of shock, he answered. "Royal Campbell."

"Royal. That's a cool name. I like it. And the tattoos."

"All right," Simmons said, a mixture of irritation and affection in his voice. "Let's go."

Daisy—*Lucy*—laughed, low and husky. "He's so easy to move along when I need to. Flirt with somebody and he's ready to rush me out the door."

"You're a real riot, you know?" Simmons said, nudging Daisy toward the door. "Call if you need anything, Deputy." But he had clearly already turned his attention to his family. "Where's Coop?"

"Running the streets wild," Daisy—*Lucy* said as they walked out of the apartment. "You did promise it would only take five minutes, and I *did* tell you we could postpone."

"So I take it Lia has him." Their family chatter slowly faded away and Royal stood exactly where he was in the middle of a very sparsely furnished apartment.

Daisy Delaney had said his name, complimented that and his tattoos. And weirder still, for a few seconds, Simmons had seemed very, very human.

He was married to *Daisy Delaney*. Had kids with *Daisy Delaney*.

Royal shook his head. What a weird-ass world Bent County was.

But he didn't have time to think about that too deeply. He had to get ready for work and clock in. Still, he couldn't help crossing the empty living room and looking out the big window.

Simmons was loading the baby into a minivan. Simmons had a minivan.

He shook his head. Unbelievable. He surveyed the rest of the street. Mostly empty this morning. Most of the shops didn't open until ten. Except the bakery.

He glanced at the door across the street as Simmons drove away. And thought *jackpot*, because his eyewitness was jogging down the stairs outside her building and turning toward the bakery door.

He hadn't *quite* figured out how he was going to handle keeping an eye on a virtual stranger, but he figured the first step was to not be strangers anymore.

Chapter Six

Franny wasn't so much surprised to find the bakery open as she was a little concerned for Lia not resting and taking time to worry about her friend. But as Franny stepped inside, the scents of pastry being made and coffee being brewed filled the air.

"Morning, Franny," Lia greeted her from where she was filling a pastry display with a tray of brownies. "How are you holding up?"

Franny slid her laptop bag off her shoulder and set it on one of the tables before crossing to the counter Lia stood behind. She was a tall woman with hair a little too dark for her fair complexion. It was always pulled back, and Franny had never seen her without a hairband fastened into her hair with bobby pins.

"That's my question for you this morning."

Lia smiled thinly. She wore a very simple gold chain around her neck and moved a hand up to fiddle with the little pressed flower pendant attached to it. "I'm worried, but a lot of people are looking for her. And you gave the police a ton to go on. We'd be lost if it wasn't for you, Franny. Really. There'd just be no hope."

The idea of no hope had a knot forming in Franny's

throat, but she swallowed past it. "Well, it was just...luck, I guess. If you can call anything about this situation luck."

"We'll take whatever we can get. So, you want the usual this morning, or something a little higher octane?"

"Are you sure you want to be waiting on people today, Lia?"

"Working keeps me from freaking out. So work it is. Besides, Zach asked me to stay open. Said there will be cops and Feds coming and going for a while yet. Good for business. And good for keeping me busy."

Zach. What made Lia on a first-name basis with Mr. Simmons? Just time? Something deeper?

"Yeah, I'll take my usual."

Franny waited while Lia plated up a cinnamon roll and poured her latte. Franny paid for both, but before she took them to a table and pretended to work, she couldn't help but ask...

"Lia... Did you know that Mr. Simmons was—"

The bell above the door tinkled and Lia's eyes flicked to the door, narrowed. But she smiled. "Excuse me, Franny," she said, moving back to the cash register. "Help you, Deputy?"

Franny looked over her shoulder to find the police officer from yesterday. She didn't remember his name. What had Copeland called him? It was lost in the blur of yesterday.

Franny moved to the table she'd left her laptop at and watched as Lia waited on the cop.

"I've been put on permanent Hope Town duty, so I wanted to go around to the businesses and introduce myself. Deputy Campbell." He held out a hand for Lia to shake.

She did so. And Franny watched with interest as Lia skirted a very fine line where she somehow seemed nothing but polite, but also made it abundantly clear she didn't like his profession. "Nice to meet you."

"I wasn't sure you'd be open this morning. I'm living across the way for a bit, thanks to Mr. Simmons. He said you guys have a killer coffee cake."

"Sure do. Want some coffee to go with it?"

"A large, please."

Franny watched with open curiosity. She didn't even bother to look away when the deputy flicked a glance at her while Lia got his order ready. Why shouldn't she observe?

"Here you go, Deputy. On the house."

"Oh, don't do that. I'll pay."

"It's on the house," Lia repeated firmly. Then turned away and walked into the back room, not giving him a chance to argue.

Franny heard the deputy sigh, then he turned and glanced at her. He gestured at her with his coffee cup. "Guessing you had a long night."

Franny smiled thinly. "It was certainly long."

"You were still at the station when I left." He moved over to her table, set his coffee down on it. "Royal Campbell," he offered, holding out a hand for her to shake.

Franny didn't know what to make of the fact he'd introduced himself to Lia as *deputy*, and to her he'd given his first name. A first name she immediately wanted to put in a book.

But she didn't say that, though it was on the tip of her tongue. She shook his outstretched hand and noted the tiniest hint of something dark at his uniform shirt cuff. A tattoo? Well, maybe that explained the long sleeves in this heat. He had big rough hands, a tall rangy build. Even though she didn't associate tattoos with cops, it fit something about him. That edginess she'd noted yesterday. He didn't hold himself like Copeland or any of the other cops she knew—though she supposed she was more familiar with detectives. Maybe that was the difference.

"Franny Perkins," she returned. Then wrinkled her nose. "I guess you knew that."

"I guess I did. You always work from the coffee shop?" he asked casually before taking a bite of the coffee cake.

"Uh, no. It's usually too distracting to write here. But I'm pretty sure if I stayed in my apartment today, I'd rot in bed all day."

"You probably earned it. Yesterday was a lot."

"Maybe, but if I let myself bed rot too much, I don't surface for weeks. And I can't even blame work. I won't write. I'll watch one-minute videos on how to make elaborate cakes that I, myself, will never make."

His mouth curved. He had very blue, yes, and his nose was just a shade crooked. There was a faint scar that ran down his jaw on the left side. And she should *not* be cataloguing the features of a deputy no matter how attractive he was.

"You mind?" he asked, pointing at the chair across from her.

She didn't think he was *flirting*, but she couldn't quite decide what this was. Still, she gestured at the chair as a sort of *have at*, and he settled himself in it. Every once in a while she could hear the faint sound of someone talking from his radio, or a crackle of static, but he didn't pay it any mind. He ate his coffee cake and drank his coffee.

"So, you're a writer," he said, eyeing her computer.

She nodded, dreading the next question.

"What do you write?"

It was an understandable question, and if it could just be that easy, she wouldn't mind it. But it was never just *that*.

"Mysteries," she answered, bracing herself for the next comments.

Like so and so? Have I heard of you? I don't like books with xyz in them. You can't make a living off of that, can you?

"That's cool. I guess Bent County has a lot of inspiration."

She stared at him for a full beat. Because...he didn't even say it sarcastically. "It does," she said, probably with a little too much earnest fervor, but so many people—her parents included—didn't understand why she found living here so inspiring.

"Plus you've got Beckett at your disposal, right? Probably pretty nice having a direct line to a detective."

Franny nodded. "I'm not sure if he's at my *disposal*," she said, biting back a laugh at the thought. "But he'd probably jump off a cliff if Audra told him to, so it *is* helpful."

"Audra is your...cousin?"

"Yes. You know Rosalie Kirk, right? The private investigator. Audra and Rosalie are my cousins. I lived with them for a while before I moved into Hope Town. Then *their* cousin who lived with us too is married to another detective, Thomas Hart. Do you know him?"

"Of him. I don't have much connection to the detective's bureau yet. I just started at Bent County three months ago."

That made sense. She didn't think she'd ever heard of a Royal Campbell before. "I've been in Bent County for three years now. It's kind of funny all the connections you'll make the longer you're here. But it's a great inspiration. Small towns and isolated ranches are a great setting for murder. Well, fictional murder, the real stuff is a lot less fun. I guess you'd know that."

He didn't say anything for a minute. Almost like he was uncomfortable. And of course he was. She was sitting here talking about murder from a writer's perspective, and he saw it from a *real life* perspective. *This* was the problem with talking to people. She always put her foot in her mouth.

"Have you lived in Bent County long or did you come

for the job?" she asked, trying to change the subject. She *would* have gone back to pretending to be writing, but he was just…sitting there.

"Ah… Well, I came here about two years ago. My sister… lives here. She liked it. We'd been…out of touch for a while. She's got all sorts of friends at the Sunrise Sheriff's Department and they convinced me to go to the police academy. She's done some work for Bent County, so it was an in."

"She's a police officer too?"

"No. Forensic anthropologist."

Since Franny didn't think there could be *two* of those hanging around Bent County, she leaned forward. "Brooke Daniels is your sister?"

He blinked once. "You know… Brooke?"

"Well, sort of. Let's see if I can get this right: Audra's friend's husband's brother is married to this woman whose brother is married to Brooke, and through that long line of small-town connections, I got introduced to Brooke so I could ask her some research questions. She's very nice."

"Yeah."

"And she was really helpful. She inspired a great twist for that book." More at ease with a connection to people he knew, she grinned at him. "I still owe her one."

He looked a little more uncomfortable than he had, but only for a second before he smiled. A smile she would categorize as…*rakish*, rather than polite.

Maybe he didn't *mean* it to be. Maybe that was just what happened when he smiled, but it sure did something fluttery to her chest. Which was so utterly ridiculous in this situation. What was wrong with her?

"Well, if you ever have any questions about being a rookie deputy in small-town Wyoming, you just let me know."

She nodded. Lamely. Really, really lamely.

He got up. "See you around, Franny."

"Sure."

She didn't *mean* to watch him go. It just seemed the natural thing for her eyes to follow him out of the bakery. Watch that confident stroll. She might have watched him through the storefront window until he disappeared, but Lia spoke, startling her.

"I think hot cop has a crush."

Franny bobbled, looking back at Lia—who she definitely hadn't known was paying any attention since she'd been out of sight. Now she stood at the cash register.

Hot cop. Yeah, well. "I think he's just doing his job, and I was polite," Franny said, a little stiffly. "Friendly."

Lia snorted. "If you say so."

ROYAL WASN'T SURE what had possessed him to answer so many of Franny's questions with the truth instead of easy evasions.

She knew his sister. Maybe it was as simple as that had thrown him for a loop. It shouldn't surprise him. Brooke and Zeke were part of the community. People knew them.

But he still wasn't used to how everyone in this huge county seemed to have *some* connection to each other.

He'd mostly kept to himself and Sunrise up until he went to the police academy. He knew the Hudsons and the Danielses and that was enough for any man.

His time with Bent County had opened up a new world of people, but he still kept himself a little separate. He didn't know who knew what about who he was or what he'd done. The sheriff knew, but Royal wasn't about to advertise he'd been to jail. That he'd been framed for murder trying to save some young girls from their terrible life in the Sons of the Badlands gang.

No matter how much of a setup the murder charge had been, he *had* been a criminal, a gang member. Maybe he'd known it was wrong, but the only way he'd known how to help was from within, which meant bending some rules.

Okay, breaking a lot of rules.

And now he was on the outside, not just following rules but enforcing them.

Which meant he couldn't let an interesting woman with dreamy green eyes and an engaging smile distract him from his purpose.

Like this job. He couldn't take it for granted that it had taken a lot to get him here. He had to make sure the sheriff was pleased with his performance. Which meant, he had to find *something* to put in his report today.

So, he went into any businesses that were open, introduced himself. Down one side of the street, then up the other. Popping into the ones he'd missed once they flipped their signs to Open, chatting with any passerby.

They were not a talkative lot in Hope Town. Not that his experience with people around here meant he expected any level of gregariousness, except Franny. She was a chatter.

He smiled in spite of himself. Based on how the day was going, that had been the most positive interaction he'd had all day.

Near lunchtime, he headed for the bookstore now that it was finally open. He was almost all the way on the other end of the street, but he kept it in his sights. Noting the comings and goings.

Like the woman who walked out of the bookstore with no bags. Her outfit wasn't distinct. Just athletic pants and a T-shirt and a green baseball hat. The T-shirt was a little baggy—not out of place considering the athletic pants, but Royal studied her figure for signs of a gun.

Because she had a brisk stride. Her hair was pulled back in a tight braid. Her eyes were careful and assessing.

Fed.

Royal didn't follow her right away, but he didn't go into the bookstore to make his introductions like he'd originally planned. Instead, he kept walking down the street, glancing backward once or twice to determine where the woman was going.

When she ducked into the antique store, he took a circuitous route there himself. Luckily he hadn't introduced himself there yet, so he could step in without it seeming off or like he knew who the woman was. Or what she was anyway.

His target was talking to a woman at the cash register. It was casual, but Royal knew just from the way the woman stood that it was an interrogation—whether the lady behind the counter knew it or not.

They both glanced his way when he stepped inside. He offered a charming smile, walked right over to them. "Morning, ladies," he said cheerfully. "Sorry to interrupt. I'm just making the Hope Town rounds today."

He held his hand out to the woman behind the counter, not giving the Fed much attention, but he saw out of the corner of his eye how she edged away from the counter and headed for the door.

"Deputy Royal Campbell," he said to the woman behind the counter. "I'm going around today and introducing myself to all the business owners."

He glanced behind him as the Fed slipped out of the front door.

Later he'd look at his body cam footage and figure out just who she was.

And what part of Albennie Ward's disappearance connected to an FBI case.

Chapter Seven

Franny chastised herself the entire time she got ready the next morning. A woman was missing, and she was doing her makeup because maybe Deputy Campbell would come back to the bakery and talk to her again?

It was gross and wrong…and it didn't stop her. She grabbed her laptop, shoved it in its bag, and then stepped out into a hot, muggy morning.

Was Albennie somewhere hot without any air-conditioning? Was she still alive? Would—

"Stop," she muttered out loud. She couldn't worry about Albennie because she couldn't *do* anything about Albennie. She had to focus on the things she could do.

Maybe Royal would have some updates. Not that she expected him to be at the bakery. He'd probably only gone yesterday as a one-off. And even if he did become a regular to get coffee to start his shift, it didn't mean they'd talk every morning.

"Because you're not going to be here every morning. This is *not* the schedule." And talking to herself out loud *outside* was not the best sign for her mental health. She made it to the bottom of the stairs and forced herself to slow down.

Just out for a casual stroll to the bakery for some food and work. She opened the bakery door, internally chastised herself for immediately searching the room for Royal. He wasn't there, although one person was. Franny was pretty sure the woman worked at the bookstore, but she'd only talked to the manager so far. This woman was chatting with Lia while Lia worked the espresso machine.

Franny set her bag down. The door's bell tinkled, and she quickly looked behind her. She was *not* disappointed that the man who stepped inside was not Royal, because she wasn't looking for Royal.

The man got into line behind the bookstore lady. They exchanged a few words, so Franny seated herself at her table and determined she was going to write a paragraph before she ordered coffee. She opened her laptop, the book document.

Maybe she'd deal with her email first. She just couldn't think clearly if she had unread mail. Especially an email from her accountant. *Ugh.* She hated numbers and reality.

"You're working here again?"

Franny looked up and realized the two customers had left while she'd been deep into crafting a response to her accountant that wasn't: *I don't know, dude, numbers aren't my thing.*

"Just for research." Franny beamed at Lia, even though she was pretty sure the woman saw right through her.

The bell jingled, and since she was proving a *point*, she didn't look behind her. She studiously hit Send on her email. Then she stood to get in line for coffee…

Only to come face-to-face with Royal. Those eyes were so *blue*. She made a noise—even she didn't know what it was. A kind of *oof* squeak.

"Morning, Franny."

She had to swallow. Plenty of people said her name, so she wasn't sure why in his low voice it felt…different. "Morning."

He glanced at her table. "Looks like you haven't ordered yet. Let me buy you a coffee," he said, stepping up to Lia and the counter.

"Oh, no." She followed him helplessly. "You don't have to—"

"She loves a latte," Lia said, oh *so* helpfully.

"A latte and a regular coffee then."

Franny glared at Lia, but she turned away to handle the drinks, so Franny had to smooth out her expression and smile at Royal. It didn't feel like a smile on her face. She felt awkward and like he could *definitely* tell she'd put on makeup this morning, because of *him*.

Stay inside where your weirdness belongs, Franny.

But Lia handed Royal the cups and Royal gestured to her table, so she had to walk back to it and let him put the latte mug in front of her computer, while he settled himself in the chair opposite.

She closed her laptop, since he was *staying* apparently. "Thanks for the latte. You really didn't have to."

"Community relations." He smiled at her, and she just... wasn't good at this. It *felt* like flirting, but maybe it *was* just community relations. How was she supposed to know?

Fictional people were so much easier.

"You looked like you were working hard."

"I wish. I was emailing my accountant. Which *is* hard work, because I'm trying to sound like I have any idea what he's talking about, and I most assuredly do not."

He chuckled. Which was... She didn't know. She didn't know what to do with *any* of this. Why had she *sought this out*?

His gaze tracked to the big window that looked out over Main as he sipped his coffee. "Listen, I don't suppose you've noticed anyone out of the ordinary poking around? Maybe asking you or Lia questions?"

She held herself very still. She refused to be disappointed. Of course he was just…working a case. *Of course he was*.

But she had to clear her throat to answer. "No one's talked to me. I haven't seen anyone talk to Lia." She thought about this morning from the lens of what she should be—a careful observer in the wake of a terrifying kidnapping—instead of…whatever this whackadoodle mess was.

"There was a guy in here this morning who I don't know. But he didn't seem to ask any questions or be unduly interested in anything. He just got his coffee and left. You could ask Lia if she knew him."

Royal glanced at the counter. Lia was in the back.

"Yeah, maybe I will." But he didn't get up and do that right away.

And since this was about the *kidnapping*, and it was *professional*, she figured that meant she could get some of her own questions answered.

"Can I ask you something about the case?"

He studied her with a wariness that felt…heavier than it should, she thought. But he inclined his head in a *go ahead* move.

"It's just, I…noticed something. About the questions you guys asked and the questions the FBI asked. Where they… differed."

That wariness turned to contemplation, and then an intense concentration that did more of that heart-fluttery thing inside her chest. "Oh, yeah? How'd they differ?"

"Maybe it's because they already knew I didn't know Albennie that well, but I heard them talking to other people and they didn't ask those people either."

"Ask what?"

"About who might want to hurt her. Ex-boyfriends or known enemies, customers who'd given a weird vibe. *You* asked people about that. Copeland too. But the Feds didn't."

He studied her, those blue eyes serious. Focused. "You sure?"

She nodded. "I started paying attention because it was just so…clear. They had a different angle. They were interested in the timing. The security cameras. More the…hows than the whys. It just made me think…" She trailed off realizing how ridiculous this was. "I'm sorry. You're a *professional*. I'm just a…bystander. You don't want to hear what I think."

"Actually I do." He leaned forward, watching her very carefully. "What did it make you think, Franny?"

Nerves danced in her chest—and they were nerves over sounding stupid and having him make fun of her, but there were also these sort of *awareness* nerves that she really didn't do well handling.

But she focused on her theory. "Well, if they weren't asking who might want to hurt her…they might already know *who*."

Royal kept *staring* at her. If she was a criminal, she was pretty sure she'd confess. Maybe even to things she hadn't done.

"They do have the description you gave, the license plate. So maybe they do know. Maybe they knew before they even got there."

Franny nodded. "Has anyone identified him yet? Found the car? Anything?"

Royal didn't answer right away. But his gaze was sharp, attentive. She imagined he was working through a couple different problems all at the same time. Or maybe he was deciding how nice to be to the crazy writer, like he'd seen *Misery* one too many times.

"No, they haven't found anything that I know of," he finally said.

Hope folded in on itself, and she just felt unaccountably... depressed. "Maybe it never mattered I got all that information then." *Maybe you should have done something in the moment.*

"It mattered," Royal said, seriously enough she looked up from her little pity party. His gaze was blue and intense. "It will matter," he said forcefully.

And it actually made her feel a little better that he thought so.

IF THERE WAS one thing Royal hated about police work, it was reports. He'd never gone to school in any traditional sense of the word. A semester with this foster family, some homeschooling lessons with that one. Nothing in the gang, *obviously*. Well, Brooke had tried when he'd been really little. The fact he could read at all was probably thanks to her.

He'd gotten his GED. He'd passed the POST test. He'd *learned*, but writing things out was just never going to be his strong suit.

He pushed away from the table where he'd been working. If he didn't take a break, he was going to be way too tempted to hurl the computer against the wall, and since it was county issued, that probably wasn't in his best interest.

He paced the apartment for a little bit, trying to get some of the pent-up energy out of his system. He'd joined a gym in Fairmont, and he was technically off duty since it was after seven, but he didn't like the idea of being gone a couple hours even if there was a deputy on call for night shift.

Maybe he could go for a run. There wasn't a great path in Hope Town, but maybe he could carve one out. Though probably not in the dark.

He walked over to the window. Hope Town was dark and quiet below. There were a few streetlights, but beyond this Main Street everything around him out there would be pitch-black nothingness.

Royal blew out an irritated breath. Along the street on the opposite side, most of the lights in the buildings were off except for security lights in the shops on the first floor. He knew most of the apartments on the second floors were rented by the women who owned or worked in the stores.

Were there any men in this town? He'd asked Lia about the man Franny had seen at the bakery this morning and had been told Ellis Sutton was on the up and up, though he'd looked into what Lia had said just to verify.

Nothing out of the ordinary, just one of the few men with a Hope Town address.

But wasn't that in it of itself w*eird*? Why did Zach Simmons only lease businesses to women? Was it some kind of…feminist outreach?

Or something more sinister.

"Not everything is sinister," he muttered to himself, mostly because he remembered that glimpse of Zach Simmons—father and husband—that had reminded Royal of the good people he'd met since moving here.

Thanks to Brooke.

Maybe Brooke knew Zach Simmons, or Zeke probably would. He could ask them what they thought.

But his mind didn't stay where it should. It flitted off.

Brooke knew Franny Perkins.

He shook his head.

"Weird-ass town," he muttered, then happened to look up to the apartment across from his. Franny Perkins's apartment.

And as if he'd conjured her, there she was in the window.

In much the same position he was in—looking out at Main Street. She was illuminated by a light in her apartment. It was hard to tell from this distance, but it *felt* like she was looking over at him. He was no doubt illuminated to her too.

As if to confirm, she raised a hand in a little wave.

Not knowing what else to do, Royal raised his own hand in waved acknowledgment.

Then she turned away from the window and lowered her blinds. He watched those closed blinds for longer than he wanted to admit, wondering what a night in Franny Perkins's apartment looked like.

None of his business. But he was putting her theory in his report. Because she was on to something there. And if the Feds knew who they were looking for, it didn't make sense—to Royal's way of thinking—to keep local law enforcement out of it. What if he saw something that would connect, but missed it because he didn't have all the details?

He shook his head, closed his curtains, and went back to his report.

Chapter Eight

Franny did *not* go to the bakery the next day. She had her pride, didn't she? And since Royal had essentially caught her *window peeping* like some kind of stalker last night—even though she'd just *happened* to look over and see his lights on, and him pacing in the warm glow of them—she was staying far away from Royal Campbell.

So, she worked from bed. And by *work* she meant: updated her website, checked her social media properties, fooled around with a pitch that was *not* her book proposal, and did a quick internet search of Royal Campbell.

With only a tiny modicum of guilt about it.

She didn't find much. The social media story posted by Bent County about his hiring. He also had no social media, no internet profile.

"What is with these people?" she muttered irritably. It was like they were all…hiding from something.

Which *did* give her a little trickle of an idea for her book. What if it wasn't just *one* person hiding in Hope Town. *One* person with secrets. What if it was a town where people went to hide? And then one of the problems they were hiding from came knocking?

With the questions percolating, Franny actually pulled

up her manuscript file and put a few sentences together. Then a few more.

When her stomach rumbled, she muttered about leaving her computer. She had a first chapter, a good idea of what would happen next, and she'd even incorporated some of her research about the history of Hope Town into her fictionalized version.

She ate lunch with some malice—it was hard to eat a packet of tuna without malice. She didn't even have a bag of chips to balance out all this *health*.

Maybe she should go to the grocery store. But she could see the next scene play out in her head and she didn't want to stop and disrupt her creative flow.

A cop with secrets. A jaded FBI agent. A town inexplicably populated by people who didn't have pasts—that they'd let anyone else know about.

Since everything was clicking, after she finished eating she let herself keep writing in bed. The whole beginning took shape. Both main characters becoming real and three dimensional even if she didn't know all their secrets yet.

Who would want to? Things would get boring. Finding the answers to the questions was a journey she didn't want to end too quickly. But eventually the haze of creative clicking started to lift. Too many ideas. Too many different ways to go.

She blinked up, noted the sun was much lower in the sky than it had been. She glanced at the time. Nearly three. And she'd actually gotten some solid words in.

That called for a reward.

She had no such rewards in her kitchen, but downstairs there might be a cupcake if Lia hadn't sold out. And since she had no expectation of running into Royal at this hour, she gave herself permission to head down to the bakery.

Everything was fine as long as she didn't *change* her schedule in the hopes she might *see* someone.

Still, she didn't head down in her pajamas and hair that was still a mess of bedhead. She got dressed and brushed her hair. "No makeup. You don't usually wear makeup. Don't be that girl."

Besides, she wouldn't see him in the bakery. It was highly unlikely she'd run into him on the walk *down her stairs and around the corner.* And even if she *did*, what did she honestly think was happening here? She was a witness to a kidnapping. A woman who was *still* kidnapped. He was a cop investigating.

So.

She grabbed her purse and headed downstairs. There was only about twenty minutes to close, and there wasn't anyone inside. Lia was already clearing out the bakery case.

"I don't suppose you've got a cupcake leftover?"

Lia nodded and plated it up. She handed Franny the plate. "I think your boyfriend missed you this morning," Lia said.

Franny took the plate, trying to figure out what Lia was talking about. "Huh?" Confusion gave way to realization at the teasing glint in Lia's eye. "Oh, don't be ridiculous."

Lia shrugged. "He asked about you."

The little flutter she was trying to quelch did the opposite of quelch. "He did?" Before Lia could confirm, Franny waved it away in irritation with herself. "Oh, who cares. It's not high school."

"Have a lot of hot cops interested in you in high school, Franny?"

"I didn't even have ugly criminals interested in me in high school, Lia." Which made Lia laugh and Franny smile in spite of herself.

"Well, he had some news on the case," Lia said, busying

herself with cleaning out the baked goods case, but Franny could see the nervous energy in it. "I guess they found the kidnapper's car, but it was abandoned. However, they're hopeful that there didn't seem to be any signs of blood or struggle. It was in Idaho, so the Feds will start focusing their attention there."

"Idaho," Franny echoed. Albennie had been taken across state lines—which explained federal involvement, she supposed. But hadn't they been involved before they knew that? Or had they known that before?

"But you know..." Lia stopped what she was doing, looked at Franny over the bakery case. "Deputy Campbell comes in here and tells me the Feds are gone, then a little while later, this lady comes in. Pretends it's casual, but it felt...purposeful. I'd have pegged her for a cop, but she's not Bent County. I'm not sure what she is."

"Did you tell Royal?"

"First-name basis now?" Lia asked, still teasing, but she must have noticed Franny's discomfort with it. Because here they were talking about Idaho and abandoned cars and still no signs of *Albennie*, and Franny didn't think *laughing* or *rolling her eyes* about Royal was the right thing to do in this moment.

Lia sighed. "Look, I've...been through my share of stuff. Danger and worry, growing up. You learn to...accept what is. Shove down all the fear, and if you deal in a little humor to distract yourself then, well, I don't know if it's healthy or not, but it works."

Franny nodded, but she couldn't quite buy in. Not right now. "I think you should tell him."

Lia bit her bottom lip. "I was thinking about telling Zach."

"You...trust Mr. Simmons?"

Lia eyed her in that way that was becoming very common. Like everyone knew what was going on but her. "I do," Lia said after a while, but she was very serious about it.

"Then maybe you should tell both of them."

Lia nodded slowly. "Yeah, you're right. Can't hurt. What can hurt?"

For a moment, just a flash, Franny saw a kind of fear and desperation in Lia's expression that Franny had never seen there before. But quickly, Lia blinked it away.

"I'll tell Deputy Campbell about the lady next time I see him. And Zach. Hell, I'll tell the sheriff if I see him. Whatever might help. But listen, I get through each day with the knowledge that Albennie's tough. She's had to be. She's going to get through this. I have faith."

But Franny knew what it sounded like when you were trying to convince yourself of something that wasn't necessarily true. Still, she wasn't about to disagree. "Me too."

ROYAL DIDN'T ALLOW himself to develop a routine, and this morning at the bakery had been a good reminder he shouldn't.

He still didn't know what had possessed him to ask the bakery manager about Franny. Why should it matter if Franny Perkins was there or not? It didn't. He was just observing.

So after grabbing his coffee, instead of doing a walking route around the town, he got in his cruiser and took a drive around the outskirts of Hope Town. He still hadn't figured out if the woman who'd been walking around yesterday was a Fed, and he didn't know what kind of car she was driving, but he kept an eye out.

If the Feds were gone, she probably wasn't here anymore, but he wanted to be sure. And he couldn't help but think about Franny's point yesterday. The Feds hadn't asked about Albennie's past.

Not that it mattered. Everyone he'd questioned that morning had basically said they didn't *know* about Albennie Ward's past. Not where she'd moved to Hope Town from, if she had family nearby or not. They'd never seen family or a boyfriend. She was a woman who'd appeared one day and mostly kept to herself.

He thought *maybe* Lia Blair knew more and wasn't saying, along with the bookstore owner he'd talked to, but he kind of wondered if they were just keeping their friend's secrets—not trying to impede an investigation. He kept expecting the sheriff to pull him. There was a time clock ticking on this—and since the Feds had announced they'd found the getaway car in *Idaho*, Royal just didn't see how much longer Sheriff Buckley could justify him being here.

Royal kept chewing over that story from the Feds. It struck him as all wrong. If a guy was going to leave a car behind—he sure as hell wouldn't leave it anywhere near where he was headed.

Royal should know. He'd left a few cars behind in his day.

After a morning of driving around and seeing a fat lot of nothing except what he always saw, he parked behind his building and got out for his foot patrol. Nothing, nothing and more nothing. Not even the odd stranger.

But the business owners he'd introduced himself to the first day tended to wave or nod or greet him. Sometimes they introduced him to one of their staff. He was considering going to the bookstore and seeing if they had any of Franny's books. What would be the harm in reading one, getting a sense of what she did?

But he heard his voice being called before he could make a move to walk toward the bookstore.

He glanced over his shoulder to find the woman who was

dominating way too much of his thoughts lately—considering he was on special assignment and he barely *knew* her.

But she bustled across the street and up the sidewalk. He met her halfway. She didn't look upset but determined. "Everything okay?"

"As okay as it can be, I guess. Are you busy? Can you come over to the bakery?" she asked, those pretty eyes intense and direct. They looked greener outside. Something about the lighting, he supposed.

And since that was *not* what he should be thinking about, he squinted across the street. "Isn't it closed?"

"Lia's closing up now, but she wanted to tell you something. She was going to do it tomorrow, but I happened to see you, so I thought I'd just act as middleman."

"All right." He followed her down the sidewalk and across the street. She knocked on the bakery door that was now locked, but Lia came right over and opened it up for them.

"I thought you could tell Ro—Deputy Campbell about that woman now, since he was right there when I walked out."

Lia looked from Franny to him. "Yeah. Sure." She wiped her hands on the towel stuck into the tied belt of her apron and held the door open for them to step inside. She didn't look *nervous* exactly, but definitely unsure. "It could be nothing."

"Which means it could also be something," he replied. "Being a cop involves all sorts of somethings and nothings."

She smiled thinly. "I've always hated cops."

"Hey, me too."

He clearly surprised a laugh out of her, and a curious look from Franny, but he listened to Lia talk about a woman who'd come in asking questions that didn't sit right with her.

He thought of the woman he'd seen yesterday. Popping

into businesses. Talking to the clerk at the antique shop. He still didn't have an ID on her. "Describe her for me."

Lia's description was dead-on to the woman he was thinking of. He frowned. The rundown sheriff had given him this morning had said the Feds had left for the time being.

But if *she* was here this morning, had they? Were they lying about this too? Or were his instincts off and she wasn't a Fed at all? Did that make *her* a sinister addition to this town?

Two pairs of female eyes studied him, clearly waiting for him to do something with the information. He could keep it to himself. Keep them out of this.

But people came and went from Lia's bakery all day long. And Franny was a witness in the kidnapping. It seemed the more they knew, the better they might be able to help.

"I saw her yesterday poking around. I think she's a Fed."

"But you told me this morning the Feds had moved out."

"That's because I'd been told they had. And maybe she did after she got one more look at the scene of the crime." But it didn't sit right. Like *maybe* he'd been told something that wasn't true at all.

"I'm going to tell Zach," Lia said.

Royal tried not to bristle. "What's Simmons going to do?"

"He used to be FBI," Franny murmured, clearly considering this new information more than what she was saying.

She lifted her gaze, noted Lia and him staring at her. She shrugged. "I did an internet search. It's no secret."

Royal had been so distracted by the case—and maybe Simmons being married to Daisy Delaney—he hadn't looked into him any deeper than making note of what all he owned in Hope Town and how long he had.

"Who else did you internet search?" Lia asked.

An interesting shade of pink crept into Franny's cheeks.

"Look. Isn't it clear the Feds and the sheriff's department aren't sharing information? Why would that be?"

"I don't know," Royal said irritably. He knew the sheriff didn't know either.

"It's why you're here, isn't it?" Lia said, nodding her chin across the way. "Why Zach let you lease that place."

He eyed her, wondering how much she knew. How much Simmons knew. It didn't matter, he supposed. The point was to pay attention to the Feds.

"Listen, if either of you see her again, you give me a call. A text. Let me give you my cell number." He rattled it off for them as they put it in their phones. "I don't care if I'm on duty or not. You see her, you let me know ASAP."

They both agreed.

So he moved for the door, held it open for Franny who stepped out with him. Lia locked the door behind them.

For a moment, Franny didn't start walking for her apartment and he didn't start working to continue his foot patrol.

He glanced down at her. He knew he should just say goodbye and move on with his day. But he couldn't quite resist… "Did you internet search me, Franny?"

She stared at him a full beat, her cheeks getting pink again. Then she shrugged. "For a unique name, there isn't a whole lot about you online."

He grinned, couldn't help it. There was just something about a woman who doubled down.

"And just so we're clear, I wasn't spying on you last night." She said this *very* formally as the blush on her cheeks just deepened.

He could not figure out for the life of him why she entertained the hell out of him. "I didn't say you were."

"I just happened to look up and…there you were."

"Same."

"Okay. So. Okay." She took a step away, then turned around to walk away. He could only categorize what she was doing as a *scurry*.

Which for some reason had him opening his mouth when he should keep it shut. "You know, you owe me a cup of coffee."

She stopped, turned. "I…do?"

"Sure. I bought you one yesterday, now it's your turn."

She opened her mouth, shut it, drew her bottom lip through her teeth—which wasn't fair considering he was on duty and had to keep *some* semblance of his attention on work not…her.

"I… I'll be at the bakery in the morning then," she said. She smiled.

So he smiled back. "Good."

Chapter Nine

Franny had a bit of a struggle getting into the swing of things once she got back to her apartment.

If she was back at the ranch, she'd be dissecting that moment outside the bakery with Royal second by second with Audra and Rosalie. Except Rosalie didn't live at the ranch anymore and Audra would be cozied up to Copeland where she belonged.

So Franny only had herself to go over that moment outside the bakery. He'd been flirting with her. She was *almost certain* he'd been flirting.

Right?

Then he'd asked her…to buy him a coffee. Which wasn't a date. He would be *on duty*. It was just…

Oh, she didn't know.

And since she didn't know—what to do about Royal, Albennie, Feds and cops alike, she figured she'd focus in on the one thing she *did* know.

Her book. So she made herself a decently healthy dinner, then settled down at her *desk* like a grown-up, and got to work.

And work she did. The words were flowing. She didn't even pay attention to the time. She wanted to ride this wave of everything making *sense*. And being within her control. No outside world allowed to invade.

But eventually…the words petered out, and she was yawning more than she was getting words down. She noted the time—well after midnight. The entire room around her was dark except for the light of her computer. Man, she hadn't been that in the zone in a while. It felt *good*.

But if she was going to get up early enough to meet Royal for coffee, she was actually going to need to set an alarm. And she needed to get *some* sleep so she didn't look like a total zombie in the morning.

Not that it mattered if she did or not, since it wasn't a date. He was working a case. The end.

She picked up her phone and started to head to the kitchen to get a drink of water, but that's about when she noted the odd noise.

It sounded like…scratching? At the door? She frowned. Had someone's cat gotten loose and was trying to get in?

You might as well throw a grenade in her apartment as allergic as she was to cats. Did she even know where her antihistamine was? She did have an inhaler in the bathroom, and one in her purse, so that was good.

And she wasn't going to let a cat in anyway, so what was she worrying about? She shook her head.

But something was *definitely* scratching at her door.

Just a cat, she assured herself, but… Why would a cat climb the stairs and scratch at her door? She crept closer to the door, put her eye to the peephole.

She couldn't see anything. *Probably because it's dark, Franny.* But usually there was a little hint of the security light over by the antique store when she looked through the peephole at night.

Maybe it was out. She almost never looked out the peephole, so maybe she'd been imagining a light before. Thinking it was anything sinister was overreacting.

Except a woman was kidnapped from this exact place just a few days ago.

Still… She looked down at her phone. 911 was over-the-top for some *scratching at her door* when she couldn't tell what it was. And she wasn't about to open the door and find out.

Maybe there was some sort of nonemergency line at the sheriff's department she could call. Ask for…advice? Or…

She opened the contact and pulled up Royal's number. She could just text him. Or even call him and just ask him to glance over at her place from his window and see what was making that noise at her door.

She'd almost talked herself out of it when the doorknob seemed to…creak, like it had moved…ever so slightly.

Her heart leaped into her throat, and she backpedaled into her room—closing the door and locking it too. She leaned against the door, fear making her feel numb. She managed to hit Call on Royal's number.

It rang four times and she was about to hang up and call 911, embarrassment be damned, when a rough, sleepy voice answered.

"'lo."

She'd clearly woken him up and felt like a complete ass. "Hi, sorry. It's late. Sorry."

There was a beat of silence, then two. "Franny?" he asked, like he wasn't quite sure.

And why would he be sure? She'd woken him up. It was the middle of the damn night. "Yeah, I'm sorry. I'm sorry. It's just, I think… I think someone is like…at my door, or something." Her heart was beating triple time, and she could hardly hear him over the sound of it so loud in her ears.

"What?"

"I almost called 911, but I'm not sure. It could be a cat. A dog. The wind? But it just…won't stop and I thought well…

I have your number and you can look over and see. And if no one is there, I can just…curl up in a ball and only be embarrassed in front of you."

She heard the sound of rustling and movement. "Someone is trying to break into your place?"

"No. I don't know. There's just this noise at my door, and then the knob kind of moved and… Everything is locked and—"

"It's too dark." His voice was firm and with it now, no sleepy notes to it. "I can't see anything. Look, I'm going to have to hang up, but you stay where you are. I'm coming over."

"Oh, don't—"

But the connection ended. And even though she felt silly for calling him over, she was *relieved* he was coming and taking her paranoia seriously.

She really wanted it to be paranoia.

ROYAL GRABBED HIS GUN, shoved his feet into the unlaced boots by his door and ran down the stairs to the street.

Before he'd even crossed the street to Franny's side, he heard the rumble of an engine getting farther and farther away. No lights anywhere, but if someone *had* been trying to get into Franny's apartment, they likely would have kept their car lights off.

Cursing, he sent a text to the night shift deputy asking him to be on the lookout for a car driving around without its lights on. Gun in hand, he moved swiftly and silently to Franny's stairs. It was dark, but he didn't see so much as a shadow or hear anything either.

Figuring a knock would unnecessarily scare her, he sent her a text to let him in the door.

It took a few seconds, but eventually she did. She was

still dressed in the shorts and T-shirt she'd been wearing at the bakery this afternoon.

"No one here," he said. He didn't have his holster on, so he couldn't put the gun away. He could see her worried gaze on it, but there was nothing he could do in the moment.

"No one," she echoed looking into the night around them. "I'm just…being paranoid. I'm so—"

Before she could apologize again, he steamrolled over her. "I don't think so. I heard an engine. Already on their way out of town when I got out. But there's not usually much going on this time of night. Doesn't feel like a coincidence. I texted our night shift guy and he's on the lookout. We'll see if he comes up with anything."

"So someone was really…"

He could hear her panic, so he thought it best to give her something concrete to do. "You got a flashlight? I left mine back at my place."

"Just my phone."

"That'll do for now. Give me some light on the outside of the door."

She did as she was told, training the light on the outside knob. Royal didn't touch the door, but he studied it. There were some scratches around the keyhole but that could have been from anything—including Franny herself not always getting the key in the first time.

He looked around at the little landing outside her door. "Anything look out of the ordinary?"

She took her time, shining the flashlight on different things. The light bobbled a little bit, but she was mostly keeping it together.

He saw it before she did, a little piece of paper tucked under her cheerful doormat. The light left the corner, but before he could ask her to bring it back, she did, focusing the beam on that piece of paper.

"That... I don't think that was there," she said.

"I don't suppose you've got any rubber gloves?"

"Uh, no."

"All right. Close the door. *Lock* the door. I'm going to go grab what I need. I'll text you when to let me back in, okay?"

She looked around helplessly, and Royal didn't know what else to do except give her arm a little squeeze, a little centering. "It's going to be okay. Just follow my instructions, all right?"

She nodded.

He stepped back from the door and waited for her to close it. She did, and he waited to hear the lock click.

Once it did, he jogged down the stairs, nearly tripping over his untied laces halfway down. Cursing himself but not wanting to stop and bother with tying them, he hurried back to his place.

He needed some stuff from his gun belt. And to put some real clothes on. The athletic shorts and unlaced boots combo wasn't exactly a professional look, but he was hardly going to put on his full clown outfit in the middle of the night.

It was too hot for a hoodie, so he grabbed the first T-shirt his hand landed on and pulled it on. Found some socks and put them on awkwardly as he went to his belt and grabbed it. Rather than fasten it around his waist he just carried it, shoving his gun into the holster.

He jogged back across the street, this time having the presence of mind to lock his own apartment up first, then he kept an eye out for movement or sound.

Nothing. With his free hand, he pulled his phone out of his pocket when it dinged. It was a text from the night shift deputy that he read as he climbed Franny's stairs again.

Haven't seen a soul.

Royal inwardly cursed, then pulled up his messages with Franny and told her to open the door.

She did so right away, light from her apartment spilling out. He handed her his gun belt. "Hold that."

"It's heavy," she muttered when she nearly dropped it. But he ignored her. He'd already gotten the gloves out of the belt. He pulled them on, then picked up the piece of paper.

It was actually more like an index card. Folded in half. Royal unfolded it. The print on the card looked like it was from a typewriter. He frowned at the odd conglomeration of codes and words.

There were some numbers and letters in the upper left-hand corner that didn't make any sense. Then: *Perkins, F.M.* Underneath it was the phrase *Dead in the River.* Before he could read the rest, Franny spoke.

"It's a card catalogue card."

"What's that?"

"They used to have them in libraries so people could find books and where they were shelved." Her voice was weird. Kind of flat. "That one's for my first book. *Dead in the River.* It's my book."

"Oh, so it's yours? You just dropped it?" He held it out to her.

She shook her head, refused to take it. "I only even know what a card catalogue is because I took a library class in college. I've certainly never seen one for my books. They don't really use them anymore. They're obsolete."

"So… This card for your book isn't yours, but it's somehow under your doormat? After you heard someone messing with your door? In the middle of the night?"

She audibly swallowed, looking up at him with big green eyes. Fear the predominate emotion there. She nodded.

It wasn't a threat *exactly*, but it sure felt like one. "We're going to have to go into the station."

Chapter Ten

Franny sat in the passenger side of Royal's police cruiser, her nerves strung tight. She clasped her hands together and looked straight ahead.

She didn't know what to think. She did know it was…terrifying. Because she couldn't think of any good reason that card should be sitting on her porch. No, not sitting. Tucked under the doormat—but visible enough she would have seen it in the morning. Picked it up and opened it.

Her imagination went in about fifty different directions. Every single one of them bad.

But the police would handle it. Royal would handle it. He'd come over and handled it when she'd called. It was relief and comfort and some semblance of security all wrapped into one thing keeping her anchored rather than in a full-blown panic.

When he'd first shown up, he'd been wearing what he'd clearly slept it. Low-slung athletic shorts and not much else.

He didn't just have *a* tattoo on his arm, he had a *plethora* of tattoos over the upper half of his body. Black-and-white and full-blown color. All down both arms, and on parts of his chest and back. And he was *built*, which was a ridiculous thing to think about, but it felt safer than her imagination taking her down the road of: *someone is out to get you.*

"You have a lot of tattoos." What a truly ridiculous thing to say. "Sorry, I'm tired. I say weird things when I'm tired." Sure, that's what it was.

"I do have a lot of tattoos," he agreed, sounding so calm. But he hadn't been calm before. Not deep down. He had a... professional *restraint* she supposed, but she'd seen something in his expression back on her porch that if she put in a book, she'd describe as lethal.

She really didn't want anything to be lethal right now. Even concerning him.

"No tattoos for you, Franny?"

She shook her head, gripping her hands tighter. Trying not to think about *lethal things*, and knowing he was trying to keep her distracted. "No, I'm pretty straight and narrow and boring."

His mouth curved ever so slightly. "We're riding to the police station in the middle of the night in my cruiser. I don't think you're boring."

She laughed, though it bordered on hysteria. No this wasn't boring. It was terrible. But she was just overreacting. If she breathed, thought it through, this was just a bunch of odd coincidences.

It had to be.

"So, look, I can't help but speculate. Occupational hazard." Because she needed this to be her imagination and nothing else. "So please tell me I'm just a writer out of touch with reality. Because what it feels like is someone involved with the kidnapping figured out who I was, found or made that card, then left it on my porch in a threatening manner—during or after trying to break into my apartment." She looked over at Royal.

His gaze flicked to her then back to the road. He said nothing.

Which did *not* help the tightening anxiety in her chest. "Tell me that's far-fetched," she demanded, knowing she sounded a little panicked.

"Okay, it's far-fetched."

"Royal."

"Do you want the truth, or do you want me to say what you want to hear?"

"I want the truth, and I want the truth to be what I want to hear."

He pulled into the parking lot of the Bent County Sheriff's Department, parked the car and then looked at her.

"I know you're scared. You've every right to be." His tone was firm and reassuring. He knew what he was doing and everything was going to be okay.

She could almost believe it.

"That's why we're going to go into the station, talk to the sheriff, and maybe Detective Beckett, and decide what to do to make sure you're safe."

She squeezed her eyes shut, any calm she'd managed to grab onto evaporating. "Oh, no, don't call Copeland."

"Why not?"

"Because he'll tell Audra. Audra will tell Rosalie. And together they'll worry and fuss and *worry*."

"Okay, I'll tell him not to tell Audra."

Franny shook her head. "He won't be able to lie to Audra."

"All the cops I know are great at lying."

"Sure. But not to the fiancée they love. Hopefully."

His expression was dubious, but she didn't want to argue about this. She wanted… Oh, God, she didn't know.

"Come on." He got out of the car, and she had no choice but to follow. He led her into the station. It wasn't bustling exactly, but there were more people and more things going on than Franny might have expected for this time of night.

Phones ringing. People talking in low murmured voices.

Royal led her into a room that looked like some kind of break room. "Sit here. Help yourself to some coffee or water or whatever you can scrounge up in the fridge. I'm going to go handle the evidence and make those phone calls and I'll be right back, okay?"

She nodded, not knowing what else to do. This felt like an utter disaster. So she sat at the table. The room was cold, the chair was cold. Everything felt cold and...out of body.

But Royal crouched down in front of her. "Franny."

She stared at him. His face was becoming familiar, which was strange. She'd had coffee with him twice. Talked to him in the street once, well twice if she counted him responding to Albennie's kidnapping. No...three times. She'd seen him in passing the first day she'd moved in. Still, it wasn't enough to be comforted by someone's presence.

Except he was a serious, capable police officer. He'd helped her, multiple times. She was in good hands. Everything would be okay, because what other option was there?

Kidnapping. Gruesome murder. Etcetera.

"Franny," he said again, more sharply this time, like he understood her panic was driving the brain bus. "The important thing is, even if this was a threat, nothing happened. They didn't break in, if that's what they were after. You called me, just like you should have, and now we've got evidence and another step to take. But most importantly, Franny, you're safe."

She swallowed at the lump in her throat. It didn't go away. The fear didn't go away. But it steadied. Because if he could look her in the eye and tell her she was safe, she could almost believe it.

THE FIRST THING Royal did was scrounge up something to keep Franny warm. The AC in the building ran high in these hot days of summer even when the nights cooled off. She had to be freezing in her shorts and T-shirt. He hadn't been issued a jacket yet since it was summer, but Vicki at the front desk had an extra sweater and let him borrow it. He brought it to Franny and she thanked him, still looking lost and afraid.

But she didn't cry. She didn't demand to leave. She didn't break down. She just sat there, waiting.

It made him...uncomfortable in ways he didn't understand. Pretty much everyone he'd known before the age of twenty-one had been through ten times worse than a little kidnap witnessing and subsequent break-in attempt, so why should he feel sorry for her?

But he did.

Still, he focused on what had to be done. He called Copeland, got cussed out for the courtesy. Still, the detective was on his way. So was the sheriff. He got the card logged into evidence.

Royal didn't let himself worry about Franny. She was holding up. He knew looks could be deceiving, but she just seemed...soft. Not jaded or traumatized by life. And still, she was holding up.

He didn't know why he felt *proud* about that. Had nothing to do with him.

Once he'd done everything that needed to be done before anyone else arrived, he went back to the break room to find her. He assumed they'd move to the sheriff's office to discuss what had happened, but not until the sheriff got here.

She sat at one of the tables, chin resting on her hand. She was doing something on her phone, but every few seconds her eyes would droop, close, then she would blink them open and straighten.

She didn't look up. So he found himself just standing

there…studying her. The harsh lights made her hair look lighter, almost red, and her skin paler. Or maybe that was the exhaustion. She just seemed…delicate. Not *fragile*. She was dealing with some stuff and she didn't break, but there was just something…*something* about her he couldn't articulate to himself.

And probably shouldn't.

"Campbell."

Royal looked behind him to where his name had been called. Detective Beckett was striding up the hall. Behind him was a pretty woman that Royal knew was the detective's fiancée. Franny's cousin. Audra.

Royal straightened, glanced back at Franny. She must have heard his name too, because she was staring at him now. Did he know he'd been watching her?

He shook his head. Didn't matter. He pointed into the room. "She's in here," he told Beckett.

Franny stood as Copeland and Audra entered the room. Her expression fell.

"Oh, Copeland. I wish you wouldn't have brought her."

"I know," the detective replied.

"I'm taking you back to the ranch," Audra said, crossing to Franny, putting an arm around her shoulders like she was going to march her right out of there. "Right now."

"I'm afraid that's going to need to wait," Royal interrupted. "We've got a lot to figure out before Ms. Perkins can leave."

Audra scowled at him, but thankfully the sheriff arrived. "Beckett. Campbell. My office." He moved on without saying anything else.

Beckett moved over to his fiancée, put his hand on her back, the touch intimate. "Take her into the detectives' office. It's more private."

Weird, weird, weird to see people who only existed in the context of work just be...real people. But Audra nodded and pulled Franny up from her chair and before they could exit the room, Royal stepped out.

Beckett led the way to the sheriff's office. Royal knew he should just follow, but he couldn't resist a glimpse back at Franny and Audra heading the opposite direction. Their gazes met for about one second before Audra dragged Franny around the corner.

When Royal forced himself to move forward, Beckett was looking at him, but Royal ignored the study.

The sheriff was already sitting behind his desk when they entered his office. It was the middle of the night, so Royal didn't hesitate. He laid it all out for the sheriff.

The potential break-in. The catalogue card now in evidence. *And* how he considered it a purposeful threat against the eyewitness to the kidnapping.

"It doesn't seem like a coincidence we get word the Feds are pulling out this morning, and this happens tonight," Sheriff Buckley said, tapping his fingers on his desk.

"No, it doesn't," Royal agreed.

"We'll have the card processed, see if we can get some prints, but if it was left there on purpose as a threat, it'll be clean," Beckett said.

Royal agreed with that too. "I'll talk to Deputy Mayfield once I'm back in Hope Town. He didn't see anything specific, but maybe there was something of note earlier in the night. Or an idea of where they would have gone to avoid him. I *heard* a car. Maybe security picked something up. I'll contact Simmons in the morning too, see if we can't get a look at some video."

The sheriff nodded. "Good first steps. But before we can

do any of that, we have to deal with what we're going to do about our victim slash witness."

"She can't go back to that apartment if she's being threatened," Beckett said.

"But if she's being threatened, she can't just go *anywhere*," Royal returned. "She has to be protected."

Before the sheriff could weigh in, Zach Simmons strode into the office. He looked a little worse for wear. He had dark marks under his eyes and his hair was wild—probably from raking his fingers through it. He did not give off the same *I've got this* aura he always had before.

"What are you doing here, Simmons?" the sheriff asked irritably.

"I need to be part of the discussion about this attempted break-in."

"How'd you find out about it?" Beckett demanded. "It's the middle of the damned night."

Simmons shook his head. "Listen. This is more delicate than you guys understand."

"So, enlighten us," the sheriff replied. "Now."

Simmons looked around the room, surveying each of the men. "Okay, but it has to stay in this room. What I'm about to explain is private, privileged information and I am only sharing it to keep everyone involved as safe as possible. It cannot go out to the department at large, or people you all may know personally. You've all taken oaths to uphold the law to *help* victims—so I need you to understand that if what I tell you goes beyond this office, you are breaking that oath."

Royal had *felt* like there was something strange about Hope Town, but this was more than strange. Especially when Simmons waited for every man to verbally agree.

"Hope Town is…complicated," he said, raking a hand

through his hair. "And there are a lot of reasons I don't tell most people about that complicated background. That's the whole point of Hope Town. Not knowing."

He looked at each of them, as if taking time to make eye contact so they'd all understand the gravity of the situation.

"It's a place for…people who are in danger to go to live a normal, *safe* life."

"So WITSEC?"

"More like…private WITSEC, with a few more complications and a little less red tape." Simmons shrugged. "Not all of these women would qualify for a federal program, and not *everyone* in Hope Town needs protection, but there are a group of women who do, who have pasts. Ones that could catch up with them if I'm not careful. And I've been incredibly careful. I realize this attempted break-in is a concern. It is for me too, but it can't get out. It can't… These women need to know they're safe."

"But one of them wasn't," Beckett pointed out.

"No. Albennie wasn't. That's part of the problem. There was a leak somewhere. Maybe it was Albennie herself. But until I know for sure, I need to keep everyone in one place. Protected. But more, so I can get to the bottom of how who took her found out where she was. The Feds are aware of Albennie's past, and they're working from that angle, but so far, they haven't gotten anywhere."

"We're handling the attempted break-in, Simmons," the sheriff said firmly. "I trust my men better than any FBI agent. We'll share what we find, but it's our case."

"Look, I don't care who does what as long as we're all on the same page. I cannot afford for any of the women in Hope Town to think they're not safe—or even more *not safe* than they usually are. It leaves too many of them open for their pasts to come back and haunt them. This break-in attempt *has* to be kept on the down-low."

"What exactly are you asking us to do?"

"Investigate. By all means. I'm not standing in the way of that, but I need Ms. Perkins to stay put. Her leaving would worry too many of the women and have them contemplating the same."

"You can't be serious," Beckett said.

"If this kidnapping has made Ms. Perkins a target? We need to use her."

"Mr. Simmons, I don't know about all that," the sheriff said. "She's a civilian. Not one of these other women with pasts."

"Yes, that's the point. *Normal* life. Not just people like them, but regular people too. If Franny runs at the first sign of danger, how do I keep anyone else calm and staying put? We'll keep her safe. I have some ideas on that. Security measures, courtesy of my company. It would keep Franny where she is, but under constant surveillance so nothing happens to her. If Deputy Campbell stays where he's at, he can man the surveillance. Keep an eye out for Franny."

"And find whoever it is threatening her, thus leading you to Albennie," Royal supplied.

Simmons flicked a glance at him. "More or less."

"You're asking Franny to be your bait?" Beckett demanded. "Not gonna happen."

"Maybe that should be up to Ms. Perkins to decide," Simmons replied with a shrug.

Royal hated that he agreed with Simmons, but it wasn't his place to throw his weight behind anybody. He was essentially just the grunt worker in this situation.

"Simmons is right," the sheriff said. "I know you've got a personal connection, Beckett, but this is the best chance to find that missing woman. And we're not putting Ms. Perkins into any more danger than she stumbled into on her own. What do you think, Campbell?"

All eyes turned to him. Royal wasn't quite sure how he'd jumped into the deep end here, being the rookie and all, but he gave his honest opinion anyway. "I agree with Simmons and Sheriff. Her leaving doesn't do anything but move the target, and not necessarily to a safer place. If Ms. Perkins will agree to it, I think her staying put with new security measures in place is the best option for all of us."

Beckett swore. "Well, someone else is telling her cousins."

Chapter Eleven

Franny was sitting with Audra in the detectives' office when Rosalie stormed in. Duncan wasn't far behind her.

"You shouldn't have called her," Franny muttered. She wasn't sure how she felt about any of this, but Audra and Rosalie feeling the need to mother her grated. It was very near infantilizing.

She could handle this. She could handle being the target of a kidnapper and his creepy threats. Hadn't Audra and Rosalie handled their own dangerous escapades over the past year? Neither one of them was too keen on leaning on help. Why should she be?

"She would have found out in the morning and been furious at both of us for waiting," Audra said, giving Franny's hand a squeeze while Rosalie approached.

"All right. Let's go. I'm taking you back to our place. We've got state-of-the-art security and—"

"No extra beds?" Franny supplied. Because Duncan and Rosalie lived in a cute little cabin on the Kirk Ranch, but it wasn't complete with *guest room*.

"We'll buy one. Rush order. Come on, Franny."

But before she could respond to that in any way, Copeland came in. Followed by the sheriff and Royal.

Everyone, even Audra and Rosalie, looked at the sheriff, waiting for him to explain.

"Ms. Perkins, we've got a request for you. And I know you're surrounded by people who care about you and have concern for your safety, but ultimately the decision is up to you."

"Decision?"

"Mr. Simmons has requested you continue to stay in Hope Town until we have a better lead on the case."

Audra whirled on Copeland. "What is this?" she demanded. And the same time Rosalie said, "Have you taken a blow to the head?" to the *sheriff*.

But it was Royal who answered. "We'll be adding a lot of security options to keep her safe, but we think this is our best chance of stopping this."

"By using her as *bait*?" Audra demanded, still glaring at her fiancé.

Before Copeland could say anything, Rosalie interjected, "I'll stay with her. Personal security. Twenty-four-seven. That's the only way she stays put."

"Sweetheart," Duncan said quietly. "We couldn't even make the drive here without having to pull over so you could throw up."

"Oh, no, Rosalie. Are you sick?" Audra's ire turning to concern as she looked over at her sister. "You shouldn't have come."

Rosalie glared at her husband. "No, I'm not sick."

"Then why would you be... Oh. Oh. *Oh my God!*"

"Oh my *God*," Franny echoed as it dawned on her too.

"Oh my God what?" Copeland demanded irritably.

"She's pregnant," Audra said. Then her eyes filled, and she went and hugged her sister. Franny followed, wrapping her arms around the both of them.

"Oh my God, Rosalie. A *baby*." She rocked with her cousins, overjoyed. Teary herself. But that might be the exhaustion. But a *baby*. It was so sweet. So great. So exciting. So *happy* in the face of all this decidedly unhappy.

"And I would have preferred not to announce that in a damn police station in the middle of the night, so thanks, Ace," Rosalie said glaring at Duncan over Audra and Franny's heads.

"Hey, it's a story. You love those."

"Uh-huh." But she pulled away from the hug, her mouth twisting and the color draining out of her face. "Hell, give me a second." She dashed out from their grasp and then out of the room.

Duncan looked after her a little helplessly. He turned back to them, shrugged. "She's going to want to help, but she's not up to it. The doctor wants her on some anti-nausea medication and she's refusing. She's okay, but she needs to take some extra care of herself, and unfortunately involving herself in this isn't the way to do it."

"She doesn't need to. I'll handle it," Audra said. "I can—"

"You have a ranch to run," Franny told Audra firmly, sad that they had to swing from the happy news of a *baby* to…whatever this was. "Copeland's got work to do. You're busy people with real lives, and this isn't… I'm not saying it's not a concern, but if the sheriff's department is looking out for me, how much safer could I be?" She turned her gaze to Royal. He stood stiff and stoic. Even though he wasn't dressed in his uniform, didn't have that gun belt slung on his waist, he looked like he was holding himself as though he was wearing a uniform.

And he was the reason nothing bad had happened tonight, she was almost sure. If he could do that… "Royal was close enough to stop it before a break-in even happened *before* we knew I might be threatened. I'm even safer now that we know I have been, sort of. I can handle this, Audra."

Audra raised an eyebrow. "Royal, is it?"

Franny shook her head at Audra, not going down that line of questioning. Not right now. She turned her attention to the sheriff.

"Sheriff, I'll stay. I want to do whatever I can to help bring Albennie home."

The sheriff nodded. "You follow instructions, Ms. Perkins, we'll keep you safe. Deputy Campbell is in charge of this for the time being. You have any questions, he's your man. Now, if you'll excuse me."

Which left her in a room with her family. And Royal.

"I can give you guys some time to talk this over," Royal said, sounding very formal and professional. "When you're ready, Ms. Perkins, I'll take you back to your apartment. Mr. Simmons is already working on beefing up the security, but I can assure you all, we won't be leaving her on her own until it's all set up."

"Yes. She won't be on her own because she's going to be with us," Audra said firmly.

"Audra. Please." Franny didn't know how to argue with Audra. It went against all her people-pleasing tendencies. But this was…important. The police wanted her to stay, and she wanted to…help. Like she hadn't been able to help when she'd watched Albennie get dragged into that car.

"You cannot just…handle this on your own," Audra said. "It's insane the police are even asking you to. Don't be stubborn for the sake of being stubborn."

"Pot. Kettle."

All eyes turned to Copeland, who'd assuredly taken his own life into his hands with those words. But he didn't back down.

"It's true. The both of you know it," he said, pointing at Audra then Rosalie as she came back into the room. "You're two of the most hardheaded women I've ever known, and I deal with criminals for a living. At least your cousin has the sense to accept *help* without putting up a fuss. That's more than I can say for the two of you when threats come knocking."

Audra and Rosalie scowled at him, but they didn't mount arguments. Because there was no argument to be mounted.

"And Franny is right. Deputy Campbell is right across the street. With the security precautions Simmons is adding, there's no reason to believe Franny won't be safe. Safer there, with surveillance and a cop always on duty in Hope Town—twenty-four-seven—than at the ranch with just you and me. Or even at the Kirk Ranch. Isolated, far away from town."

The room was silent for a few humming minutes. Audra turned to Franny. "I don't like it."

Franny met her cousin's gaze. "I didn't ask you to."

Audra closed her eyes and shook her head, but that was how Franny knew she'd won.

Royal was choking down some dregs of coffee that had probably been made twelve hours before and had since kind of burned at the bottom of the pot. But it was the only thing keeping him awake at the moment.

Everything was taken care of on his end—Beckett would handle the evidence. Simmons was off getting the security arrangements ready. He couldn't ask the businesses for their security footage until actual morning.

So he was just standing around waiting for Franny to be done with her family so he could take her back to her apartment.

He understood her cousins' reservations. He understood their desire to save and protect.

Brooke had tried to protect him like that. He'd never appreciated it. He wondered why he couldn't accept it back then when he'd needed it most. Why now, when he didn't need anyone protecting him, he could look back and understand what she'd been doing and appreciate it.

Life was a hell of a ride.

He looked up from his coffee mug at the sound of footsteps. Franny stepped in, looking back over her shoulder with some concern.

He dumped the terrible coffee, rinsed out the mug. "Ready to go?"

She nodded. "I distracted Audra with baby talk and ran, so we might want to hurry."

He chuckled, led her back outside. There was the hint of a sunrise on the horizon as they got into his car. At first, they drove in silence.

He didn't really know what to say to her. He wanted to offer reassurances, but then wondered if that was too personal. And she wasn't sitting there airing her worries, so maybe she wasn't worried. Maybe she had it all under control.

He flicked a glance at the way her hands were gripped in her lap. Like all her stress was centered there.

Yeah, she didn't have it under control. She probably needed a good night's sleep and a decent meal. Then she'd have the reserves to deal. She *had* agreed to stay, and not everyone would be brave enough to do that.

Should he tell her she was brave? While he was trying to decide, she sighed.

"I love watching the sunrise here," she said as they drove toward the one bleeding out in front of them. "I rarely do it, because I also love morning sleep, but… It's different here, isn't it?"

He looked at the little sliver of sun peeking its way over the horizon, the colors in bright pinks and oranges slashing out across the sky. He glanced at her, because the sunrise looked the same to him no matter where he was. But he didn't want to argue. "Sure."

She *almost* chuckled. "Maybe you're just so used to it you don't know. Did you grow up here?"

Uncomfortable, Royal didn't allow himself to shift. He kept his gaze resolutely on the road. "No."

"Where'd you grow up?"

"Why are you interrogating me all of a sudden?"

"I'm not trying to interrogate you. I'm trying to stay awake." She blew out a breath. "And not think about how on edge I'm going to be in my apartment knowing someone tried to break in."

"So why'd you agree to this?"

She turned that gaze on him, and he *refused* to meet it. Not because he was a coward, but because he was *driving*. Obviously.

But she repeated the question. "Where'd you grow up, Royal?" she demanded this time.

He sighed. He didn't want to talk about *growing up,* but if she was going to be stubborn about it… "South Dakota."

"Ooh, the Mount Rushmore state."

"Never been."

She leaned forward, staring at him. "You grew up in South Dakota and never went to Mount Rushmore?"

You don't tend to go to tourist sights when you spend most of your childhood in a dangerous biker gang. It was on the tip of his tongue to say it. Not just to shock her, but because he was curious how she'd react.

But not *that* curious. "There weren't a lot of family vacations when I was growing up." Unless moving from outskirt nomad campsite to outskirt nomad campsite counted. Unless the one nice foster family he'd been with taking him to their biological kid's baseball game in Brookings counted. Which hadn't been half bad, compared to all the other stuff in his life.

But it wasn't Mount Rushmore.

"Well, next time you go home to visit you'll have to rectify that," Franny said, as if he had a home to go visit. "It's great. We went when I was like…twelve, I think. I loved it. Of course, I was a little history nerd."

"Yeah, well, I've got no plans to return." Maybe his father was in jail, for good this time. Maybe the Sons were dead and buried. But there was nothing for Royal back in South Dakota except bad memories.

He could feel her studying him. He could practically hear gears in her head turning, deciding what question to ask next. If she wasn't such an odd little thing, she'd probably make a good detective.

But he didn't want to be studied, asked or figured out. So he went on the offensive.

"Why'd you agree to this, Franny?"

She looked hard at the road in front of them, or maybe that sunrise she thought was so different in Wyoming. "I watched Albennie get shoved into that car. I watched and I didn't do anything." She didn't say it with a hitch to her voice. She was very firm, very matter-of-fact. "Now it's been days, and nothing I *did* do has helped find her or bring her home. So, if I can do something, even if it's scary or a bit dangerous, I'm going to do it."

He understood, better than most people, what it felt like to witness terrible things, and to have no recourse. He'd spent a lot of time blaming himself pretty hard for that, but Franny shouldn't. She was just…a good person. A *normal* person. Not like him. "What could you have done?" he asked gently, because he wanted her to really think about that.

Sometimes bad things happened, and no matter what you *wanted*, there was no way to fix that.

"I don't know," she said, leaning back in her seat. "Maybe nothing. But now I *can* do something. So I'm going to do it."

Despite her clasped hands, the exhaustion written plain on her face, she said that with conviction.

"And I'm going to keep you safe while you do," he promised.

Because *this* was why he'd let Brooke talk him into the police academy. *Protecting* was why he was here.

He wasn't about to fail at that.

Chapter Twelve

Franny felt like she was in a movie. Mr. Simmons and his partner, a man he'd introduced as Cam Delaney, were doing all sorts of things to her apartment that felt more suited for a spy.

They'd already done most of it by the time Royal walked her up to her apartment, and Mr. Simmons gave her the rundown while Mr. Delaney finished up.

"As you know, there was already a security system in place, but we beefed it up. Now, do you know what the first step to any security system being successful is?" Mr. Simmons asked her.

She blinked at him—not sure if it was ignorance or exhaustion that made her mind completely blank.

"Turning it on," he finished—some censure in his tone, but it wasn't unkind.

"I do! Before I go to bed." When he raised an eyebrow, she wrinkled her nose. "I just hadn't gone to bed yet last night."

"Now you turn it on at all times, even if you're inside and awake. We've made the doorbell camera more sensitive, and we're going to connect it not just to your phone but to Deputy Campbell's as well. On top of that, we've added another camera—this one hidden—that encompasses the entire doorway and stairway. All video will be available to Deputy Campbell and the sheriff—in real time, and as video later on. Should they decide they want to add anyone else who can access that, that'll be up to them, but they'll have to disclose that information to you."

Right. Cameras. Security. All for her safety.

"You've got a camera set up in this living area," Mr. Simmons continued, pointing to a little square on the top of her bookshelf that she barely noticed. "It will pick up sound. Obviously for privacy we've left any equipment out of the bedroom and bathroom, but we've added cameras on the outside of the building at each window point, and more sensitivity to the window alarms. I went ahead and bolted the bathroom window shut, as that seemed the best security option there. All alarms will be connected to the deputy's phone, so that he can respond as needed. Deputy, I'll need your phone to program that real quick."

"Sure," Royal said, fishing the phone out of his pocket and handing it over to Mr. Simmons.

Cameras. In her house. It was for her safety, but the idea of Royal and the sheriff being able to watch her, like, cook *dinner* was not exactly one she relished. Still, she had to admit it would give her a certain level of reassurance no one was trying to get in her door—and if they *were*, someone would stop them before it happened.

"It's a lot, and it's going to feel awkward. I don't think anyone expects this to be easy or feel normal," Mr. Simmons said, frowning at Royal's phone as his fingers moved across the screen.

"If it might help catch whoever has Albennie or took her, then I don't care how it feels," Franny replied, happy she sounded surer of that than she was.

Mr. Simmons smiled warmly as he handed Royal his phone back. "Good. Now there is one more thing. This one is optional. Up to you and Deputy Campbell here." He pulled out two cases. They looked like earbud cases.

"These are a bit like a walkie-talkie, in layman's terms. Let's say Ms. Perkins heads down to the bakery while Deputy Campbell is driving out to the Temperance Ranch for a disturbance call. You both have one of these in your ears, and you can talk to each other—and only each other—without anyone having to know that's what you're doing. They're small. They're wired to only each other. How and when you'd want to use them are up to you, but it'd give you a direct line to each other if you need that."

He handed them out and Royal and Franny had no choice but to each take one.

"I'm going to go do one last sight check on the outside cameras. Call if you need anything, including tech support. Franny? You set that system once Deputy Campbell leaves."

Franny nodded, looking at the little case in her hands. It was like being a spy, except all of her privacy was being invaded. She couldn't—wouldn't—complain about that. She knew what she was doing it for.

She looked over at Royal sheepishly. "I guess we're about to be ear buddies." *Ear buddies. Oh my God, Franny Perkins, what is* wrong *with you?*

Royal smiled—which was really very kind of him considering how ridiculous she sounded. "I'm glad it's an option. I want you wearing them anytime you leave the apartment. Just text me your schedule."

Franny nodded. "Right. Sure." Maybe she'd just never leave the apartment again.

"I've got to get going. I'm going to be late for my shift."

She trailed after him to the door. "But you didn't sleep."

"I got a few hours before you called me. It's okay. Part of the job."

"Royal..." She didn't know what to say. *Thank you* seemed so lame. *I'm terrified* was definitely not his problem.

Royal gestured down to where Mr. Simmons stood with Mr. Delaney, discussing something underneath her back window. "Did you know he's married to Daisy Delaney?" Royal asked.

Franny blinked at the odd segue, but then she nodded. "My friend Vi? Her husband is friends with Mr. Simmons, so she *met* her."

"So did I. She was in my apartment. Foisted a baby off on Simmons while he was getting me set up." Royal shook his head. "Hell of a thing."

"I desperately want to ask her a million questions for a million book ideas, but that feels pretty... I don't know. Crass." And it was nice, to end this strange interlude on something that wasn't threats and fear.

She supposed that's why he'd brought it up.

"Crass," he repeated. Then shook his head. "I've got to go. You should get some sleep. I'll come back tonight after my shift, and we'll talk about how...all this works."

She nodded. "Yeah. That sounds good."

"You're worried about something, you call me. You need to leave after you've gotten some rest, text me. We'll try these out." He held up the earbud case.

"Got it."

"And remember to—"

"Set the security. I know, I know." She tried to smile at him. "I appreciate...all of this."

"You appreciate having your life upended by witnessing a crime?"

She laughed in spite of herself. "No. Not even a little. But I do appreciate what everyone is trying to do to bring Albennie home and keep me safe in the midst of it."

ROYAL JOGGED DOWN the stairs, hoping he'd be able to catch Simmons before he left. There were things he wanted to discuss without Franny hearing.

Not that she didn't deserve to know everything, but he needed to make sure his suspicions were on the right track, and he wanted to get a better sense of Zach Simmons.

That story back in the sheriff's office, about women who came here to hide from pasts, it made sense. Hell, he knew firsthand just how complicated pasts could be. Simmons's information explained the predominance of women, the businesses leased to *only* women. It explained a lot.

And if it was true, Royal couldn't help but respect it. It was a hell of an idea. He could have used it for a few of the girls stuck in the Sons' life.

But it also led them to where they were now, which was putting Franny in danger all because she'd *seen* something. Because he'd leased her an apartment to add "normal" people to the town.

It wasn't right.

Simmons was at the back of the building now. His partner was nowhere to be seen. Which was good. Royal wanted to keep as many things on the down-low as possible.

"Simmons, I need to talk to you."

"Sure. Have at."

"This break-in, this threat. Is it my imagination, or is the timing suspicious?"

"Suspicious how?" Simmons asked, poking at something on his phone then looking up at the roof of the building. Presumably checking different security checkpoints.

"Somebody shows up at Franny's door *after* the car she IDed is found in Idaho. The Feds, allegedly, pull out of Wyoming to focus on Idaho."

"Likely the kidnapper ditched the car in Idaho, then doubled back here to make his threat."

"Likely, yeah. But only if that meant they'd dropped Albennie Ward off with someone." He didn't come out and say *if she was still alive*. Royal figured her being dead was just as possible, but he also knew that sometimes kidnapping people for information or ransom was a more complicated endeavor.

He assumed whatever past Albennie Ward had leaned more to that than quick, easy murder. Otherwise someone would have taken her out here.

"What's your point, Deputy?"

"My point is, this only makes sense if the guy who kidnapped Albennie was for hire. He drops off the kidnapping victim, ditches the car, but he knows he's got a loose end. The woman who saw him. I'm worried even when we get him, he'll have no connection to the real brain behind this, and we'll be exactly where we are right now, except Franny will be safer."

Simmons was quiet for a long humming moment. "I don't love that theory, deputy, I've got to say."

"Then what's yours?"

"Runs similar to yours at first. Yeah, I'd wager a bet he's a kidnapper for hire. He drops Albennie off with whoever actually wanted her. There's no on-paper connection." Simmons shrugged like that was obvious. "But when we catch him? There's no honor amongst thieves, Campbell. None that I've seen. He'll talk, and it'll lead us to whoever really has Albennie."

"If you have the right kind of ringleader, loyalty is a hell of a drug. It's not honor amongst thieves, it's…belief." He thought of the way his father had worshipped Ace Wyatt, leader of the Sons. Like the man was God himself. His dad would have done *anything* for Ace. Kept any secret, weathered any punishment, because he'd believed that someday, somewhere, there'd be something in it for him.

"You know what else is a hell of a drug?" Simmons asked. "Threat of the death penalty."

"For kidnapping?"

Simmons sighed, shoving his phone into his pocket. "That's where things are…tricky." He started walking to his car, so Royal fell into step next to him.

"The Feds know who did this, don't they?"

"Know? No. Have some ideas? Yeah, that's my take, but as many friends as I have, as many strings as I can pull, I'm not FBI any longer. I don't have access to everything they know. I can only wager some guesses based on how things have gone, based on what little information I was given when Albennie came here."

"So, when are they going to come back?"

"They're not."

"What?"

"They don't know about the break-in. If I can help it, they won't."

"Why the hell not?" Royal demanded. He wasn't too thrilled with the Feds keeping things from local police, but he happened to feel like right now the more law enforcement agencies were working on this, the better.

"Because I'm starting to worry that Albennie's location was leaked somewhere on their side of things. It shouldn't have been possible for anyone from her past to find her. So unless she gave herself away, which I just can't fathom, it's there. Somewhere in there."

"Then why'd you involve them in the first place?"

Simmons just spared him a look.

"It's complicated. Right," Royal muttered. But it made

him remember the strange woman he'd assumed was a Fed. "Did you know all the agents who were here after the kidnapping?"

"Not all of them personally."

"But you know. Who should be here. Who shouldn't."

Simmons narrowed his eyes. "Sure. Or I could find out. Why?"

"What about a brunette, brown eyes, mid-thirties. Five-six, a buck twenty, maybe more. She had some muscle on her. A tiny trio of moles on her chin, and I *think* a birthmark, faint, on the back of her neck."

"That doesn't describe anyone I can think of off the top of my head, but I can poke into it deeper."

"I've got footage of her on my body cam."

"If you send me that or a still of the woman, I'll look into it. But you'd have to trust me to do that."

Royal wondered why he did. What had changed. He supposed everything this man had said in the sheriff's office this morning. And how he'd handled Franny's security now. "All that stuff up there, you claim only the sheriff and I have access to it."

"I don't just claim. It's true. Professional guarantee. Not saying I don't have the skills to hack into anything if I had a mind to, but CD Corp is on the up and up. You could hire an unbiased third party to make sure of it, but it'd take time and I sure as hell hope this is done soon."

"Yeah, me too."

"Look, Deputy, I get the suspicion. Respect it even. Law enforcement requires a certain level of it. I know that from experience. But my entire goal is to bring Albennie Ward back home without anyone getting hurt."

Royal's gaze tracked up to Franny's apartment. "Yeah, mine too. I'll send you that picture."

Chapter Thirteen

Franny did sleep. It wasn't a great, restful sleep but it was sleep nonetheless. She couldn't seem to drag herself out of bed until late afternoon—half dozing and half worrying the day away. Then she tried to read, to write, to watch a movie on her computer, but her mind kept wandering to the cameras surveilling her apartment.

Eventually, her stomach demanded sustenance, cameras be damned. It was nearly seven by the time she felt presentable enough to be *constantly video monitored* and shuffled out into the living area.

She needed to make herself a decent dinner, not just do what she wanted to do and eat chips and maybe a block of cheese. She opened her pantry and then refrigerator, surveying the contents.

"Spaghetti it is," she said out loud, then nearly groaned remembering she was on *surveillance* and anyone who watched or listened would in fact *observe* her talking to herself. *Fantastic*.

Irritated and jumpy, she set about making dinner. She wanted to turn some music on, or the TV, anything to drown out the sound of her own thoughts screaming: *you are being recorded*, but what if someone came up the stairs? What if another threat came?

What if, God forbid, she started *dancing and singing along* to something?

And even if she didn't need to be listening for a threat or constantly monitoring her own behavior, Royal would be coming whenever his shift was done. Which should be soon, shouldn't it? Maybe she should make enough spaghetti for him.

She stared at the boiling water, debating her choices. She stopped herself from saying *to hell with it* out loud and dumped the entire contents of the box in the water. If she had enough leftover spaghetti for a week, so be it.

The *least* she could do was offer him some food when he came by. So she focused on putting together a decent dinner. Made some garlic toast with what pieces of bread she had left. Her only vegetable option was a can of green beans that didn't exactly go with the rest, but hey, it was green.

She was just straining the pasta when her text notification went off. She glanced at the screen. From Royal.

On my way up.

She looked at the text, then at the door. There was no reason to be nervous. Or feel weird. She was going to eat dinner. He could join if he wanted while they discussed strategy, or he could watch her eat while they did.

Either way, this was her life now. She crossed to the door, disengaged the alarm, then opened it.

He'd changed into a T-shirt and shorts. His hair was damp like he'd run through the shower before he'd come over. He stepped inside and closed the door behind him, then he gestured toward the door, a nonverbal *set the alarm again*.

She did, even though it felt a bit like being in *jail*, but that was the price to pay for safety and she was determined to be reasonable about that.

"I was just finishing up making dinner. Spaghetti. If you're hungry, you can…have some. There's plenty."

"Oh—" He glanced at the kitchen, and she couldn't quite read the expression on his face, but she was worried it was discomfort. Like he felt *bad* for her and would *pity* accept.

"But you don't have to. Just extra, if you want. If you're hungry. I'm going to eat, because I'm hungry." Jeez, she was a mess.

"Well, sure. I…haven't eaten yet."

"Great," she replied, no doubt sounding *far* too cheerful. She walked back to the kitchen, finished up preparations then handed him a plate. "Help yourself. What would you like to drink? I've got water. A variety of zero-calorie pops. And milk that expired three days ago."

He chuckled a little at that. "Water's fine."

It was very awkward to share the tiny kitchen space with someone so…big. He smelled like soap and she was having a hard time not cataloguing all the tattoos on his arm when what she needed to do was get him a glass of water and get her own dinner sorted.

Once that was finally done, they took a seat at the little dining table that had come with the apartment or she wouldn't have bothered with. She preferred to eat on the couch. Or in bed.

Now she sat across from Royal eating very basic spaghetti and canned green beans at her kitchen table.

"So, I'm on duty seven to seven here in Hope Town. Deputy Mayfield handles the night shift." He covered his spaghetti in an alarming amount of the parmesan she'd put on the table. "Simmons has all the alarms connected into my phone, so anything that happens should wake me up even overnight. Plus, I've got my phone set so a call or text from you goes through no matter what."

"What about days off?"

"Usually it'd be weekends, but Sheriff and I thought it'd be best to just work through this. Ideally, we get to the bottom of things before I work too many days in a row. What about your schedule?"

She was stuck for a moment, not sure if she was supposed to insist he take days off or if she should just accept that he and the sheriff were doing the right thing. It's not like this was *for* her exactly. It was to find Albennie.

"Well, I usually like to go down to the bakery for my afternoon coffee and baked good, but I certainly don't have to anymore. At some point this week I probably need to go to the grocery store. But I can really just…hermit down with the best of them."

His mouth curved into an almost…half smile. It was kind but not patronizing. Kind of like she *amused* him, in a good way.

She didn't know what the hell to do with that. So she ate her dinner and they worked out how they'd handle surveillance monitoring. When he'd be watching, when they should wear the earbuds.

It wasn't that complicated, all in all. *Weird?* Yes. Complicated? No. But they were both still eating once they'd determined the logistics and an uncomfortable kind of lull fell over the table.

Franny didn't know why it was uncomfortable, or why she couldn't seem to think of anything to say except to interrogate him about his life because she was desperately curious.

Was he curious at all about her? *No, because you are not that interesting.* But she had invited him to dinner, and he was *protecting her*, so it was probably her job to keep conversation going.

Or you just want to know about him. "So you grew up in South Dakota. Your sister is a forensic anthropologist and you're a cop. Law enforcement run in the family?"

He laughed, not an amused laugh but a full-on maybe even a little caustic laugh. "No. Not at all."

She knew a red light when she saw one. Curiosity was a hard thing for her to tamp down, but she did when she knew the questions weren't wanted, wouldn't be welcomed. She was uncomfortable enough in her own skin half the time, she hated to make anyone else feel uncomfortable.

But just because she knew she couldn't ask all the questions she wanted to didn't mean she knew what to say. So another awkward silence descended.

"Why do you have so many questions about me, Franny?" Royal asked her.

For a moment she just met his gaze, her heart fluttering around in her chest. The truth was, she always had questions about people, but she didn't always *voice* those questions. Not everyone interested her.

He did. For a lot of reasons. But she wasn't going to tell him *that*.

"People are interesting," she said, trying to sound casual. "People are kind of my job. Writing stories is just…discovering how people tick. I guess sometimes that just slips out into trying to be a normal human being making conversation. And if you haven't gathered, normal isn't one of my top qualities."

His mouth curved, ever so slightly. But his blue eyes were very serious. "So, if Brooke and I were characters in your book, what would make us tick?"

She could play this a couple different ways. It was a challenge of sorts, she could recognize that, though she didn't know what he was hoping to gain from the challenge. So she just told him the truth.

"Well, based on the way you laughed at me asking if your family was in law enforcement, and the fact that you were quite adamant you'd never want to go back to South Dakota, my fictionalized version of that childhood—which is usually what makes people tick—would be…raised by criminals, saw awful things, so grew up wanting to protect people. Because you weren't protected when you were vulnerable."

He studied her for a long time. Long enough she had to look away or she'd start blushing. Or start staring *very* hard at the tattoo on his right bicep that peeked out under his T-shirt sleeve.

It looked like the bottom half of a heart, and she desperately wanted to know if it had something inside like: *Mom* or a woman's name.

What kind of woman would prompt Royal to get her name tattooed on his arm?

When he finally spoke, it was with a kind of gravity that had her looking back up.

"Maybe your fictions aren't far off." He downed a gulp of water like it was hard liquor that might take the sting away. He set the glass down, fixed her with that intense stare of his. "You ever heard of the Sons of the Badlands?"

She blinked once, swallowed, feeling unaccountably nervous and not really sure why. Except, she supposed, nothing about the Sons of the Badlands was *good* conversation. "The biker gang cult group?"

"Yeah. What do you know about them?"

"Well, uh, my second book, the reason I first came to live with Audra and Rosalie in fact, was because I was researching cults to base my fictional one on. I mainly focused on the Order of Truth. That old cult from the seventies that lived out near Sunrise? I was interested in the religious fanaticism and the isolated location, but I wanted something more criminal, so I fell down a little Sons of the Badlands research rabbit hole. For the story, I liked their whole nomad thing, and their broader scope. Much more menacing. Combining the two created a nice fictional hybrid that suited my purposes."

She wasn't surprised he was staring at her a bit like she'd grown a second head. Because she was yammering on about what she liked about *cults* for God's sake. "Fictional purposes, obviously," she tacked on lamely. "That stuff is all interesting to me for my…fictional world." She shut her mouth, because how bizarre must that sound to someone who didn't write?

But Royal didn't look confused or horrified. He still looked very, very serious. "Brooke and I were born into the Sons."

He just…said that. Like it was a normal thing to tell someone. *I was born into a notorious, murderous biker gang.*

"Oh," was all she could think of to say.

"Brooke managed to get us out when I was pretty young, but we got separated and the foster families I was tossed around to weren't much better. So I went back."

Franny nodded along like this was a normal conversation she knew how to deal with. Her with her privileged upper class, only child upbringing.

He studied her, like he was keeping track of every last reaction she had to this information.

"You've got eight million questions, but you won't ask them," he said. "Why? Because it's *crass*?"

She shifted in her chair. That was the word she'd used when they'd discussed Daisy Delaney. It wasn't the only word that applied here, and she wasn't sure what he wanted from her. She wasn't sure what was the right way to deal with this. Maybe just…try to keep it simple.

"Yeah, it is. I like to research. I use a lot of real-life stuff in my books. I follow a lot of…stories and things that interest me because people interest me. But I'm not going to make you uncomfortable to get some questions answered for a book I might write someday. That's not nice or right, and I like to be both. If I can."

She didn't have to tell him she was already thinking about how she could fit it into her current book. Giving her federal agent hero *or* her cop heroine a background of having actually grown up in a cult, or at least something dangerous, had about a million new ideas springing to life.

Maybe that sowed a lot of distrust when they had to work together—the fed didn't trust a cop from such a background? Maybe they both came from horrible backgrounds and bonded over it?

But she wasn't going to let her mind go down that road right now.

He shook his head. "You're just about the strangest woman I ever met."

She felt a little stung and knew that was stupid. But it didn't stop the words from falling out of her mouth. "You are not the first person to say that to me, but I'm not going to lie it's far more insulting coming from a cop that grew up in a biker gang."

Then he laughed. Really laughed. Not caustic or bitter or anything. "Hell, Franny." He shook his head. "I'm not trying to insult you. You're interesting. *I* don't find people very interesting as a whole. I tend to want to know as little about everyone as possible, because more often than not, people suck."

She thought about that. He hadn't really asked any questions about her. Maybe he was right and he didn't have any—considering she had approximately eight million for him.

But…not being interested in people, believing they all sucked, didn't add up. "You wouldn't have gone into helping people if that were totally true."

He looked down at his plate, a puzzled kind of expression on his face. Then he got to his feet. "I should get going. Thanks for dinner. Can I help you clean up?"

Franny shook her head. "No, don't worry about it."

Still he collected his dishes and took them to the sink. For a moment, she just sat there, then she finally pushed herself into a standing position.

Obviously, he'd done what he'd come for. He wasn't just going to hang around all night. He had his own place, and he was probably exhausted since he'd had to work twelve hours today. Not just lie in bed all day like she had.

"I really appreciate not having to make myself a meal for once," he said as he moved for the door.

Right. He really was kind, but it was clear he wanted to head for the hills, and who could blame him?

But he didn't stride right out. He turned and gave her a kind smile. "And the company's not bad."

"Except for the poking into your tragic past, I would assume."

"Pretty sure I gave that up of my own free will. It's not something I just go around telling everyone." He studied her in that intense way of his. She wondered if he did that to criminals or if she was special.

You are not special in this scenario, Franny. A step above criminal maybe, but not special.

"So what's your childhood story? You didn't grow up here."

"No. Washington state. My dad is an engineer. My mother is a math teacher. Aside from being a dreamy, head-in-the-clouds artistic type, which made and makes no sense to my parents at all, I had a very easy, lovely upbringing. Probably even spoiled thanks to my health issues."

He frowned. "Health issues?"

She waved it away. "Oh, it's all sorted now. Just some allergies and asthma. It just took a while to figure out, so I had a few hospital stays when I was very little to freak my parents out. Kinda stuck with all of us. Trauma for them, trauma-lite for me."

"Trauma-lite," he echoed.

"Should we call yours extra-mega trauma?"

He laughed again, the nice one not the harsh one. "Yeah. At the very least. But I guess it makes sense then. I'd rather be a sick head-in-the-clouds dreamer than a sick realist."

It was…shockingly astute. She had used books and fiction and her own little stories to take her mind off her allergy issues growing up.

"And I'd rather be just about anything other than a math teacher," he added.

It made her laugh, because *same*, but then he moved for the door again. He was leaving, and of course he *should*. He needed to. But…

The thought of being there alone with her thoughts and security camera and…everything, it caused a little spiral of panic to move through her.

He reached for the door, and she just couldn't bear the thought.

"What about dessert?" she asked, desperately she could admit. To herself anyway.

But Royal studied her like he fully understood. "You know, if you're afraid to be alone, you can tell me that. You've every right to be afraid."

"Says the guy who escaped from a biker gang and became a cop."

"Am I going to regret telling you that?"

"Probably." What was the point in pretending? "Why did you?"

"I don't know. I don't know why I do a lot of things when it comes to you." He said it with a smile, but his eyes were serious. They were always serious. And he did tend to look at her…

She didn't have words for it, and she had words for everything. There was just this…weight to it. Like he looked at her and *saw* her.

Surely she…was just imagining things.

"Night, Franny."

She should say good night. He wanted to leave, needed to leave, and she had no right to keep him there.

But…

"Okay, I admit it. I'm afraid. I don't want to be alone in here. It freaks me out. Not just some guy out there wanting to threaten me or worse, but being in here with cameras so you can hear my every talking-to-myself moment if you want to."

"You talk to yourself?"

"I could make cookies," she said, totally desperate now. "And you could just stay a little longer. Just… Please, I know it's silly and intrusive and a million other things you didn't sign up for, but…"

"Sure." He took his hand off the knob. "I like cookies."

Relief swelled through her like a tide, and since she desperately wanted this to be okay, to not be ruining his life, she walked over to the couch, grabbed the remote and handed it to him. "You can watch TV if you want. I've got the streaming services in the first row, and then if you scroll a little bit, I've got a baseball subscription. There should be a few games on tonight."

He took the remote but looked at her dubiously. "*You* like baseball?"

"Why do you say it like that?"

"Because you just don't seem like the type. You told me yourself you're head-in-the-clouds artistic."

"Sure, but sports are stories, Royal. And baseball is stories *and* history. Baseball has marked the *time*."

"Did you just quote *Field of Dreams*?"

"Obviously. Besides, I don't know if you noticed, my cousin-in-law is Duncan Kirk."

"I noticed."

She grinned. "I've got his rookie card. Signed now—though I didn't ask until the wedding was over so as not to be *crass*."

"Well, as long as you weren't that." He narrowed his eyes. "You've got a baseball card collection?"

"Yes. At the ranch. I didn't have room to store it here." Which kept her from talking about all the other collections she had: unicorn figurines, antique toasters, her late grandmother's gigantic salt and pepper shaker collection.

"Well, you're going to have to show it off sometime."

She really wished her heart would stop doing this *fluttering* thing. "Sure. Yeah. I… I better get started on those cookies. It shouldn't take more than fifteen," she said, turning back to the kitchen, hoping she had all the ingredients necessary. She *knew* she had chocolate chips and butter—she always had chocolate chips and butter.

She scrounged enough of everything together to create a kind of half batch. It was funny how much more relaxed she was with him there.

They were still being filmed. It didn't change anything whether he was here or across the street watching, but it *felt* different. It felt safe. But once he ate some cookies she was going to have to let him go and that filled her with such dread.

Be a grown-up, Franny, she scolded herself as she pulled the cookies out of the oven. She piled them up on a plate.

"Here we…" She trailed off. He sat on her couch, head slightly bowed, though his arms were crossed over his chest. His breathing was steady and even and his eyes were closed.

She stared at him there, sleeping soundly in an upright position on her couch. Poor guy was working overtime just to keep her safe. She knew it was his *job*, but it still felt like he was going a little above and beyond.

She knew that wasn't about *her* personally, but that didn't mean she couldn't have gratitude. Surely not every police officer who would have been assigned to this job would be quite so…kind about it.

She should probably wake him up, but she couldn't bring herself to do it when he seemed so deep in it. She'd just… let him sleep.

Selfish, Franny.

Maybe, but it made her feel better knowing he was there.

So she got some blankets, a pillow, and wrote a little note. Then she turned off the TV and left him there sleeping and went to bed herself.

With the cookies, of course.

ROYAL WOKE IN the dark, a sharp pain his neck, and a bunch of old, ugly memories prickling at the edges of his brain.

Had he really told Franny all that about himself? What the hell had possessed him?

Well, that was easy if uncomfortable. Sympathetic green eyes and that careful way she held herself. It reminded him of someone who'd been beaten—always waiting for the next blow. He didn't think that was her issue. She probably would have mentioned it and not called her "health issues" trauma-lite. But there was something there. A vulnerability she wasn't any good at shoring up.

He should not like her for that alone. You had to be tough to get through life, and she was just…soft.

And sweet.

He blew out a breath, stretching his neck to one side and then the other, before doing a full neck roll.

He didn't have a clue how his life had twisted and turned to wind up here. It felt even more unimaginable when he said things like *born into the Sons* and she said things like *engineer dad and math teacher mom.*

Upper middle class for God's sake.

They didn't have a thing in common, and yet he found her endlessly fascinating. She was just…unique, and there was something about her curiosity, her bravery in the face of all this that life had in no way prepared her for, and the open vulnerability that drew those protective instincts he'd honed somewhere along the way.

You either wanted to protect or you wanted to be the monster. Those were the only two options in the life he'd been born into. He didn't consider himself that great of a guy, but he'd never had any interest in being the monster. He supposed that was the only thing that had led him *here*.

That and Brooke. He'd learned to forgive his sister—and it wasn't as though she'd done anything to him that she needed his forgiveness for. It was just he'd gotten through his adolescence and some of his young adulthood by blaming her, by thinking she'd had it better somehow. The grudge had been a crutch.

And it had taken some work to get over it, just like it had taken some work to accept all the people ready and willing to help him build a real life outside of everything that had happened to him and everything he'd done.

He knew those people were *willing* because of Brooke, but getting to know his sister as an adult these past two years had made him fully understand why anyone and everyone rallied around Brooke.

She was a good, kind person. It was at the very core of who she was. No time in the Sons or in a crappy foster home had dulled that.

He wasn't sure he'd ever had it to be dulled.

Franny had it. It was the only explanation for him telling her about the Sons.

He'd *seen* the questions building up inside her, but she hadn't voiced a one. She would, he thought. In the next few days, she wouldn't be able to resist. He could have offered more, explained it deeper.

He'd wanted her to see only the surface of it. A stop sign.

Because it felt a bit like they were on a strange precipice. Neither quite sure what to do with each other. Both a little too…attracted.

Polar opposites. Maybe it made sense. Not that he should *let* it make sense. He should be erecting very clear boundaries to a very complicated and odd situation.

Instead, he had…fallen asleep on her couch. The lights were out but the glow from the microwave clock allowed him to make out the shadows of furniture. He could smell cookies, but the scent was faint.

Hell, how long had he been out? He pulled his phone out of his pocket. Four. He'd slept for like…at least six hours. He shook his head and clicked on the phone flashlight. On the coffee table in front of him were a stack of blankets and a pillow with a little piece of paper on top.

He picked up the note, read it in the light of his phone.

Royal,
I thought it best to let you sleep. Text me when you need to leave, and I'll get up to set the security system. Otherwise, I set my alarm for six and I'll wake you up so you can get to your shift. Feel free to use whatever you need. Bathroom is in the hall.
—Franny

Like he wouldn't have known who'd written the note. Which made him smile, but not as much as the little PS at the end.

I'm sorry, but I ate all the cookies.

It was four in the morning. It'd be silly to wake her up now to set her security system. He might as well just try to get another hour or two of sleep on the couch.

He grabbed the pillow and tossed it behind him. He didn't bother with the blanket. Even though he could hear the air-conditioning working, it was hot up here.

He lay back and stretched out. He was usually a little too big for a couch, but this was a good size. Cushy. They pillow smelled fresh and clean, kind of like her. He looked up at the dark ceiling.

What the hell was he doing? Getting in way too deep, that was for sure.

Which was just impetus to see this through. Get it done. Once Albennie Ward was found and it was certain Franny was out of danger, they'd go back to passing each other on the street or bumping into each other at the bakery every *once* in a while.

Things wouldn't feel quite so...tenuous then. He was sure of it.

Almost.

Chapter Fourteen

Franny woke up to her alarm and groaned. She turned it off immediately wondering whose bright idea it was to set it for six in the damn—

She sat bolt right up in bed. If her alarm was going off, Royal had...slept on her couch. Had he woken up at some point and decided to stay? Or had he slept in that horrible upright position?

Was she going to have to wake him up? She couldn't let him be late for work. Not after he'd been so kind as to *stay*.

God, she'd slept so much better knowing he was there. Did that make her pathetic? Well, she was alive and not kidnapped so maybe she didn't care if she was a little pathetic.

What she did care about was having to go out there and wake him up. That was just...awkward.

But she could hardly let him be late for work. She threw the covers off her. She ran her hands through her hair, trying to tame it as she moved around trying to find some clothes. She didn't have a mirror in here. Why didn't she have a mirror in here?

Six in the morning was never her friend, so running around grabbing random items of clothes and then rejecting them wasn't what she *wanted* to be doing, but usually she didn't have to actually *think* before a cup of coffee.

She finally pulled on a pair of yoga pants and an oversized T-shirt. She was about to open her door when she stopped herself.

"Bra. My God, Franny, put on a bra." Thank God there were no cameras in here. She backtracked, put on a bra, and then took a deep breath, let it out.

This was not the panic-inducing moment she was making it out to be.

Rolling her eyes at herself, she opened her bedroom door and stepped out into the hallway. She heard the faint sound of movement and edged into the main area.

Royal was standing, looking at something on his phone—the light from it and the hint of early sunlight from around the blinds were the only things illuminating the room.

Unerringly he looked up at her when she took one more step.

She held her hand up in the most awkward wave of all time then turned the main overhead light on. She managed a smile, hoped it didn't read as awkward as it felt. "Morning."

"Morning," he said, his voice gruff. Which was hot. Because he was hot. And she could not be thinking about *that* right now.

"I know it's silly, but I slept *way* better knowing you were here, so I really appreciate your willingness to humor me."

He shoved his phone in his pocket and put the pillow on the stack of blankets he hadn't used. "I appreciate you not waking me up. Probably got a solid eight in. Your couch isn't half bad."

"Good."

He made a gesture for the door. "I better get back to my place so I can be ready for my shift on time. Just text me if you plan on going somewhere. Sound good?"

She nodded.

Before he could move, or she could offer coffee or breakfast or something, a knock sounded at the door. They both looked at it, then froze. Neither making a move one way or another.

Maybe he was as little of a morning person as she was, because he didn't immediately tell her what to do or do anything himself.

"Well, kidnappers don't really knock, right?" She managed a shaky kind of laugh and moved for the door. "I'll look out and see who it is." She moved to her toes, looked out the peephole.

It was... Copeland. She fell to her heels. She didn't dare look back at Royal. This looked... Well, surely Copeland wouldn't jump to weird conclusions. He'd understand.

But she was *nervous* now. "Uh, it's Copeland," she offered. Then disengaged the alarm and unlocked the door.

"Franny, sorry for the..." His gaze tracked beyond her to Royal, his expression immediately hardening. "What the hell are you doing here at six thirty in the morning?"

"Protecting me," Franny said firmly. She stepped between Copeland's angry gaze and Royal. "Remember?"

"Yeah, how far is that going?" Copeland demanded of Royal.

"It's not...going." Franny couldn't look at Royal or she'd turn beet red. "And even if it was, absolutely none of your business, Copeland."

"Look—"

"I know you and Audra have a very sweet meet cute from protecting her, but this isn't...that. So stop making things *weird* and explain to me why *you* are here at six thirty in the morning."

He was still glaring at Royal, kind of like the older brother she never had, which was almost sweet. If she didn't feel so damn embarrassed. He stepped inside and she closed the door behind him.

Then his gaze moved to her, and there was an alarming kind of…regret there. "I just got some…disturbing news. I wanted to tell you in person. Both of you. Didn't imagine you'd both be together, but—" He sighed. "There was a fire this morning at the library in Sunrise. The fire department called me once they saw what was being burned."

"Which was?" Royal demanded, speaking for the first time since Copeland stepped in the door.

"A stack of your books, Franny."

She leaned against the door, slowly let out her exhale as if she could control her breath she could control the jump of fear in her chest. "Well, that's not good."

"If it was burned, how do they know they were Franny's?" Royal asked.

"It's possible they weren't *all* Franny's titles," Copeland said. "But…there was enough left of some of the covers it feels…likely they all were. I talked to the librarian. You know Dahlia, right?" he asked Franny.

She nodded. She liked the librarian out in Sunrise. The library was tiny, but they had a lot of information on the Order of Truth, so she had spent some time there researching that book.

"She said all your books that the library carries were checked out the day before by someone who claimed they were new to Sunrise and got a library card. So, we've got something to go off of. But it is another threat, and I want you both aware of it."

"Why the Sunrise library?" Royal asked. "The Bent County library in Fairmont would have more of her books, wouldn't they?"

"Yes, but if I had to guess, the size of the library worked

in the suspect's favor. No surveillance, minimal security. Dahlia can describe the person who got the library card to us, and she will, but…"

"It'll be like me describing the kidnapper. It'll do a fat lot of nothing," Franny said with some level of disgust.

"Or it doesn't. We just don't know." Copeland glanced at her. "I want you to be aware so you're always making an informed decision. If you want to come to the ranch, or have Audra—"

"I think we all know and agree that the safest place for me is here with all this security," Franny managed. "Audra has enough on her plate even with your help, as do all of you. I'm staying put."

Copeland eyed Royal. "Well, if anything changes, you let me know."

"Was it a man or woman?" Royal asked, seemingly out of the blue. "The person who got the library card."

Copeland looked at Royal. There was distrust in his eyes, but eventually he answered. "Dahlia said it was a woman. I'm going to run the information she gave, but I don't have much hope there. Why?"

"Just need to know who to look out for. Is there going to be a sketch?"

Copeland nodded. "She's going to come by the police station this morning. I'll make sure you and Mayfield get a copy of it, and whatever we work up on the ID, even if it's fake."

"As soon as you can," Royal said. "And any other information you get."

"I will. I need to get into the station. Walk me out, Deputy."

Since Copeland didn't say it as a request, Franny felt like she had to step in. Even if she felt a little out-of-body trying to wrap her mind around someone burning her *books*, she had to protect Royal from…whatever Copeland thought he was doing. "He's not going to walk you out because you're going to do some ridiculous male law enforcement posturing, and I don't want any part of it."

"That's why we're going to do it outside."

"No, you're not." She put her hands on Copeland's chest and gave him a shove. "Bye."

He scowled down at her, but she watched him relent. "I'll have those sketches to you as soon as I've got them, Campbell. Franny, if anything changes—"

"*Bye*, Copeland."

"Bye," he muttered, and turned on his heel and stalked out the door.

Franny locked the door behind him, then stayed staring at the door trying to breathe through the tears that threatened. She wasn't going to cry in front of Royal. She wasn't going to feel *helpless* when she had all these people looking out for her.

"Well, that's…not great." She turned and tried to smile at Royal. "But I guess it doesn't change much for me. Does it?"

"It's a step. Every time they do something, there's a chance they leave clues behind. So, it's actually good."

"Good?" She wanted to believe that, but she knew he was mostly just saying it to set her mind at ease.

"Look, Franny, I have a theory. I'm going to work on getting to the bottom of it."

"Why didn't you tell Copeland this theory?"

Royal studied the door, then moved his gaze back to her. "I want to talk to Simmons first. It's not that I don't trust… your friend there. I just think we have to be more careful. Sometimes when a lot of people know something, even a lot of well-meaning cops, everything gets too complicated."

"You trust Mr. Simmons?"

"I don't know. I guess I'm starting to."

Franny chewed on her bottom lip, trying to work through *any* of this, but... He had to get to work. And she should probably try to get some work done too. She unlocked the door, opened it for him, and tried to force her mouth to curve upward. "Thanks again for last night."

He nodded, moving for the door. But he stopped, reached out, but his big hand on her shoulder and squeezed. "It's going to be okay, Franny."

"Of course," she said brightly.

But she figured they were both lying.

ROYAL GOT READY in a rush. He tried not to think about how...down Franny had looked when he'd left. She had every right to be worried *and* down, and it wasn't his job to cheer her up.

The fact he wanted to make it all right for her was completely and utterly foreign. He'd just never before believed he could make something awful *right*. Better maybe. Put a stop to something terrible. But not actually make it right.

There had been too much awful all around him to ever make right.

But Franny hadn't grown up like that, and he found himself...needing to fix this so she didn't have to live with any *bad* hanging on her shoulders.

He shook his head as he let himself into his temporary apartment. That was a little ridiculous. He needed to...screw his head on straight today. Focus on the case. He couldn't decide if this was an escalation of threat—sure, fire was worse than a piece of paper, but the piece of paper had been on her doorstep. The fire had been miles away.

Though it didn't really matter what *he* thought, did it? It mattered what the person doing the threats thought. And he had the background to know that even if you *thought* you understood a bad person, that understanding could change on a dime.

The fact it was a woman bothered him. And that so easily could be a coincidence, but... It just didn't feel like one. He should call the sheriff. Hell, call Beckett. But Simmons worrying about leaks left Royal needing to be cautious.

He was probably being overly paranoid. But if there was anything his childhood had taught him it was to listen to all those looming *bad* gut feelings. It usually meant something was wrong.

Simmons had said he'd get in touch once he had information on the picture of the woman. And if she *was* a Fed, it'd be something for Simmons to look into, not him. But what if she wasn't? What was next?

Royal worked through that question as he did his Hope Town patrol duties.

It was nearing lunchtime when he saw Simmons was pushing a giant stroller down the sidewalk toward the bakery Royal had considered hitting up.

Maybe as an excuse to text Franny and ask her if she wanted anything.

So he was pretty glad for the distraction, because that would have been foolish and unnecessary. He'd spent the damn night on her couch. She was certainly fine for a few hours.

He thought back to her saying she slept so much better with him there, and he couldn't for the life of him figure out what to do with the...sense of purpose and satisfaction that gave him.

Simmons offered a wave and started pushing the unwieldy stroller toward him, so Royal walked toward him instead of away. He couldn't resist looking around to see if Daisy Delaney was going to appear.

"My wife isn't here, if that's who you're looking for," Simmons said somewhat irritably when they met on the sidewalk. "Lucy's out of town, so I'm on kid duty and let's just say we all needed some fresh air before we all started crying."

Royal peered into the double stroller. A kid clutched a giant plastic dinosaur and was fast asleep. The baby—the one that had been crying the other day—was sitting there babbling to herself happily. She held a sock in one pudgy hand and was waving her bare foot around like she'd amazed herself at what she was capable of.

For a second, he was struck by the idea that Brooke would have one of these soon enough. It was kind of a nice thought. She'd have a baby to push around in a stroller and who would grow up and run around that big ranch, happy and protected and loved. So unlike everything they'd been given.

But that was the future and this was the present.

"You got anything for me on the woman?"

"I'm still pulling a few old threads, but no one I know and trust at the FBI knows who she is. I can almost guarantee she's not a Fed, but it worries me you thought she was one. When this all started, the sheriff seemed to think you'd have a good eye for that kind of thing."

"Yeah." Royal ignored the speculative look from Simmons, considered this new information. "What about other agencies? Maybe not FBI. Would ATF or someone be involved? You know what Albennie Ward is mixed up with better than I do."

"Yes and no." Simmons shook his head. "I don't want to poke too hard, raise any suspicions, so it's *possible* she could be with a random department, but..."

"It feels off." Royal studied Main Street around them. It was a quiet day. "I have a theory. I can't confirm yet, but someone started a fire with Franny's books in Sunrise this morning. Apparently, yesterday a woman no one knew got a library card at the Sunrise library and checked out all Franny's books."

"A woman... You think it's the same woman."

"It's not the male kidnapper. So... It's a theory. Copeland is running the woman's name, but it'll be fake."

"I guess you could try to get an APB out, or something through Bent County, but..."

Royal could read Simmons's reluctance. "It's delicate. I feel like... This is a case where we don't want to tip anyone off. We need to keep things close to the vest."

Simmons nodded. "Agreed, Deputy."

Which brought him back to the thought he'd been ruminating over all morning. He'd figured if he went through with it, he wouldn't tell anyone, but maybe... Maybe Simmons was the guy to tell. "I—I know someone who might be able to figure out who she is. Under the table. Not exactly...within the law. But they'd be able to do it without anyone knowing. I can't go through the sheriff for this one."

"Does this person know what they're doing?"

"Probably better than you or me."

Simmons was clearly dubious, but he didn't mount any objections. "How much you think they'll charge?"

Royal shook his head. "It'd be a favor. I just... It's the right course of action, don't you think? Find out who this woman is kind of under the radar? If you weren't worried there was some kind of FBI leak, you'd have them do it, wouldn't you?"

Simmons nodded. "I would."

"All right." Royal couldn't help but be a little concerned

that by not taking this to the sheriff he was stepping out of his lane, risking his job.

But he couldn't go against his gut instincts that this was right, and the best option to keep Franny safe.

He was distracted momentarily by some grunting and groaning sounds. He looked into the stroller again. The boy was waking up, wriggling and noise making enough to earn his sister's wide-eyed attention.

"Keep me in the loop, Campbell," Simmons said, pushing the stroller forward. "If I have to fall on the grenade, let me know. Sheriff can't fire me."

Royal laughed in spite of himself. "I'll hold you to that."

More roaring from the little boy in the stroller.

"I better get him something from the bakery before he turns into a pint-sized monster."

The boy squealed. "I'm a T-Rex! Not a *monster*."

"Oh boy, here we go," Simmons muttered under his breath. "Let me know, Campbell."

Royal nodded, watched Simmons go for a few seconds, trying to reconcile having that conversation over two cute kids. He shook his head. Well, life was weird.

And about to get weirder, because now he had to figure out how to ask Zeke for a favor.

Chapter Fifteen

Franny didn't leave her apartment. She didn't even leave her bedroom except to eat. The writing wasn't going *quite* as well as it had the other day. As much as she wanted to think about fictional worlds, lose herself there, her brain kept wandering back to book burning.

Her books.

So when the writing couldn't distract her from the creepy, crawly *targeted* feeling, she let herself be distracted by the internet. About the only thing that took her mind off her anxiety was watching videos of a concert she'd never attend. Then she called Audra back—because of course Copeland had run his mouth and told her about Royal being there this morning.

"He just spent the night on the couch because he fell asleep, and I didn't want to wake him up, because he's running himself ragged watching out for me."

"Hmm," was all Audra had said.

"Trust me, Audra. He's like…" She thought about everything he'd told her about the Sons. About foster homes. She was so…pampered and privileged in comparison. There was just no way he saw anything interesting in her. "He's not into me."

"You've never been a very good judge of that."

"I swear, Audra. He's touched me all of three times. And it's that friendly cop-to-victim attagirl pat each time."

"Cataloguing it?"

"Well, sure. He's hot. He has tattoos."

Audra snorted. Luckily for Franny, Audra had a million things to do at the ranch, so she'd been able to move the conversation quickly along, promising to go over to the ranch for dinner once this whole *surveillance* thing was over. She got an update on Rosalie—sick as a dog but finally taking the anti-nausea medication. Then she said goodbye.

And spent the next two hours doomscrolling.

When it got to be close to seven, she forced herself out of bed. She'd make dinner again. Maybe Royal would stop by and she could con him into staying again. Probably not fair. Probably not what she should *try* to do.

But she was just so much more at ease when someone was here. Not just *any* someone, because there were *cameras*. It had to be someone she was comfortable with, and since Audra had ranch business and Rosalie had puking and baby-growing business, and Vi had her ever-growing family to contend with… Royal was just going to have to suck it up.

Or tell her no.

Before she could talk herself out of the sinking feeling in her stomach at the thought of him *refusing* and how embarrassing that would be, her phone chimed.

Coming up.

It was from Royal. She appreciated that he texted first, so her heart didn't jump into her throat in fear at an unexpected knock. But why was he here? Did he *want* to eat dinner with her every night?

"Don't be ridiculous," she muttered, turning off the security system and then going to unlock the door and open it.

He looked just about the same as he had last night, in fresh clothes and wet hair like he'd run through the shower after his shift. There was just *something* that happened inside of her every time she saw him. It wasn't just thinking he was hot—she thought plenty of guys were hot. It was something in the eyes, the serious cast of his mouth pretty much always, even when he laughed.

Because his childhood was the worst, Franny. Not because he's a brooding romance hero.

"Hi." She shifted out of the doorway so he could come in, but he didn't move forward right away.

"Hey. You busy?"

"Oh, no. Just…figuring out what to eat for dinner. Um, I can make enough for two if you want to stay again."

"Actually, I promised my sister I'd have dinner at her place tonight. Something we try to do once a week."

She *refused* to feel disappointed. She *refused* to let her expression fall. She kept her smile bright, but before she could think of what to say like, *please don't*. He kept talking.

"I came over to see if you want to come with."

"Come…with." She had no idea what to do with that invitation or how to feel about it. She wanted to, *obviously*, but this was his sister and… If it was pity, she didn't want his full-blown pity.

Did she?

"Sure. I'm picking up a pizza. And you've already met, right? So, nothing crazy. Just be two hours probably." He shrugged, all casual and at ease while her lungs seemed to tie themselves into a knot.

"Is this because you feel sorry for me, or because you literally think I'm in that much danger?" She wouldn't allow herself to think about any third option, or Audra saying she never recognized when men were into her.

He most assuredly was *not*. This was business. Protection. His *job*.

He studied her for a long drawn-out minute, standing there in her doorway. He had a way of standing that *seemed* casual, but then she caught that intensity in his eyes, and it dispelled her of that notion right quick. But it certainly didn't stop the obnoxious fluttering thing her heart was doing.

"I don't feel sorry for you," he said very carefully. "I don't think you're going to wind up dead if I leave you here, but I have…concerns if I'm out close to Sunrise and you're here. It's just too much space. But Mayfield's a good cop from what I've seen. If you want to stay, I can turn over the surveillance stuff to him until I get back."

She was already shaking her head. "No." Maybe she should be fine with any cop handling her surveillance, but it had set her on edge enough and she knew, trusted, *liked* Royal. She'd never even met this Mayfield. "I'll…go with you." She looked down at her outfit—the same thing she'd put on this morning in a panic. "I need to change first."

"You look fine for pizza."

She waved him in, shaking her head. "You're a man who looks good in whatever you put on. You don't understand."

"You look good," he said closing the door behind him.

She could *not* engage with that. Because if she did…she might read into it. He was just being polite. "No, you said I look *fine*, and I don't. I look like… I've been rotting in bed all day. Because I *have*."

"Does it matter?"

She fisted her hands on her hips and gave him her best glare. "Do you want to keep arguing or do you just want to let me get dressed?"

He made a waving motion for the hallway. So she went into her room, inwardly groaned that she could not take her time thinking this through. What did you wear for a pizza dinner at your protector cop's sister's house? When you were the sad victim, not an actual guest.

Match Royal's vibe. Casual. Relaxed. She changed out of her yoga pants into jean shorts with a plain blouse—slightly elevated from a T-shirt but not fancy. Then tennis shoes, because if she remembered correctly, Brooke lived on a ranch. Footwear should match the location.

Hair? No mirror. She grabbed a clip off her dresser, twisted her hair up, then used her phone to use the camera as a kind of mirror.

Once she was satisfied—or at least as satisfied she was going to get in a few minutes—she went back out to the main room. Royal was standing in front of her bookcase.

And she was back to thinking about someone purposefully burning all her books.

"You got a favorite?" he asked, pointing at the shelf where she'd arranged her own books.

"Of my books?"

He nodded.

She wasn't sure why he'd ask, but she gave it some thought as she walked over to stand next to him. The physical representation of the past seven years of work. "I don't know that I have a favorite. They all mean…something different, I guess." She reached out, tapped her fourth one. "This one though? Rejected by my first editor, so selling it to a new publisher—and then having it do well—probably the one that brings the biggest smile to my face."

He chuckled. "Spite determines your favorite?"

"Spite is a great motivator."

His mouth curved. "Yeah, I guess it is."

"You're not a police officer out of spite."

"Maybe not, but it didn't hurt thinking about how much my dad would hate it when the academy was annoying as hell. Kinda spitey."

"Kinda," she agreed, amused. More…thrilled than she had any sensible right to be that he understood.

"Well, we better head out," he said. "I promised Brooke I'd pick up the pizza, and she likes to remind me you shouldn't leave a pregnant woman hungry."

"Oh, she's having a baby? Isn't that great?" She grinned at him as they left the apartment. She locked the door and set all the alarms. "Uncle Royal."

"Yeah, I guess." He grunted, leading her down to a car that wasn't his police cruiser. "Kinda weird."

They settled into the car. "I love being an aunt—well, honorary aunt, because I don't have siblings. But I got to help Vi when she had Magnolia, so I became Aunt Franny, though Mags calls me Geen."

"Why?"

"Not a clue, but even now that she's stringing full sentences together, I'm still Geen. It's cute. And then Fox came along, and he's the sweetest little pudge ball. And now Rosalie is having a baby? It's the best. You get to spoil and play and be fun instead of having to worry about keeping a whole other human alive twenty-four-seven."

"Not sure I know how to *be fun* with an infant."

"Oh, it's easy," Franny said waving that away as they drove. "I'm guessing the teenage years will be the hardest, but then you just take them to the R-rated movie their parents don't want them to see or buy them the energy drink their parents won't let them have."

He eyed her. "You're really planning on walking on the wild side."

She laughed, even though he was kind of making fun of her. "Wild is my middle name."

"I just bet," he replied with a grin that had the damn *flutter* taking it up a notch, but he pulled into the pizza parlor parking lot. "I'll be right back." It only took a few minutes before he reappeared with a big box of pizza and a bag balanced on top. He secured the pizza in the back seat, then drove again.

Conversation did not naturally return, and the silence made her nervous, so she figured he was going to have to deal with her annoying questions.

"So, Brooke is married to…somebody from the Hudson family from Sunrise?"

Royal shook his head. "No. Zeke Daniels. His brother and sister are married to Hudsons."

"Right. Okay. And Zeke is a rancher?"

"Yeah. Or trying to be anyway. Him and Brooke seem to like figuring it all out."

She could hear the bafflement in his tone. "No ranching aspirations?"

"Not a one. I had my fill of living out in the great wide open."

"Bent County isn't exactly a thriving metropolis."

"Yeah, I haven't got any interest in that either. I don't want extremes. I want something…straightforward. Besides, I wanted to settle somewhere close to Brooke more than I cared what kind of place that was."

She didn't point out that straightforward was *not* exactly how she'd describe Bent County, because him wanting to be close to his sister was sweet.

He turned off the highway onto a kind of bumpy lane. In the distance was a house. It was a lot like Audra's. A little…sagging around the edges, age and weather taking their toll, but a lot of effort to make it look like…home, she supposed. Lace curtains in the windows. A porch swing painted a pretty blue. Flowers planted along the base of the porch that popped in colorful summer blooms.

Royal parked his car next to a big truck and got out. Franny followed suit and the front door opened.

A dog came running out, barking up a storm as he rushed over to Royal, tail wriggling in excited pleasure.

Franny froze. It had been so long since she'd been in the kind of situation where she went to someone's house that she didn't know, she'd forgotten to ask.

Royal greeted the dog by crouching down to pet it. He let the dog lick his face while Franny stood out of the way, stock-still. He glanced over at her. Franny could practically see the fur flying through the air and toward her. Her eye almost twitched in anticipation.

"Afraid of dogs?"

"Uh. No. I love them actually, but I'm…fairly allergic."

He narrowed his eyes. "What's *fairly* mean in Franny world? Deathly?"

"I won't…die." She always had her inhaler in her purse. And it wasn't a cat. But she didn't think she had any of her antihistamines with her. She was just so good at managing her exposure, she didn't carry around all the things she needed. Or *had* been good at managing exposure.

Royal straightened, studying her with that expression that was vaguely disapproving, but not in a way that got her back up. She didn't know how to describe it. It was closer to concern than…disapproval.

"Well, it's not too hot out with the sun setting. I'll suggest to Brooke we eat outside. She's got furniture out here on the porch." He got the pizza out of the back, holding it up high so the dog couldn't jump at it. He started moving toward the porch and Franny scurried after him.

"You don't have to do that. I can handle a little dog fur." Maybe. She hadn't had any allergy shots since moving to Wyoming, but what was a few hours? She'd take a pill when she got home, shower off all the fur, and be *fine*. Ish.

"Don't be a martyr, Franny," he told her as he began to stride toward the door where Brooke now stood. She had an arm draped over an adorable baby bump and was smiling in warm welcome.

"You mind if we eat out here on the porch?" Royal said as he approached. "Franny's allergic to dogs."

"Oh, sure. No problem. I'll have Zeke put her inside. Come here, Viola." Brooke patted her thigh and the dog came running.

"Oh, you don't have to—"

At Royal's sharp look, she shut her mouth. "Thank you."

"Good girl," he murmured.

Which should be insulting. Not kinda hot.

Dinner was...nice, actually. Not that Royal had expected it to be *bad*, just maybe a little awkward. But Brooke and Franny seemed to have endless topics to discuss. It made it easy to relax a little, and he figured it was good for Franny to get out. Feel normal, even for a few hours.

She could go have a meal with her cousins, but he had a feeling she hadn't asked for that because she knew they would just worry and hound. Dinner out here was like pretending nothing was wrong.

Royal was just biding his time, waiting for a chance to talk to Zeke alone. When Franny asked Brooke about some flower and they got up to peruse Brooke's gardens, Royal hung back with Zeke. At some point, Brooke took Franny inside to show her something, so Royal finally had the privacy to discuss what he'd come there to discuss with Zeke.

"I've got a favor to ask."

"What kind of favor?"

"A former secret agent who still keeps in contact with all those other former secret agents favor."

"I'm retired." Zeke leaned back in his chair and crossed his arms over his chest. "And I don't help cops."

"Since when?"

Zeke looked him up and down. "Since *you* became one."

Royal snorted in spite of himself. He and Zeke had found a lot of even ground, what with both wanting the best for Brooke, but part of that even ground was giving each other a hard time.

"Will this favor help your…friend?" He jerked a chin toward the door Franny and Brooke had gone in.

"She's not a friend. She's a *witness* I'm protecting." Which felt like a lie. "But yeah, it's to help her."

"All right. Shoot."

Royal filled Zeke in on the suspicious woman in Hope Town—and a few of Royal's theories. "If she's not a Fed, I want her identity. Especially if she started that fire."

"Dahlia was pretty upset about it."

Reminding Royal that everything in Bent County was connected. Because Zeke's siblings were both married to Hudsons—and Dahlia the librarian was married to a Hudson.

"Email me the picture, and your bodycam footage if you can. I should be able to get a look at Dahlia's description myself, but it wouldn't hurt to send it my way if you get a sketch. I'll look into it. If I can't figure it out, I'll send it up the former secret agent chain. We should be able to ID her."

"Thanks." It eased a little of the tension inside of him,

though it would no doubt wind back up again if this took too long.

"Just a warning. Brooke's matchmaking."

"Matchmaking what?"

"You and your friend, I mean *witness*. She heard you were bringing a woman, and she immediately started picking out wedding decorations."

Royal scoffed. "Surely she's not that delusional."

"Romantic bliss will do that to you."

"Bliss with you? My ass," Royal grumbled. "Let me know when you figure out who the picture is. I've got to take my *witness* home." He pushed out of his chair at the same time the door opened.

"Royal, I think you better take Franny home," Brooke said, worry written all over her face.

"I'll be fine, really," Franny said, sounding…weird. Kind of squeaky. "I just have to take a shower, an antihistamine, and I'll be—" She sneezed. Twice. "—back to normal."

"You sound *horrible*."

She looked over at him, and he thought maybe she was trying to glare, but…

"And your eye is…swollen or something."

She sneezed again. Her eyes were watering and the swollen one looked like it was…pulsing.

"I'm so sorry, Franny," Brooke said again. She held out a wet washcloth. "Why don't you try to wipe your face again?"

Franny took it, wiped it over her face. "Please don't be sorry." Sneeze. "It's my own…" Sneeze. "…fault. I forgot how bad…" Sneeze. "…it can get, and I should have asked if you had a cat." Sneeze. "I haven't been around any in a while and…" She trailed off and sneezed three times in quick succession.

Royal took her by the arm, tried not to notice his sister's expression going from worry to *notice*.

"Let's get you home," he told Franny.

She held out the washcloth to Brooke, but Brooke refused. "You take it with you. Royal will bring it back. No worries."

He led her down to the car. She sneezed the whole way, sputtering out thanks and goodbyes and apologies as her face turned redder and her eye seemed to get even *more* swollen. He went to the back of his car and grabbed a box of tissues. When he slid into the driver's seat, he handed it to her. "Here."

She shook her head. "I'm allergic to tissues."

"What?"

"It just makes it worse. I have to use handkerchiefs or napkins or paper towels or…" She went into another sneezing fit.

"Why'd you go in the house?" he asked, baffled by this entire thing. He left the ranch, pushing the speed limit more than he usually would.

"Brooke had the book I wrote that she helped with, and she wanted me to autograph it, so I did that." She sneezed. "I *am* terribly allergic to dogs, but it would have been fine. I'm usually fine for a little bit. But there was a cat…" She gestured to her face.

And sneezed, four times in a row. "Cats are worse. Still, it's been a long time and maybe I was a little optimistic I'd grown out of the allergy. You know, they change every seven years."

She said it so earnestly he found himself with twin urges to laugh and just…gather her up and take care of her.

He resisted both. "Do I need to take you to the hospital?"

She shook her head. Sneezing through another sentence.

"I just need to get home. Run through the shower, take an allergy pill. I'll be good as new."

She fumbled with her purse, then pulled out a little contraption. Once she put it to her mouth he realized it was some kind of inhaler.

"Franny…"

She took another big breath of air from that thing, still shaking her head. "A shower. That's all."

He was more than a little concerned she needed an entire hospital stay, but he followed her instructions and just drove back to Hope Town while she kept sneezing and wiping her face with the washcloth Brooke had given her.

He pulled up next to her stairway, parked illegally. She got out of his car about as fast as he did, fumbling through her purse again.

"Give me your keys," he muttered.

She handed them over while she fumbled with her phone to turn off the security alarm. She wasn't sneezing quite as much, but she was still red and looked miserable.

Once they were inside, she handed him her phone. "You can set the alarm and leave if you want. I'm going to run through the shower." Then she made a beeline for the hallway.

He looked down at her phone in his hand. He obviously wasn't going to *leave*. He set it on her kitchen counter, then paced the small area.

What could he do? He wanted to…do *something*. Fix it. Hell, it was practically his fault. He'd taken her over to Brooke's. He could have just left her under Mayfield's watch. That's what he *should* have done.

And he could tell himself a lot of reasons why that had been, *had* told himself a lot of reasons. But he knew none of them mattered as much as the non-police one.

He liked being around her. He'd wanted to see her with Brooke. He'd wanted…something he couldn't quite articulate to himself.

Or maybe he could, thanks to Zeke. *Matchmaking*. He scoffed, taking a few steps toward the hallway.

She was pretty and funny and interesting, but what was he? A kid from a biker gang. He'd done terrible things in his life. Maybe mostly for good reasons, or to try to protect people, but… They were still there, living inside of him. His record could be expunged, but his memories couldn't.

And Franny was privileged and…*nice*. She'd probably never had so much as a speeding ticket. She'd gone into that house to sign his sister's book to be nice.

She was kind. Down to the marrow.

And you want a piece of that.

Yeah, maybe he did.

As little as he *should*.

Chapter Sixteen

Franny felt mortified. She tried to let the hot spray of the shower wash away that feeling along with all the allergens.

It didn't work. Well, she stopped sneezing. The throbbing behind her eye was starting to fade. Eventually the antihistamine would kick in. She'd probably be a little tired, but by the morning she'd feel good.

Well not *good,* because the humiliation settled deep.

She'd just wanted to feel *normal*. Instead she'd proven to literally everyone involved she was the opposite. When it had been so nice to leave the apartment, to leave Hope Town, to not worry about library cards or burned books or Albennie.

Brooke was so nice, and Franny kind of missed being on a ranch. Or maybe she just missed it because it had felt like freedom.

On a deep, only *slightly* wheezy breath, she turned off the water. Her eyes had stopped watering, and she hadn't sneezed in a while.

She hadn't grabbed clothes before she'd come in there. Well at least she had a towel or that would be *really* embarrassing if he hadn't left.

Surely he'd left. Hightailed it back to safety. He was probably talking with Brooke right now about what a strange little weirdo he'd been assigned to protect.

She dried her hair then wrapped the towel around her, just in case. She stepped out of the bathroom then stopped short. Royal was standing there. For a moment, they were both perfectly still, staring at each other.

Then he jerked his head up, looking at the ceiling.

But there was that...brief second where his gaze had drifted...down.

Wasn't there?

"Sorry. I thought you'd...be dressed," he said, sounding gruff. "I just wanted to... Do you need anything? I'm still worried about you."

Worried. That was...sweet. But she was *in a towel*. "All my clothes are in my room. So I'm just going to..." She sidestepped, holding the towel tight. "Get dressed. I'm good. I'll...be out in a minute." She nearly *leaped* for her door and then closed it very firmly behind her.

It was silly. The towel covered what any dress would. Well, maybe not *any* dress as she wasn't prone to wearing anything that short, but still.

It didn't matter. He wasn't looking at her any way, and the *worry* was that the woman he'd been assigned to protect might die from cat allergy instead of crazed kidnapper she'd IDed.

Frustrated with herself on just about every level, she pulled on some baggy athletic shorts, and because she couldn't be bothered to put on a bra, an athletic top with support built in. She left her hair damp and down, because it didn't matter *how* she looked.

He'd seen her use her inhaler. She needed to stop holding on to some strange little seed of hope that the hot cop who'd grown up in a *biker gang* thought there was anything even remotely interesting about her.

She stepped out of her bedroom, determined to play all of this as just *normal*. Something that could happen to *anyone*. Ha. Ha. *Ha*.

But he was standing there still. Right across from her room door. Waiting for her.

She tried to smile but wasn't sure she managed. "All better," she said brightly.

But he crossed the small space between them. He studied her face very intently, then framed her face with his very large, very rough hands and tilted her face up toward the light.

For signs of allergic reaction, Franny. Stop letting your imagination play tricks on you. Because in her imagination this would lead somewhere *very* different. In her imagination, she was the kind of woman who knew how to issue an *invitation*.

And then knew how to behave if such invitation was accepted.

"Are you sure you're okay?" he asked very seriously.

"Yeah." She nodded. He didn't move his hands, so her cheeks just kind of brushed up against the rough palms. *God.* "I'm a big girl. I know how to take care of myself."

He cocked his head.

"Well, you know, with how to handle an allergy attack. Not so much the whole kidnapper threatening me thing." She tried to smile, but he was so *close*. "See? I haven't sneezed once since I got out of the shower."

"Yeah, an improvement, but your eye's still swollen." And then his thumb swept under said eye, and she forgot all about the pounding in her temples, that swollen feeling when she blinked, how much her eyes itched.

Because he was touching her with such gentleness and touching her at *all*. Even though she knew he was doing it in like a first responder, worried about her health way, she couldn't get that message through to all the pleasure receptors in her body.

"Well, uh, the allergy meds will take a little while to kick in. But I already feel ten times better. And learned my lesson that I did not, in fact, grow out of my terrible dog and cat allergy."

She should move her head. Step away. She knew she should, but her body wasn't listening.

And *he* wasn't moving. His hands were still on her face. His expression had changed slightly. He didn't look...concerned.

He looked intent.

Stop. Dreaming.

But she didn't heed the warning in her head. She stayed very still. She was afraid to move. If she moved, he might move. And she wanted to stay right there for as long as humanly possible.

What happened to not imagining things?

But then he was closer. His head tilting toward hers, his hands still on her face. She could feel his breath across her mouth, the warmth of his body. She could smell...something on him. Soap or cologne or...

His mouth was just a whisper away from hers, and she could think of no rational reason for it. Checking her pulse? Making sure her eye hadn't fully swollen shut?

No, none of that made sense, the only thing that made sense...even though it *didn't*, was that he was...going to kiss her.

And he did. Kind of. His lips touched hers. She barely felt the contact. It was so light. Like a test. For both of them.

She'd always enjoyed acing tests, so she moved to her toes, touching her hands to his chest as balance.

And then it wasn't light at all. His grip on her face changed, somehow firming and gentling at the same time. The kiss wasn't...*wild*, but she didn't know what it was. Serious, like him. Intent and thorough and absolutely mind-emptying.

And it just seemed to *last*. He lingered, and she lingered, and surely she was just hallucinating or something, but she'd take it. If it felt this good, she'd sure as hell take it. Especially since she could feel the unsteady beating of his heart under her palm.

He eased away, but for a moment their lips still faintly brushed, their breath a little ragged, mingling. She inhaled deeply, opened her eyes. To his blue ones staring intently at her.

Then he kind of *sighed*, slowly dropping his hands. Then stepping back, leaning against the wall opposite her.

Franny didn't breathe. Her skin *buzzed*. And there was not one useful thought in her head. Not *one*.

He had kissed her, and she could not rationalize that simple fact away.

Royal cleared his throat. "I... I should apologize."

Apologize. Right. *The humiliation continues.* "Okay."

"It's just... I shouldn't be..." At least he seemed *almost* flustered. He wasn't *trying* to humiliate her.

Just succeeding at it.

"You don't have to explain," she said, proud of how... calm her voice sounded. "You didn't like it. You don't have to manage my feelings." She even smiled at him, because he *didn't*. That was her job. And she was damn good at it.

But he didn't move out of the way. He frowned down at her. "Didn't like... That's not why I'm sorry. It was a good kiss, Franny."

She opened her mouth, but...no, she had absolutely no words ready to respond to that. He'd really emphasized the word *good*.

"But this is my job. My *new* job. Maybe I'm off field training, but I'm still on probation for six months. They can fire me for *no* reason if they want, and I came into the job with reasons, Franny. I don't want to give them another one. If I'd been stupid enough to do that about ten feet to the left, it would have been on *video*. And I'd have been out on my ass."

Well, *that* was a sobering thought.

"I crossed a line. One I can't afford to cross again." He said it so...forcefully. Maybe she hadn't fully realized until right now just how *important* his job was to him. She knew, just from what she picked up on, that getting on the right side of the law meant something to him, but *this* job in particular wasn't something he was going to jeopardize.

She could accept that. It was actually very honorable—though she didn't think he quite saw himself that way. But *she* did. Maybe... Maybe she could find a way to show that to him. Just how far he'd come, if he wasn't willing to accept it himself.

She desperately wanted to do that. He *deserved* that. So she smiled at him. "So, hypothetically, when this is all over...assuming you know, I don't get murdered by some crazed kidnapper in the process, a kiss like that could...repeat itself. Once the job was over?"

Royal still didn't know what had possessed him. Well, he understood the *inclination*, just not having the control to *stop* the actual *acting* on the inclination.

She just looked... Something about the wet hair and the swollen eye and her smiling at him like she was *fine*, when she was a bit pathetic, it undid something in him.

It shouldn't. It didn't make sense that it did. And yet he couldn't seem to rationalize all these...impulses when it came to her away.

He desperately wanted her to be safe and comfortable and happy and... Boy, if he started inserting himself into her life that was not going to lead to any of those things.

He wanted to say so many things. Mainly that there were no hypotheticals about it. The minute it didn't threaten his job he wanted his mouth on her. Among other things.

But that was the problem.

"I don't think you understand..." He didn't know how to articulate that this was a *him* issue. She seemed so certain... Saying he didn't like the kiss when he'd been the damn one to initiate it. She seemed so sure of herself, but those little uncertainties shone through and just...

She needed someone who... Who was *actually* the guy he pretended to be. *Actually* honorable and dedicated to the law, through and through. Not a screwed-up kid from a biker gang trying to make some kind of weird amends to his sister and maybe himself.

"Franny, I'm not a *good* guy. I've done and seen some... truly awful things."

She studied him with those big green eyes, all soft and considering, like she *understood* him, but not in the way he wanted her to. In some deeper way he didn't fully grasp.

"Royal, I think the fact you've become a police officer, that you want to do good things in the face of all the bad you were surrounded with is something to be proud of. It's brave."

He had no words. *Brave*. He'd mostly called any *brave* he'd demonstrated survival. Because that's all it really was. Sometimes you had to face fear not because you wanted to, not because you were *brave*, but because you wanted to survive.

Franny had probably never considered *survival* in her life, and he was glad for that. Glad something awful didn't weigh on her. He didn't want it to.

But for a brief, painful moment, he wanted to be as *brave* as she thought he was. Instead of just someone who knew how to survive.

Before he could decide what to do with that, or *this*, his phone rang. He pulled it out of his pocket. The readout was the sheriff's department.

"I better take this," he said, swiping to answer and stepping away from her. "Deputy Campbell."

"Campbell. Sheriff here. I've just gotten a call from one of the FBI agents who was here. They've found Albennie Ward. I don't have the details yet, but they're bringing her back to Bent."

For a moment, Royal was speechless. *Found.* "What about who took her? The kidnapper?" The woman that had been creeping around that the sheriff didn't know about?

"Like I said. No details."

"If we don't know if the kidnapper has been apprehended…"

"You can keep an eye on Ms. Perkins until we have the details. Once I get more information, we'll reevaluate your assignment."

"Yes, sir." He ended the phone call with the sheriff, looked over at Franny.

"They…found her."

"She's okay?" she asked, wide-eyed and hopeful.

"The sheriff doesn't have details just yet, but she's alive and on her way back to Bent." Relief crossed her features and she kind of sagged there against the wall. He wanted to offer support. An arm to hold her up, a body to lean on.

He stayed where he was, tried to order his thoughts. Tried to think like a *police officer*. Not someone who wanted to make everything okay for Franny.

He could call Simmons and probably get more answers and quicker, but he thought of the stroller and the kids and the late hour. He could wait. They could wait. Sheriff had told him to stay put.

"We don't know who's been arrested, so we continue on tonight just like we've been doing until we know for sure the kidnapper is behind bars."

"Can I tell Lia? I have to tell her. She'll be… God, it'll just take such a weight off."

"We don't have any information. Albennie could be hurt. There could be more to this. I don't want to sound cynical. I just don't want to get anyone's hopes up that everything is great when we don't know that for sure."

Franny nodded along. "But… You're not wrong, Royal, but Albennie's *alive*. Even if it's not all sunshine and roses, she's alive and coming home. Lia needs to know."

He couldn't argue with that. "All right. Just make sure to be clear we don't have any details. There's nothing we can do right now except wait for morning."

"Of course," Franny agreed. She made a move for the living room, but Royal couldn't…just stay there. "I should probably go."

She stopped, slowly turned. "Oh."

He forced himself to move forward. To be a damn police officer. "For now, I still want you following all the same precautions, okay? I don't have enough information to be sure they've got the kidnapper locked up, and we still haven't figured out the identity of that woman." He made a beeline for the front door. "We're still keeping you safe, Franny. Until it's all for sure."

She trailed after him.

"You could stay again." Her smile was a little wobbly. It wasn't an *invitation*, in that sense of the word. It was because she was still worried about her own safety, like she should be.

But he had a bad feeling if he stayed, it could *turn* into an invitation he wouldn't have the sense to refuse. He sent her a kind smile. "I better not." And those big green eyes were a *big* reason why.

"Okay." She was clasping her hands together like she did when she was nervous, but he couldn't stay and manage her nerves. They had surveillance, they had alarms. He was right across the street.

And with that barrier maybe he could talk some sense into himself.

"Security. Locks. Call or text if you need anything."

She nodded, got her phone out of her purse on the counter. She disengaged the alarm and he unlocked the door and stepped out onto the porch. He waited for her to close the door behind him, listened to the locks click into place. He knew she'd set the alarm. She'd take all the precautions she should.

It took more self-talk than it should to force himself to walk down the stairs and across the street. He surveyed the dark street, saw no signs of life except the occasional light from one of the buildings.

In the dark, everything looked more ghost town than quaint small town. The shadows seemed to loom. Everything was eerily quiet. But when he got to his side of the street, looked up at Franny's building, the lights behind the windows shone like a beacon.

A beacon you aren't answering, buddy.

He'd been so sure if he just…tested the waters she would back off. Instead, she'd pressed her mouth to his, her hands on his chest, and upended something inside of him he'd thought too cynical to *ever* be upended.

Maybe he'd blame Brooke and her happiness and her baby bump.

Maybe he'd blame allergies and asthma.

Maybe he'd blame his own damn self for being foolish enough to think there was anything good on the other side of everything he'd been through.

Disgusted with himself, he went up the stairs to his apartment. Once inside, he double-checked all the surveillance equipment just to make sure everything was up and running like it should be. Maybe there was a little niggling *impulse* to see if she was on camera, if she was talking to herself, but he wouldn't do that.

It was crossing a line, and maybe he'd been raised to cross lines, *erase* lines, *destroy* every last line. But he'd left that behind. The fact that the impulse still resided in him was what he'd been trying to get through to Franny.

And she'd called him *brave*.

Why did that hit him like a *blow*? Like when Brooke said horribly insightful things about…building a life that the Sons never got to touch. Even if all those scars existed inside them still. Always.

He pulled out his phone, pulled up Franny's contact information and clicked Message. He studied the empty box for a few minutes before he typed up what was on his mind.

Hypothetically, I didn't stay because I don't trust myself around you. He considered the text for a good ten minutes. Let it sit there without sending. It wasn't *smart* to send it.

But she had *hypothetically* been talking about an after.

He should nip that in the bud. Instead he was acknowledging it?

She'd thought he didn't like the *kiss*. He still couldn't get over it. She was so damn pretty and funny and *sweet*, but she didn't necessarily see it. Not enough to think *he* might see it.

He hit Send on the damn text. Then stomped around his apartment, irritated and frustrated, getting ready for bed. He was going to sleep and sleep well. Tomorrow he'd have answers and…

And maybe an *after* to think about, but until then, it didn't matter.

He turned off all his lights, got into bed, then lay there staring at the ceiling.

She tasted like *spring* was all he could think. That sharp, bright slice of hope after a long, dark winter. And he shouldn't think or feel or accept that.

His phone dinged, and he all but lunged for it, figuring Franny would have responded.

But it wasn't Franny. It was a text from Zeke.

We've got a problem.

Chapter Seventeen

Albennie was safe, but even after Franny spoke to Lia, and even though she was exhausted from the allergy attack, Franny still didn't sleep.

Not because she was afraid. Not because her allergic reaction hadn't fully gone away. She didn't sleep because she was *obsessing*.

About that kiss.

About Royal Campbell.

About what was *next* if Albennie was safe and sound in one piece and coming *home*.

It was a relief, but there was such a lack of answers, it was hard to relax and just…believe everything was going to be okay. She had expected Lia to be ecstatic when Franny had called with the news, but she'd been…reserved. Kind of like Royal. Like they were afraid to hope for the best.

It reminded her that Lia had made a joke about hating cops. Maybe it wasn't a joke. Maybe she had a background like Royal did.

Royal.

Her phone pinged. She felt twin pangs of worry and excitement when she saw it was a text from Royal. She opened the text, then just…stared.

Hypothetically, I didn't stay because I don't trust myself around you.

She stared at that text, her heart fluttering in her throat. Didn't *trust* himself around her?

She might actually for the first time in her life understand the word *swoon*. Maybe she shouldn't find that sweet. And hot. And romantic.

But she did.

Except she didn't have the first clue how to respond. She wanted to say something flirty, but she didn't have any experience being that. So she lay there in bed, agonizing over how to respond, but it seemed in only a blink she woke up to the sun streaming through her windows, the phone cradled to her chest.

She'd forgotten to shut the blinds yesterday. And clearly the allergy meds had conked her out, because she'd never responded to Royal's text and it was morning. Late morning at that.

"Way to go, Franny," she muttered, but she didn't even have time to consider self-recriminations because she realized someone was knocking on her door.

And when she looked at her phone screen to see what time it was, she saw she had three new texts from Royal.

I'm giving it two more minutes then I'm breaking down the door, came the last one.

She jumped out of bed, hurriedly typing as she moved for the front door. Because she was pretty sure he would do just that, and even though she was *tempted* to want to see it, she knew she'd feel foolish later.

I'm awake, she texted, then opened the alarm app on her phone and disengaged it. Then she unlocked the front door to Royal standing there, scowling.

He had a to-go cup of coffee in one hand and held it out to her. "Thank you for scaring five years off my life."

She took the coffee he offered her. "I... I'm sorry. I'm a little out of it. The allergy pill really knocked me out last night."

"Lucky," he muttered. He didn't look at her. He surveyed the room. Continuing to speak before she could parse the *lucky*. "The sheriff wants us both to come into the station this morning."

It was so silly to want to just...put her mouth to his and see what he would do. Which was definitely a pre-coffee, post–allergy pill thought. Not a sane one in response to what he'd just said.

"Why?"

"I assume to go over what the FBI have told him about Albennie's return. And what that means for your surveillance and so on."

"Oh, right." Important stuff. Not kissing stuff.

"You might want to get dressed. And brush your hair."

Her free hand flew up to her hair. She could *feel* the rat's nest at the back of her head. Usually she slept like the dead after an allergy pill. Apparently last night she'd slept like the restless dead. And since her hair had still been damp from the shower, it was no doubt a hopeless mess.

His mouth curved, for the first time a spark of something behind the cop facade. "I mean, it's a real cute look and all, but it looks like you've been up to something."

She could feel her cheeks *heat*. She wished she was the kind of woman who had the guts to say something like *I wish we'd been up to something*. But she wasn't Rosalie.

She was just tongue-tied.

"Go on and get ready, Franny," he said, very gently, but his mouth was still curved. Amused at her in a way that never felt condescending.

She nodded and went for her room, because this was important police business stuff.

Then she remembered his text last night.

Didn't *trust* himself.

She blew out a breath. Well, she was just going to have to concern herself with both. She had to contain multitudes.

She tried to find a suitable outfit for the police station quickly so she wasn't leaving Royal waiting, but her mind kept wandering because he'd sent that text and he'd…

He liked her. He was interested in her. It wasn't imagination or wishful thinking. He'd *kissed* her. She hadn't forced him to do that. And he didn't strike her as someone who… would go against his own truth to soothe someone else. He *was* a soother, but it was like…honest soothing.

She shook her head, pulled on some jeans since the police station was freezing. A T-shirt, a jacket she tied around her waist. Her hair was hopeless, but she tried to detangle it a little bit before using a rubber band to create a messy bun that looked purposeful instead of wild.

Then she grabbed the cup of coffee and guzzled down as much as she could.

A latte. Because he knew what she drank. Because he liked her. Didn't trust himself around her. And maybe there was a hope that could all mean something, but they had to step over this whole *kidnapping* business first.

And it was about to be over. It had to be, right? Albennie was coming home. The surveillance would be over. And maybe she and Royal could…go out on a date or something.

Because he *liked* her, and whether that worked out or not wasn't important in this moment. What was important in this moment was not talking herself out of what he'd made perfectly clear.

That and going to the police station.

She went back out into the main part of the apartment. Royal stood at her window, looking down over Main Street, but he turned when she came in.

For a moment, neither of them said anything. They just stared at each other. And she hoped he was reliving that kiss at least a *little*, because that's where her brain had gone.

"There are things you should know about me, Franny. Things that would change the way you look at me."

He was so serious. Even more serious than his usual. Her heart tripped over itself, but when she spoke her voice was calm. Even if her heart wasn't. "Do I look at you a particular way?"

"Yeah, you do. Like you think I'm good or brave. I'm not."

She wanted to argue with him, but he said it with such *conviction*. So she had no words, just an ache in her heart. Because he could tell her a million things, but she didn't think he'd ever be able to convince her he wasn't good or brave. No matter what he said.

"I've been to jail."

Well, she hadn't expected *that*. But it didn't add up. Not yet. "Then how did you become a police officer?"

"My record was cleared. It was…gang stuff, a frame job. But there were things I did in that gang. I broke the law. I hurt people."

"Because you liked it or to protect people who weren't as strong as you?"

He didn't answer that right away. She hadn't thought he would. She wasn't surprised that he didn't really answer the question at all. Just side-stepped it.

"I belonged there."

She shook her head. She knew she was in out of her depth here. She could never imagine what it was like to grow up with all that awful around you. It broke her heart that some people had to.

But more, it amazed her the strength of spirit to walk out of it. He didn't see that, and maybe she couldn't convince him of it.

But God she had to try. And not just because she wanted some…chance to see where that kiss would go. But because he deserved to see himself as he was.

"If your record was cleared, that makes it sound like you didn't. And the law itself didn't think you did. And the entire Bent County Sheriff's Department certainly doesn't think you did either."

"What I did? None of it was heroic."

She tried to really put herself in his shoes. Understand how he might view it. But she couldn't get past the fact…too many people loved him, trusted him. He'd been given too many chances not to be the man he seemed like he was. "Wasn't it?"

ROYAL DIDN'T KNOW why they were having this conversation. She'd just looked at him and he'd seen…too much in her eyes. Hope and care and just what he'd told her—she looked at him and he felt as brave and good as she saw him.

But he wasn't, and she had to know. With that kiss rattling around in his head acting like some kind of…precursor to a bigger change than he'd counted on, he had to make sure she *knew*.

Before they took one more step forward. She had to understand. She could not look at him and see him as her hero.

He had failed too many times to be anyone's hero, and the thought of failing *her* in this moment, in any moment, it hurt too much to bear. It was bad enough when it was Brooke, but Brooke was his sister, his blood. She was stuck with him, with that belief in what he could be.

Franny didn't need to be mixed up with or chained to… all the bad he was. Deep inside.

But Franny crossed the space between them. She stopped only when they were practically toe to toe. She met his gaze, her green one serious and kind. Her hand came up to his bicep.

She could be so awkward and unsure of herself, but the way she saw people was so astute. She'd had him pegged before he'd really told her anything about himself.

So maybe you could listen to her.

But it just felt wrong. Bone-deep wrong. To let anyone think he was anything better than what he was.

"The tattoo you have right here," she said quietly, intently, squeezing his bicep. "When you're wearing a T-shirt, I can only see the bottom of it. But it looks like the bottom of a heart."

He didn't know where she was going with this, or maybe worse, he was afraid he knew exactly where she was going. Because she just seemed to be able to see through him, read him, and it should feel wrong. It *was* wrong.

But he didn't move.

"What is it?" she asked.

He didn't want to tell her, but that would make this line of questioning a bigger deal than it was. "Yeah, it's a heart."

"For what?"

"They don't all have meaning." These days, some just served as a reminder of who he'd been, what he'd allowed, all he'd failed.

"For what, Royal?" she repeated, very calm but the kind of calm he could recognize wasn't going to falter or be pushed away. He had to tell her. Somehow…she'd know if he lied.

"The people I couldn't save." It came out on a rasp. A secret he'd never told anyone. That heart on his bicep. A reminder that he could make himself stronger and strong and stronger.

But it'd never save those girls in the gang he hadn't been able to get out.

"Do you have a tattoo for all the ones you did save?" she asked in that same gentle tone. But she knew.

He didn't know how, but he knew she did.

He couldn't speak. Even if he'd had any words, his throat was locked shut. This was…too much, too big, and he had to get her to the police station. He had to…

"I'll never be able to imagine what you've been through, Royal. I would… I would be more than happy to listen if you ever wanted to talk about it. But nothing you could say is going to change what I've seen, what I know. Anything you did to survive the horror you grew up in was brave. Anything you feel like you failed at wasn't *your* failure."

He knew that. Brooke had tried to impress that upon him over the years. And he blamed everything on the evil men who'd hurt him and all the people around him. But it didn't bring back the people who'd been lost.

Nothing did. If he'd been stronger though…

"You chose this," she said, tapping his uniform. So earnest. So sure. "You worked for it. You earned that badge and now you wear it with pride. So you can stand there and tell me a lot of things—you can tell me I'll never understand, you can tell me you *feel* like you failed, but you cannot tell me you aren't good or brave, because that is the *heart* of who you are. Period."

Everything in his chest *hurt*. Like he was being cracked open. Worse, that her eyes were shiny like she might cry. Like she meant all this and it meant something to her.

He meant something to her.

"We should go," he managed to grind out, sounding gruff and pained to his own ears.

She sighed, blinked a few times, then nodded.

Chapter Eighteen

When he moved for the door, Franny followed, not trusting her voice. She didn't know what to do with that entire conversation. It was so deep, so profound, and yet...

She hadn't gotten through to him. Did that make *her* a failure?

She did everything she needed to do to secure her apartment, and hoped it was the last time she had to go through that rigmarole.

She climbed into his police cruiser. She didn't dare look at him, because she wasn't going to lose the battle with tears. She wasn't going to look desperate. Not when she was *right*.

They hadn't driven far when Royal's phone rang through the car's Bluetooth system. Since it was connected, she could see the caller ID pop up on the screen of the car. Zach Simmons. "Why is Mr. Simmons calling you?" Franny wondered aloud.

Royal didn't say anything at first. When he spoke, it was very...detached. And she didn't think it was *all* to do with their conversation at her apartment. "I'll call him back."

Which wasn't an *answer*. It was an evasion.

But then her own phone chimed, a text from Audra in the family group chat about Copeland saying Albennie was saved and demanding to know why Franny hadn't told them.

So Franny had to craft a quick, breezy text about her allergy pill knocking her out the night before and how she was on her way to the sheriff's department to get an update now. Once she was satisfied and hit Send, she realized the car had come to a stop.

She looked up at the police station. Then over at Royal. He was already getting out of the car, so she followed suit. He didn't offer anything as they walked up to the building. No words of support. No encouragements.

Because she'd had to open her big mouth and tell him he was brave and good. Well, she wasn't going to feel bad about that. She *refused*.

When they stepped inside, Copeland was waiting there, which had a little pit of worry forming in her gut. He didn't look happy or relieved. He had that detective stoicism going on.

"Is everything okay?"

Copeland looked from her to Royal. "Let's go hear what the sheriff has to say and find out."

This was the last place Royal wanted to be right now. He needed to talk to Simmons about the information Zeke had given him, and what that meant for...everything, but he supposed Albennie being found would trump his own investigation.

Unless...

He didn't let himself think about the unless. Not yet. He put that away like he put away the conversation with Franny. He stood stiff and still and listened to the sheriff.

"Ms. Ward has some minor injuries. While they took care of those in Idaho, she requested her own doctor to check her out on arrival, so no one local has had a chance to talk to her yet. The Feds will share their *public* reports with us, but they're being closemouthed about the entirety of the case."

"So you don't know who did it?" Franny asked. She was the only one sitting. The sheriff had offered her his chair. So it was an odd tableau—sheriff, deputy, detective standing in front of her like she was the boss.

She was looking a little wide-eyed and concerned to be the boss. *Beautiful though.*

A very unhelpful thought.

"*I* don't, but the FBI do. I suppose that's going to have to be good enough."

"With all due respect, sir, it isn't."

The sheriff sent him a sideways glance. Royal should have taken it as censure, but he couldn't help himself.

"Until we have confirmation that the kidnapper Franny witnessed has been arrested, there is still a chance she's in danger even if Ms. Ward isn't."

"I think that's highly unlikely, Deputy Campbell."

"I don't," Beckett said. "I think he's spot-on. Look, we were all operating under the theory the kidnapper was hired muscle. Even if he doesn't connect to Ms. Ward's disappearance in a full-blown way, that means Franny being able to identify and implicate him in a crime is *still* a risk."

The sheriff shifted uncomfortably. He looked from Beckett to Royal to Franny. He smiled at her. Thinly. "Ms. Perkins, would you mind waiting outside for a few moments?"

Franny's gaze moved to his. For a moment that felt too much like that moment in her living room, their gazes just held. Like they could have full-on conversations without speaking.

But they *couldn't*. So Royal gave her a little go-ahead nod. The sheriff would speak more freely if she wasn't there, and he and Beckett could too.

Because this wasn't over for Franny just yet. And no matter what she thought of him, no matter what she'd said this morning, he was going to be right there making sure she was safe. He wasn't failing her, no matter how much it messed with his head.

"Maybe Albennie will tell us," Franny offered as she got out of the seat. "What's going on. Who the kidnapper was. Maybe we don't have to wait for the FBI to."

The sheriff smiled at her. "Maybe." But then he waited for her to leave, and he closed the door behind her.

Royal stood feeling pulled in way too many directions. The conversation he'd had with Zeke last night about the identity of the woman weighed on him. Because it wasn't something he could bring up to the sheriff. It was under the table stuff that could get him fired.

Just like kissing Franny.

He wanted to talk to Simmons about the woman's identity—a former FBI agent was *definitely* a problem as Zeke had said. Instead he had to convince the sheriff that Franny wasn't safe until they had absolutes. And that irritated the hell out of him.

"Sheriff, Franny's own recount of the kidnapping was that Ms. Ward had a hood secured over her head. It's possible she never saw her attacker. It's possible Franny remains the only witness that can pin this on him, *especially* if he was hired muscle and not connected with the group the FBI may or may not have apprehended. With the threats that have been leveled against her, that's a problem."

"And a crime," Beckett tacked on. "Harassment and threats are a crime. One that happened in our county and we have an obligation to solve."

"That you can continue to investigate, Detective. But we can't surveil her indefinitely," the sheriff replied with a kind of calm detachment that grated against Royal's nerves. "And until there's another threat on Ms. Perkins *after* Ms. Ward's return, I don't see how I can justify it. If she still feels unsafe, she can hire her own security. But our responsibility only goes so far."

"I think it should go at least as far as ascertaining who has been arrested for what."

The sheriff stared him down, and Royal couldn't help but have some concerns that *I kissed the witness and have definitely gotten too deep* was written all over his face.

"You know he's right, Sheriff," Beckett insisted, and Royal was glad for some backup here, even if it came from a personal attachment of Beckett's own.

"At the very least, I'd like to request maintaining the Hope Town assignment," Royal said. "Until we know everything for sure."

The sheriff looked from him to Beckett. Then sighed. "*If* the kidnapper is still on the loose, and that's confirmed by the FBI, I can give you a week to continue the Hope Town assignment, along with Mayfield on nights. But if it goes beyond that, I can't afford it."

The sheriff's assistant poked her head in the door. "Sorry, gentlemen. Sheriff, that FBI agent is waiting for you in the conference room."

The sheriff's scowl deepened. "All right. I'm headed that way, Miranda. You two are dismissed," he said, striding out of the room.

Royal didn't follow right away. He needed to get a grip on himself before he dealt with Franny. In so many different ways.

"Maybe she *should* get private security," Beckett muttered, still standing next to Royal.

Royal knew the irritation was with the sheriff, but he

didn't like the suggestion either way. "She trusts me." She shouldn't but she *did*. So he'd be what she needed him to be, even if he couldn't change all those past parts of himself.

Beckett made a considering type of noise.

Royal sent him a sidelong glance. "What?" he demanded.

Beckett shrugged. "If you've got a personal stake in this, Campbell, it'd set my mind at ease. And my fiancée's."

Royal looked back at the door. "I don't know what that means."

"Yeah, you do."

Maybe he did. But he wasn't about to address it with Beckett. So he moved for the door, but he couldn't *quite* help himself. "Nothing's happening to Franny on my watch."

Chapter Nineteen

Franny sat making small talk with the sheriff's administrative assistant in between the phone calls she fielded. She watched the sheriff leave at Miranda's insistence, then waited for Royal and Copeland to follow.

It took them a few minutes, which made her uneasy. But she fixed a smile on her face when they finally came out. Royal looked irritated. Copeland looked a little smug—which she supposed meant he'd been poking at Royal.

"I'm going to work on getting to the bottom of the FBI stuff," Copeland told her. "Whether they want to tell us or not, we deserve to know. You deserve to know. The sheriff will be diplomatic. I don't have to be."

"Well, don't get fired or anything. You'd drive Audra crazy being around all the time."

"Ha," he replied sarcastically. "Let Royal take you back to Hope Town. Keep locked up with the security. Maybe get some work done. Let us handle it."

Franny nodded. Not because she was going to *let* anyone do anything, but because arguing with a brick wall was pointless.

So she followed Royal back out to the parking lot. He wasn't saying anything. He was clearly thinking, or planning. She could tell from the expression on his face he'd put earlier into some kind of box and shoved it deep down underneath what needed to be done.

"I could talk to Lia," Franny suggested when they were in the car driving back to Hope Town. "Maybe Albennie has told her or she even knows. Maybe she'll tell me now that Albennie's safe."

"Maybe," Royal agreed, still deep in thought as he drove. "Maybe that's not a bad backup plan."

"Backup?"

"Yeah, my plan first. We're not going back to your apartment just yet."

"We're not?" She was more than a little shocked he wasn't bustling her away.

"We're going to Simmons's house."

"Why?"

He sent her a sidelong look. "Because Simmons and I had a discussion about the woman Lia and I saw poking around Hope Town after the kidnapping. And I took the information to someone who has some...skills at finding out who people are."

Franny considered that sentence. What he was saying. What he wasn't. She was pretty sure the only time he'd left Hope Town, or talked to anyone not directly in Hope Town or connected to the police department was when they'd gone to dinner at his sister's ranch last night.

It was natural to extrapolate from there. "Zeke."

He frowned, sent her a quick glance. "How did you know that?"

"Well, I didn't *know*. I guessed. You likely could have missed dinner with your sister, but instead you took me with you. So you could talk to him when Brooke was distracted. Besides, there's something about Zeke that makes it...easy to believe he'd have said skills. It explains last night better than…anything else."

"I don't need Brooke to be distracted. He probably told her about it anyway. I invited you because I didn't like the idea of being that far away if something happened, like I said."

Franny didn't say anything to that. She felt petulant and weird. Uncomfortable and…maybe she'd blame the allergy med hangover on not quite knowing how to navigate *all* of this.

"Brooke likes you," he said, out of nowhere. In a careful way that didn't quite make sense.

"I like Brooke. And Zeke. I even like their animals, even if their cat inadvertently tried to kill me. They've got a sweet little ranch, and you can tell they're…happy together. Settled. It's like my cousins. It's nice watching people build things."

Build. She sighed in spite of herself. She'd watched her cousins and friends *build*, and she felt the exact same as the day she'd moved to Wyoming three years ago.

Until Royal Campbell had kissed her last night. Which was a wild leap, but all *chances* started with tiny seeds. Maybe they didn't all grow, but they all had a *chance*.

He just had to get past…his whole traumatic childhood. *Sure, Franny, why shouldn't he do that just because you told him to?*

"My point is… If you were annoying or whatever, I'd hardly cart you around or stick by your side." He didn't say it begrudgingly exactly, but he was frowning while he said it.

Maybe that's why she said what she did. "You didn't last night."

He flicked her another dark blue glance. "I told you why."

"I think there's a compliment in there?"

Royal blew out an irritated breath. With her? The situation? Both? She didn't know, but he kept talking.

"The point is, Zeke found this woman's identity. She *used* to be an FBI agent. Briefly. I want that to mean that she's only connected to Albennie Ward."

"But?"

"Look, library card catalogue card and burning books? It just doesn't strike me as the kind of threat you get from hired muscle. And we know a woman was involved with checking the books out of the Sunrise library. I want it to be a coincidence, but until I know for sure it is, I'm worried you're not out of the clear. If they didn't catch these people, then the kidnapper, and maybe this woman, knows you can still implicate them. You're a liability to them."

She *really* didn't like that. Unfortunately, she agreed. She desperately wanted it to be over, but it wouldn't be until the person she'd identified was behind bars. And if this woman was connected to him…yeah, her too.

Royal drove through Hope Town, not stopping at their apartments. He drove on out to the outskirts of town, where some of the big showpiece houses were.

When he pulled through a big wrought iron gate, Franny leaned forward in her seat.

"Wow." Franny stared at the house. It shouldn't surprise her considering Mr. Simmons's wife was a famous country singer, whose father had been a famous country singer. That meant money. But…

It was a beautiful old house, with all sorts of interesting features—architecture and windows and a huge wraparound porch. Landscaping and hanging baskets of blooms complemented everything.

Royal came to a stop in the driveway. For a moment, they both just sat and took in the house.

"And I thought him affording a whole damn town was something," Royal muttered.

Franny chuckled in spite of herself, glancing over at him. His mouth quirked into an amused smile as their gazes caught.

She sighed. Now wasn't the time, but... "Royal..."

"Come on," he muttered. He got out of the car so Franny followed. Not the time.

She could hear the squawk of chickens and noted there was a little coop off to the side toward the back. It was painted red and looked as cute as any Pinterest page.

"It's gorgeous. This would be the perfect place to set a murder." At Royal's sharp look, she smiled sheepishly. "I meant fictionally."

He shook his head and moved up the porch steps, rapping on the door.

Mr. Simmons opened it, a baby on his hip. The image made Franny smile, just like every time she saw Thomas carting around his and Vi's brood. There was just something really nice about watching a man be a good father. Which made her think of Rosalie and Duncan. They'd make such cute babies.

"Thanks for meeting me here," Mr. Simmons said, over the sounds of explosions and dinosaur roaring in the background. He bounced the baby on his hip. "Lucy's supposed to get back today, but I'm solo parenting until she gets home. This whole county is crawling with family, and do you think a one of them could spare some babysitter duties? No. Why? Because we all have too many damn kids."

He led them into a big living room. For as gorgeous and formal as the outside looked, inside was warm and cozy and covered in kid paraphernalia. On a huge screen, *Jurassic Park* was playing.

A little boy was hanging off the arm of the big couch, his eyes on the TV, but he glanced over at them briefly.

"I'm not scared." The boy's eyes were wide and serious. He didn't *look* scared, but the statement spoke of concern.

"Wow. You must be brave like your daddy," Franny offered.

The boy flashed a grin, then his gaze went back to the movie.

"I keep waiting for him to grow out of the dino phase. Hasn't happened yet. Look, I've got some things in my office I'd like to show you, Royal, but…"

"I can take her. Watch him," Franny offered, holding her arms out for the baby. "I'm the aunt babysitter in my family. Lots of practice." Besides, kids were simple. They didn't make her heart ache like Royal's serious blue eyes did.

"Well, she's kind of particular," Mr. Simmons said, but he handed the baby over. Then he watched the baby, who looked up at Franny with serious eyes like her father. But she didn't express negative feelings.

"Huh," Mr. Simmons said.

Franny smiled at him, made a face at the baby. "I'm a natural. I'll keep an eye on things here. You go show Royal whatever you need to."

Mr. Simmons waited a few more seconds, watching the baby for signs of distress, then shrugged. "All right, Campbell. Follow me."

ROYAL WAS *NOT* weirded out by Franny holding a baby. That off feeling in his gut, like when Brooke talked about her own baby plans and futures and families, was a product of spending an entire childhood not being able to trust the future.

It wasn't about *babies*, in particular, it was just like this looming future. That he somehow had to believe in and yet struggled to get past the idea that death or evil was always just waiting in the wings to destroy any kind of happiness or real life.

That his failures meant…whatever waited him on the other side of the Sons wasn't anything *good*.

Except the Sons were gone, and he was a *cop*, and maybe he had to take Brooke's example and start building on… faith.

Franny had tapped his badge and told him he'd earned it. Had he?

Thinking about it left an uncomfortable tightness in his chest, and an itch behind his shoulder blades he couldn't reach. He was almost grateful he didn't have the time to parse it.

Simmons led him into a big office-type room and Royal was glad to have work to focus on over homey living rooms and cute kids.

And pretty brunettes with big green eyes.

Royal relayed the information Zeke had found to Simmons. "This woman's real name is Holand Meyer. She's got a few aliases, but Zeke couldn't connect any of them to Wyoming over the past month. She was an FBI agent stationed in Michigan for about six months five years ago, and then she disappears, more or less. He can make the connection to the aliases, but not much else. He'll keep digging, but the FBI connection is a problem."

"Yeah, it is." Simmons tapped his fingers on his desk. He had at least three computers, and all looked far more complicated than Royal could ever hope to understand. "There's got to be a leak somewhere. Someone who knows about Hope Town in the FBI knows Holand Meyer and fed her that information. Purposefully or not."

"I agree."

"But what's the connection? What connects a kidnapper, a former FBI agent and Albennie Ward?"

"You know," Royal said, tired of people beating around the bush. "Maybe you don't fully know, but you know what Albennie Ward is mixed up in. Or was. You have enough information from your FBI contacts and whatever you do for these women when they come to Hope Town. She's back. She's safe. Now we need to make sure Franny is safe before the sheriff pulls the entire police department. I've got a damn week."

Simmons studied him intently for a few seconds. "You know, I was skeptical about some rookie cop handling this, but I agreed because I figured I could push him around if he was bad at his job."

Royal said nothing. He'd swallow a lot for a chance to succeed at this job, but he'd be damned if he was going to be pushed around by some ex–FBI agent when it came to keeping Franny safe.

"You're not bad at your job, Campbell. I can't disclose Albennie Ward's case, for a lot of reasons. But now that I've got a name, I can look through what I know about it and see if there's any connection to Holand Meyer."

"All right." It wasn't much, but it was better than nothing. "And you'll send me the list of people arrested if you get it before the sheriff's department?"

"Right away." Simmons studied him. "What are your next steps?"

"I don't know. Wait I guess."

"You any good at waiting?" Simmons asked.

Royal thought about the time he'd spent back in the Sons. The things he'd seen and done with an end goal of protecting some of those girls. Any of those girls. He'd had to bide his time back then, too, and play a hell of a lot of games.

"Yeah, I'm a damn expert at waiting," he muttered, turning away from Simmons and walking back out to where they'd come from.

When they got back into the living room, the boy was lying across Franny's lap, still watching the movie intently, but he had one hand gripped on Franny's arm. The baby was sitting next to them, and Franny was dangling a little bird toy in front of her, making her gurgle with laughter.

"She literally doesn't like anyone but me right now," Simmons said, clearly baffled.

Franny looked up at them, a relaxed smile on her face that hadn't been there in days. "I have been called the baby whisperer a time or two."

She carefully disentangled herself from the boy, then lifted the girl and handed her off to Simmons.

Simmons studied her curiously. "You looking for a babysitting job?"

Franny laughed. "Sure, now and then. You've got my number."

He walked them out into the bright light of morning. Franny said cheerful goodbyes to both kids, but with every step toward his cruiser he watched the tension creep back into her shoulders.

"So?" she asked as they climbed into the car.

He wished he had a better answer for her. "Leads, I guess, but not answers."

Franny blew out a breath. "Well, leads are better than nothing."

He slid a glance at her before returning his eyes to the road. She was trying to be positive. She was always trying so hard to…make everything okay for anyone in her orbit.

Case in point, when he parked next to her building rather than his, she turned that warm smile on him. "You don't have to walk me up."

He didn't. The cameras and alarms were all in place, but he went up just the same. Something about the whole day just felt *off*. Was it him? Her? This...*thing* about her that seemed to jumble up his previously held certainty? All those things she'd said to him...

It didn't matter. He wasn't letting her out of his sight until he had some answers. He walked up the stairs with her. "Have you had breakfast? We could go down to the bakery and—"

That off feeling finally had a place to land. He grabbed her arm before she could reach forward and put her key in the lock. "Don't open the door."

Chapter Twenty

Franny stopped on a dime. Royal's expression was so serious her heart had leaped to her throat. And his grip on her arm was tight. This was an order, through and through.

Danger.

He was frowning at the door as he studied it, keeping his grip on her even though she'd immediately stopped her forward progress.

"See here," he said, pointing to the frame around the latch with his free hand. "That splintering wasn't there before. I studied this lock the first time someone tried to break in. This wasn't here."

She noticed the crack in the door frame now that he pointed it out, but she wasn't sure it hadn't been there before. She'd never paid much attention to the door frame. "Are you sure?" She glanced up at him.

He was sure.

He took her by the elbow, cop gaze moving around as if assessing a threat in every air molecule. "Come on." He led her down the stairs, then across the street, then up the stairs to presumably his apartment.

"What do you think…" But the question died before she could get it out. She wasn't sure she wanted to know what he thought. The idea of someone getting into her apartment was scary enough, but trying to look like they *hadn't* been in there?

Definitely worse.

They made it to his door, but he didn't immediately unlock it. He studied that too.

He shook his head. "Someone's been in here too. Trying to break in or succeeding." He turned in a slow circle on the landing. His gaze zeroed in on something at the bottom of the door. He released her enough to crouch, study it.

"What is it?"

When he didn't speak, her heart started to thud harder, because to her it looked like a smear of…blood. She swallowed. Why would there be a smear of blood going *into* his apartment?

"Royal?"

He stood slowly. He didn't seem at all panicked, even though that's what was starting to hammer in her chest. His blue gaze was intense, but she didn't see even one ripple of fear in it.

"I'm going to take you to… I'll take you to Simmons. He's got that big-ass house. He can keep you hidden away." He'd already grabbed her again and was pulling her back down the stairs.

She jerked her arm away halfway down the stairs. "No."

He looked up at her from where he stood a few stairs down. "Franny, I'm not sure what's going on. I need to get you somewhere safe. This isn't safe anymore."

"If this is dangerous, and it sure as hell seems dangerous if that was *blood*, I'm not going near anyone's *kids*."

"Okay, fair." He shoved a hand through his hair, the first sign this was more than a simple decision for him. "What about your cousin's ranch?"

She didn't really want to pull Audra into the middle of this either, but Audra *did* know how to shoot a gun. If they were in danger, Audra could at least defend herself. It felt safer than going to Mr. Simmons with his adorable kids around.

"If we're to our last resort," Franny said very carefully, wishing she could come up with something else. "We can go to my cousin's ranch." Blood did feel kind of…last resort. A very bad last resort.

"We might just be getting there." He was back to pulling her along. She could certainly follow him without the hand on her arm, but it was a kind of nice having some kind of anchor.

He wouldn't like that either, would he? Him being her anchor. He wouldn't trust it. But right now, in the midst of danger, neither one of them had the time to consider that.

"What do you think is happening, Royal?" she asked him once they were in his car—his personal one, not his cruiser. He was still in his uniform though. He was still a *cop*, but she knew taking this car meant he was acting as Royal Campbell, not anyone's deputy.

His expression was grim. "I'm not sure, but nothing good, Franny. Nothing good at all. Someone broke into your apartment and mine, bypassing all security systems. There's blood on my stoop. I have a bad feeling if we'd gone in there, we'd have found…worse."

"We need to tell Mr. Simmons. It's his security system. You don't think he…"

"No, I don't think he's got anything to do with this. Not on purpose anyway. You're right. We need to tell Simmons. And Beckett. Someone was in our apartments for a reason, and I can't imagine it was a good one."

"You drive. I'll handle telling them."

He flicked her a glance, then nodded. "Text. That way they can't try to argue with you about what we should do."

"Good thinking. But what…are we doing?"

He drove. "I'm working on it."

ROYAL DROVE WITHOUT a full idea of what his destination was. He had to work out what had just happened.

There would have been more blood inside his apartment. Not his. Not Franny's. That was something. But why blood at all?

He thought about the splintering on Franny's door frame. It had been obvious—maybe not to a layman, but someone had to know she had police protection. The break-in at his place was way less obvious, the smear of blood inconsequential. He wouldn't have noticed it if he hadn't been looking because of *Franny's* apartment.

He couldn't help but wonder if it had all been a kind of trap. That he was *meant* to notice Franny's place had been compromised. Rush to his and…

Something bad was inside. He knew that without going in. But what he wasn't sure of was the purpose. A threat? Maybe he should have checked it out, but with Franny…

No, best to leave to someone else. Beckett could handle it. Royal had to admit he was coming around to trusting Beckett.

"Mr. Simmons is going to check the security," Franny said, reading from her phone. "I gave him permission to access all the footage. He'll text me back when he's gotten something. Copeland, on the other hand…"

"Wants us to come into the station," he finished for her. No surprises there.

"Yeah."

Maybe it was best. Maybe it only felt wrong because of his old gang-member, knee-jerk responses, but the sheriff wanting to pull Franny's security still irked. Going back to a place where they thought she should be *fine* whether they knew if the kidnapper was in jail or not felt wrong.

Still, she'd be safe there. Surrounded by cops and all those detectives she knew. If he dropped her there, slipped away to handle this...she'd be safe. Beckett could make sure of it. He glanced at her as he drove down the mostly empty highway in the opposite direction of Bent.

She lifted her gaze to meet his. Her eyes were full of trust. And panic, but underneath that panic and worry was *trust*. He didn't deserve it.

But her words from this morning kept coming back to him. How much belief and trust she had in him. No, she didn't know his past.

But she did know his present. And she was so...smart. So intuitive. Couldn't he trust her instincts better than his own?

Maybe he didn't deserve her trust, her belief, her thinking he was good or brave, but maybe... Maybe he could be all those things because she *did* think them of him.

Maybe he had to be.

"It's not a bad idea to go to the police station," he said, his voice gruff. "The sheriff won't be able to ignore the fact someone broke into your place. That's a crime. You could officially report it, and we could just...stay put until we have more information."

He glanced in the rearview mirror, ready to make a U-turn on the highway, head back to Bent and trust the establishment he'd bought into when he became a cop. How was he ever supposed to move forward if he was still thinking like a scared teenager who couldn't trust anyone or any system?

That wasn't why he'd stayed put near Brooke, his only family. That wasn't why he'd gotten through the police academy or applied at Bent. He'd taken all those steps as part of an acceptance that he was an adult now. He had the power, and he wanted to use that power to help where he could—in a way that mattered.

Good and brave.

But he caught a flash of another car in that rearview mirror. He might not have thought anything of it, but a car that same color silver had pulled onto the highway as he'd left Hope Town proper. He thought it had turned off back at the exit to Bent County, but it was still there.

Far enough away to be a tail.

Or it's a different car, or some old lady driving at the speed of molasses. Don't jump to conclusions. This isn't the Sons.

Since the coast was clear, he made the U-turn. If that person followed them back the other direction, then he'd know for sure. And if they did—he'd be headed to the police station. If they didn't, well, he was getting Franny to safety either way.

Franny's phone pinged. "It's another text from Copeland. He says, 'Second thought, don't come to the police station. Dead body of kidnapper found.'" Franny looked up at him wide-eyed.

"Well, we're good then. He's dead and we're on our way to the station. You can ID him and…"

Franny cleared her throat. "There's more, Royal." Her voice shook. "They found the body…in your apartment."

Yeah, definitely not good.

Chapter Twenty-One

Franny had managed to settle her panic a bit, until the last part of that text. Why would the dead body of the kidnapper be in *Royal's* apartment? She knew her writer brain wasn't based in reality, but the only thing that made any kind of sense to her was that...

"Someone...set you up?"

"Maybe."

He was so calm. So detached. "What do you mean, maybe?" she demanded, unable to be any of those things. "There's a dead body in your apartment. *You* didn't put it there."

"No," he agreed easily.

"Royal."

He flicked a glance at her, but there was nothing behind it. No heat or ice or anything. Just a kind of blankness that chilled her. "I'm going to take you to the police station."

"No, we're not going anywhere near the police station. Copeland told us not to." She waved her phone at him as if that would get through to him. "We're going to listen."

"I'll just drop you off."

"Royal." She couldn't let him do that, but she couldn't quite think of what to say that might get through that *cop* facade. She'd seen Copeland and Thomas put that on. So easily shutting off any...*person* underneath this job they did. The only thing she could do when they did that was maintain being reasonable. Find some cop facade of her own.

"I understand you think getting me out of the way would be safe," she said, hoping her voice sounded as calm as his. "But Copeland is telling us to stay away. *Us*. We need to listen to him, so we don't complicate whatever they need to investigate with the..."

"The dead man in my apartment?" he replied blandly, but she *saw* the flicker of irritation. Whether at her or the murder she wasn't sure, but emotion felt like progress.

Before she could continue to convince him they needed to turn back around and head away from Hope Town *and* Bent, he swore viciously.

He was glaring at the road, so Franny looked out. There was a car on the opposite side coming toward them. Why did it look familiar? But she couldn't consider that, because she realized the car was not driving on its side of the street.

"Royal, is that car..." The car kept going *faster*, and it was *clearly* in their lane, heading right toward them.

"Hold on, Franny."

She gripped the door, because there was no way that car was not careening right toward them. She squeezed her eyes shut, braced for some kind of impact even as Royal jerked the wheel and tried to avoid the collision.

But she felt the impact, the sound of crunching metal and shattering glass exploding around her as the car seemed to move at a completely bizarre angle. Franny jerked against her seatbelt at the impact, but holding on to the door and the odd angle of the force of collision kept her from bashing her head against anything.

But they kept...moving. Spinning? Something hit the back of her head, but it was all kind of surreal. She tried to open her eyes, but the force of everything made it impossible to do anything but tense her entire body and wait for it all to be over.

Finally, the car stopped moving. Once she realized that, Franny opened her eyes. They'd twisted around so they were facing the wrong way. The collision must have happened to the back end of the car because the front end looked perfectly fine. Which meant they were okay. They could be okay even though the airbags hadn't gone off.

She frowned at that. They should have, shouldn't they? That had been a hell of a jolt, even if it had been to the back of the car. Oh well, as long as they were okay.

"Roy—" She looked toward him. He was crumpled over the steering wheel.

He wasn't moving.

Panic speared through her, and she lunged for him, but she was held in place by the seatbelt. "Royal. Royal. *Royal!*" She slapped at her seatbelt, desperate to get it off, to get over to him. He wasn't moving.

Why hadn't any airbags gone off? Why wasn't he *moving*?

She managed to get the seatbelt out of her way, but now that she'd had enough time to think, she was scared to try to move him. What if he'd hurt his neck or spine? If she moved him to see what was wrong, she'd make it worse. Wouldn't she?

She wouldn't let her mind go there. "It's okay, Royal. It's okay. It's going to be okay." She said it more for her benefit than his, because it kept the panic from turning into hysterics.

She fumbled with her phone. Since her text to Copeland was still open on the screen, she just hit the call button at the top. He'd have a better idea of where they were to send help rather than trying to explain her location to a 911 dispatcher.

With shaking hands and her teeth chattering, she reached out with her free hand and grabbed Royal's wrist. She knew how to find a pulse, and a pulse would mean everything could be okay.

"Franny? I can't talk right now."

"Cope..." She thought she felt a pulse. Didn't she? The steady thump of life? Or was she hallucinating?

Copeland's voice in her ear was kind of a buzz.

"We...had an accident." She was pretty sure she got those words out. It was weird. She didn't think she'd hit her head, but it was kind of aching now. And her words didn't... sound right.

She sucked in a breath, trying to focus. Royal needed help. He had a pulse. She was *determined* he had a pulse. So she needed help.

But before she could manage to put those words together, the passenger door flung open. A woman stood there. For a blinding moment of pure hope, Franny thought they were saved.

Then she saw the woman's sharp smile and remembered that a car had been careening *at* them. And if it hadn't been someone's medical event that led to the dangerous speed and direction, it had been done very much on purpose.

Considering there was a dead body in Royal's apartment, well....

"God, this couldn't be more perfect." The woman laughed, actually *laughed*. "Well, F.M. Perkins, come on out. We've got places to go."

She must not have seen the phone in Franny's hand. Franny's body and face might be blocking it. For a moment of pure adrenaline and clarity, Franny knew that she would need her phone.

She swallowed, angling her body even farther and doing

everything she could to shove the phone—the call with Copeland still going—into her pocket without the woman seeing.

"Damn, that's a hell of a party trick," the woman said, which made absolutely no sense to Franny. The woman must have read that in her expression. "You've got a shard of glass really lodged in there." She said, pointing at the back of Franny's head.

The pain in her head. A shard of glass? She reached up with a shaky hand.

"I wouldn't. Gonna hurt like hell. Besides, we've got places to be," the woman said, she patted her hip and that's when Franny realized she had a gun in a holster. "Out of the car now."

Franny didn't know what else to do but obey. Royal no doubt had a gun on that belt of his, but she could hardly get to it, get it *out* of the belt, *and* shoot it in any defensive fashion before this woman shot her.

And if the woman shot her, what might she do to Royal?

So Franny got out of the car. Help was coming. Copeland would get help. Everything would be okay if she could keep this all from…escalating.

She winced and tried not to groan in pain, but for as much as she thought she'd managed to not get hurt since she wasn't unconscious, everything screamed in protest at moving.

Especially her head. Every move, every step sent a searing, slicing pain down the back of her skull. She lifted her hand again but was a little too afraid to try to touch anything. A shard of glass *stuck* in there sounded…really bad.

The woman—and it had to be the woman Royal had seen poking around Hope Town in the beginning of this. What had he said her name was? Holand something.

So, this was the former FBI agent, somehow connected

to Albennie. But why was she after Franny? Why… She swallowed at the lump in her throat as she thought of Royal slumped in that car. He needed medical attention. They needed help.

She hoped and prayed that came across to Copeland.

"We're just going to get a ways off this road here. So no one sees us before I'm ready. You go on and walk ahead of me. You try to run—well that glass will probably stop you, but a bullet will too."

Franny took a staggering step forward. She tried to walk softly and slowly as much to delay any possible harm until help got there as because of the pain. But the waves of pain just throbbed through every inch of her until tears were filling her eyes. She couldn't think straight from all the hurt, except to move forward one excruciating step at a time.

She *felt* the woman walking behind her. She wasn't holding the gun. It was just in a holster at her hip. Maybe Franny could run…or fight, but the thought of trying to do either with this horrific pain in her head kept her from actually trying.

She didn't know how long they walked. Into the trees. Oh, she shouldn't have come this far. But what else was there to do? The woman had a gun. Royal needed help. What was she supposed to *do*?

With no warning, something…happened to the back of her head. She screamed out in pain, her hand flying instinctually up to the source. Her hand came away wet with blood. She stared at the woman who now held the bloody shard of glass that had been *in her head*.

Holand must have yanked it out.

Franny's vision wavered and she couldn't stay upright. She managed not to fully pass out. Just kind of crumpled to her hands and knees, nausea sweeping through her. She breathed raggedly, staring at the ground where tears and blood dripped.

"Yeah, why don't you pass out?" Holand said. "That'd make this a lot easier on all of us now that we're here."

But Franny had to breathe through the pain. Stay awake. It was her only chance. Royal's only chance.

She could feel the blood dripping down the back of her neck. Oh God, maybe neither of them had any kind of chance.

"Now, we're going to have to make this look a little bit more…believable." She cocked her head to one side, studying Franny. "The glass is clearly from the accident, so we need a struggle. Don't we?"

Then, without any kind of warning, she lifted her foot and kicked hard into Franny's side so Franny fell over. The shock of the blow elicited another howl of pain, but as the woman was gripping her shirt and tearing it, Franny fought back.

She kicked out herself, she wriggled, she pushed. It was instinct beyond avoiding pain. Not letting this woman hurt her any more than she was already hurt. The screaming agony in her head was a distraction, but it didn't make her *stop* fighting back. But there was so little she could do.

She managed to get on her butt and scoot back, but the woman was getting to her feet, brushing the dirt off her clothes.

"There we go. Now we've got a struggle."

Franny looked down at herself. Her shirt was bloody and torn. There were scrapes on her hands. Dirt all over her pants.

"What are you doing? Why?" Franny demanded, because everything just hurt, and she couldn't tell if the liquid on her cheeks was blood or tears or both. She was so baffled and just hurting.

"Look, you learn a lesson real quick in the real world. You can't trust a man as far as you can throw him. If there's any complaint I have about your books, it's that one."

"You... My *books*?"

"Sure, had to do some research on the witness, didn't I? They're not half bad. I have some critiques, but they pass an evening all right. Except for the idea that there are *heroes* in this world, F.M. But I guess that's why it's classified fiction."

Franny could only gape at this woman. Discussing the believability of her *books* while Royal was unconscious, and she was bleeding at an alarming rate. This woman had *crashed into them* and she had *critiques*.

"In the *real* world, there are the users and the used. You gotta be smart enough to be a user. I used Tony for what he was good for, and when he couldn't do that right?" She shrugged. "Well, collateral damage is a term for a reason. You see, I'm a pretty good writer too. I've got all sorts of ideas. So, we're working this story out. Brainstorm with me."

Franny stared up at her. Did any of those words make sense? If they did, maybe she had a worse head injury than she thought.

"So, the police will come upon the scene I left for them. The second scene. They'll blame your cop boyfriend for Tony, the first scene, since the body was in his place. But you saw the cop off Tony. Oh no! He's got to get rid of you too. He drives you out to the middle of nowhere. He's dragging you out of the car. Here because he thinks the bears will get you and he won't have to explain *your* body. In his head, he'll get back to take care of Tony before the cops know the difference."

Franny looked around. Sure there were bears in Bent

County, but she didn't think one happening upon her dead body was much of a plan for body removal.

And why was she actually considering this like a *book*, when this was her *life*?

"But I happen to drive by," Holand continued, really getting into it. "I see him. Hero that I am, because it's fiction, right? But even in real life stupid people want to believe in heroes. I run into his car to stop him. But it's too late. I call the police, then disappear. Neat and tidy like. We all win. How's that for a happy ending? If I didn't have to kill you, I'd let you write that one. Your books aren't bad. Could use an editor."

Franny was almost positive this had to be a very lucid dream. But she didn't wake up. No reality came calling. She sat there on the ground, *bleeding*, and stared at this woman. "No one would ever believe any of that. In real life *or* in one of my books. There's a million plot holes."

The satisfied look on the woman's face turned into a scowl. "Says you."

"Says…reason and rationality. Royal is still in the car. He hasn't moved. How did he kill me then crawl back into the crashed-out car? He's *unconscious*." She forced herself to add the next bit even though she didn't want to say it out loud. "He might be *dead*."

The woman lifted her chin. "I've got that figured out. Don't you worry about it." She flashed a smug smile again.

"I won't. But you should worry about this. The police know who you are. They all know who you are, *Holand*. So you can run, but you can't disappear. They're already looking for you. Thanks to Royal."

Franny had a glimmer of satisfaction as the smile slid off the woman's face. The woman stood very still. Enough of a moment that Franny felt a bubble of hope.

But then the woman shrugged. "That's a shame. Because if I can't frame him, I don't have time to mess around with you." And as she raised the gun, Franny realized she'd made a fatal mistake.

ROYAL CAME TO on a stab of pain and a wave of nausea. He coughed, pain wracking his system. Something came out of his mouth when he coughed.

Blood.

Hell.

"Franny?" he croaked. He managed to lift his head, even though it hurt worse than he'd ever been hurt—and he'd been beaten and shot and all manner of things.

Her seat was empty, her door open. She must have gone to get help. That was good. He could just…rest until help came.

He managed to sit up, sort of, lean his head back. Sunlight gleamed off the car and it hurt his head. He closed his eyes, and closing his eyes seemed to help steady his jumbled thoughts.

He swore.

That hadn't just been some car accident. Someone had hit them on purpose. He'd tried to swerve out of the way, but he hadn't been willing to risk Franny, so he'd swerved in the only way he could to keep his side of the car the target.

The airbags hadn't gone off. That was…wrong. Someone had to have messed with his car.

Everything was wrong.

Which meant Franny likely hadn't gone for help. She'd likely been taken by whoever had crashed into them.

He heard a sound. Turned his head toward it. The passenger door was open. Someone was out there. The car that had rammed into him was there in the road, and someone was out beyond the road. In the trees.

He had to get out. Find Franny. He had to… He looked down at his uniform. His walkie wasn't turned on, but he was wearing it.

Gritting his teeth together, he lifted his hand to turn it on. He was greeted by the steady sounds of radio traffic and the occasional burst of static. With what little strength he seemed to have, he managed to depress the talk button. He croaked out his department serial number, and his location, best as he could remember it. "Car accident."

He needed them to know it was dangerous though. No accident. Who had been the driver of the car if the kidnapper was dead in his apartment?

The only other person he'd been looking into. Holand Meyer. He managed to give a description. Or thought he did.

"Units have already been dispatched, Deputy Campbell," the dispatcher said. "ETA is a few minutes."

Already been dispatched? How? Had someone seen something?

It didn't matter. A few minutes was still too long if Franny wasn't *here*. Ignoring the rest of the radio noise, he put all his focus on getting his door open. It didn't go at first. Most of the damage had been done to the back end of the car, but enough that it made his door stuck.

He had to fight it, and the pain, and every other damn thing, but he finally wrenched it open. He was having a hard time breathing. Probably a cracked rib. Maybe worse. Couldn't think about it. Had to stay conscious and find Franny.

He managed to get out, get to his feet, and then he had to lean against the car, close his eyes, breathe. Just breathe. It wasn't just the hurting. He was dizzy, nauseated. Rough shape. Maybe he should just wait for backup.

Then he heard that sound again. Someone in pain.

Franny.

He pushed himself off the car and started walking for the trees. His vision was blurry, but he just kept moving by sheer force of will.

He fumbled with the latch on his holster but finally got it free and got the gun out. His left arm screamed in pain no matter how he moved it, but he gripped the gun in his right and kept moving.

He just had to stay conscious long enough to stop the threat. Hell, he could *die* after that, which felt like a real possibility at the moment.

Gun in one hand, he tried to use the other hand to lean against a tree, get his bearings, but his arm screamed in pain at any pressure put on it.

Not good. None of this was *good*.

He thought he'd spared Franny the worst of the accident, but what if he hadn't? He had to find her.

He blew out a breath, concentrated on getting his eyes to focus while he ignored his body. He'd had to learn, hadn't he? Pain didn't matter. Pain was weakness. You had to ignore the pain. To survive. Survive. *Survive.*

He was so damn sick of surviving. So tired of everything hurting. Pain and suffering and the whims of horrible people ruining *everything*. He'd been fighting it for so long, why did he keep doing it?

Because there'd always been a voice in the back of his head. Brooke's voice, urging him to be better, do some good.

But Brooke was well and taken care of and what did *he* matter anymore?

Franny.

She was out there. All because she'd *seen* someone do something bad and tried to stop it. He couldn't let her be another horrible person's victim. She deserved more than survival.

Hell, they all did.

She thought he was brave and good, no matter what he'd told her. She'd held on to that belief, so he had to hold on to it now.

Something was going to change after this. He didn't have the presence of mind to know what just yet, but once he could think, once he could *breathe* without this searing pain, he was going to figure it out.

He kept moving forward, trying to be quiet, but with the agony radiating through his body and the odd drumming in his ears, he didn't know for sure if he was being stealthy or as subtle as a Mack truck.

There were tracks in the dirt. Not clear ones, but indentations in the dry ground, the sweep of dried pine needles moved by someone's footsteps.

The occasional drop of blood. He followed them, focusing only on finding Franny and nothing going on in his own body.

He thought he heard voices, so he stopped, tried to focus his vision. In the distance, between trees, he saw a flash of something. He didn't know what, so he just kept moving for it.

After a few more yards, he could make out the scene clearly.

The woman he'd seen skulking around Hope Town stood, gun in hand, back to him. She wasn't a brunette now, but a blonde. Franny sat, bloody and dirty. Royal couldn't quite make out what they were saying—not because they were far away or quiet, but because his ears were just kind of a low buzz.

But Holand Meyer didn't turn around to face him, so she

must not know he was there, but he saw what was coming the moment Franny did. Her eyes went wide. And that was enough to have Holand turning, gun in hand, raised to aim at him.

Royal didn't wait, didn't think. He just lifted his own gun and shot.

Of course, so did she.

The force of the bullet hit him dead center. And he fell back, which hurt more than the bullet to his vest.

His *vest*. He wanted to laugh, might have if he wasn't in so much damn pain.

Being a cop had saved him after all.

Chapter Twenty-Two

Franny raced forward on an outraged cry. She'd shot Royal. She'd shot him. He'd fallen over and *oh God, oh God*. Franny wouldn't let her shoot again.

But there was nothing to be done because Holand was also on the ground. She was bleeding. It seeped out of her side. Franny stood above her, watching her move and writhe. For a moment, Franny did nothing but stare, a bit like she'd been detached from her own body.

Royal had shot Holand too. She was *shot*. She didn't even have her gun anymore. But Franny realized that's where Holand's eyes were trained. The gun a few feet away from her outstretched hand.

Her whole body shaking, Franny managed to grab it before Holand could wriggle close enough to. Then she rushed over to Royal, stumbled onto her knees by his side. His eyes were closed.

"Royal."

"It's too damn bright out here," he muttered.

Oh, *God*, he'd spoken. He'd spoken. He was still alive. He was… "I thought she killed you," Franny managed to choke out.

"Vest. Hell of a thing."

Everything fell apart then. He had a vest on because and

only because he was in uniform. He wasn't dead. Oh, he was so hurt, but he wasn't dead. She simply lowered her forehead to said vest and wept into it.

She felt a hand on her shoulder and whirled, ready to fight or shoot or whatever she had to do.

But it was Copeland. A few deputies. Copeland easily swiped the gun out of her hand.

"Damn, Franny, you're bleeding like hell. We need to get you to a hospital too." He looked over at some people, shouted orders.

"I'm okay. I'm better than he is. She shot him. She *shot* him. Copeland, you have to..."

Some EMTs rushed over with a stretcher. They talked to each other as they worked to get Royal moved onto it.

Copeland helped her to her feet, and out of the way. He held her in one place while deputies and EMTs swarmed the area. She wanted to be with Royal. She wanted...so many things, but her mind couldn't seem to make a decision.

Except... She had the truth. Answers. Sort of. She looked up at Copeland helplessly.

"Copeland, she told me everything. I mean, not *why*, but...that she killed the kidnapper. That she was framing Royal. She was going to frame him for me too, but the story didn't make sense."

"We'll take your statement once you're checked out," Copeland said gently. "I'm sure it'll corroborate whatever angle the damn Feds are working from." The EMTs were moving Royal, and Franny took a step toward him, but Copeland held firm.

"You can't go with him, Franny. Hey, Bowman. Come check her out, huh?"

Another EMT came over, had Franny sit down on the

ground. "I'll clean this up and get a bandage on it, but she's going to need to be transported too."

"I'm fine."

Both the EMT and Copeland gave her a disapproving look.

"We'll get another ambulance here soon as we can. She'll hold up all right," the EMT said. She could feel his hands on her hair and she winced.

The pain she'd nearly forgotten in all her fear and panic was back, tenfold, throbbing through her body like a drumbeat. She was so, so tired all of a sudden that the EMT had to hold her up.

She looked up at where Copeland stood, still coordinating everything with that blank cop mask on.

"Copeland, it's over now, right?"

He looked down at her, a flicker of emotion in his gaze now. Sympathy. Relief. "Yeah, Franny. It's over."

THE BEEPING WAS going to drive him insane.

It was the first coherent thought Royal'd had in what felt like a very long time. When he blinked his eyes open, nothing fully made sense except if that beeping didn't stop he was going to...

Well, not a whole lot because he couldn't seem to move the way he wanted to. He could turn his head, and when he did, he came face-to-face with his sister.

"Chick." His voice sounded rough.

Brooke smiled, but she'd been crying. It was all over her face. Red eyes and puffy cheeks. "You're really getting shot way too much for my personal comfort."

"Had a vest this time."

"Thank God."

He tried to shift in the bed, but he didn't feel in control of his limbs just yet, and he realized one of said limbs was in a cast. His left arm. He stared at it, not fully making sense of it. A broken arm. Must have been from the accident.

Accident. "Franny?"

"She's doing all right. They stitched her up. She had to stay overnight, but they released her today. Just a nasty gash on her head, but otherwise she's fine." Brooke scooted closer to the bed, peering at him. "She's waiting to see you. Refuses to leave until they let her. They were only letting family sit with you while you were coming out of the anesthesia."

"She should go."

Brooke frowned. "She wants to see you. Why should she go?"

He had answers for that, but he couldn't seem to find them in the swimming feeling in his brain. "Am I dying or something?"

"No. Broken nose, broken arm, concussion, bruised and cracked ribs, honestly too many bumps, bruises and lacerations to count, but you're going to be okay. If I have to personally see to it."

"You need to take care of yourself, Chick." She was *pregnant*. She shouldn't be worrying over him. She didn't say anything to that, just frowned disapprovingly at him.

Royal sighed. It hurt, but not the way it *had*. Pain killers, probably. Or that anesthesia Brooke was talking about. How long had he been out of it? He kind of remembered arriving, but everything around that was a blur.

One thing was clear though. "I wasn't fast enough. Not the first time. Couldn't get the car out of the way. I should have seen it coming. I should have *known*."

Brooke studied him for a long time, that serious study that always felt like she saw more than he'd ever understand.

She brushed at the hair on his forehead, like she had when he'd been a little kid. Before they'd been separated.

"You are incredibly brave, Royal. A hero. The people you've saved in your life would have *died* otherwise. So you don't get to be hard on yourself."

He didn't argue with her. He *wanted* to, but he supposed now wasn't the time.

Hero? With them all beat up like this? He didn't think so.

But he heard Franny's words in his head. *You cannot tell me you aren't good or brave, because that is the heart of who you are. Period.*

Brooke stood. "I'm going to go get Franny."

"What if I don't want you to?" He had things to work out, and he wasn't strong enough to stand up to how much he wanted… So much he wanted…

"You're wrong," Brooke said simply. "And you'll have to tell *her* that. I'd suggest not." She swept out of the room. Mad at him. Which wasn't fair.

He didn't think.

Didn't matter. He had to think of the right words to get Franny to leave, and his brain wasn't firing on all cylinders, so it'd be a challenge.

She came in, clasping her hands together. She had a bandage wrapped around her head, and the clothes she was wearing were too big for her, clearly not hers. Hers had been ripped and bloody.

He could see her there. On the ground. It gripped him, all that fear sweeping through him again even as she moved across the room to hover over his bed, cleaned up, bandaged up and okay.

He'd been so sure he'd tell her to go away. To give him space. He couldn't get the words out, because just looking at her made everything okay.

"Hi," she said. Her green eyes were shiny with tears.

"Hi," he managed, wanting to take those tears away.

But she smiled. It wobbled, but it was a smile. "I... I don't know how much Brooke told you, but Holand made it through surgery. She's going to go away for a very long time. The Feds still won't give a lot of details, but basically this woman has been a kind of informant of sorts, using her inside FBI knowledge to work for hire. The group that kidnapped Albennie hired Holand to find her, then *she* hired the kidnapper. I haven't talked to Mr. Simmons yet—he'll probably have more information—but it seems like everyone involved at every step is now in jail."

Royal didn't really understand the words—he'd blame all the drugs in his system for now, but she just kept talking, standing there, hands clasped. Nervous and upset.

He'd been so sure this was it. He'd put a wall up. Look what had happened to her in just a few days of being involved with him? He was bad luck. A harbinger.

But she just babbled on about everything that had happened. How many stitches she'd gotten, how many times Rosalie had thrown up in the waiting room. Such silly little details and he just...couldn't stand the thought of suddenly not having Franny in his life.

He didn't want to be bad luck anymore.

He wanted...a future. To be the brave and the good she saw. Wasn't that why he'd become a cop? Wasn't that why he'd stayed here in Bent County? A future meant believing he deserved one. He didn't deserve her.

But he'd work at it.

She sat abruptly in the chair Brooke had vacated, looked pained. "I'm probably giving you a headache."

But she wasn't. "I like hearing your voice."

Her mouth curved and she leaned forward, touching a spot on his forehead. "I like seeing your eyes open."

For a few quiet moments, they just stared at each other, maybe reassuring themselves the other was all right.

"When I'm on my own two feet again. And you don't have that bandage on your head. We're going to go out."

She blinked once. "Out?"

"To dinner. A movie. Whatever. A date." He tried to move, winced when it hurt. "Like normal people."

"A date?" she repeated.

"Yes," he said firmly.

"Oh. Well, okay."

"You want to, don't you?" he demanded.

She was looking at him with serious green eyes. "Yes. Though I don't know how normal I can be. But I can try."

He laughed. It hurt. But somehow that was…just right now too. "Well, okay then. That's what we'll do. But don't try to be normal. Just be you."

"I think that's a compliment," she grumbled. "Are you sure you're not delusional?" she asked, leaning forward. "Hyped up on pain killers and anesthesia. You might change your mind."

He stared at her. After everything, all this, his whole damn life, she still made him smile. "I'm sure. I won't. I like having you in my life, Franny."

She swallowed hard. "You're a real hero, Royal."

Well, it wasn't going to be easy. He shifted, winced at the pain. "I don't know about all that."

"I do. That Holand woman… She said heroes are fictional. But she's wrong. Maybe heroes aren't all perfectly good, but there *are* heroes." Her eyes filled with tears again, but they still didn't fall. "People who do the right thing in the face of bad things, hard things. That's you."

He didn't want to believe it, but Brooke had said it. Franny had said it. How could he argue with two of the best, strongest women he knew?

"Well, then it's you too, Franny."

She looked puzzled for a minute, then straightened her shoulders. "You know what? I'll take it."

He managed a little bit of a laugh, even if it hurt.

Maybe he'd learn to take it too. With her.

Epilogue

Three Months Later

Franny was in the bakery talking to Albennie and Lia over coffee, marveling inwardly at how much Albennie looked like her old self. Even though she'd only been kidnapped a few days, she'd come back looking skinny and haunted.

These days, she looked like she had before. Strong and sure and happy.

She didn't talk about the kidnapping, and the police still only knew that whatever Albennie had been involved in was related to a federal case, but the people who'd wanted her were all behind bars. Where they belonged.

As long as she was safe, that was what mattered.

So life was good, and Franny knew how to appreciate that. Especially with her book almost done.

The bell on the door jangled and all three women looked to see Royal striding in. He wasn't in uniform, but he had his serious cop expression on.

"God, he's hot," Albennie muttered before he made it over to them.

"I know," Franny said with a grin. "And all mine." He even spent most nights at her place now. He volunteered for the Hope Town sector whenever he had the chance.

Three months had been exactly what Franny had always hoped a real, adult relationship might be like. Not perfect, not always romantic. Solid. Real. Nothing she could write in a book because it was cooking meals together or drinking their coffee or arguing on which team had the better starting rotation.

They were building something like her cousins had with their significant others, and that filled Franny with all kinds of hope.

"Bragger," Lia muttered. "Except who wants a cop?"

Before Franny could answer that, Royal linked his arm with hers. No greeting. Just: "We have to go."

"Where?" she asked as he pulled her along, a little worry fluttering low in her stomach.

"Brooke's having the baby."

"Oh!" Worry turned to excitement. Except…she shouldn't be coming with. She'd spent more time with Brooke and Zeke since she and Royal had been dating, but this was still…a family thing.

"Brooke probably doesn't want non-family in her hospital room. It's a sacred place, Royal."

"Zeke said it was okay. His brother and sister are going to be there with their kids and everything. I can't face a baby *alone*, Franny. She's going to want me to hold it."

"Him, Royal. The baby is a boy."

"Right, right. See, that's why I need you." She liked seeing him flustered, because he only ever was about truly wonderful things. And she thought…maybe someday they'd get to a point where good things and babies and building families didn't fluster him so much, and she wanted to be around to see that.

Maybe she had lots of dreams about the future, but she didn't need everything to happen at once or quickly. In fact, it was nice to just enjoy dating somebody. While Rosalie grew her baby, and Audra planned her wedding, Franny was getting to know her boyfriend.

And apparently his new nephew.

Royal was glad he'd dragged Franny along, because he didn't know what the hell he was supposed to do in the waiting room, waiting for updates. But Franny chatted with Zeke's family and in-laws. She entertained Zeke's brother's toddler and had a very serious discussion about Taylor Swift with his brother-in-law's teenager.

Because she just had a *way* about her.

When Zeke came out to the waiting room, everyone was desperate for an update. "Baby's here," he said, raking a hand through his hair like he couldn't quite believe he'd said those words. "Brooke's...amazing. Everything's great. She wants to see Royal first." Zeke looked as unsteady and winded as Royal had ever seen him—and he'd seen him face down men with guns. "You come on too, Franny. We'll do the families one at a time."

Royal didn't stiffen at the word *families* like he once had. Maybe Franny wasn't his family, but he liked where they were going. And luckily, in the moment, he could focus more on other people's babies than his own stuff.

Zeke led them down a hall and into a room. Royal immediately crossed to his sister sitting in the hospital bed, a little bundle wrapped in her arms.

Everything that had been stacked against them from the start didn't matter now. She'd brought life into this world. His sister was a mother, and he knew she'd be the best one in the world.

Brooke smiled at him, tears in her eyes. "Well, hello, Uncle Royal."

"Heya, Chick." He pressed an uncharacteristic kiss to her forehead, relieved she looked happy and whole. He peered down at the little baby and its—*his*—red and scrunched-up face.

"Royal."

He looked back at Franny's tight voice. She was looking at some little card on the bassinet thingy. He squinted at the card. It read *It's A Boy*, and then underneath had all the pertinent details written out.

Like name. "Campbell Royal Daniels." He looked back at his sister, emotion clogging his throat. "Hell, Chick. What did you do that for?"

"Because our names mean something. Something good now. Because we fought for it. And I hope he never has to fight for *anything*," she said, looking down at the tiny baby in her arms. "But if he does, he'll have some fine examples." She smiled up at him, tears glimmering in her eyes. "Now sit down so you can hold him."

"I told you she'd make me," Royal muttered to Franny as they moved over to a little bench under the window. He was unsteady, unmoored and so…damn happy.

Yeah, their names meant something now. Something good. Something brave.

Zeke brought the bundle over and Franny instructed Royal how to hold his arms. The baby was so tiny. A little fluff of nothing. And yet the biggest, brightest thing in the world. His little nephew.

"Oh, Brooke, isn't he just the handsomest little thing?" Franny said, running a finger along one of the little wrinkles on his forehead.

"Yes," Brooke said emphatically.

They stayed a little while. Royal was happy to hand the baby back to Brooke. He was determined to be a damn good uncle and involved as hell, but…maybe a little less hands on until the baby firmed up a little bit.

He walked out of the hospital hand in hand with Franny. "Thanks for coming with me. The moral support was appreciated. But now you have to be there every time I'm forced to hold him before he gets old enough for that not to be terrifying."

She smiled at him. "Anytime."

They reached his car, but he didn't let her go. In the fading autumn light, he kept her hand in his. She looked up at him quizzically.

There were better ways to do it, to say it, but it was this moment that gave him the courage he'd been lacking for a while now. That his sister had built a family. That he'd… come to this moment. Where he had a life and some peace and too much good to deserve.

But that just meant he had to take it. "Franny, I love you."

She looked up at him, didn't say anything right away. Sometimes he thought he knew exactly what was going on in her head, and sometimes he didn't have a clue.

As the silence stretched out, he didn't have a damn clue. Especially when a little nervous flutter started up in his chest.

"Well?" he finally demanded, because what the hell? Why had he done this in a hospital parking lot? He should have planned it out. He should have… Made sure she was going to say something *back*.

But she just stared at him. "Well what?"

"Aren't you going to say something?"

She inhaled, then slowly let the breath out, still staring at him with all that vibrant green. "I was trying to think of… the right thing to say."

"It's pretty damn simple, isn't it?"

"Yes, and no." She reached up, put her hands on his cheeks, like she was about to let him down gently, and he didn't know what the hell to do with *that*.

Well, he'd... He'd figure out a way to fix it. He could be patient. Maybe she wasn't ready yet, and that was okay. It would be okay. He'd *make* it okay.

"You are my hero," she said very seriously.

"I hate it when you say that," he muttered, trying to move his head out of her grasp, but she held firm.

"I know. But I don't think you'll hate this. I love you too, Royal." She pushed up onto her toes and pressed her mouth to his. It was a sweet kiss, and he could have deepened it, but... He pulled away.

"What the hell did you put me through the ringer for?"

She laughed, and he loved the sound of it. Loved *her*. Even if she had just about scared him to death.

"I wasn't *trying* to. I was trying to enjoy the moment. Commit it to memory. *Savor*."

He grunted in irritation, but she kept her arms around his neck and that wasn't irritating at all.

"Just think, when Campbell is like fifteen, I'll be able to say, your uncle told me he loved me for the first time the day you were born. And then, because he'll be a teenager, he'll be like, 'ew, gross, why would you tell me that?' And we'll both have a good laugh."

Royal couldn't imagine anything fifteen years down the line. Certainly not that little wisp of a baby being a teenage boy, but he liked the part where Franny was by his side still. Laughing.

Yeah, that was pretty much perfect.

* * * * *

COMING SOON!

We really hope you enjoyed reading this book. If you're looking for more romance be sure to head to the shops when new books are available on

Thursday 26th March

To see which titles are coming soon, please visit
millsandboon.co.uk/nextmonth

MILLS & BOON

LET'S TALK
Romance

For exclusive extracts, competitions and special offers, find us online:

- **f** MillsandBoon
- **X** @MillsandBoon
- **◉** @MillsandBoonUK
- **♪** @MillsandBoonUK

Get in touch on 01413 063 232

For all the latest titles coming soon, visit
millsandboon.co.uk/nextmonth